D0058131

Fourth Grave Beneath My Feet

Also by Darynda Jones

Fourth Grave Beneath My Feet

Darynda Jones

ST. MARTIN'S PRESS ❧ NEW YORK

This is a work of fiction. All of the characters, organizations, and events portrayed in this novel are either products of the author's imagination or are used fictitiously.

FOURTH GRAVE BENEATH MY FEET. Copyright © 2012 by Darynda Jones. All rights reserved. Printed in the United States of America. For information, address St. Martin's Press, 175 Fifth Avenue, New York, N.Y. 10010.

www.stmartins.com

ISBN 978-1-250-01446-7 (hardcover)
ISBN 978-1-250-01447-4 (e-book)

First Edition: November 2012

10 9 8 7 6 5 4 3 2 1

For Quentin,

part-time pimp, full-time ninja, who,
even at his age, still says things like,
"Thank you, Easter Bunny! Bok, bok!"

Acknowledgments

This book owes a lot of things to a lot of people, not the least of whom are my amazing agent, Alexandra Machinist, and my incredible editor, Jennifer Enderlin. Thank you guys so much! You are both awe-inspiring, and I'm convinced each of you lead secret lives as superheroes.

Thank you to everyone at Macmillan Audio and a special shout-out to the ever-so-lovely Lorelei King for breathing life into my characters. Literally. Speaking of which, thank you to all at St. Martin's Press, Macmillan, and Janklow & Nesbit Associates.

A special thanks to Jacquelyn Frank and Natalie Justice for naming this book while waiting for a shuttle, war-torn and tattered after a lively three-day conference where the effervescent Natalie mastered mechanical-bull riding and Jacki won my heart over a game of X-rated Round Robin. You guys are the bomb.

Thank you so much to Mary Jo, Mary Ellen, and Bette for the consultations and advice on PTSD. You guys went above and beyond to help me, especially considering the fact that I only had three days to turn in the book. I am so grateful.

Thank you to Danielle "Dan Dan" Swopes for brainstorming with me even when your brain was almost as mushy as mine, and to your wonderful family whom I consider my own. And thank you to my actual family—you know who you are—for being so supportive and understanding when I miss holidays and birthday parties in the name of all things writerly. As soon as I make my next deadline, we are so having a cookout.

A *huge* thanks to Cait Allison for reading this book in its infancy, painful as it must have been, to give me feedback. I appreciate it more than you can know.

And, sadly, I have to say that at least three of the best lines in this book did not come from my own warped . . . er, vivid imagination, but that of the enlightened and sometimes terrifying musings of Jonathan "Doc" Wilson and Quentin "Q" Eakins. You guys are like crazy on whole wheat: fun and good for the digestion.

And most of all, thank *you,* esteemed reader, for making all my dreams come true. Or most of them. I have this one where I'm naked at an airport and . . . no, you're right. That's better left to the professionals. Either way, thank you so much! I hope you enjoy reading this as much as I enjoyed writing it.

Fourth Grave Beneath My Feet

1

Only two things in life are certain.
Guess which one I am.
—Charley Davidson, grim reaper

I sat watching the Buy From Home Channel with my dead aunt Lillian and wondered what my life would've been like had I not just eaten an entire carton of Ben & Jerry's Chocolate Therapy with a mocha latte chaser. Probably about the same, but it was something to think about.

A midmorning sun filtered through the blinds and cut hard streaks of light across my body, casting me in an ultra-cool film noir effect. Since my life had definitely taken a turn toward the dark side, film noir fit. It would have fit even better if I weren't wearing *Star Wars* pajama bottoms and a sparkly tank top that proudly proclaimed EARTH GIRLS ARE EASY. But I just didn't have the energy that morning to change into something less inappropriate. I'd been having lethargy issues for a few weeks now. And I was suddenly a tad agoraphobic. Ever since a man named Earl tortured me.

It sucked.

The torture. Not his name.

My name, on the other hand, was Charlotte Davidson, but most people called me Charley.

"Can I talk to you, pumpkin cheeks?"

Or pumpkin cheeks, one of the many pet names involving the fall fruit that Aunt Lillian insisted on calling me. Aunt Lil had died some-time in the sixties, and I could see her because I'd been born the grim reaper, which basically meant three things: One, I could interact with dead people—those departed who didn't cross over when they died— and usually did so on a daily basis. Two, I was super-duper bright to those in the spiritual realm, and the aforementioned dead people could see me from anywhere in the world. When they were ready to cross, they could cross through me. Which brought me to three—I was a portal from the earthly plane to what many refer to as heaven.

There was a tad more to it than that—including things I had yet to learn myself—but that was the basic gist of my day job. The one I didn't actually get paid to do. I was also a PI, but that gig wasn't paying the bills either. Not lately, anyway.

I rolled my head along the back of the sofa toward Aunt Lil, who was actually a great-aunt on my father's side. A thin, elderly woman with soft gray eyes and pale blue hair, she was wearing her usual attire, as dead people rarely changed clothes: a leather vest over a floral muumuu and love beads, the ensemble a testament to her demise in the sixties. She also had a loving smile that tilted a bit south of kilter. But that only made me adore her all the more. I had a soft spot for crazy people. I wasn't sure how the muumuu came into play, with her being so tiny and all—she looked like a pole with a collapsed tent gathered about her frag-ile hips—but who was I to judge?

"You can absolutely talk to me, Aunt Lil." I tried to straighten but couldn't get past the realization that movement of any kind would take effort. I'd been sitting on one sofa or another for two months, recover-ing from the torture thing. Then I remembered that the cookware I'd been waiting for all morning was up next. Surely Aunt Lil would under-stand. Before she could say anything, I raised a finger to put her in pause mode. "But can our talk wait until the stone-coated cookware is over? I've been eyeing this cookware for a while now. And it's coated. With stone."

"You don't cook."

She had a point. "So what's up?" I propped my bunny-slippered feet on the coffee table and crossed my legs at the ankles.

"I'm not sure how to tell you this." Her breath hitched, and she bowed her blue head.

I straightened in alarm despite the energy it took. "Aunt Lil?"

She tucked her chin in sadness. "I—I think I'm dead."

I blinked. Stared at her a moment. Then blinked again.

"I know." She sniffled into the massive sleeve of her muumuu, and the love beads shifted soundlessly with the movement. Inanimate objects in death carried an eerie silence. Like mimes. Or that scream Al Pacino did in *The Godfather: Part III* when his daughter died on those steps. "I know, I know." She patted my shoulder in consolation. "It's a lot to absorb."

Aunt Lillian died long before I was born, but I had no idea if she knew that or not. Many departed didn't. Because of this doubt, I'd never mentioned it. For years, I'd let her make me invisible coffee in the mornings or cook me invisible eggs; then she'd go off on another adventure. Aunt Lil was still sowing her wild oats. A world traveler, that one. And she rarely stayed in one place very long. Which was good. Otherwise, I'd never get real coffee in the mornings. Or the twelve other times during the day I needed a java fix. If she were around more often, I'd go through caffeine withdrawal on a regular basis. And get really bad headaches.

But maybe now that she knew, I could explain the whole coffee thing.

I was curious enough about her death to ask, "Do you know how you died? What happened?"

According to my family, she'd died in a hippie commune in Madrid at the height of the flower power revolution. Before that, she really had been a world traveler, spending her summers in South America and Europe and her winters in Africa and Australia. And she'd continued that tradition even after her death, traveling far and wide. Passport no longer needed. But no one could really tell me how she died exactly. Or what she did for a living. How she could afford to do all that traveling when she was alive. I knew she'd been married for a while, but my family didn't know much about her husband. My uncle thought he might've been an oil tycoon from Texas, but the family had lost contact, and nobody knew for certain.

"I'm just not sure," she said, shaking her head. "I remember we were sitting around a campfire, singing songs and dropping acid—"

I used every ounce of strength I had to keep the horror I felt from manifesting in my expression.

"—and Bernie asked me what was wrong, but since Bernie had just done a hit of acid himself, I didn't take him seriously."

I could understand that.

She looked up at me, her eyes watering with sorrow. "Maybe I should have listened."

I put an arm around her slight shoulders. "I'm so sorry, Aunt Lil."

"I know, pumpkin head." She patted my cheek, her hand cool in the absence of flesh and blood. She smiled that lopsided smile of hers, and I suddenly wondered if she'd perhaps dropped one hit too many. "I remember the day you were born."

I blinked yet again in surprise. "Really? You were there?"

"I was. I'm so sorry about your mother."

A harsh pang of regret shot through me. I wasn't expecting it, and it took me a moment to recover. "I—I'm sorry, too." The memory of my mother's passing right after I'd been born was not my favorite. And I remembered it so clearly, so precisely. The moment she parted from her physical body, a pop like a rubber band snapping into place ricocheted through my body, and I knew our connection had been severed. I loved her, even then.

"You were so special," Aunt Lil said, shaking her head with the memory. "But now that you know I'm a goner, I have to ask, why in tarnation are you so bright?"

Crap. I couldn't tell her the truth, that I was the grim reaper and the floodlights came with the gig. She thought I was special, not grim. It just sounded so bad when I said it out loud. I decided to deflect. "Well, that's kind of a long story, Aunt Lil, but if you want, you can pass through me. You can cross to the other side and be with your family." I lowered my head, hoping she wouldn't take me up on my offer. I liked having her around, as selfish as that made me.

"Are you kidding?" She slapped a knee. "And miss all the crap you get yourself into? Never." After a disturbing cackle that brought to mind the last horror movie I'd seen, she turned back to the TV. "Now, what's so groovy about this cookware?"

I settled in next to her and we watched a whole segment on pans that could take all kinds of abuse, including a bevy of rocks sliding around the nonstick bottom, but since people didn't actually cook rocks, I wasn't sure what the point was. Still, the pans were pretty. And I could make low monthly payments. I totally needed them.

I was on the phone with a healthy-sounding customer service representative named Herman when Cookie walked in. She did that a lot. Walked in. Like she owned the place. Of course, I was in her apartment. Mine was cluttered and depressing, so I'd resorted to loitering in hers.

Cookie was a large woman with black hair spiked every which way and no sense of fashion whatsoever, if the yellow ensemble she was wearing was any indication. She was also my best friend and receptionist when we had work.

I waved to her, then spoke into the phone. "Declined? What do you mean declined? I have at least twelve dollars left on that puppy, and you said I could make low monthly payments."

Cookie bent over the sofa, grabbed the phone, and pushed the end-call button while completely ignoring the indignant expression I was throwing at her. "It's not so much declined," she said, handing the phone back to me, "as canceled." Then she took the remote and changed the channel to the news. "I've put a stop to any new charges on your Home Shopaholic store card—"

"What?" I thought about acting all flustered and bent out of shape, but I was out of shape enough without purposely adding to the condition. In reality, I was a little in awe of her. "You can do that?"

The news anchor was talking about the recent rash of bank robberies. He showed surveillance footage of the four-man team, known as the Gentlemen Thieves. They always wore white rubber masks and carried guns, but they never drew them. Not once in the series of eight bank robberies, thus their title.

I was in the middle of contemplating how familiar they looked when Cookie took hold of my wrist and hefted me off her sofa. "I can do that," she said as she nudged me toward the door.

"How?"

"Simple. I called and pretended to be you."

"And they fell for it?" Now I was officially appalled. "Who did you talk to? Did you talk to Herman, because he sounds super cute. Wait." I screeched to a halt before her. "Are you kicking me out of your apartment?"

"Not so much kicking you out as putting my foot down. It's time."

"Time?" I asked a little hesitantly.

"Time."

Well, crap. This day was going to suck, I could already tell. "Love the yellow," I said, becoming petty as she herded me out of her apartment and into mine. "You don't look like a giant banana at all. And why did you cancel my favorite shopping channel in-store credit card? I only have three."

"And they've all been canceled. I have to make sure I get paid every week. I've also funneled all of your remaining funds out of your bank account and into a secret account in the Cayman Islands."

"You can funnel money?"

"Apparently."

"Isn't that like embezzling?"

"It's exactly like embezzling." After practically shoving me past my threshold, she closed the door behind us and pointed. "I want you to take a look at all this stuff."

Admittedly, my apartment was a mess, but I still didn't know what that had to do with my card. That card was a tool. In the right hands— like, say, mine—it could make dreams come true. I looked around at all the boxes of super-cool stuff I'd ordered: everything from magical scrubbing sponges for the everyday housewife to two-way radios for when the apocalypse hit and cell phones became obsolete. A wall of boxes lined my apartment, ending in a huge mountain of superfluous products in one specific area of the room. Since my apartment was about the size of a Lego, the minute amount that was left was like a broken Lego. A disfigured one that hadn't survived the invasion of little Lego space aliens.

And there were more boxes behind the wall of boxes we could actually see. I'd completely lost Mr. Wong. He was a dead guy who lived in the corner of my living room, perpetually hovering with his back to the world. Never moving. Never speaking. And now he was lost to the ecology of commerce. Poor guy. His life couldn't have been exciting.

Of course, it didn't help that I'd also moved out of my offices and brought all my files and office equipment to my apartment. My kitchen, actually, making it completely useless for anything other than file storage. But it had been a necessary move, as my dad had betrayed me in the worst way possible—he'd had me arrested as I lay in a hospital bed after being tortured by a madman—and my offices had been above his bar. I had yet to discover what possessed my own father to have me arrested in such an outlandish and hurtful manner. He'd wanted me out of the PI biz, but his timing and modus operandi needed work.

Sadly, the bar was only about fifty feet north of my apartment building, so I would have to avoid him when coming and going from my new work digs. But since I hadn't actually left the apartment building in over two months, that part had been easy. The last time I left was to clear out my offices, and I'd made sure he was out of town when I did so.

I surveyed all the boxes and decided to turn the tables on Cookie. To play the victim. To blame the whole thing on her. I pointed at an Electrolux and gaped at her. "Who the hell left me unsupervised? This has to be your fault."

"Nice try," she said, completely unmoved. "We're going to sort through all of this stuff and send back everything except what you'll actually use. Which is not a lot. Again, I would like to continue collecting a paycheck, if that's not too much to ask."

"Do you take American Express?"

"Oh, I canceled that, too."

I gasped, pretending to be appalled. With a determined set to her shoulders, she led me to my own sofa, took boxes off it, piled them on top of other boxes, then sank down beside me. Her eyes shimmered with warmth and understanding, and I became instantly uncomfortable. "Are we going to have the talk again?"

"I'm afraid so."

"Cook—" I tried to rise and storm off, but she put a hand on my shoulder to stop me "—I'm not sure how else to say that I'm fine." When she looked down at Margaret, who sat nestled inside my hip holster, my voice took on a defensive edge. "What? Lots of PIs wear guns."

"With their pajamas?"

I snorted. "Yes. Especially if they're *Star Wars* pajamas and your gun just happens to resemble a blaster."

Margaret was my new best friend. And she'd never funneled money out of my bank account like some *other* best friends who shall not be named.

"Charley, all I'm asking is that you talk to your sister."

"I talk to her every day." I crossed my arms. Suddenly everyone was insisting that I seek counseling when I was fine. So what if I didn't want to step out of my apartment building? Lots of people liked to stay in. For months at a time.

"Yes, she calls and tries to talk to you about what happened, about how you're doing, but you shut her down."

"I don't shut her down. I just change the subject."

Cookie got up and made us both a cup of coffee while I stewed in the wonders of denial. After I came to the realization that I liked denial almost as much as mocha lattes, she handed me a cup and I took a sip as she sat next to me again. My eyes rolled back in ecstasy. Her coffee was so much better than Aunt Lil's.

"Gemma thinks that maybe you need a hobby." She looked around at the boxes. "A healthy hobby. Like Pilates. Or alligator wrestling."

"I know." I leaned back and threw an arm over my eyes. "I considered writing my memoirs, but I can't figure out how to put seventies porn music into prose."

"See," she said, elbowing me. "Writing. That's a great start. You could try poetry." She stood and rummaged through my box-covered desk. "Here," she said, tossing some paper at me. "Write me a poem about how your day is going, and I'll get started on these boxes."

I put the coffee cup aside and sat up. "For real? Couldn't I just write a poem about my ultimate world domination or the health benefits of eating guacamole?"

She rose onto her toes to look at me from behind one of my more impressive walls. "You bought two electric pressure cookers? Two?"

"They were on sale."

"Charley," she said, her tone admonishing. "Wait." She dipped down then popped back up. "These are awesome." I knew it. "Can I have one?"

"Abso-freaking-lutely. I'll just take it out of your pay."

This could work. I could pay her through my Buy From Home purchases, though that might not help her keep her lights on or continue to have running water. But she'd be happy, and wasn't happiness the most important thing in life? I should write a poem about that.

"You do realize that to use any of this stuff, you have to actually go to the grocery store."

Her words shoved me deeper into the pit of despair often referred to as buyer's regret. "Isn't that what Macho Taco express delivery is for?"

"You'll have to buy food and spices and crap."

"I hate going to the grocery store."

"And you'll have to learn to cook."

"Fine," I said, letting a defeated breath slip through my lips. I had a fantastic flair for the dramatics when needed. "Send back everything that involves any kind of food preparation. I hate to cook."

"Do you want to keep the Jackie Kennedy commemorative bracelet?"

"Do I have to cook it?"

"Nope."

"Then it stays." I lifted my wrist and twirled the bracelet. "Look how sparkly it is."

"And it goes so well with Margaret."

"Totally."

"Pumpkin butt," Aunt Lil said.

I looked up from my Jackie Kennedy commemorative bracelet. Now that she knew she was dead, I would never have to go through that surge of panic at the prospect of her insisting on cooking for me for two weeks straight. I almost starved to death the last time. I held up the bracelet. "Do you think this bracelet is too much?"

"Jackie goes with anything, dear. But I wanted to talk to you about Cookie."

I looked in Cookie's direction and frowned in disappointment. "What has she done now?"

Aunt Lil sank down beside me and patted my arm. "I think she should know the truth."

"About Jackie Kennedy?"

"About me."

"Oh, right."

"What in the world does this monstrous machine do?" Cookie asked from somewhere near the kitchen. A box appeared out of nowhere, hovering unsteadily over a mountain of other boxes.

I smiled in excitement. "You know how sometimes we order coffee and it comes with that incredible foam on top?"

"Yeah."

"Well, that machine does the magic foam trick."

Her dark head popped up. "No."

"Yes."

She looked at the box lovingly. "Okay, we can keep this. I'll just have to carve some time out of my schedule to read the instructions."

"Don't you think she should know?" Aunt Lil continued.

I nodded. She had a point. Or she would have if Cookie didn't already know. "Cook, can you come here a sec?"

"Okay, but I'm working out a system. It's in my head. If I lose it on the way over, I won't be held accountable."

"I can't make any promises."

She sauntered over, shaking another box at me, a disturbing kind of joy in her eyes. "Do you know how long I've wanted a salad spinner?"

"People actually want those?"

"You don't?"

"I think that was one of those four A.M. purchases where I'd lost all sense of reality. I don't even know why anyone would want to spin a salad."

"Well, I do."

"Okay, so, I have some bad news."

She sat in a chair that catty-cornered the sofa, a wary expression on her face. "You got bad news since you've been sitting here?"

"Kind of." I tilted my head discreetly to my side, indicating a *presence*. Cookie frowned.

I did it again.

She shrugged in confusion.

With a sigh, I said, "I have news about Aunt Lillian."

"Oh. Oh!" She looked around and questioned me with a quirk of her brows.

I gave a quick shake of my head. Normally, Cookie would play along, pretending she could see Aunt Lil as well, but since Aunt Lil had finally caught on to the fact that she could walk through walls, I didn't think that would be appropriate. I put a hand on hers and said, "Aunt Lil has passed away."

Cookie frowned.

"She's gone."

She shrugged in confusion. Again.

"I knew she'd take it hard," Aunt Lil said by my side. She sniffled into her sleeve again.

I wanted so badly to roll my eyes at Cookie. She was not getting my hints. I'd have to try harder. "But you know how I can *see the departed*?"

A dawning emerged on Cook's face as she realized Aunt Lil had caught on at long last.

I patted her hand. Really hard. "She's here with us now, just not as you will remember her."

"You mean—?"

"Yes," I said, interrupting before she could give anything away. "She has passed."

Cookie finally grasped the entire concept. Not just a little corner of it. She threw a hand over her mouth. A weak squeak slipped through her fingers. "Not Aunt Lil." She doubled over and let sobs rack her shoulders.

Subtle.

"I didn't think she'd take it *this* hard," Aunt Lil said.

"Neither did I." I looked on in horror as Cookie acted out that scene from *The Godfather*. It was even more eerie from this close proximity. "It's okay," I said, patting her head. Really hard. She glared through her fingers. "Aunt Lil is with us incorporeally. She sends her love."

"Oh, yes," Aunt Lil said with a delirious nod. "Send her my love."

"Aunt Lil," Cookie said, straightening and looking beside me. Only on the wrong side.

I nodded in Aunt Lil's direction again, and Cookie corrected her line of sight.

"Aunt Lil, I'm so sorry. We'll miss you so much."

"Aw, isn't she the sweetest thing? I always liked her."

With a smile, I took Aunt Lil's hand into mine. "I always liked her, too. Until about fifteen minutes ago."

I decided a shower was not out of the question and hopped in as Cookie took inventory and Aunt Lil decided to see what Africa looked like from her new perspective. I wondered if she'd ever figure out how long she'd been dead. I certainly wasn't going to tell her.

Hot water was one of the best therapies in the world. It washed away stress and soothed nerves. But Rottweilers were even better. Ever since a gorgeous Rottie by the name of Artemis had died and become my guardian—against what, I had no idea—I found my showers more challenging than usual. Mostly because Artemis loved showers, too. She didn't come around that often, but the minute I turned on the water, there she was.

"Hey, precious," I said as she tried to catch a stream of water in her mouth.

She barked playfully, the loud yelp echoing off the walls of the tub. I reached down and rubbed her ears. The water ran straight through her, so she was dry to the touch, but she tried so hard to catch the thick droplets on her tongue.

"I know how you feel, girl. Sometimes the things we want most seem completely out of our reach."

When she jumped up on me, her stubby tail wagging with delight, her weight sent me crashing against the tile wall. I clutched on to the showerhead to keep my balance, then let her lick my neck before another stream of water captured her attention. She dived for it, almost knocking my feet out from under me. I totally needed a shower mat. And shaving my legs with a Rottweiler chasing every splash of water known to man was like taking my life into my own hands, but it had to be done.

After semi-successfully shaving my legs with minimal blood loss, I turned off the water and nuzzled her to me. She licked my left ear, her front teeth scraping the lobe and causing goose bumps to spread over my skin, and I laughed out loud. "Oh, thank you. I needed that ear cleaned. Thank you so much."

With another yelp, she realized fun time was over. The wonderful world of waterworks had stopped, so she dived through the exterior wall and disappeared. I wondered if it was wrong that I took showers with a dog.

I dried my hair and pulled it into something that resembled a ponytail, dressed in jeans and a white pullover with a zippered collar, then inspected myself in the mirror. No idea why. I'd only change back into my pajamas in a couple of hours anyway. Why did I get dressed? Why did I bother? Why did I shower, for that matter?

I pumped a dollop of lotion onto my palm and rubbed my hands together as I examined the nasty scar on my cheek. It was almost gone. On anyone else, it would have remained a constant reminder of events better left forgotten. But being the grim reaper had its benefits. Namely, quick healing and minimal scarring. Nary a shred of visible evidence to support the reasoning behind my sudden case of mild agoraphobia. I was so stupid.

I took the lotion I'd been rubbing into my hands and smeared it across the mirror. White streaks distorted my face. A definite improvement.

Growing more annoyed with myself by the second, I strolled to the window to see if my traitorous father was at work yet. He seemed to be coming in later and later. Not that I cared. Any man who would have his own daughter arrested while she lay dying in a hospital bed after being tortured almost to death didn't deserve my concern. I was just curious, and curious was way on the other side of concern. But instead of seeing my father's tan SUV, I caught sight of one Mr. Reyes Farrow, and my breath stilled in my chest. He was leaning against the back of Dad's bar, arms folded at his chest, one booted foot leveraged against the building.

And he was out.

I knew he would be, but I had yet to see him. He'd been in prison for ten years for a crime he didn't commit. The cops caught on when the guy he'd supposedly killed tied me up and tortured me. I was glad he'd been freed, but to get there, Reyes'd used me as bait, so we were once again at an impasse. I was mad at him for using me as bait. He was mad at me for being mad at him for using me as bait. Our relationship seemed to hinge on these impasses, but that's what I got for falling in lust with the son of Satan. If only he weren't so deliciously and dangerously hot. I had such a thing for bad boys.

And this particular bad boy had been dipped in a lake of beauty when he was born. His arms corded with muscles across a wide chest; his full mouth, too sensual for my peace of mind, sat in a grim, moody line; his dark hair, forever in need of a trim, curled at his neck and tumbled over his forehead. And I could just make out his thick lashes as they fanned across his cheeks.

A man walked past him and waved. Reyes nodded, but then he must have felt me watching him. He looked down in thought then up directly at me. His angry gaze locked on to mine, held it for a long, breathless moment, and then slowly, with deliberate purpose, he dematerialized, his body transforming into smoke and dust until there was nothing left of it.

He could do that. He could separate from his physical body, and his incorporeal essence—something I could see as easily as I saw the departed—could go anywhere in the world it wanted to. That didn't surprise me in the least. What surprised me was the fact that, while incorporeal, no one else could see him. But that man had waved. He'd seen

Reyes standing there and waved. That meant his physical body had been leaning against that brick wall.

That meant his physical body had dematerialized, had vanished into the cool morning air.

Impossible.

2

Doing nothing is hard.
You never know when you're done.
—T-SHIRT

It took every ounce of strength I had to tear myself away from the window, wondering if Reyes Farrow had just dematerialized his human body. Then another thought hit: What the hell was he doing out there? And then another: Why was he so angry? It was my turn to be angry. He had no reason to be. And I would have told him that very thing if I'd felt any incentive to leave my apartment and hunt him down. But my apartment was cozy. The thought of leaving it just to get in a fight with the son of evil incarnate made about as much sense as flying ants. Where was the logic in that? Ants were scary enough without giving them the ability to fly.

I walked into my living room, shaken and disoriented. "Reyes Farrow was outside. Just leaning against the bar. Watching the apartment."

Cookie jumped up. She gaped at me for about ten seconds before hurdling the couch and stumbling into my bedroom, nearly crashing through the window. She was almost agile where men were concerned. I didn't have the heart to tell her she'd have had a better view from the living room, from pretty much right where she'd been sitting. Nor did I have the heart to tell her that he was already gone.

"He's not there," she said, her voice agitated and panicked.

"What?" I asked, pretending to be surprised. I hurried over and peeked out the curtains. Sure enough, he was gone. "He was there a minute ago." I scanned the entire area.

She frowned at me. "You knew he was gone."

I cringed, ashamed. "Sorry. You were just so into your gymnastics routine, I didn't want to break your concentration. Do you know how hard it would be to explain to the cops if you'd crashed through the window and plummeted to your death?" I refocused on the spot where Reyes had been standing. "But I swear, if that man is tailing me—"

"Hon, you have to go somewhere to be tailed. This would be more like stalking."

She had a point. One that I could throw in his face if I were ever going to speak to him again.

I bowed my head as Cookie continued to search the parking lot in the hopes that he would show up again. I could hardly blame her.

"While we're on the subject, I think he dematerialized his human body."

She jumped in surprise. "I thought that was impossible. Are you sure?"

"No." I walked back into my cluttered living room, because another thought hit. Freaking ADD. "So, be honest. How broke am I?"

Cookie drew in a deep breath and followed me. She regarded me with a sad expression before answering. "On a scale of one to ten, you're not on it. You're more like a negative twelve."

"Crap." I studied my Jackie Kennedy commemorative bracelet with a great and terrible weight on my chest, then opened the clasp. "Here, send this back, too."

She took it. "Are you sure?"

"Yeah. I was only pretending it went well with Margaret, anyway. Now, if it were black with skulls on it . . ."

"Sadly, I don't think Jackie wore skulls all that often. You know, we still have a couple of clients who owe us."

"Really?" This was promising. I wound around boxes to Mr. Coffee. He was the only action I'd been getting lately.

"Yep."

When she hesitated, I knew something was up. I refreshed my cup and questioned her with a quirk of my brows. "Like who?"

"Like Mrs. Allen."

"Mrs. Allen?" I stirred in creamer and fake sweet stuff. "She pays me in cookies. I'm not sure how that will help with the bills."

"True, but she didn't pay us the last time you found PP."

PP, otherwise known as Prince Phillip, was Mrs. Allen's rabid poodle. She should have called him Houdini. That dog could escape a locked bank vault. But actually, Cookie was wrong. Guilt had me biting my lip as I stirred, averting my gaze.

She gasped. "Mrs. Allen paid you?"

"Kind of."

"And you didn't share?"

"Well—"

"An entire plate of cookies, and you didn't share? After I did all the legwork?"

My jaw fell open. "The legwork? You walked over to the window and spotted him by the Dumpster."

"Yes, and I *walked*—" She crisscrossed her fingers to demonstrate a walking motion, which I found humorous. "—to the window with my *legs*."

"Yes, but I was the one who chased that vicious little shit seventeen blocks."

"Three."

"And then he bit me."

"He has no teeth."

"Gums hurt, too." I rubbed my arm absently, remembering the horror of it all.

"He's a poodle. How hard can he gum?"

"Fine, next time you can chase him down."

After exhaling loudly, she said, "What about that Billy Bob guy? He still owes us money."

"You mean Bobby Joe? That guy who thought his girlfriend was trying to kill him with peanuts? He traded that out."

"Charley," she said, her tone admonishing, "you have got to learn to keep it in your pants."

"Not like that," I replied, appalled. "He painted the offices for us."

After a long, exasperated stare, she asked, "You mean the offices we are no longer in?"

I offered her a sheepish shrug. "Yeah, I forgot to cancel, and he painted them after we moved out. He was really happy that they were so clutter free."

"Well, that's just fantastic."

Her enthusiasm seemed disingenuous. It was weird.

"Surely, someone else owes us money," she said.

Then it hit me. The answer to all our prayers. Or at least a couple of them. "You're right," I said. Reyes Farrow owed me and owed me big. I grinned at Cookie. "I solved a case. I am due my usual rate, plus medical expenses and mental anguish."

She looked hopeful. "What case? Who?"

The determined set of my jaw told her exactly who I was talking about. She got that faraway, dreamy look in her eyes. "Can I help collect?"

"Nope, you have to get all this stuff sent back. How else are we going to eat for the next month?"

"I never get to have any fun."

"It's your own fault."

She cleared her throat. "How is any of this—" She spread her arms wide. "—my fault?"

"That's what you get for leaving me unsupervised. Don't you have return receipts to fill out?"

She lifted a handful. "Yes."

"From your apartment?"

"Fine."

She took the receipts and started to leave me to my own devices. She would never learn.

"Oh," she said before opening the door, "I took your remote, so don't even think about it."

That was so uncalled for.

After she left, I sat down and tried to think up a plan of action. If only I could get ahold of Angel. If anyone could find that low-down, dirty—

"How did you do that?"

I jumped at the sound of a voice coming from behind me. It was high. The jump. Not the voice. I pressed my hands to my heart and turned to the thirteen-year-old departed gangbanger who went by the name of Angel Garza. He stood in my apartment, wearing his usual jeans and dirty T-shirt with a bandanna wrapped around his head. "Angel, what the hell?"

"What do you mean, what the hell? What did you do?"

"What?" I asked, trying to calm my heart. I didn't normally get that scared when Angel popped in.

His dark brown eyes narrowed in question. "How did you do that?"

"I don't know. What did I do?"

"I was at my cousin's *quinceañera* one minute, then here the next."

"Really?"

"Did you do that?"

"I don't think so. I just thought about you, and you were there."

"Well, stop it. That was weird." He hugged himself and rubbed his arms.

"This is cool. You never come when I need you."

"I'm your investigator, *pendeja*, not your lapdog."

"I can't believe that worked."

"What are all these boxes?"

"Did you just call me *pendeja*?"

Then he noticed me at last and got the familiar look in his eyes. "You're looking good, boss."

"And you're looking thirteen." Throwing his age in his face always worked. He bristled and turned to study my new cheese pot. He wouldn't like what I was about to ask him, so I stood and faced him head-on, my stance set, my expression hard. "I need to know where he is."

Surprise straightened his shoulders a moment, but he caught himself and shrugged. "Who?"

He knew exactly who I was talking about. "He was just here a minute ago, standing outside my apartment building. Where is he staying?"

Frustration slid through his lips. "You've stayed away from him for weeks. Why now?"

"He owes me money."

"Not my problem."

"It will be when I can't pay your salary." To pay for his investigative services, I sent an anonymous cashier's check to his mother every month. He couldn't use the money in his rather sparse condition, but she could. It was a perfect arrangement.

"Shit." He disappeared through a wall of boxes. "Every time you get near him, you get hurt."

"That's not true."

He reemerged but only partly. "What's a Flowbee?"

"Angel." I put a finger under his chin and stroked the barely emerging growth of hair that peppered his jaw. "I need to know where he is."

"Can I see you naked first?"

"No."

"You want to see me naked?"

"No. And yuck."

He straightened, offended. "If I was still alive, I'd be older than you."

"But you aren't," I reminded him gently. "And I'm sorry for that."

"You aren't going to like it."

"That's okay. I just need to know where he is."

"He'll be at Garber Shipping in the warehouse district tonight."

"At a shipping warehouse?" I asked, surprised. "Is he working there?"

Reyes had money. Lots and lots of money. His sister told me. So why would he be doing manual labor for a shipping company?

After Angel took a long moment to nibble at a hangnail, he said, "Depends on your definition of work."

After being stunned speechless by Reyes's new job title, I walked toward my front door, wrapped a hand around the knob, then rethought what I was doing. I was going to face Reyes Farrow. Unarmed. Reyes had never tried to hurt me directly, but he'd been out of prison for two months. Who knew what the man was capable of? He'd probably learned a lot of bad habits since leaving the big house. Like cheating at poker. And urinating in public.

Even though I wasn't much for carrying firearms—every time I carried a gun, images of it being wrestled away from me and used to end my life always flashed before my eyes—I headed back to my bedroom for Margaret. I figured, when facing a dirty, lying scoundrel like Reyes Farrow, one couldn't be too careful. Or too armed. So I slid a belt through the loops of my jeans, holstered the Glock, then snapped the clasp closed.

After another deep breath, I headed out the door only to lose steam when I came to the stairs. The same stairs I'd taken a gazillion times before. They looked steeper somehow. More dangerous. My hands shook on the rail as I paused on each step, working up the courage to take the next, wondering what in the name of thunder was wrong with me. True, it'd been a while since I'd ventured out, but surely the world hadn't changed that much.

When I finally made it down two flights of stairs to the first floor, I studied the steel entrance door to the complex. It sat ajar, not quite closed, and daylight streamed in around the edges. I forced one foot in front of the other, my breaths shallow, my palms slick with a nervous energy. I reached a quaking hand for the vertical handle and pushed. Daylight rushed in, flooding the area and blinding me. My breath caught and I pulled the door shut. Leaning against the handle for support, I took in long gulps of air, and tried to calm myself.

One minute. I just needed a minute to gather my wits. They were always running amok, wreaking havoc.

"Ms. Davidson?"

Without thought, I drew the gun from my holster and aimed toward the voice coming from the shadowy entranceway.

A woman gasped and jumped back, her eyes wide, gaping at the barrel pointed at her face. "I—I'm so sorry. I thought—"

"Who are you?" I asked, holding the gun so much steadier than I thought possible, considering the irrational state of my insides.

"Harper." She held her hands up in surrender. "My name is Harper Lo—"

"What do you want?" I had no idea why I was still holding the gun on her. Normally, nice women with no hidden agenda whatsoever didn't scare me. It was weird.

"I'm looking for Charley Davidson."

I lowered the gun but didn't holster it. Not just yet. She could turn out to be psychotic. Or a door-to-door salesperson. "I'm Charley. What do you want?" I cringed at the sharpness of my own voice. Why was I behaving so badly? I'd eaten a good breakfast.

"I—I'd like to hire you. I think someone is trying to kill me."

I narrowed my eyes, took in her appearance. Long dark hair. Tall and curvy, full figured in a very pretty way. Soft features. Neat clothes. She had a baby blue scarf tied loosely at her neck, the ends tucked into her dark blue coat. Her eyes were large, warm, and captivating. All in all, she didn't look crazy. Then again, neither did most crazy people.

"You're looking for a PI?" A girl could hope. I hadn't had a job in two months. Apparently. I glanced up toward Cookie's apartment.

"Yes. An investigator."

I took a deep breath and holstered Margaret. "I'm kind of in between offices at the moment. We can talk in my apartment, if that's okay."

She nodded briskly, fear evident in every move she made. Poor thing. She clearly didn't deserve my surly side.

With head hung in shame, I started back upstairs. They were much easier to climb than to descend. That wasn't usually the case. Especially after a two-month veg-a-thon. My muscles should have atrophied by now. "Can I get you anything?" I asked when we reached my apartment. I was only slightly out of breath.

"Oh, no, thank you. I'm fine." She was eyeing me warily. Not that I could blame her. My people skills needed a good honing. "Are you okay?" she asked.

"I'm fine. The wheezing will go away in a minute. It's been a while since I took those stairs."

"Oh, does this building have an elevator?"

"Um, no. You know, I'm not sure it's wise to go into someone's apartment who just pulled a gun on you."

She'd been busy perusing the mess that was my office-slash-apartment-slash-ballroom-area-when-the-dancing-bug-hit. She dropped her gaze in embarrassment at my words. "I guess I'm a little desperate."

I offered her the chair and I took the couch. Thankfully, Aunt Lillian still wasn't back from Africa. After picking up a notepad and pen, I asked, "So, what's going on?"

She swallowed hard and said, "I've been having strange things happen to me. Bizarre things."

"Like?"

"Someone has been breaking into my house and leaving . . . things."

"What kinds of things?"

"Well, for one, I found a dead rabbit on my bed this morning."

"Oh." Taken aback, I crinkled my nose in disgust. "That's not good. But I'm not sure—I mean, maybe it was suicidal."

She rushed in to stop me. "You don't understand. A lot of things like that have been happening. Rabbits with their throats cut. Brakes with their lines cut."

"Wait, brakes? As in car brakes?"

"Yes. Yes." She was starting to panic. "The brakes on my car. They just stopped working. How do brakes just stop working?" She was scared. It broke my heart. Her hands shook and her eyes filled with tears. "And then my dog." She buried her face in her hands and let the emotions she'd been holding at bay rush forth. "She disappeared."

Now I really felt bad about the Margaret thing. I chastised her with a glare. Margaret. Not Harper. Sobs racked her body as all her fears spilled forth. I scooted forward and put a hand on her shoulder. After a few minutes, she began to calm, so I started my questions anew.

"Have you called the police?"

She pulled a tissue from her coat pocket and dabbed at her nose. "Over and over. So much so, they actually assigned an officer to vet my calls."

"Oh, really? Which officer?"

"Officer Taft," she said, a hard edge leeching into her voice. Definitely no love lost there.

"Okay, I know him. I can talk to him to get—"

"But he doesn't believe me. None of them do."

"What about your brakes? Surely they could tell if they'd been tampered with?"

"The mechanic couldn't say it was foul play specifically, so they just dismissed that like they did everything else."

I leaned back and tapped my notebook in thought. "How long has this been going on?"

She bit her lip, glanced away in embarrassment. "A few weeks now."

"What about your family?"

Her fingers smoothed the edge of her scarf. "My parents aren't really the supportive type. And my ex-husband, well, he'd just use it against me every chance he got. I haven't told him."

"Do you suspect him?"

"Kenneth?" She scoffed softly. "No. He's an ass, but he's a harmless ass."

Proceeding with caution, I asked, "Is he paying you alimony?"

"No. Not any. He has no reason to want me dead."

I wasn't so sure about that, but decided to go along with it for now. "What about work colleagues?"

I'd embarrassed her again. She blanched under my questioning gaze. "I don't really—I don't work. I haven't had a job for a while now."

Interesting. "How do you pay your bills?"

"My parents are very well off. They basically pay me to stay away from them. It works out well for the both of us."

I couldn't help but conclude that if she weren't around, they'd no longer have to carry her. Perhaps her parents were even less supportive than she imagined.

"What do they think of this situation?"

She shrugged. "They believe me even less than Officer Taft."

She had me at Officer Taft. While we weren't exactly enemies, we weren't really friends either. We'd had an encounter once that ended in him cursing at me and storming out of my apartment. I tended not to forget such encounters. That one involved his sister, who'd died when he was very young. He got testy when I told him she'd stayed behind for him. Some people were so touchy when I told them their departed family members had taken up stalking.

"Okay," I said, "I'll take this case on one condition."

The tension seemed to ooze out. I wasn't sure if that was because I was taking her case or she really was that afraid for her life. "Anything," she said.

"You have to promise to be honest with me. Once I take this case, I'm on your side, do you understand? Think of me as your doctor or your therapist. I can't repeat anything you tell me in confidence without your express permission."

She nodded. "I'll tell you everything I can."

"Okay, first, do you have any idea, any suspicion at all of who would want you dead?"

Most people, when threatened, did, but Harper shook her head. "I've tried and tried. I just have no idea who would want to hurt me."

"Fair enough." I didn't want to push her too hard. She seemed fragile as it was, and my shoving a gun in her face couldn't have helped.

I took down the names of her closest family and friends, anyone who might be able to corroborate her story. Attempted murder was no laughing matter. Neither was stalking or harassment. The fact that her immediate family wasn't taking her seriously alarmed me. I'd have to pay them a visit ay-sap.

"Do you have a place to stay besides your house?" I asked when I was done.

Her hair fell forward with another soft shake of her head. "I haven't thought about it. I guess I really don't. Not anywhere safe."

That could be a problem. Still . . . "You know, I might have just the place. It's like a safe house, only it's a tattoo parlor."

"Oh . . . kay."

She seemed open to the idea. That was good. "Awesome. You sit tight while I get this information to my assistant across the hall, then I'll take you over."

With an absent nod, she studied a box on the sofa beside me of collectible Kiss action figures.

"Yeah," I said, agreeing with her bewilderment, "a lot of caffeine went into that decision."

"I can imagine."

I started across the hall, thrilled about the prospect of rubbing my new client in Cookie's face—not literally, though, as that could be awkward—and almost ran down Mr. Zamora, the building's superintendent.

"Oh—hey, there," he said. He was shorter than me, pudgy with salt-and-pepper hair that always seemed to be in need of a good conditioning. And he always wore sweatpants and T-shirts that had seen more abuse than narcotics. But he was a good landlord. When my heater stopped working in mid-December, it took him only two weeks to get it fixed. Of course, it took me knocking on his door in need of a warm place to sleep to get it that way, but one night on his sofa, where I'd suddenly developed night terrors and epilepsy, and that puppy was running like a Mercedes the next day. It was awesome.

"Hey, Mr. Z."

He was carrying a small ladder, a drop cloth, and a gallon of paint. And he was headed to the apartment at the end of the hall. What the heck? When I'd first moved in, I wanted that apartment. I begged. I pleaded. But no. The owners weren't willing to shell out the money it would take to renovate it. And now he was renovating it? Now they were willing?

"What's going on?" I asked as nonchalantly as possible.

He drew to a stop in front of me, key at the ready. While Cookie's apartment and mine were right across the hall from each other, the end apartment spanned the length of both of ours with the door perpendicular to the main hall. It was like taking both of ours and putting them together. Since it'd suffered major water damage a few years ago and the owners lost the insurance money at the casinos before they could finish the renovations, it'd sat vacant for years. Which made no sense to me whatsoever.

"Finally finishing up this apartment," he said, pointing with a key. "Got some construction guys coming in this afternoon. Might get noisy."

Hope blossomed in my chest like a begonia in spring. My apartment was way too small now with all my new stuff. I could totally use bigger and better digs. "I want it," I said, blurting it out before I could stop myself.

He raised a brow. "Can't let you have it. Already have a tenant."

"No way. Mr. Z, I've wanted that apartment since I first looked at this place. You promised to put me on the list of possible tenants."

"And you are on the list. Right below these people."

I gasped. "You mean, you cheated?"

"No. I took a bribe. Not the same thing."

He started for the door again. I took a menacing step in front of him. "I bribed you, too, if you'll remember."

With a snort, he said, "Was that a bribe? I thought it was a tip."

I was now officially appalled. "And I offered to pay you more than what I was paying for this cracker box."

"You dissing my building?"

"No, your ethics."

"If I'm recalling this right, you offered to pay fifty dollars more a month for this apartment."

"That's right."

"For an apartment that's twice the size of yours."

"Yeah, so? It's all I had at the time."

"From my understanding, the new tenant is paying three times what you pay for yours. And paying for all the repairs."

Crap. I probably couldn't afford to do something like that. Maybe if I sent back the espresso machine. And the electric nail gun. "I cannot believe you went behind my back like this."

He picked up the ladder. "I don't think renting out an apartment is going behind your back, Ms. Davidson. But if you feel that strongly about it, you can always kiss my ass."

"In your dreams."

After a soft chuckle, he disappeared into the apartment. I got a peek at the new drywall lining the walls, all fresh and unpainted. Clearly, I'd missed something.

I strode through Cookie's door, cursing my bad luck. And bad hearing. "Did you know Mr. Z rented 3B?"

Cookie looked up from her computer. "No way. I wanted that apartment."

"I did, too. Who do you think our neighbor will be?"

"Probably another elderly woman with poodles."

"Maybe. Or maybe a serial killer."

"One can dream. What do you have?" She nodded toward the paper in my hands.

"Oh, right. We have a client."

"Really?" Her surprise wasn't completely unexpected. It'd been a while. But it was a little offensive.

"Yeah. She just showed up. Maybe those ads we're running on late-night radio are working."

"Possibly, but I still think they'd work even better if they were in English. Not many people speak Japanese around here."

"Honestly, Cook, you act like I don't even *want* any new clients."

She reached over and snatched the paper out of my hands. "I wonder where I got that idea from."

With a confounded shrug, I glanced behind me to make sure Harper wasn't at the door; then I spoke softly to Cook. "I need you to find out everything you can about her. I need family members, work and volunteer history, parking tickets, whatever you can get."

"You got it. Where are you going now?" she asked as I headed for the door.

"Harper believes someone is trying to kill her, so I'm taking her to the safe house."

"Sounds like a plan." After the door clicked closed, she yelled out, "We have a safe house?"

3

After a battle of epic proportions, where my legs wanted to go one way while my head told them to go another, I strode with Harper past my dad's bar and down the alley toward our makeshift safe house. I couldn't help but scan the terrain like a soldier in hostile territory. Oddly enough, Harper did the same thing. We looked like tweakers as we passed businesses, college students, and the occasional homeless person.

I decided to try to lighten the mood. "So, what did you always want to be when you grew up?" I asked Harper.

She walked beside me, arms crossed at chest, head down, and fought to smile.

"It's just up here," I said, saving her from having to respond. "Pari's a saint. Only with full sleeves and a bad attitude. Other than that, you can totally count on her. Mostly for questionable advice, but we all have to be good at something, right?"

"Do you think you'll catch him?" She couldn't quite wrap her head around anything other than her immediate danger. Clearly she did not suffer from ADD.

"I'm going to do my best, hon. Cross my heart."

"I'm so tired of feeling helpless. Guess I should've taken karate or something, huh?"

I liked her thought process, but even martial arts didn't guarantee a long and prosperous life. "Don't beat yourself up over this, Harper. There are crazy people out there. People you can't reason with or even begin to understand without being a licensed psychotherapist. There's no telling what set this guy off."

She nodded, acceding to my expertise on crazy people. I grew up with one in the form of Denise Davidson, the stepmother from hell. She could teach the son of Satan a thing or two.

"Here it is," I said, pointing to a screen door. Remnants of red paint framed the wood around the back entrance.

Harper stopped and looked around the alley. We were at the back entrance of a seedy tattoo parlor. Her confidence in me seemed to wane a bit.

"It's totally safe. I promise."

After a hesitant nod, she said, "Okay. I trust you."

Maybe she really was crazy. "And Pari has a really cute apprentice."

A shy grin spread across her face. She seemed so innocent and unworldly, yet she was simply beautiful. I wondered what her life had been like. Hopefully, I'd find out as the case went on.

"A teacher."

I was just about to open the door when she'd spoken. "I'm sorry?"

"A teacher. You asked me what I'd always wanted to be. A teacher."

I gave her my full attention. "Why didn't you become one?"

She shrugged and looked elsewhere. "My mother didn't approve. She wanted me to be a doctor or a lawyer."

While I couldn't imagine her as a lawyer, I could definitely see her as a doctor. She seemed the nurturing type. Then again, doctors weren't all that nurturing. Maybe a nurse. Still, I could definitely see her as a teacher. She would've made a great one. "I hope all your dreams come true, Harper."

"Thank you," she said in surprise. "I hope yours do, too."

I offered an appreciative smile. "Most of mine involve a man who is more trouble than he's worth, but it's a nice thought."

She laughed softly, covering her mouth with a hand. Her mouth was too pretty to be covered.

We stepped inside Pari's shop. She had a desk up front, but her office sat in the back, past the studio, a corner space the size of a moth's testicles with a nice view of the Dumpster across the alley. I heard a few huffing sounds coming from underneath the desk, so I strolled in, half hoping to catch her doing something illicit. Her apprentice was hot.

She had computer guts scattered over her desk. Wires and gadgets of all shapes and sizes littered every available inch of counter space.

It seemed like every time I walked into her parlor, she was busy with something technical, which seemed to go against the grain of her artistic nature. Then again, she always was a little grainy.

A thumping sound wafted toward me, eliciting an evil grin. I was such a perv. "Hey, Par," I said, hitching a hip onto her desk to peer over it nonchalantly.

After a mighty struggle that involved a sharp crack and a few gurgling sounds, she popped her head up. Her hair, a thick black mop that some would call a mess while others—namely me—would call a work of art, seemed to have grown attached to the wires she was working on. She spit out a microscopic piece of plastic while fishing the wires out of her do with one hand and shielding her eyes with the other.

"Fucking hell, Charley." She closed her eyes and felt around her desk blindly for her sunglasses. Pari had been able to see what normal folk referred to as ghosts since she'd had a near-death experience when she was twelve. She couldn't make out the shapes or communicate with the departed. She just saw them as a gray mist, so she always knew when one was near.

But me she could see from a mile away. My brightness seemed to grate on her. It was funny.

After inching her sunglasses away from her reach a third time, she opened her eyes and glared at me. It must have been painful. I could only hope she didn't have a hangover.

She sighed and ducked back under the desk.

"Is your guy down there with you?" I asked.

"My guy?" She grunted, apparently trying to reach something. "I don't have a guy."

"I thought you had a guy."

"I don't have a guy."

"You have an apprentice."

"That's not a guy. That's Tre."

"Who is a guy."

"But not that kind of guy. How did you get in here? My office door was locked."

"No it wasn't."

She popped her head back out and glanced around. "Really? It should have been locked."

After she ducked back down, I asked, "Why? What are you doing?"

". . . Nothing."

She'd hesitated far too long. She was totally up to something. I leaned over to inspect her work. "Looks to me like you're rewiring your phone line."

"No, I'm not," she said defensively. "Why would I do that?"

If liars were the main course at a Shriners convention, she'd be a pork chop.

"Okay, fine, don't tell me. I need to leave a client with you a few days. Can we use your spare room?"

"There's only a couch, but it's comfortable."

"That'll work. This is Harper. Harper, this is Pari."

"Hey, Harper," she said, but before Harper could respond, a shower of sparks lit the area. A rustling sounded from under the desk and was followed by a solid thud as Pari slammed into the underside of it for the umpteenth time.

Doubtful that phone lines sparked like that, I leaned over again. "Seriously, what are you doing?"

"Did you see a spark?"

"I'm going to show Harper to her room. Try not to kill yourself before I get back."

"Okay, lock the door on the way out."

"O—"

"Wait!" She popped up again, an idea lighting her face. Her heavy liner narrowed as she patted the desk, searching for her sunglasses again. I let her get them that time. She slid them onto her face, then said, "I'm doing you a favor."

I hitched my hip back onto her desk. "Yes."

"And favors need to be repaid, right?"

Wondering where she was going with this, I said, "Yes."

"Go on a date with me."

"You're not really my type."

"Come on, Chuck. One date and I'll never ask again."

"No, really, you're not my type."

"You know how you have this incredible gift for being able to tell when someone is lying?"

I glanced at Harper. She seemed very interested all of a sudden. I shrugged. "Yeah."

"Well, I'm thinking about dating this guy, but I can't quite get a read on him. You know, I can't tell if he's being truthful with me or not."

"Do you suspect him of anything in particular?"

"Not really. I just thought you could *show up*—" She added air quotes to emphasize the deception "—then just sit with us a minute. You know, just long enough to get a read on him."

"I don't really read people."

"Feel him, then."

"Fun, yet awkward."

"You know what I mean. Tit for tat, lady. Take it or leave it." She looked past me. "No offense, Harper."

"Oh, none tak—"

"So?" Pari said, interrupting poor Harper, who was finally getting a word in. "My couch for your mad skill."

"Well, since you put it that way."

"Sweet. I'll text you the place and time."

"Wonderful. I'm going to show Harper the couch."

"Okay."

I figured our conversation was over, but no sooner had she ducked behind the desk than she popped right back up again. She reminded me of a toaster pastry minus the icing.

"Wait a minute. Where have you been?"

"Around. Just kind of hanging out in my apartment."

"For two months?"

"Pretty much."

"Hmm. Okay, well, lock the door!" she yelled. She was so pushy.

"She's interesting."

"Yes, she is." I led Harper around a tight corner, made tighter by the boxes of supplies, and into a small back room. "It's not much, but no one will think to look for you here, I'm certain of it."

She took it all in with a gracious nod. I could tell she wanted to scrunch her nose in distaste, but refrained out of kindness. "This is perfect," she said instead. What a great sport.

"Okay, I'm off to do investigative stuff. I'll come back later tonight. You gonna be okay here?"

"Sure, I'll be fine."

I put a hand on her arm to draw her attention away from her new surroundings. "I'll do everything in my power to find whoever is doing this to you. I promise."

A tiny smile lit her face, and if I wasn't mistaken, she was a little relieved. "Thank you."

After leaving Harper standing in the middle of the tiny room, I spotted Pari's apprentice, Tre. He was working on a girl's tat who looked torn between anguish and desire. I could hardly blame her. Tre was like a Long Island iced tea: tall, unassuming, delicious enough to wet your whistle as well as other places, and packed a lethal punch when you least expected it.

"Hey, Chuck," he said, nodding at me between buzzes of the needle. The fact that deep down inside, tattoo artists must enjoy the infliction of pain on others was not lost on me. I wondered if that trait spilled over into his personal life. I could handle pain if that's what he was into. Not a lot, but . . .

"Hey, you," I said, only a little worried I'd make him mess up. Mistakes were so permanent. Like nine-months-after-prom permanent.

He paused his efforts to ask, "Do you just call me *you* because you can't remember my name?"

My shoulders wilted. "Darn. You caught me. No, wait, it's here somewhere." I tapped my temple in thought as he went back to his task. "Oh, right, is it Serving Tray?"

He shook his head, his brows drawn in concentration.

"Is it Lunch Tray?"

"No," he said with a soft chuckle.

"Is it Ashtray?"

He paused again, and the girl shot daggers at me with her huge dark eyes. She was either jealous or in so much pain, she just wanted it over with, and I kept interrupting.

"Forget I asked," he said, a boyish smile lighting his features.

What a heartbreaker. No wonder Pari's female client base had tripled since he started working with her.

"See ya round, handsome."

He winked and went back to work with a grin sparkling in his eyes. I felt sorry for the girl.

On the way back, I cut through the parking lot and made a beeline for Misery, my cherry red Jeep Wrangler. In the semi-open space of downtown Albuquerque, I felt naked. I'd been naked in public once, so while this definitely synthesized that level of discomfort, this was different. More raw. More acute. More feral.

"He misses you, you know."

I spun around to see a statuesque African American woman walking past me toward the back of Dad's bar. I'd seen her a few times in the last few weeks and figured she was the new bartender Dad had been planning to hire when I refused the job. He'd wanted me to give up my PI business and work for him. Silly rabbit. She stopped and offered me a friendly, I-come-in-peace smile. To say that she was stunning would have been an understatement. She was like a shimmering skyscraper, jutting proudly into the sky and daring the world to try to knock her down.

"Your father," she said, elaborating. Her exotic eyes held me captive for a full minute before she turned back to the bar. "You're all he talks about."

Clearly she knew about our falling out, but I had no use for anything she'd just told me. Even if it were true, my father did not deserve my forgiveness at that moment. Nor my attention.

I climbed into Misery and sank into her faux leather seats. She fit like a big red glove and felt just as warm. Well, not literally. The weather was chilly and her plastic windows were frosted over. I turned the key to let her warm up. She roared to life, then settled into a purr. It'd been a while since the two of us had had any alone time together. We'd have to talk later, but for now, we had places to be and suspects to see.

Harper had given me her address, and I wanted to check out her dwelling before diving in too deep. If the person stalking her had left another threat, I wanted to see it for myself. One could judge a lot about a person by how they left threatening evidence. Was the culprit violent or just menacing? Would he really harm her or did he just want to get that rise out of her? That control?

She lived in the gated Tanoan Estates, and I didn't know if entrance would require Harper's express permission or not. I dragged out my PI license just in case. It might help. It might not.

After pulling up to the gate, I offered the uniformed security guard a placating smile.

He stared, unimpressed.

"Hi," I said.

He offered a brisk nod. Still unimpressed. I'd have to up my game.

"My name is Charley Davidson. I'm investigating a situation with one of your residents. Have you had any break-ins recently? Any alarms going off?"

He lifted a shoulder. "Alarms go off every now and then, mostly by the residents themselves. And we have the occasional break-in, but they're pretty rare here. Can I ask who hired you?"

"Harper Lowell. She lives on—"

"I know where she lives."

When I raised my brows, he tipped his hat back to scratch his head.

"Look, we've gotten a couple of calls from her, but we've never found any evidence of foul play on site. No signs of a break-in. No footprints or cars parked near her house. And she never could describe the intruder. If there was an intruder."

"So, you think she was lying?"

"No," he said with a noncommittal shrug. And now it was his turn to lie. "Not so much lying as . . . mistaken."

"You mean paranoid."

He thought a moment. "Overzealous."

"Ah. Okay. Well, you don't mind if I check it out, do you? Ms. Lowell gave me the key and the security code."

"Knock yourself out. I'll just need to record your license-plate number."

"Do you record the information of every nonresident who comes through?"

"Sure do."

I offered him my best smile. "Is there any way I can get a copy of the most recent pages?"

He shook his head. "Not without a warrant."

Darn. I made a mental note to set Cookie on that. She had a knack for getting protected documents without a warrant. I was pretty sure that was her superpower.

After he took down my information, I drove through the estates until I came to Harper's house. Tanoan was one of the nicer parts of Albuquerque. At least Harper's parents did that much for her.

And Harper was doing everything right: Gated community with uniformed security guards. Active security system. Triple locks on all the doors. I went from room to room, checking for any signs of foul play before I hit the kitchen. It'd been something like an hour since I last had a cup of coffee. Surely she wouldn't mind.

To my utter delight, she had one of those machines that used those individual cups and made one serving of coffee at a time. I may have ordered one of those. I'd have to go through the boxes when I got home.

I searched her cabinets, wondering where I'd be if I were a K-Cup before coming to the conclusion that I'd be in heaven, that's where. Filled to the brim with grinds of shimmering black gold. I opened the last cabinet door and jumped back in surprise. A stuffed white rabbit sat against a can of beets. Normally white rabbits, especially stuffed ones, didn't bother me, but there was something creepy about having one in a kitchen cabinet.

Staring.

Judging.

I started to reach up and take it down, then stopped myself. This was evidence. True, it wasn't particularly incriminating or overtly threatening, but it was evidence nonetheless.

And it was scary. Its eyes weren't on right, and its neck looked like the stuffing had been pulled out so that it sat lopsided on its little shoulders.

I left it there and exited Harper's house unnerved and un-caffeinated.

After informing the security guard of what I found, leaving him unimpressed again, I gave him my card and made him promise to keep an eye out for anything out of the ordinary. Then I started for home with my tail tucked between my legs. According to Angel, Reyes was going to be at that warehouse tonight, so I had some time to kill. I could do that on my sofa just as easily as I could running around Albuquerque like a chicken with my head cut off.

Wait. Somehow the word *chicken* struck a chord. I played with it in my mind. Rolled it over my tongue. Then came to a conclusion: It was me. I was a chicken butt. I was suddenly scared of everything.

I pulled off Academy and into a shopping center to stew in my own astonishment. I was a chicken of the most cowardly kind. Like a roosting hen. How can the grim reaper do her job if she's a roosting hen? Suddenly every sound, every movement, caused an adrenaline dump the size of Australia to flood my system. This would so not do. I had to get my act together.

I looked at Misery's dash. Being with her was comforting on some level, but not as comforting as my sofa. Then it hit me. An atrocity I'd overlooked for years. I'd never named my sofa. How could I do that to her? How could I be so callous? So cold and selfish?

But what would I name her? This was big. Important. She couldn't go through life with a name that didn't fit her unique personality.

Filled with an odd sense of relief at the new goal in life, I put Misery into drive. I could worry about being a roosting hen later. I had a sofa to name.

With renewed energy, I pulled back onto Academy—after hitting a drive-through for a mocha latte—and had just started for home when my phone rang.

"Yes?" I said, illegally talking on the phone while driving within the city limits. Scoping for cops, I waited for Uncle Bob to stop talking to whomever he was talking to and get back to me.

My uncle Bob, or Ubie as I most often referred to him, was a detective for APD, and I helped him on cases from time to time. He knew I could see the departed and used that to his advantage. Not that I could blame him.

"Get that to her, then call the ME ay-sap."

"Okay," I said, "but I'm not sure what calling the medical examiner ay-sap is going to accomplish. I'm pretty sure his name is George."

"Oh, hey, Charley."

"Hey, Uncle Bob. What's up?"

"Are you driving?"

"No."

"Have you heard anything?"

Our conversations often went like this. Uncle Bob with his random questions. Me with my trying to come up with answers just as random. Not that I had to try very hard. "I heard that Tiffany Gorham, a girl I knew in grade school, still stuffs her bra. But that's just a rumor."

"About the case," he said through clenched teeth. I could tell his teeth were clenched because his words were suddenly forced. That meant he was frustrated. Too bad I had no idea what he was talking about.

"I wasn't aware that we had a case."

"Oh, didn't Cookie call you?"

"She called me a doody-head once."

"About the case." His teeth were totally clenched again.

"We have a case?"

But I'd lost him. He was talking to another officer. Or a detective. Or a hooker, depending on his location and accessibility to cash. Though I doubted he would tell a hooker to check the status of the DOA's autopsy report. Unless he was way kinkier than I'd ever given him credit for.

I found his calling me only to talk to other people very challenging.

"I'll call you right back," he said. No idea to whom.

The call disconnected as I sat at a light, wondering what guacamole would look like if avocados were orange.

I finally shifted my attention to the kid in my backseat. He had shoulder-length blond hair and bright blue eyes and looked somewhere between fifteen and seventeen.

"You come here often?" I asked him, but my phone rang before he could say anything. That was okay. He had a vacant stare, so I doubted he would have answered me anyway.

"Sorry about that," Uncle Bob said. "Do you want to discuss the case?"

"We have a case?" I said again, perking up.

"How are you?"

He asked me that every time he called now. "Peachy. Am I the case? If so, I can solve this puppy in about three seconds. I'm heading down San Mateo toward Central in a cherry red Jeep Wrangler with a questionable exhaust system."

"Charley."

"Hurry, before I get away!"

He gave up. "So, the arsonist just got serious."

Sadly, I had no idea what he was talking about. Uncle Bob was a homicide detective and rarely worked anything but murders and the like. "Okay, I'll bite. Why are you trying to find an arsonist? And why is he just now getting serious? Was he only kidding before?"

"Three questions, one answer." He mumbled something to another officer, then came back to me. "And that answer is because our arsonist is now a murderer. The building he torched last night had a homeless woman in it. She died."

"Crap. That would explain why you're on an arson case."

"Yeah. Have you heard anything?"

"Besides the Tiffany Gorham thing, no."

"Can you put out some feelers? This guy is getting sloppy."

"Wait. Is this the one who makes sure the buildings are empty before starting the fires?"

"The one and only. We've linked him to four fires so far. Same MO, right down to the timing device and accelerant. Only this time he didn't get everyone out. This homeless woman didn't happen to visit you, did she?"

"No, but I'll see what I can dig up."

"Thanks. I'll bring the folder on this guy over tonight."

"Sounds good." He was only coming over for Cookie. He had such a crush.

"So, have you talked to your dad?"

"Oh, no, you're breaking up. I can hardly—" I hung up before he could question me further. Dad was not open for discussion, and he knew it.

The minute we hung up, my phone rang for a third time. I answered. "Charley's house of Cheerios."

"Your uncle called," Cookie said. "He has a case he wants you to look at."

"I know," I replied, faking disappointment. "I just got off the phone with him. He told me all about how he needed you to contact me immediately, and you refused. Told him you had better things to do. Like funnel money into offshore accounts."

"Did you know you ordered a neck massager? This thing is great."

"Are you getting any actual work done?"

"Oh, yes! I got the addresses you needed, but there's not much on the brother. He's never received a single utility bill."

"Maybe his parents are paying his utilities, too."

"That makes sense. I'll check into their accounts, see what all they're paying for. But I do have a work address on him and an address for Harper's parents."

"Perfect. Text them to me."

"Now? Because this feels amazing."

"Only if you don't want me to file embezzlement charges against you."

"Now it is."

4

You can't fix stupid,
but you can numb it with a 2 by 4.

—T-SHIRT

Having already driven across town, I'd gone from being fairly close to Harper's parents' house to way out in the boondocks. I pulled a uey amidst a blaring horn—mine—and headed back that way only to be blocked by another gate when I got there. One made of intricate iron surrounded by a high brick wall. I pushed a button on the speaker box.

An arrogant male voice crackled out of the speaker. "Yes?"

I must've been in the midst of old money. The massive expanse of mansion that loomed before me was a testament to two things: The Lowells were rich, and the Lowells liked people to know it.

When I glanced back at the speaker box, I said, "Yes, I'd like a taco with extra salsa." When he didn't ask if I'd like something to drink with that, I tried again. "I'm here to see Mr. and Mrs. Lowell." I smiled into the video camera mounted above the box, then took out my PI license and held it up. "I've been hired by their daughter, Harper."

When I received no answer, I decided to change my tack. "I just need to ask them a few questions."

After a long moment in which I kept smiling at the dead kid in my backseat, trying not to contemplate how awkward the moment was becoming, the arrogant guy came back on.

"Mr. and Mrs. Lowell are not receiving."

What the hell did that mean? "I'm not throwing a forty-yard pass. I just have a few questions. I think their daughter is in danger."

"They are not accepting visitors."

What a caring bunch. "In that case, I'll have the police over in a few. I apologize beforehand if they come with lights flashing and sirens blaring."

Rich people hated nothing more than scandal. I loved scandals. Especially the kinky kind with illicit affairs and CEOs photographed in heels and feather boas. But I did live in my own little world.

"You will have five minutes," he said. He did the clenched-teeth thing much better than Ubie. I'd have to mention that next time I saw my surly uncle. Maybe he could take lessons.

After rolling up a long driveway that turned into a cobblestone entrance, I lifted Misery's emergency brake and glanced in my rearview. "Don't even think about going for a joy ride, buddy."

His blank gaze didn't flinch. He was fun.

A self-assured man who was dressed much more casually than I'd expected met me at the massive white door. The house looked more East Coast than most houses in New Mexico. Without saying a word, the man led me to what I could only assume was a drawing room, though there were no art supplies anywhere. Since I couldn't draw, I decided to snoop. Pictures lined the walls and shelves, but there was not a single candid shot among them. Every photograph was a professional portrait, and each one had a color theme. Black. Brown. Navy blue. Four in the family: the parents, one boy, and one girl—Harper. They all had dark hair except the boy, and he didn't particularly look like the others. I wondered if the rooster had gotten out of the henhouse. A blond rooster. The parade of portraits mapped out the development of the Lowell children, from around four or five until the kids were in their early twenties. Clearly the parents had a firm grip on their children. In one portrait, they got almost crazy and wore white.

These people were scary.

"How may I help you?"

I turned to a woman, the matriarch of this here hoity-toity club, if the pictures were any indication. By the upturn of her nose, she held herself in high regard. Either that, or she found my fascination with her drawing room distasteful.

I didn't offer my hand. "My name is Charlotte Davidson, Mrs. Lowell. I'm here about Harper."

"I've been told you are a private investigator?"

"Yes. Your daughter hired me. She believes someone is trying to kill her."

A lengthy exhalation told me she probably didn't care. "Stepdaughter," she clarified, and my hackles rose instantly.

I wondered if my stepmother did the same with me. Corrected people when they called me her daughter. Cringed at the usage. The very thought.

"Has Harper mentioned the fact that she's being stalked?"

"Fact?" she said, her expression full of a peevish kind of doubt. "Yes, Ms. Davidson. We've been through this with her ad nauseam. I can't imagine you could bring anything new to the table."

The woman's indifference floored me. It was one thing not to believe Harper, but another altogether to be so blatantly unaffected by her stepdaughter's distress. Then I got a clue that might shed some light.

"May I ask, is Harper's brother your stepson as well?"

Pride swelled her chest. "Arthur is mine. I married Harper's father when Art was seven. Harper was five. She didn't approve, and these antics of hers began soon after."

"Antics?" I asked.

"Yes." She waved a dismissive hand. "The drama. The theatrics. Someone is always after her, trying to scare her or hurt her or kill her. You can imagine how hard it is to take this seriously when it has been happening for over twenty-five years."

That was interesting. Harper hadn't mentioned that part. "So this started when she was young?"

"Five."

"I see." I took out my notepad and pretended to take notes. Partly to look official, but mostly to give myself a minute to get a well-rounded read off her. From what I could tell, she wasn't lying. She didn't believe Harper's accusations were real. She didn't believe Harper's life was in danger.

Then again, my stepmother had never believed a word I'd said growing up either. Mrs. Lowell's indifference meant nothing in the grand scheme of things besides the fact that she was petty and vain.

"According to her therapists," she continued, her tone waspish to the extreme, "seven therapists, to be exact—it's not unusual for a daughter to feel neglected and crave attention when her father remarries. Her biological mother died when she was an infant. Jason was all she had."

"Is your husband home? May I talk to him?"

She chafed under my forwardness. "No, you may not. Mr. Lowell is very ill. He can hardly entertain Harper's delusions of doom, much less those of a hired private investigator."

Mrs. Lowell's expression would suggest she thought I was nothing more than a charlatan, out to take Harper's—aka her—money. Since I was quite used to people believing me a charlatan, the snub didn't irritate. But the slight to Harper did. She clearly harbored no genuine affection for her stepdaughter. She saw her as a nuisance. A burden. Much like my own stepmother thought of me.

"And," Mrs. Lowell continued, a thought having occurred to her, "she disappeared for three years. Three! Off the face of the Earth, as far as we knew. Did she tell you that?"

While I wanted to say, *I would have, too, with a stepmother like you,* what I said was, "No, ma'am, she didn't."

"See. She is completely unstable. When she finally deigned us with her presence, she said she had been on the run for her life. Of all the ludicrous . . ." Mrs. Lowell shifted in irritation. "And now she hires a private investigator? She has gone over the edge."

I wrote the word *psycho* in my notebook, then scribbled it out before she saw. I was letting my own biases guide me on this case, and that would get me nowhere. Taking a mental step back, I took a deep breath and tried to see this from Mrs. Lowell's perspective, as difficult as that might be. I didn't often identify with rich bitches, but they were people, too. Weren't they?

So Mrs. Lowell marries a man, a rich man, only to find out the man's daughter hates her with a passion and despises the relationship her new mother has with her father, so much so that she makes up wild stories about someone trying to kill her. To get back at her new mother? Her father for abandoning her?

Nope. I didn't buy it. Mrs. Lowell was a cold bitch. She most likely married for the money, not that I could blame her entirely for that—a girl's gotta do what a girl's gotta do—but to dismiss Harper's fears out-right and so callously bordered on neglect, in my opinion. Jason Lowell was her meal ticket, and his daughter was part of the deal. I couldn't help but feel a little ambivalent toward Harper's father. Where was he in all this? Why was he not here supporting his daughter? Taking up for her?

I cleared my throat and said, "You mentioned drama. Can you give me an example?"

"Oh, goodness, you name it. One minute someone is leaving dead rabbits on her bed, and the next minute a party popper made her throw up all over her cousin's birthday cake. A party popper. Then there were the nightmares. We used to wake up to her screams in the middle of the night, or we would find her standing beside our bed at three in the morning."

"She sleepwalked?"

"No, she was wide awake. She would say someone was in her room.

The first few times, Jason would jump out of bed and go investigate, but the therapist told us that was exactly what she wanted. So, we stopped. We started to ignore her and told her to go back to bed."

"And would she?"

"Of course not. We'd find her the next morning asleep under the stairs or behind the sofa. And searching for her would always make us late to this or that. Her antics were absolutely exhausting."

"I can only imagine."

"So, we stopped searching for her altogether. If she wanted to sleep in the broom closet, so be it. We let her and went about our usual routine. But the doctor insisted there was nothing wrong with her. She said the more attention we gave Harper, the more she would act out. So we stopped paying attention."

A dull ache ricocheted through the cavern of my chest. To know what Harper went through with no one to support her. No one to believe her. "So you did nothing?"

"As per her doctor's instructions," Mrs. Lowell said with a sniff. "But her outbursts escalated. We went through the nightmares and the panic attacks night after night, and did nothing but order her back to bed. So, she stopped eating to get back at us."

"To get back at you?" I asked, my throat constricting.

"Yes. And then she stopped bathing, stopped combing her hair. Do you have any idea how humiliating that is? To have a child who looks more like a street rat than a proper young lady?"

"That must've been awful," I said, my tone flat and unattractive.

My sarcasm was not lost on the foul woman, and I regretted it instantly. She shut down. Any information I might have gained was now lost to the frivolity of my mouth.

"I think your time is up, Ms. Davidson."

I chastised myself inwardly and asked, "Is Harper's brother around? Can I talk to him?"

"Stepbrother," she corrected, seeming to sense my chagrin. "And he has a place of his own." The statement wrenched an interesting rush of indignation out of her. I sensed no small amount of displeasure from Mrs. Lowell that her son had moved out. But he had to be in his thirties, for heaven's sake. What did she expect?

She had her housekeeper show me out before I could ask anything else. Like who trimmed her lawn, because day-um, I had no idea bushes could be clipped into the shape of a Kokopelli.

"Have you worked here long?" I asked the young woman as she escorted me to the door, knowing she couldn't have. She looked around twenty.

She glanced nervously over her shoulder, then shook her head.

"Can I ask how long you've known the Lowells?"

After opening the door, she scanned the area again before saying, "No. I just started here a couple of weeks ago. Their long-term housekeeper retired."

"Really?"

She seemed to want me out of the house. Bad. And I didn't want to get her in trouble. I knew how these people worked, and their employees were not to speak of anything that happened at their house or they would lose their jobs immediately, but we were talking about the well-being of one of their own. "How long had the last housekeeper worked here?"

"Almost thirty years," she said, seeming as baffled by the idea as I was. How someone could last thirty years under the reign of that woman was beyond me. But if anyone knew what happened in a house like this, it was the hired help.

"Thank you," I said, offering her a wink. She grinned shyly.

I left the Lowell mansion with way more questions than I'd had when I went in, but at least I had a clearer picture of what Harper had endured growing up. Still, she didn't tell me how long this had been going on. While I could guess why—nobody believed her, why should I—I would need to confront her as soon as possible. I was missing pertinent information that could help us solve this entire case.

But one thing stuck out in my head. Everything Harper had done, all the nightmares and delusions and lashing out, pointed to one thing: posttraumatic stress disorder. The tip-off was the party poppers. I had taken enough psych in college to recognize the most basic symptom of PTSD: extreme response, like shaking and nausea, to loud noises.

Being stalked could cause posttraumatic stress to a degree, especially if the situation was life-threatening, but Harper's symptoms would indicate a more severe form. Surely a licensed psychotherapist would know that. Maybe I needed to visit these seven therapists Mrs. Lowell was telling me about.

I called Cookie to have her find out exactly who Harper was seeing and when. "Also, I want to talk to their housekeeper who recently retired, and then I need more info on the Lowell family."

"Housekeeper. Got it. But info?" she asked, typing away at her keyboard.

"Dirt, Cook. I need you to scrounge up all the dirt you can get on them. Any family with that much hot air has something to hide, and I want to know what it is."

"That kind of dirt rarely makes the headlines, but I'll see what I can dig up."

"And I want to actually talk to the therapists the Lowells were sending Harper to. She's been seeing them since around the age of five."

"That could be difficult."

"Are you saying you can't do it?"

"No," she said, a smile in her voice. "I'm saying it's about time you gave me a challenge."

"I was hoping you'd say that."

The second I hung up, I called David Taft. Officer Taft worked the same precinct as Uncle Bob and had a departed little sister who liked to visit me at the worst times possible. Namely any. We weren't exactly friends, Taft and I. Which might explain the cold reception.

"Taft," he said when he picked up.

"Hey, Charley Davidson here." When he didn't say anything, I continued. "I have a client who says you're her liaison at the precinct. Harper Lowell?"

"Doesn't ring a bell. So, you're back?"

"I was never gone. She claims someone is stalking her. Trying to kill her."

"I know who you're talking about. We never got anything on any stalker."

"Do you believe her?"

"I didn't. Until I spoke to her parents."

Well, well. I was starting to like him. "Why is that?"

"I don't know. They seemed a little too eager to convince me their daughter was crazy."

"I got the exact same feeling."

"So, she hired you?"

"Yep. Did you ever find any evidence at all?" I couldn't hide the hope in my voice.

"Nothing that couldn't be explained away as a crazy woman seeking attention. Stuffed rabbits aren't exactly life-threatening."

"When they're not stuffed and they're placed on your bed while you sleep with their throats cut, they are."

"Look, I'm not arguing with you. We just never found any evidence to corroborate her story."

Just when I was starting to like him. "And I'm sure you tried really hard."

"I tried, Davidson," he said, adding a sharp edge to his voice.

"Okay, okay. You don't have to get obstinate."

"Have you seen my sister?"

Taft's sister died when they were young, and she'd recently decided that haunting me was more fun than following her brother around day in and day out. It took him a while to believe that I could see her and talk to her and grow uncharacteristically homicidal by her annoying habit of asking question after question. But once he realized I was the real deal, he'd decided to keep tabs on her through me. Joy of joys.

"Not lately," I said. "She's spending a lot of time at Rocket's."

"You mean that abandoned mental hospital where you talk to ghosts?"

"Yes, and I only talk to one ghost. Rocket. He has a little sister, and she and your little sister get along famously. I'm going to check on them soon. I'll let you know how she is."

"Thanks. I really appreciate—"

Yeah, yeah. "If you hear anything."

"You'll be the first to know."

"In case your sister asks, are you still dating skanks?"

A light chuckle filtered into my ear. "No. Well, not for the most part."

"Okay. Don't make me come down there and kick your skank-lovin' ass."

"I'll try not to let that threat keep me up nights."

"Good luck."

I hung up and took in a long breath, deciding it was time. Harper's brother would have gone home for the day by now, and I still didn't have a home address on him, so I'd have to catch him at work on the morrow. If Cookie was right, he worked for some kind of energy-conservation company, but tonight I had bigger issues. I straightened my shoulders and tightened my grip on the steering wheel, because tonight I had a dragon to slay. A dragon named Reyes Farrow.

I steered Misery through the warehouse district of Albuquerque near the railroad tracks downtown. A cold rain tumbled in sheets down my windshield, but one never complained about the rain in such an arid climate. Complaining about rain in Albuquerque would be like complaining about sunshine in Seattle. So I wasn't complaining so much as bemoaning the fact that I had to drive in it. Hard rain made it almost impossible to see the road. Hopefully, whoever owned those trash cans I'd sideswiped would understand that.

After idling on a side street for a bit, watching through chain link as car after car entered a fenced-in area, I decided to grow some balls and go through, too. How bad could this be? I removed Margaret and stuffed her under my seat before heading in.

A gigantic man in a black plastic poncho held up a hand to stop me the minute I drove past the entrance. I stopped. Partly because he was massive and partly because pulling off that look was awe-inspiring.

I unzipped my window, wondering if I should think about getting a car with all the latest gadgets. I could do without unzipping windows, but Misery was such a part of me, I couldn't imagine my life without her. Unless my new ride sported a jaguar on the hood. Then I'd kick Misery to the curb faster than a crushed aluminum can.

I patted the dash. "Just kidding, girl. I'd never abandon you. Unless you catch fire and I have to run for my life."

As if launching a comeback, she sputtered and shimmied before returning back to her normal purr. Such sass. We were totally made for each other.

"You a cop?" the poncho guy asked.

"No, but I dated one once."

He raised a flashlight and scanned Misery's innards. Sadly, all he'd find was a mishmash of files, a couple of jackets, and basic survival gear that consisted mainly of Cheez-Its and an emergency stash of Thin Mints. Frickin' Girl Scouts. Those things were way too addictive. They had to be laced with crack.

I couldn't see Poncho Guy's face past the darkness of the night and the shadows of his hood. But he did the menacing bit well. His head tilted to the side. "Were you sent here by cops?"

"Not today." I smiled, pretending rain was not pelting me in the face.

"Did you get an invitation?"

"I got an invitation to Nancy Burke's slumber party in the sixth grade. We played spin the bottle. I had to kiss a turtle named Esther."

"Yeah? Well, I don't know you, and I don't give a shit."

"Oh!" I jutted my hand out of the window. "I'm Charley."

He backed away and motioned for me to turn around. "No entrance. Go back the way you came in."

Damn. I totally should have dressed sexy and called myself Bunny. "Wait!" I felt under the dash for my emergency mocha latte money. "I'm just here to talk to Reyes Farrow."

He seemed unimpressed. "Farrow doesn't talk. Now go or I'll drag your ass out of your vehicle and beat the shit out of you."

That was totally uncalled for. As if in involuntary reaction, my fingers felt blindly along the door until they found the lock. Just in case. Then I held out the fifty-dollar bill and decided to play his game. The forlorn girl so in love with the god Reyes that I'd do anything to get in. Anything to see him. "Please. I just want to see him. I just . . . want to watch."

With a loud sigh, he took the fifty out of my hand. "If I catch you recording anything, I'll drag your ass out of that building and beat the shit out of you."

Holy cow, he liked to drag and drop. "Thank you." I blinked a few times in concession, only partly because rain was still pelting me in the face. "Thank you so much."

He frowned and swept the flashlight to the left, showing me where to park. I followed his directions, grabbed one of the cast-off jackets from the backseat as a makeshift umbrella, saluted a good-bye to the kid sitting there, staring off into his own little space station, then hurried to a side door, where I'd seen a couple run in earlier. Sadly, I was stopped again. By another big guy in a black plastic poncho. Who wanted money.

"Fifty bucks," he said, his tone flat.

No way. "Fifty bucks? I just gave that guy a fifty to get in."

I could just make out the lower half of the guy's face. He smiled. "That was just to park. To get in, it's another fifty."

Well, crap. Being broke sucked ass. I pulled out my wallet while a group of men moaned behind me.

"It's raining, lady. Hurry it up."

"This is going to be so badass," another said, ignoring his friend.

"No shit. I hear he's undefeated."

"Damn straight he's undefeated. Have you seen that guy? He moves like a fucking panther."

Knowing exactly who they were talking about, I tore through my wallet, looking for my *other* emergency mocha latte stash. This was the last of anything and everything I had, and it'd damned well better be worth it.

"I don't know. I think I could take him," another guy said.

I looked over my shoulder as his friends gaped at him.

The guy grinned. "If he were unarmed and I had an AK-47 in my hands."

They laughed along with their buddy until they noticed I'd stopped looking for money. One of them shouldered me, pushing me a solid three feet forward. "C'mon, honey. We have an ass-kicking to watch."

"Fuck, it's already started."

I heard a loud roar as an audience cheered beyond the door.

"Here," one of them said, handing the guy a fifty, then sidling past me. The others followed suit, and I soon knew what it felt like to be a washing machine in spin cycle. They pushed me into Black Poncho Guy number two, and oddly enough, a fifty-dollar bill just sort of materialized in my hand. Probably because I jacked it as the last guy slid past me, in that moment where both the giver and the receiver thought the other had it.

"Here it is." I held up the fifty with a little too much enthusiasm. The bouncer didn't seem to notice. He snatched it out of my hand, then offered me help inside by way of a none-too-gentle shove. Geez. I stumbled forward as more people entered behind me, so I hurried toward a bright spotlight in the middle of an otherwise very dark and very empty warehouse. The smell of dirt mingled with the aromas of beer and smoke and manly cologne. I liked manly things. Especially cologne.

Still, I strode forward on high alert.

As I drew closer to the action, I realized the crowd was way bigger than I thought it would be. People, mostly men, stood cheering around a chain-link cage like the ones on TV, only rougher. The crude structure had no padding around the bars, and the gate to get in was chained and locked from the outside. That couldn't be good.

By the sounds of the crowd's cheers, they thirsted for blood more than the beer that flowed freely. Drinks were bought. Bets were made. Fists were thrown. I was actually rather surprised at how many women were present, then realized they weren't cheering like the men. They were watching, all eyes focused on one thing. That's when I saw it. Him. Reyes Alexander Farrow. Through the grid of chain link, I focused on the action, the show the crowd had come to see.

5

Angel wasn't kidding. Reyes had taken up cage fighting. It was such a foreign concept, I thought he'd said cat fighting at first. I pushed my astonishment aside and hurried closer for a better view, shouldering through the crowd. The fighters didn't wear traditional boxer's shorts. Reyes's opponent wore sweats while he wore jeans and nothing else. His hands had been taped, and he had bandages around his torso and over one shoulder. An injured fighter would never have been allowed to compete in a sanctioned fight. This was about as legal as shoplifting.

The moment he felt me close, his eyes raised from the task at hand—a task that involved blood and sweat and a three-hundred-pound opponent—and locked on to mine. The surprise that flashed across his face was so minute, so fleeting, I doubted anyone saw it but me. He caught himself instantly. His expression hardened, his corded muscles tensed, and the guy he had folded into a full-body lock yelled out in pain a split second before he tapped the floor of the cage, indicating his surrender.

It must've been hard for a man like that, clearly a seasoned fighter, to tap out, to admit defeat, but the pain Reyes inflicted had to be excruciating.

And yet Reyes didn't stop. He didn't let up. A makeshift referee ran into the cage as the guy tapped again. The pain twisting his features had me cringing inwardly, but Reyes's eyes wouldn't leave mine. He stared, his sparkling gaze angry, his jaw set as he tightened his hold even more. The ref was going crazy, trying to drag Reyes off the opponent. Two other men rushed into the cage, but they didn't have nearly the enthusiasm the ref did. They approached more warily as the crowd roared in excitement. Begged for blood. Or, well, more blood. The man's pain was too much. It pulsed in sharp, liquid waves through my veins as surely as hemoglobin did.

I lowered my head but not my eyes and whispered, "Please, stop."

Reyes released the man immediately and fell back on his heels, a salacious warning glimmering across his impossibly handsome face.

He didn't want me there—that much was obvious—but it was more than that. He was angry. He who'd set me up just to watch me fall. He who could bite my lily-white ass a thousand ways to Sunday was mad at me. Of all the nerve.

The opponent lay on the canvas wheezing and writhing in agony. That last little exertion on Reyes's part must've damaged something. Reyes ignored him. He also ignored the ref, who was pummeling him with verbal warnings, and the guy who started to put a hand on his shoulder for support before thinking better of it. Jumping to his feet, he strode out of the cage like he had somewhere else to be. Cheers and congratulatory whoops abounded as he navigated through the crowd. He ignored those, too. Thankfully, the crowd had enough sense to move out of the way when he got close.

He swam through it with ease, then ducked inside a door that led to a large, boxy construction in the far corner. Offices, maybe. The trainers helped the other guy to his feet and led him away in the opposite direction while a custodian mopped blood off the mat.

My feet followed where every eye led. To the rooms in the corner. I shoved past the feral crowd and lovelorn women. Several of them hovered near the door but didn't dare go inside. The fact that the door was completely unguarded surprised me. Another guy walked out, shorter and stockier than Reyes, his hands wrapped in tape, his fists at the ready as he shadowboxed his way to the cage.

And the crowd went wild.

I stepped through the door into a type of industrial locker room. Not the kind in gyms, clean and bright, but the kind in old factories, dingy, dark, and dirty. Three rows of the metal units cut the steam-filled room in half. On the left were several walled offices and a desk. On the right—

"And they want you to make it last longer." A male voice echoed toward me from that very direction. "We talked about this, remember?"

I followed it, walking past the lockers until I came to an open area with benches and a couple of tables. The showers were past that, and someone was apparently taking advantage of them. Steam billowed around Reyes as he sat on one of the tables. A man who must've been his trainer stood in front of him, wrapping his hands in white tape, just like in the movies. His jeans hung low on his hips, showing just enough of the dip between hipbone and abdomen to weaken my knees. Bandages and more white tape adorned a shoulder and encircled his ribs, and I fought to tamp down my concern. As for the rest of him, his coppery skin stretched with fluid grace over a solid frame of hard muscles and long sinewy curves. He was simply magnificent.

The first time I saw Reyes, I was in high school and my sister Gemma and I had spotted him through the kitchen window of his apartment late one night. It was a bad part of town, and what I saw proved it. A man—a man who I would later learn was Earl Walker, the monster who raised Reyes and who, years after that event, had tortured and almost killed me in my own apartment—was beating him. Reyes was nineteen at the time. Fierce. Feral. And beautiful. But the man was huge. His fists were slamming into Reyes until he could no longer stand. Could no longer defend himself.

To stop the man from killing him, I'd thrown a brick through the kitchen window. It'd worked. The man stopped. But that brick was like putting a Band-Aid on a gunshot wound. I found out years later that Reyes had spent over a decade in prison for killing Earl Walker, only to be told that Earl wasn't really dead. He'd faked his own death, and Reyes had gone to prison for a crime he didn't commit. The problem lay in the fact that Reyes escaped from prison to prove his innocence and used me as bait to get Earl Walker to come out of hiding. I almost died as a result. Cookie and her daughter, Amber, were put at risk as well.

Those things combined with the fact that Reyes was literally the son of Satan, forged in the fires of sin and degradation, were proving a little hard to get past. But he was also the dark entity that had followed me my whole life. Had saved it more than once. His actions contradicted everything I was raised to believe about such darkness. Such ambiguity.

And now, I stood at the precipice of a great divide. Did I dare trust him again? Did I dare believe anything he had to say? I had spent two months in my apartment pondering that very thing.

His heat reached me then, and I stepped closer. The familiar warmth that radiated out of him in soft nuclear waves was like a stinging ointment, soothing and unsettling at the same time. I stood under the glaring fluorescent, but he didn't look up. It gave me a chance to study him more closely, to assess how freedom had changed him. Not a lot, I quickly realized. His hair was the same length it was two months ago. Thick strands hung down over his forehead and curled behind an ear. His jaw—that strong, stubborn set he always carried—was shaded with a day's worth of growth. It framed his full mouth to such delicious precision, my own mouth watered in response.

I forced my attention off his face to his wide shoulders, laid bare for the fight, exposing the ancient tattoos he'd been born with. The tattoos that doubled as a map, a key to the gates of hell. I could read a map as well as the next girl, but how did one use such a map to travel onto the other plane and traverse the desolation of infinity to get to a place nobody wants to be?

Without looking up from the trainer's ministrations, Reyes asked, "What are you doing here?"

He was so startlingly beautiful, it took me a moment to realize he was talking to me. I hadn't seen him in two months, and even before that, I'd seen him in the flesh on only a few fleeting, harried occasions, each one eliciting similar feelings of preoccupation and light-headedness. No matter how angry I seemed to be, his attraction, his raw succulence acted as a magnet. And I was apparently a paper clip. Every cell in my body urged me forward.

The trainer glanced up in confusion, then realized someone else was in the room. He turned to me, a sharp disapproval lining his face. "You can't be back here."

"I need to talk to your fighter," I said, thrusting as much authority into my voice as I could muster, which admittedly wasn't much.

Finally, and with infinite care, Reyes raised his lashes until I could see the shimmer of his rich brown eyes. I tried to force my heart to keep beating, but it stopped dead in its tracks. His lips parted slightly, and my gaze fell to his mouth again. It thinned in response, and he said, "You need to leave."

Ignoring the rush of heat that flooded my body at the deep, sensual sound of his voice, I squared my shoulders, stepped forward, and handed him the paper I'd crumpled the minute I saw him in the cage. "I brought your bill."

His thick black lashes lowered, and he reached for the paper with his free hand. "My bill for what?" he asked, perusing what I'd written.

"For my services. I found your father for you. Almost died in the process. My private investigations business is just that, Mr. Farrow: a business. Despite what you might believe, I am not your personal errand girl."

He quirked a brow the moment I used his surname but recovered quickly enough. He turned the paper over. "It's written on a Macho Taco receipt."

"I improvised."

"And it's for a million dollars."

"I'm expensive."

The barest hint of a grin lifted one corner of his mouth. "I don't have a million on me at the moment."

"We can go to the nearest ATM, if that would help."

"Sadly, no." He folded the paper and stuffed it into a back pocket, and the only thing I could think was how I would've loved to be a Macho Taco receipt at that moment in time. "I'm broke," he added.

Even without reading his emotions, I knew that was an outright lie. Good thing, because I wasn't getting much in the way of deceit. Lust, maybe. A hot, visceral desire that had my knees fighting to stay locked. But no deceit. Speaking of which . . .

"Why are you fighting?" I looked around at the paltry conditions. Even illegal fights should be sanitary. This was crazy.

"I told you, I'm broke. I need the money."

"You're not broke," I countered.

He shook off the man wrapping his hand and rose from the table.

I stepped back in a wary retreat. He followed, every movement fluid. Powerful.

I had a few tricks up my elastic cuff. Time to shock and amaze. "You have a cool fifty million just waiting for you to wrap your hot little hands around."

He stilled, which was his tell. Where others gasped or rounded their eyes when surprised, Reyes stilled, so I knew I had him.

"You're mistaken," he said, his voice like silk over cold, hard steel.

"Your sister told me," I explained. Though not biologically related, Reyes was raised with a girl whom he considered to be his sister in every way. They were both subjected to extreme abuse, though in very different ways. Earl Walker, the man who tortured me, also raised them. In his own sick kind of way, he would refuse Kim food and water until Reyes would comply with his horrendous demands. Kim and Reyes both grew up in a nightmare at the hands of a monster, and in an effort to keep Kim safe, Reyes disavowed any knowledge of her when he was arrested for Walker's supposed murder. And yet, he had somehow managed to make her a millionaire while in prison.

He bit down. "That's not my money. That's hers."

I folded my arms. "She won't spend it. She swears it's yours."

"She's wrong." He took another step closer. "And I thought we agreed that you'd stay away from my sister."

We didn't agree so much as he threatened, but I decided not to bring up that point. "This was a while ago, after you'd escaped from prison. You'd been hurt and I was concerned."

"Why do you care?" Another step. "Last thing you said to me was fuck off."

I made myself stand my ground. He was only coming toward me to force a retreat, a tack he took when he needed to exert his authority. "I only said that in my head."

"The look on your face said it all."

"The same face with the huge gash in it where your father sliced it in two?" He walked right into that one. "That face?"

He blanched. "He's not my father."

"I know. But fighting here like this is crazy. It's like you have a death wish."

"You're one to talk."

"What is that supposed to mean?"

His jaw worked in frustration before he answered. "I'm trying to keep my distance, as per your wish." He stepped closer, and this time I had no choice but to retreat. But one more step brought me up against a cinder block wall. He braced one hand above my head just to tower over me. "But you're not making it very easy."

A surplus of emotion shuddered deep in my core. Reyes Farrow ignited every cell in my body as though I were made of gasoline, one spark away from being engulfed in flames. He knew what he did to me. He had to. And that alone kept me sane. Kept me from reaching out and running my fingers along the bandages at his ribs. Dipping them into the front of his jeans.

I drew in a steadying breath instead. "I saw you this morning."

A soft frown stole over his face, so I explained further.

"By my apartment building. I saw you standing there. Are you stalking me?"

"No," he said, dropping his arm and turning away from me. "I'm hunting another animal altogether."

"And that animal just happens to live in my building?"

He smoothed the tape on his hands. "No, but what that animal wants most does."

His words caused my pulse to quicken, my breath to shorten. The only thing that wanted me, the only animal Reyes would hunt, was a demon.

Then he was in front of me, his hand around my throat holding me when I wanted to run. "You reek of fear."

I fought his hold to no avail. "And whose fault is that?"

"Mine, and I apologize again, but you have to get the fuck over it." He pressed into me until my skin had no choice but to absorb the heat radiating off him in waves. I breathed it in, gasped as it pooled deep in my abdomen and washed down my legs. "They love it," he said at my ear. "It's like a drug. In the same way the smell of blood lures sharks, the smell of fear lures *them* closer, drives them into a frenzy. It is both bait and aphrodisiac."

"And you would know this how?"

"Because I was one of them, and I want nothing more than to drag you into those showers, rip off your clothes, and have my way with every inch of you."

I closed my eyes at the image he offered me. "You want to do that anyway."

"True, but this is stronger. You're the reaper, and nothing on earth is more mouthwatering to one of my kind than the prospect of licking fear off your skin."

He'd never told me that. He'd never told me a lot of things, but that particular tidbit would have been nice to know.

"I never told you, because it's never been an issue," he said, startling me.

He did it again. Read what I was thinking. I looked up at him in surprise.

"It's all over your face, Dutch."

There it was again. Dutch. The mysterious name he called me. A name I had yet to understand.

"I can see it," he continued. "Your confusion. Your doubt. I can't read your mind. But like you, I can read your emotions. And it's never been an issue, because you've never been afraid before. Not like this."

"You're wrong," I said, my words breathy with a combination of awe and trepidation. "I've always been afraid of you."

That seemed to give him pause. He loosened his hold long enough for me to scramble out of it. And scramble I did. I rushed out of his grip and backed warily away from him. He kept one arm braced on the wall and inhaled deep gulps of air as though trying to get a grip on his emotions.

"You need to leave before I change my mind about letting you."

I shook my head. "I'm not leaving until you promise to stop fighting."

He snapped to attention. "Are you kidding?"

"Not at the moment." If I ever had any power over him, now was certainly the time to use it. I raised my chin to face him head-on. "I forbid you to fight."

A sudden burst of anger hit me like a wall of fire. He straightened and advanced.

"You are the one who insists I keep this body. Now you want to tell me what I can and cannot do with it?"

He was right. I'd insisted he keep his mortal body once when he'd wanted to let it pass away. And it was a decision I still stood by. "Pretty much," I said, squaring my shoulders.

"Well, then, what exactly would you like me to do with it?"

What an amazingly loaded question. He was towering over me again, stepping closer, forcing me back until I hit the table he'd been sitting on. His heat seeped into every pore on my body.

"I need answers, and I can hardly get them if you end up dying in an illegal cage fight. Do they even have an EMT on duty?"

"Dying?" he asked, scoffing at the very idea.

I pointed to his bandages. "You're not as indestructible as you might think."

He laughed, a harsh sound that echoed against the metal lockers. "Do you honestly believe a human could do this to me?"

It took a moment for realization to sink in. When it did, I felt my jaw drop as I gaped up at him. "They . . . you mean—"

"Rey?"

I recoiled, fought to keep the room from spinning as I grasped his meaning. Demons. They were here. Back on Earth. And he was fighting them.

I looked past him toward a woman walking into the room.

"Are you ready for the next fight? They're asking for you."

He didn't look at her. Didn't take his eyes off mine.

"Wendell wants you to make this one last," she said, her voice weak, uncertain. I could feel anxiety coming off her from where I stood.

When a tall woman with short blond hair stepped into the light, I realized who she was and almost seized. Elaine Oake? The woman with the website? The woman with the museum dedicated to all things Reyes Farrow, stocked with dozens of items stolen from Reyes and smuggled out of the prison by guards? Guards that she paid? She was here? With Reyes?

When I thought of how she was nothing more than a prison groupie, a rich woman who had stalked Reyes the entire time he was in prison, who'd paid guards to get information on him, to steal items from his cell and take pictures when he wasn't looking, my astonishment shifted from the thought of demons roaming the hills and valleys of Earth to the thought of this woman roaming the hills and valleys of Reyes's body. An acrid and infuriating kind of jealousy erupted in my chest and surged out of me in a humiliating burst of resentment.

I fought to tamp it down, but she had to see the utter shock on my face. Hers showed, too. As well as her insecurity. Reyes was dangerously close, and clearly she didn't like that. Then recognition flitted across her face, followed by another tangible wave of shock.

"Rey?" she asked again. "Do you know who this is?"

He released a heavy breath from between his suddenly clenched teeth. "Yes."

"Oh, okay." She stepped over to us. "Are you here on a case?" she asked me, the hope so evident in her eyes, I almost felt sorry for her.

"I'm here collecting on one, yes."

"Oh, well, whatever it is, I can pay it. I'm Reyes's manager." She turned toward him and placed a timid hand on his arm. "You need to get ready. This fight is almost over." Then she forced a smile. "They're all here for you anyway. That fight was just a filler, something to cleanse the palate between rounds."

He was fighting again tonight? And she was cool with that?

My knee-jerk reaction was to rip out her short, perfectly coiffed hair, and I chastised myself inwardly. Reyes was not mine. I had no say in anything that he did, including the fights, and he knew it. He'd been in prison for over a decade for a crime he didn't commit, and here I was trying to control him. Just like they did. Every single day for over ten years. Every movement, every thought, controlled by a trustee or a guard or a warden.

But still, Elaine Oake?

"And we need to get home before the new sponsors show up," she added. "They're very eager to meet you."

I almost fainted. Home? He was living with her? The depths of my astonishment seemed to know no bounds. I was lost for a moment, reeling as each new discovery sank in.

Reyes examined my face, watching every move, every reaction.

"Can you give us a minute?" he asked, and I wasn't sure which one of us he was talking to. Wasn't sure if I cared.

"O-okay," Elaine said. She strolled off slowly, as if it took every ounce of strength she possessed to do so.

"You're living with her?" I asked under my breath. "Do you have any idea who she is?"

"Yes." He waited a moment, then added, "And yes."

A soft laugh of astonishment escaped before I could stop it. I turned to leave, but he took hold of the table and blocked my path. I shot a look toward Elaine. She'd stopped just past the wall of lockers and didn't miss the maneuver. And I didn't miss the hurt in her eyes.

Welcome to the world of Reyes Farrow.

"You need to move," I told him.

"You didn't answer me. What would you like me to do with this body you insist I keep?"

I raised a hateful glare at him. "Send it back to hell."

His smile was like a hot poker in my stomach. Was he enjoying this? My bewilderment? My pain? "Can't do that when there's so much to entertain me here on Earth."

"Entertainment? Is that what I am to you?"

A man walked into the room. His trainer. "You're on."

"Well?" Reyes asked again, still waiting for a legitimate answer.

This was getting ridiculous. I noticed Elaine just outside the door, looking in, her brows crinkled in concern. "Your girlfriend is fretting," I said, trying to change the subject.

"Jealous?"

"Not in the least."

" 'Cause you seem jealous."

"I'm not jealous. I just can't believe—"

"My abs?"

My stomach flip-flopped. I took a calming breath, and said, "Your taste."

"My taste is just fine." He lifted my chin with a taped hand. "You don't want me around, so why do you care anyway?"

"I don't."

"Then why are you here?"

"You owe me for my services."

"Aw, so all those times I saved your life?"

I shrugged a shoulder. "Bill me."

He leaned in and whispered, "I would rather fuck you."

"I would rather you let go."

"But you haven't answered my question." He put his mouth at my ear, his breath fanning over it, down my neck, and spilling onto my shoulder in an intoxicating wave of delight. "What do you want me to do with my body, Dutch?"

After a solid minute, I said, "Take it to go see your sister."

Mentioning his beloved sister was like throwing ice water in his face. He cooled instantly, his body tense, rigid.

"You're on," the trainer said more forcefully. "Get out there and—"

When Reyes turned on him like a cobra ready to strike, the man stepped back. His eyes widened for a fraction of a second before he raised his hands in surrender. "We're going to lose this spot if you don't get out there. That's all I'm saying."

Reyes seemed to calm. He turned to me, wrapped his fingers into my collar, and pulled me forward until his mouth was only centimeters from mine. "Go home." He let go with a soft shove, and I swatted at his hand in response. But he was already headed for the door.

Go home, my left ass cheek.

6

Why kill them with kindness when you can use an axe?

—T-SHIRT

I stood in a less crowded area of the warehouse, still dumbfounded. He was living with her? That woman? That stalker? To say that I was astonished would have been the biggest understatement since "Houston, we have a problem." I was thunderstruck.

But holy cow, he was living with her? My jealously seemed endless, and I hated it. I would rather be attacked by rabid fire ants than be jealous. The superfluous emotion was a combination of fear, rage, humiliation, and insecurity. I looked down at the expanse of girl parts I carried on my chest, also known as Danger and Will Robinson. Clearly, I had no reason to be insecure.

As much as I did *not* want to see Reyes fight again, I sidled into a dark corner to do that very thing. He wouldn't be able to see me from here and get his panties in a twist. Thankfully, the platform was high enough for me to see the action over the crush of spectators. But I stepped onto a cement pylon a metal beam was bolted to, wrapped my arms around the beam, and searched for Reyes.

He'd been talking with his trainer and turned to go into the cage, but after walking up the first step, he paused. Looked down. Took a deep breath. Then placed a pointed stare right on me. I scooted farther into the corner. How could he possibly see me? Maybe he was looking at someone else. He tilted his head before lifting a long arm and pointing to the exit behind me.

In one choreographed wave, the sea of heads turned to investigate. I turned, too, so they wouldn't know he was talking to me. When I looked back, he'd crossed his arms over his chest and glared. I jumped off the pylon and crossed my arms, too. Only mine were crossed in defiance. If he wanted me out so bad, he could come drag me out himself.

Wait, no, that probably wasn't a good idea.

Before I could decide what to do, the crowd started to cheer again as Reyes's opponent appeared out of the rooms opposite him. Reyes shifted his focus when the guy emerged on the stairs. I could see why. He was even bigger than the last, more muscular. Reyes was a big guy, but he was lean, solid, built for speed just as much as for strength. This guy was all strength. He looked more like a professional bodybuilder than like a fighter. And as awesome as Reyes's reach was, this guy's had to be at least four inches longer.

My heart jumped and lodged in my throat at the sight of him. I knew Reyes was a supernatural being, but he was wounded and this guy was huge. I took a step forward as he entered the cage. But Reyes stayed on the stairs outside his entrance. Watching. Studying. He'd dropped his arms and dropped his head and stood eyeing the guy from underneath his lashes as though he were waiting for something. But what?

The crowd fell silent as they waited with bated breath. The opponent had stopped dead in his tracks and was staring back at Reyes. Then he frowned and looked down as though confused. That's when I saw it: A blur in his movements. A disturbance in his aura. He shook his head as though to clear it. A heartbeat later, his eyes were locked on to mine. They widened in surprise as recognition flashed across his face. I had no idea why. I'd never seen the guy. But when he let out an animalistic shriek, fear rocketed down my spine and across my skin.

I stumbled back as the guy ignored the exit gates and bounded over the cage with the speed and grace of an animal. A huge animal with a deep-seated hatred twisting his features. I tried to slow the world, to stop his progress—I'd done it in the past, before the Earl Walker incident— but it wouldn't happen. I couldn't control anything, including the raging beat of my pulse in my ears.

Somewhere in my periphery, I noticed Reyes as he tried to intercept him. He'd scaled the cage in one leap and launched himself into the air, missing the guy by inches. He reached back, grabbed the top of the cage, executed a magnificent turn in midair, and launched himself again. The cage walls buckled under the pressure of his weight and the force it must have taken him to catapult himself into the crowd.

Then he disappeared behind the opponent. The hulking fighter landed only a few yards away from me and barreled forward, pummeling any- one who stood in his way like a battering ram, his face a mask of furious determination.

And I didn't even know the guy.

I tried to turn and run. With every ounce of strength I had, I tried to force my feet to head in the opposite direction, but I could only stare. Watch as he got closer and closer. Drool rolled out of his shrieking mouth like the foam of a rabid dog. He wanted me dead. And he craved my death like addicts craved their next high. I could feel it. In one caustic blast, his murderous intentions hit me a microsecond before he did.

He slammed into me with the force of a freight train, knocking me senseless, but he had only enough time to send me crashing against the wall behind me before he went down. Probably because an equally an- gry Reyes was on his back. He tackled the guy to the floor, wrenching a loud scream from the guy's throat as he tried to shake Reyes off. Still, the guy kept coming forward. Kept fighting and crawling and inching

toward me as I pressed against the wall, stewing in my own bewilderment. And agony. My head had whipped back when I hit, and a startlingly sharp jolt of pain ripped through me like a tornado hell-bent on
eating half of Barbara, my brain.

Faced with such bizarre and violent behavior, the crowd panicked.
Several were hurt the moment the guy landed, but more were getting
hurt in the crush of bodies, some trying to get out, some angling for a
better look. Screams and shouts erupted and grew louder and louder as
the guy did everything in his power to get to me.

"Go!"

I looked at Reyes. Keeping the man subdued was taking all his strength,
and that's when I knew the guy could not possibly be human. Or at least
not all human.

He fought for a better hold and wrapped the guy in a headlock before
offering me another glare. "Charley, for fuck's sake, go!" he shouted
through clenched teeth.

I scrambled to my feet as the guy elbowed Reyes's jaw, loosening his
hold just enough to gain another six inches. He refocused on me, his face
contorted with a hateful sneer, saliva bubbling out of his mouth, blood
gushing from his nose, but his only goal was to get to me. He clawed forward, his nails scraping on the cement floor, breaking as he fought for
ground.

The chaos around me took on a life of its own. It rose to a cacophonic
frenzy. Screams echoed from all corners of the warehouse as the spectators ran for the doors. I doubted any one of them even knew what they
were running from at that point. People were screaming. People were
running. And that was good enough for them. They followed suit only
because not to do so would be detrimental to their health. They simply
had no choice.

I'd started for the door when I noticed a kid in a Slipknot hoodie. He
fell and would be trampled in a matter of seconds if no one went to his

aid. I tried to rush forward, but the throngs of frenzied spectators pushed me back. I lost sight of the kid altogether.

Then I heard another growl. I had to turn back, to check on Reyes. The man had made some headway. He was once again only a few feet from me. As I placed one foot behind the other, unable to take my eyes off Reyes and the Hulk, a darkness emerged from him, the opponent, the crazy guy clawing toward me with a rabid fervor. For a split second, another head emerged out of his own. As black and dark as the outermost fringes of the universe. Teeth sharp as an obsidian razor and honed to a needlelike point. Then the beast was back inside him and I realized what I was looking at. A demon.

No. I stepped back again. No. A man possessed by a demon. I'd seen demons before when they'd tortured Reyes. Their spiderlike bodies. Their sinewy limbs that bent and twisted at unnatural angles. Their eyeless heads that consisted of teeth, teeth, and more teeth. And one was inside this man. He quaked with a fierce, animalistic need to rip me to shreds. He wanted me so badly, the hunger of it radiated toward me.

He gave one last, valiant effort to shake Reyes off, but Reyes was too strong. He wrestled him to the ground, and in one sharp move, he twisted the man's head to the side and broke his neck. The surreal crack that followed, the unorthodox angle of his neck, the life draining out of him in seconds flat, caused another gallon of adrenaline to dump down my spine. And his smell, like rotten eggs, assaulted my senses.

A wave of nausea swept over me. I glanced around, tried to steady myself and to see who had witnessed Reyes break a man's neck. The warehouse was almost empty now. A few stragglers stood in the shadows, mostly the bouncers and a couple other workers, their faces frozen in shock as they took in the dead guy.

Then Reyes was up. He grabbed my jacket and jerked me to attention. "What is it going to take to get you to listen to me?"

The colossal adrenaline dump that had overloaded my system now needed a place to go. With every ounce of strength I had, I pushed him off, rushed to the wall, and emptied the contents of my stomach onto the concrete foundation.

It was weird. I'd never had that kind of reaction to being attacked. I was usually much more composed. Or if not composed, vertical at least. But this time, I could barely stand. The world spun around me as my stomach heaved violently. That would explain the shaking and why I had an inexplicable compulsion to double over. But why? Why now? Why this guy?

Reyes didn't give me time to finish, to catch my breath. He grabbed the back of my jacket again and dragged me toward the door. I thought about fighting him, but that would take an energy I just didn't seem to possess. I felt like a rag doll in his grasp, my limbs hanging at my side, limp and useless. So I argued instead. I always had the energy to argue.

I wiped my mouth on my sleeve, swallowing back another lurch of my stomach, and said in a muffled voice, "Let me go."

He didn't. He continued to drag me across the floor like a used mop. I felt his manhandling unnecessary and uncalled for, but fighting to keep bile down was taking all my mental energy.

I managed a few words between a heave and a swallow. "What was that?"

I knew, of course, but it was just too unreal. Too horrible for me to fully absorb. I had no idea humans could really be possessed. Figured it was just a movie device to cause goose bumps and nightmares. Or something preachers said to keep their parishioners in line.

But that man had been possessed, sure as I was standing there. Or, well, being dragged across the floor there.

We were halfway to the door when Reyes whipped me around to face him, clutching my shoulders in a death grip, his expression more angry than, say, understanding. So, naturally, I got annoyed. I'd just barfed. Did he have no sense of decency? Sadly, I could do nothing about it at the moment. I swallowed again and tried to push at his arms.

"Get in that Jeep of yours and get out of here, or I swear by all that is holy—"

While I was totally into the conversation and had every intention of listening to his seven thousandth threat, certain I'd take it to heart, I heard another crack. It was quickly followed by a guttural moan. Then another crack. And another moan that seemed more like the screech of a wounded owl.

I looked to my left, to where Reyes's opponent lay dead. Only he wasn't dead. He was up on all fours, craning his neck from side to side as though popping it after a long night's sleep. Blackness swirled around him again as though the demon inside him had a hard time staying within the confines of the physical body it inhabited.

Reyes jerked me forward until his face was inches from my own. "Leave."

Then it leapt. Like a tiger in the tall grasses of India, the man launched himself toward us. Toward me. Reyes pushed me down so hard, my head bounced, this time off the cement foundation. But the stars that followed were upstaged by one thing. As Reyes stepped protectively in front of me, tensed, readying himself for the attack, another growl, deep and guttural, echoed from the deepest corners of the universe.

With a ferocious snarl, Artemis jumped out of nowhere and ripped through the guy as he leapt forward. His physical body drifted forward, then landed with a hard thud, skidding across the floor, while the demon shrieked and writhed beside it under the attack of my guardian. Its teeth clamped down on Artemis's neck. Its claws swiped at her back. She let out a yelp, but kept at it, her head shaking the agonized demon, her teeth tearing until a blackness, like a gaseous blood, seeped out, crept along the floor, then dissipated just like the demon itself.

I spared a quick glance at my attacker. No doubt about it this time. The man was dead. His eyes stared at nothing, fixed and lifeless.

Then Artemis turned toward me, lowered her head, bared her fangs, and let another guttural growl rumble out of her chest. And I thought we were friends. But Reyes had turned around as well, and damned if he didn't do the same. I got that feeling of insecurity, like when I had something stuck in my teeth. Only they were looking over me, just past my head.

That's when I felt the cold desolation of hatred at the back of my neck, and I knew there was another one. I looked up and into the vacant eyes of the boy in the Slipknot hoodie. He was much smaller than the Hulk, but his curious determination, and the saliva dripping off his chin, was no less scary. Just as he pitched toward me, Artemis shot across the floor and bolted straight through him like a dart. She tore the demon out of him and proceeded to maul the thing to its smoky death.

The boy dropped the second the demon left him. He curled into a ball, and that's when recognition hit. It was the kid from my backseat. The kid I thought was dead. His blond hair was matted and dirty. His blue eyes somehow darker. Had the demon occupying his body sent his soul somewhere else? Maybe there wasn't room for the both of them.

I blinked in startled realization until Reyes lifted me off the ground. Again. Being manhandled by the son of Satan was getting old, but I was too weak to do much about it. He started dragging me toward the door once more.

"Wait," I said, fighting his hold. "Get the boy."

"No."

With a jolt of stubbornness, I twisted and jerked out of Reyes's grip. He stopped and glared.

"Fine. Glare, glower, scowl, I don't care, but I am not leaving this warehouse without that kid." When Reyes crossed his arms over his chest, I continued. "He was possessed. An innocent boy."

Artemis leapt up to me then and barked playfully. I kneeled down and nuzzled against her before looking up at Reyes again, thrilled that she hadn't attacked him.

"Why would they choose a boy like that?"

"They have their reasons. The same reasons you need to leave."

"Can he be possessed again? Will they come after him again?"

He looked back in thought. "It's possible."

I rushed over to the boy, knelt down to push his hair back from his dirty face. Artemis came over and tried to lick it. When she realized she couldn't, she hunched down beside him. "How can we make sure they don't?"

Reyes knelt, too, and checked the kid's pulse. Artemis seemed completely uninterested in him until he reached for the kid. "They can't touch him on hallowed ground," he explained as Artemis scooted forward and licked his wrist.

"Really?" I asked, surprised by both the information and Artemis's reaction to him. I was worried that since he was the son of Satan, she'd try to rip out his jugular. "You mean like churches and cemeteries?"

"Yes." He offered her ears a quick rub, then turned the kid's face up and lifted his eyelids. "He's in shock."

"We have to get him to safety." I put a hand on his forearm. "Please, Reyes." Artemis whined as though asking for his help as well.

Fighting the frustration he felt, he bent down and lifted the kid into his arms. He wasn't exactly small, but Reyes had no difficulty rising to his feet with a sixteen-year-old kid in his arms. Artemis barked in excitement, offered me one last nuzzle, then disappeared to wherever she'd come from, leaping into the earth beneath us. I couldn't help but be in awe. Where the heck did she stay?

I looked back at the other man who'd been possessed, Reyes's opponent. A current of guilt jolted through me. He'd been innocent, too.

"Not that one," Reyes said, kicking the door open. Most of the cars were gone. Thankfully, the rain had stopped. I followed beside them, watching the boy carefully.

"Which one?"

"The man inside. He was not worthy of your sympathy."

"But he was innocent." I hurried around and unlocked the passenger's door.

"No, he wasn't. Pull the seatback forward."

I noticed the kid's incorporeal essence was no longer in my backseat. Was he back in his body? Is that how it worked? I pulled the seat forward and Reyes deposited the kid in the back.

"Keys."

"Wait—are you driving my Jeep somewhere?"

"I'm driving you away from here. Give me the keys and get in."

"I can drive myself, thank you very much."

"And what if he gets possessed again while you're driving up I-25?"

I tossed him the keys. "The transmission sticks a little."

He climbed in the other side as sirens sounded from the east. We headed west, skidding through the wet parking lot and swerving onto Second. "Where are we taking him?" he asked.

"I know just where to keep him for now. They'll know what to do. Just get to Central and head east."

Only after the sirens grew too distant to hear did I remember that we'd left Elaine Oake at the warehouse. I wondered if I should mention it, then realized I had to get over my pettiness. She could be in danger. "We left your girlfriend back there."

One corner of his mouth lifted in indifference.

"And we just left a crime scene."

Another shrug of indifference.

"I can't just leave a crime scene," I said, realizing what I'd done.

"You can this time."

I looked over my shoulder. "Maybe we should go back. They're going to want to know how that man died."

He didn't seem to care about that either. "Are you broke?"

The last thing I wanted to talk about were my financial woes. I wanted to discuss demons and possession and how innocent children suddenly became pawns in this war Reyes had been warning me about. But I decided to placate him. Maybe my cooperation would help him open up.

"I moved out of my offices," I said, trying to block the pain of my father's betrayal. Reyes would be able to feel it anyway. "And I just haven't gotten back on my feet after the accident."

"You're calling what Walker did to you an accident?"

"It makes me feel better, so yes." I didn't enjoy pondering the fact that what Earl Walker did to me was no accident. He'd come after me with two goals in mind: Interrogate through the use of torture, then kill. But the word *accident* seemed to make the whole thing more palatable.

Reyes's fingers tightened on the steering wheel. "I'm sorry, Dutch. I never thought he'd come after you."

Hoping to dismiss the conversation, I folded my arms in suspicion. "Are you trying to get out of paying your bill?"

He almost grinned. "How did you come up with a million dollars?"

I plucked a string off my jacket. "I added my regular daily charge plus expenses, then rounded up."

After a quick sideways glance, he asked, "You're not very good at math, are you?"

Since we were on the subject of changing the subject, I decided to ask a question of my own. "Why are you staying with her?"

He looked at me just as a passing car's headlights lit his face, the low beams shimmering in his rich brown eyes. "She offered."

"You could stay with Amador and Bianca," I said, mentioning the only true friends he seemed to have.

He turned back to the road. "I could stay with you."

I snorted. "Not likely." Though it was a ridiculously nice thought, one that sent a spark of interest jolting through my nether regions. Since we were being civil to each other, I said, "I'm glad you're out."

"Prove it," he said as a wicked grin spread across his face. I ignored the flip-flop of my stomach.

"I'll expect a check soon. Don't make me come looking for you again. It's just up here." I pointed to a building that sat perpendicular to one of the oldest churches in Albuquerque. A sign outside it read THE SISTERS OF THE IMMACULATE CROSS.

"You're taking him to a convent?" he asked.

"It's hallowed ground." And they would take him in. I looked back at the kid. How could they not?

Reyes slowed to a stop beside the adobe building and put Misery in park. A single light illuminated the front door.

Instead of getting out, I turned to my chauffer. "I have to know more about this, Reyes. If they're after me, I have the right to know what's going on."

He turned off the motor and gazed out his window. "I'm still working on the hows and whys."

"That's fine. I'll settle for the whats."

When he didn't elaborate, I climbed out and pulled my seatback forward with every intention of dealing with him later. The kid was still unconscious, but he stirred. Reyes got out and came around the car just as another thought hit me. One I'd completely forgotten about.

"I meant to ask you, when I saw you this morning outside my dad's bar, another man waved at you."

He leaned against Misery's quarter panel and folded his arms at his chest. "That happens sometimes. We live in a crazy world."

"No, I mean, you were there, right? Your physical body?"

"Why do you ask?" he asked with an uncomfortable shift.

"Because you dematerialized. You. All of you."

A devilish grin played upon his sensual mouth. "Dutch, you know that's impossible."

"But—"

The boy stirred again. I glanced at him. At his blond hair as it fell over his handsome face. At his long lashes and his strong jaw. He was going to be a lady killer, no doubt about it.

With a smile of appreciation, I looked back at Reyes, but he was gone. I turned in a circle, scanned the area, walked around Misery, searching. He was definitely gone, vanished as soundlessly as smoke.

No way.

7

Happiness isn't good enough.
I demand euphoria!

—T-SHIRT

Clearly Reyes didn't want to answer any of my questions. Then again, we were on hallowed ground. Maybe he couldn't step foot on sacred soil? But could he really dematerialize his physical body? The mere concept left me flummoxed.

I crawled into the Jeep beside the boy and pushed his hair out of his face. He woke up with a jolt and pushed away from me, half in confusion and half in fear.

"It's okay," I said, showing my palms in surrender. "You're okay, but I need to get you inside."

His gaze darted around wildly, squinting every time he looked at me as though looking into a bright light, and I realized, with no small amount of shock, that he was like Pari. He could see my light, and it was obviously disturbing him. I reached into the front and brought out my sunglasses.

"This will help." When he didn't take them from me, I unfolded them and leaned in to slip them on his face, taking care to move slowly. He let me but kept his muscles taut, wary. "Is that better?"

He examined his surroundings, then returned his wary expression to mine.

"Oh, right. This is my Jeep, Misery, and I'm Charley." The moment I said it, I wished I could take it back. Why would I introduce my vehicle to a kid who was, as far as he was concerned, being held captive in it? That would be like introducing Jonah to the whale after the fact and expecting them to get along.

"Misery didn't have anything to do with this, I promise."

"Why am I here?" he asked, and I realized why he wasn't answering my questions. He didn't use his voice. He used his hands.

"Are you Deaf?" I signed back to him.

He seemed surprised. "Yes."

"Well, then, I'm Charley," I signed, taking a couple of seconds to finger-spell my name. I was suddenly very grateful I'd been born knowing every language ever spoken in the history of the world, including the vast and varied array of signed languages.

"Who else?" he asked, and I furrowed my brows in confusion. "You introduced someone else."

"Yeah," I said sheepishly. "I introduced my Jeep." I indicated her with a sweep of my hand. "Her name is Misery."

"You named your car?"

"Yes. And please don't ask what else I've named. You're too young."

The barest hint of a smile crossed his mouth. "My name is Quentin," he said, finger-spelling his full name; then he raised his left arm and placed a Q on the outside of his wrist with his right hand, indicating his name sign.

"Nice to meet you," I said, and as per custom, he reciprocated the sentiment, even though I doubt he meant it. "I brought you here for your safety. Do you remember what happened to you?"

He glanced to the side. "Some things."

Crap. He would totally need counseling.

I waited for him to turn back to me, and said, "It could happen again."

When he stilled and a ripple of fear wafted toward me, I said, "I'm so sorry. I need to get you inside this building. You'll be safe there."

He leaned forward to take a look.

"Do you have family here in Albuquerque?"

"*A-B-Q?*" he asked, not recognizing the abbreviation, so I finger-spelled the whole thing. No easy feat.

"Yes, you are in Albuquerque, New Mexico."

The shock on his face needed no interpretation.

I put my hand on his shoulder for a minute, let him absorb that latest bit of intel, then asked, "Where are you from?"

After a moment of recovery, he said, "Washington, D.C."

"Oh, you're a long way from home. Do you remember how you got here?"

He turned away from me to hide the tears that had pooled in his eyes. I took that as a no. He must've been possessed before leaving D.C.

"I can contact your family. I'll let them know you're okay."

He covered his face with a hand, and a blanket of sorrow fell over my heart. I put a palm on his shoulder again. Rubbed. Soothed. He didn't have to say anything for me to realize he had no family. I wondered if he was homeless.

His sorrow had me struggling for air. To be so lost. So alone.

"Are you going to come in anytime soon, because it's getting really late."

I jumped in surprise to see Sister Mary Elizabeth standing outside Misery.

Awe swelled inside my chest. "Did the angels tell you we were coming?"

"No, I saw you pull up."

"Oh." That was kind of anticlimactic.

"And the angels never tell me anything. I just kind of overhear their conversations."

"Right. I forgot."

I coaxed Quentin out of Misery and introduced him to Sister Mary Elizabeth and the three other sisters who'd come out to greet us. They huddled around him like mother hens, checking a scrape on his face and a large cut on his wrist. A couple of them even knew ASL, to my utter delight. He'd be fine. For now, at least.

They herded us into the convent, made us soup—which tasted much better than the vomit that still lingered in my mouth—and hot chocolate, and then proceeded to ask me a million questions about what it was like to be the grim reaper and what it was like when people passed through me until the mother superior came in and broke up our party. Sister Mary Elizabeth had told them all about me, so it was only natural they'd be curious. I couldn't help but notice how they skirted the issue of Reyes. They knew who he was, what he was, and how we were connected.

I turned to Quentin. He'd been having a riveting conversation with Sister Ann about how Xbox had the best graphics and the best live streaming. Sister Ann knew her game systems, and she had completely disarmed the shy youth.

He put the sunglasses back on so he could understand me.

"You're going to stay here awhile—is that okay?" I asked him.

"Can I stay with you?"

"No, you need to be on holy ground to be safe. My apartment is more, well, unholy."

He nodded and looked around him, pretending not to be affected by the prospect of staying in a house with a bunch of nuns, though he did seem kind of relieved.

"If you need anything, text me." I handed him my card. "Wait, do you have a phone?"

He patted his jacket and jeans pocket, then pulled out a phone with a huge smile. Then it faded as he tapped on keys. "Dead," he signed with one hand.

"I can get you a charger," Sister Mary Elizabeth signed, her enthusiasm endless.

"Thank you," he said gratefully. Then he asked me, "What's your name sign?"

I bowed my head in mortal shame. "I don't have one. None of my Deaf friends will give me one. Every time I ask, they say they're still thinking about it. It's like they're avoiding the issue."

"Why?"

"I think it's because I have so many good qualities, they can't decide which one to focus on for a name sign."

He chuckled softly. "Hearing people are crazy," he said, his signs vague, as though pretending I wouldn't understand him.

"Oh, yeah?" I asked, puffing up my chest. "Well, Deaf people talk with their mouths full." I burst out laughing at the oldest joke in the Deaf handbook.

Quentin rolled his eyes, and I took the opportunity to go in for a hug. At first he stilled; then he almost draped himself over me, hugging me back like his life depended on it. We stayed in that embrace until Quentin loosened his hold. I kissed his dirty cheek as we pulled apart, and he bowed his head in that sweet, shy way of his.

"I'll be back soon, okay?"

"Wait," he said, suddenly worried. "Do nuns eat bacon? I really like bacon."

Sister Mary Elizabeth tapped his arm to get his attention, then signed, "I love bacon. I'll make some for breakfast, okay?"

He nodded, then let the sisters, thrilled with the prospect of protecting him, usher him out to show him the living quarters where he could bathe and get a fresh change of clothes. He seemed relaxed and grateful, which made me relaxed and grateful. And I could tell the mother superior had taken a shine to him. Something deep inside her stirred when her eyes met his, something warm and maternal, and I wondered what memory surfaced when she looked at him.

After everyone left, I pinned Sister Mary Elizabeth to her chair with my infamous fluster stare. She didn't seem to get flustered, though, if her

bright, slightly ADD gaze was any indication. A gaze I could totally re-
late to.

"I know what you're going to ask me," she said in that rushed way
of hers.

"Good, then I don't have to ask. What have you heard?"

Sister Mary's superpower lay in her ability to hear the angels. Literally. Like a supernatural wiretap without the wires. It was how she knew
about me and about Reyes and about Artemis. She'd been listening to
supreme beings talk about us for years. I could only wonder what they
had to say. I wasn't that interesting.

She bowed her head and stared into her tea. It was unlike her. She was
about to give me some very bad news.

"They've discovered a way to track you."

Oh, well, that didn't seem too bad in the grand scheme of things.
"Who? The demons?"

"Yes, the fallen. They've devised a new plan."

"They're possessing people," I said in disgust. "Is that their big plan?
To take over humans' lives? To destroy them? They possessed that boy for
no reason."

"They had a reason." She ran a fingertip through some spilt sugar gran-
ules. "They're only possessing people who are sensitive to the spiritual
realm. Who are clairvoyant."

I looked to where they'd led Quentin. "So, Quentin is clairvoyant?"
"Yes. Quite."

"Cool, but what does that have to do with me? Doesn't clairvoyance
mean you can see into the future?"

"Not necessarily. It encompasses all persons with clear vision. Those
who can see into the spiritual realm. Some people are born with the ability. Some come by it through other means, like near-death experiences."

I thought of Pari. She could see ghosts ever since she'd had a near-
death experience as a child. "But, why target them? What do they have
to gain?"

"Because they can often see auras."

"Okay," I said, still not catching on.

"And if they can see auras"—she put a hand on my arm—"they can see you."

I did a mental slap to the head. Sometimes I was so thick. "Of course. That explains why they chose Quentin. He can see the light around me."

I'd have to check in on Pari, make sure she hadn't been possessed since I saw her last.

"That's how they can track you. And according to the latest conversations, the demons are closing in. That's why they sent you a guardian. Why they sent you Artemis. They knew this was going to happen."

Damn. I figured there had to be some ghastly reason full of gloom and doom. Artemis couldn't have just been a belated housewarming gift. "Can they hurt her?" I asked, suddenly concerned. "Can the demons hurt Artemis?"

"I don't know. I haven't heard." She cleared her throat and took my cup. "Would you like some more tea?"

"Sure, thank you," I said absently.

The mother superior walked back in and sat down as Sister Mary Elizabeth gathered our cups and stood to make more tea.

She planted her best disdainful expression on me.

I smiled. Inspected the craftsmanship of the cabinetry. Thrummed my fingers on the table. Checked my watch. Or checked my wrist where a watch would have been had I not forgotten it.

"You know," she said after a long moment of reflection, "it took me a long time to—" She struggled to find the right words. "—to believe in Sister Mary Elizabeth's abilities."

Oh, cool. This wasn't going to be about me and my shoe box full of sins. Because we could be here awhile if that were the case. "I understand," I said, trying to be understanding. "It takes people a long time to believe in mine, too. There's nothing wrong with that."

"Actually, there is. She was sent to us by God, and I questioned it. I questioned his gift. That is something I'll have to answer for when the time comes."

That seemed kind of harsh. "I don't think using logic and human instinct is a sin."

Her smile was more congenial than affirming. "From what she has told us, there is a great and terrible war on the horizon."

"That's right," Sister Mary Elizabeth said, nodding in enthusiastic confirmation as she sat back down, handing me a fresh cup of tea. "And it will be brought forth by an impostor."

"An impostor?" I asked.

The mother superior placed a hand on Sister Mary Elizabeth's arm to stay her.

"No way," I said, looking back and forth between the two of them. "You have information that I could use, and you won't hand it over?"

"It is not our place," the mother superior said. "This information is sacred. It was given to us so that we may pray."

"I can pray," I said, insulted. "Just tell me what to pray about. I'll totally put it on my to-do list."

The woman's iron demeanor relaxed a little as a smile twitched at the corner of her mouth. "Prayer must be lived, not checked off a laundry list of duties."

Crap. She was right. "But we're talking about my life here."

"And the lives and salvation of everyone on Earth. You are destined to play a part. You simply must decide which part to play."

"Riddles?" I asked, unimpressed. "You're giving me riddles?"

Sister Mary Elizabeth's eyes were wide with innocent ardency as she watched our exchange. She looked like a kid watching her favorite Saturday-morning cartoon.

Fine, they were keeping the good stuff to themselves. "Can you at least tell me what I'm capable of?"

The sister's mouth spread wide. "Anything you can imagine."

"I don't know," I said, trying not to be disappointed. "I can imagine a lot."

The mother superior patted her protégée's arm. "Time for bed," she said, her voice maternal, caring.

That was my cue to leave. They promised to keep an eye on Quentin until it was safe for him to venture out, but they knew more than I did. I tried not to feel resentful. Not hard, but I did give it an ounce of effort before I gave up and resented the heck out of the entire human race. Not sure why. Fortunately, I was over that by the time I got to Misery, dripping wet, as it had started to rain again.

I called Cookie. She knew where I'd gone and would be frantic with worry. Or driven to the brink of insanity with lust. Reyes did that to her. He probably did that to a lot of girls.

"Well?" she asked when she picked up.

"Do you think we're really alone in the universe?"

"Were you abducted by aliens again?"

"No, thank goodness. Once was enough for me."

"Oh, whew. So, what happened with Reyes? Did you see him?"

"Saw him. Argued with him. Barfed."

"You vomited?"

"Yes."

"On Reyes?"

"No, but only because I didn't think of it at the time. I'm going to Pari's to check on Harper before I head home. No need to let the fact that I'm wearing a bra go to waste."

"Wonderful, then you have a few minutes to fill me in."

I figured as much. I explained everything that had happened in the shortest sentence structure possible. Pari didn't live that far away. Brevity was of the utmost importance. By the time I got there, every molecule in my body was vibrating. It would seem that recaps of Reyes were almost as good as the real thing. How could any man be so inhumanly perfect?

Probably because he was inhuman. His presence seemed to cause a disturbance in my space–time continuum. I felt disoriented around him. Unbalanced. And hot. Always hot.

"What about the bill?" she asked, her voice full of hope.

"I told him to send a check."

"A check?" She seemed appalled. "Couldn't he just work out what he owes us?"

"Maybe, but he owes me much more than he owes you. I think he only owes you like two dollars."

Her voice turned deep and husky. "I could do a lot of damage for two dollars. Send that boy over here, and I'll prove it."

She scared me sometimes. I ended the call after promising I'd brush the vomit taste out of my mouth as soon as possible. But my mind drifted back to the problem at hand. Or, more specifically, problems. As in multiple. They were back. The demons in all their glory. And they had a plan. I made plans sometimes, too, but they rarely involved world domination. Hot dogs on a grill, maybe. Tequila.

After searching for a space, I parked behind the tattoo parlor in front of a sign that said NO PARKING. Since it didn't specify to whom it was referring, I figured it couldn't possibly be talking to me. I hurried through the rain. Got drenched again anyway. I had every intention of complaining to Pari and Tre, but they were both busy evoking whimpers of agony from their patrons, so I left them to it and cruised to the makeshift guest bedroom. Harper, who seemed to have taken an interest in Pari's wall texture, jumped up the minute I walked in.

"Did you find anything?"

"Not a lot. How are you doing?" I asked, sitting on the sofa and motioning for her to sit beside me.

She did reluctantly. "I'm okay."

"I talked to your stepmother today. Why didn't you tell me this has been going on since you were a kid?"

She stood again and turned her back to me, embarrassed. "I didn't think you'd believe me. No one ever believes me, especially when I tell them the whole story."

"I'll tell you what," I said, knowing exactly how she felt. "You promise to trust me, and I'll promise to trust you, okay?"

"Okay."

I finally convinced her to sit back down, but she hid behind her long dark hair.

"Can you tell me what happened? How all this got started?"

"I don't know. I don't remember."

"Your stepmother said it started right after she married your father."

Harper rolled her eyes and faced me. "She always says that, because this is all about her. All about their marriage. It couldn't possibly have anything to do with me, with the fact that I've been traumatized almost my entire life." She threw her arms up in frustration, and I liked the glimpse of her she offered me. The fighter. The spirited and capable woman I knew she was if she'd put up with a psychotic stalker her entire life.

I let an appreciative smile slide across my face. "Better."

"What?" Her pretty brows crinkled together.

"Never mind. Why don't you give me your version of what happened?"

She drew in a deep breath, leaned back, and said, "That's just it. I don't remember. They got married. Yes, against my wishes, but I was only five, so I really didn't have much of a say. They went on their honeymoon. I stayed with my maternal grandparents in Bosque Farms while they were away." She focused on me again. "My real grandparents on my biological mother's side, who were wonderful. Then we came back and that's when everything started. Right after their honeymoon."

I took a memo pad out of my bag and started taking notes. It seemed like the right thing to do. "Okay, tell me exactly how it all started. What do you remember noticing first?"

She shrugged. "I've gone over this so many times with therapists, I'm not even sure which parts are real and which parts I made up. It was so long ago."

"Well, I'm glad that you realize some of your memories could have been a product of years of prodding by professionals. They could have been a fabrication of your own mind trying to cope with the circumstances. But let's just say, for argument's sake, that they aren't. That every single thing you remember really happened. What can you tell me?"

"Okay. Well, I guess it started when I found a dead rabbit on my bed."

"So, a real rabbit? Dead?"

"Yes. I woke up one morning and there it was. Lying dead on the foot of my bed."

"What happened?"

"I screamed. My dad came running in." Her gaze darted toward me, then away. "He took it away."

She was still in therapy mode, worried what I would think, how I would analyze her every move. "I get it, Harper. Your dad came to your rescue. So, maybe that was a way to get his attention, yes? Is that what you learned in all those years of therapy? That you were just seeking your father's attention?"

She wilted. "Something like that. And maybe they're right."

"I thought we had an agreement." When she turned back to me, I continued. "I thought we were going on the assumption that you are not making things up. That you did not imagine or fabricate any of this." I leaned in closer. "That you're not crazy."

"But it makes sense."

"Sure it does. So does exercise, but you don't see me doing it on a regular basis, do you? And if it would make you feel better, I could analyze you myself. Tell you all the reasons why you've pulled these accusations out of thin air. I minored in psychology. I'm totally qualified."

A timid smile emerged from behind her hair.

"I know how you feel. I've been analyzed to death as well. Not, like, professionally, though I did date a psych major who said I had attention issues. Or at least that's what I think he said. I wasn't really paying attention. Anyway, where was I?" When she didn't answer in less that seven-twelfths of a second, I continued my rant. "Right, so what I'm trying to say is that—"

"You're crazier than I am?" She crinkled her nose in delight.

With a laugh, I said, "Something like that. So, what happened with the rabbit?"

"Nothing really. My dad said the dog brought it in, but the dog wasn't allowed in the house."

"Can you describe the rabbit? Was there any blood?"

She thought back. Her brows furrowed in concentration; then a slight rush of fear flitted across her face. "Nobody's ever asked me that. In over twenty-five years, not one person has asked me about that rabbit."

"Harper?"

"No. I'm sorry, no, there was no blood. None. Its neck was broken."

"Okay." She seemed to be making a connection in her mind of some kind. I wondered if she was still talking about the rabbit. I kept silent awhile, let her absorb whatever she needed to, then asked, "What happened later? What led you to believe someone was trying to kill you?"

She blinked back to me with a shake of her head. "Oh, well, just little things. Strange things, one right after another."

"Like?"

"Like the time my stepbrother set my dog's house on fire. With him in it."

"Your stepbrother did this? On purpose?"

"He says it was an accident. I believe him now, but I didn't at the time."

"Why not?"

"Because that same night, my electric blanket caught fire."

"With you in it," I said knowingly.

She nodded. "With me in it."

Well, asshole stepbrother just jumped to the number one position of possible suspects.

"But they always happened like that: in twos."

"What do you mean?"

"I had a birthday party about a week after the first incident, the dead rabbit thing. And my stepmother's sister came to the party with her two horrid children." She actually shivered in revulsion. "They were so aggressive. Anyway, she gave me a rabbit. A white rabbit just like the one in my room, only someone had torn a small hole in the back and had taken out part of the stuffing so that its head flopped to the side."

"Like its neck was broken."

"Exactly."

What a loving family. I didn't want to bring up the rabbit I'd found in her kitchen. It could have been the same one, or it could have been placed there more recently, but I was afraid if I mentioned it, I'd lose her altogether.

"Everyone laughed," she continued, "when I got upset. My aunt held it up to me, flopping its head from side to side. She had a shrill laugh that reminded me of a jet engine during takeoff."

"And you were five?" I asked, horrified.

She nodded and proceeded to pick lint off her dark blue coat.

"What did your father do while all this was going on?"

"Working. Always working."

"What else happened?"

"Just odd little things. Jewelry would go missing or my shoelaces would be tied in knots every morning for a week."

Things that could definitely be chalked up to a bratty brother playing practical jokes.

"Then I started seeing someone in my room at night."

"That's creepy."

"Tell me about it."

"And you never recognized who it was?"

After shaking her head, she said, "But it didn't get really bad until I was around seven. My stepbrother gave me a plastic ring with a spider on it." She grinned sheepishly. "We liked spiders and bugs and snakes and things."

"Spiders are cool as long as they respect personal boundaries," I said. "Namely mine. But why do I get the feeling it doesn't end there?"

"That night, the same night he gave me the ring, I was bitten three times on the stomach by baby black widows as I lay sleeping. They found two of them in my pajamas."

"Someone could have put them there while you slept."

"Exactly."

"Do you think your brother had anything to do with it?"

"I wondered for a long time. We weren't very close at first, especially after the doghouse thing. But we grew to love each other very much. He was the only one in my family who believed me, stood up for me even against my stepmother. It infuriated her."

"I can imagine."

And I could. Harper's stepmother was about as loving as my own, but mine never set a black widow on me or lit my electric blanket on fire. There was a time when I thought she was trying to microwave my brain cells with the remote control, but I'd been on a three-day *Twilight Zone* marathon with too little sleep and too much coffee. And I was four at the time.

"So, this went on your whole life?" I asked.

"Yes. I'd find dead mice in my room or dead bugs in my shoes. One time I poured a cup of milk, and in the time it took me to put the milk in the refrigerator and butter my toast, someone put a dead worm in it. Another time I came home from a sleepover and found that all my dolls were bald. Someone shaved their heads. Of course, no one saw anyone go into my room. It was just me trying to get attention again."

I pressed my mouth together in disapproval. "What are we going to do with you?"

She chuckled and I was glad I could help her sprinkle a little humor onto an otherwise horrific situation. It always helped me cope. Life was too short to be taken seriously.

I decided to find out where she'd run off to for three years. That is a long time to sow the old oats. "Your stepmom said you disappeared."

"Yes. When I hit twenty-five, I'd finally had enough. I told them to kiss my butt and left. Completely disappeared. I changed my name, got a job, even took some night classes. But when my dad got sick, I had no choice. I had to come home."

"When was this?"

"About six months ago."

"But how did you know your father was sick?"

She bowed her head, her face softening in remembrance. "I had a contact," she said; then she curled the edge of her jacket into her fingers. "But my stepmother was hardly happy to see me. I stayed with them at first, despite the glares of disapproval."

"I swear our stepmothers were conjoined twins in another life."

"Then another dead rabbit showed up on my bed, and everything came rushing back to me. I realized then that I'd willingly walked back into a recurring nightmare." Tears pushed past her lashes.

I gave her a minute, then asked, "Can I ask you, when your father passes away, who inherits the estate?"

She sniffed. "I do. My stepmother and brother have a sizable sum coming to them, but I get the house and about seventy-five percent of the assets. It was part of the agreement when they got married. I think she signed a prenup."

"So, if anything happens to you, then what?"

"My stepfamily gets it all."

That's what I figured.

8

Insanity does NOT run in my family.
It strolls through, takes its time,
and gets to know everyone personally.

—T-SHIRT

I tucked Harper in, harassed Pari and Tre a bit, then headed home. The good news was that it'd stopped raining again. The bad news was that my hair was still wet underneath but the top layers were dry and it created that frizzy, homeless look I was so not fond of. I totally needed a better conditioner.

All the parking spots in front of my building were taken, so I had to park in the back of Dad's bar. When I grabbed Margaret and climbed out of Misery, I realized the SUV in my spot belonged to my uncle Bob. He would pay and pay dearly. With his life. Or a twenty. Depending on my mood.

I took the stairs to my floor and heard hammering coming from the end unit when I got there. I looked at it longingly. Lovingly. It had the coolest kitchen I'd ever seen. Mine had a kitchen, but comparing the two would be like comparing the *Mona Lisa* to a drawing I once did of a girl named Mona Salas. Her head kept ending up on her left shoulder and she had really big boobs. We were in kindergarten. Though I liked to think of that drawing as some form of extrasensory perception, because when

Mona got boobs, she got boobs to spare. Clearly that drawing was irrefutable proof that I could see into the future.

"Where have you been?"

I stepped into my apartment and met Uncle Bob's glare with one of my own. "Out trying to pass myself off as a movie producer to get hot guys to sleep with me. Where have you been?"

Uncle Bob ignored my perfectly worded question and handed me a file. "Here's what I've got on the arsonist. He sticks to old buildings and houses, but that probably won't last."

Without missing the look of concern that flashed across his face when he saw Margaret in my arms, I placed her along with my bag on the breakfast bar and took the file. "I need to do a little research," I said, heading for the bathroom and my toothbrush while reading. "I know the basic psychological profile of the everyday arsonist, but nothing that would impress anyone of import. And now that he's killed someone—"

"He didn't," he said, interrupting. "The homeless woman was already dead when the building went up. From what the ME could tell, she probably died of pneumonia about two days earlier."

"Oh, but you're still on the case?" I asked, studying the guy's profile while squeezing toothpaste onto the bristles.

"Decided to stick around, give a hand. And you went out," he said, his tone pleased.

I said through the bubbles of toothpaste, "Had to. I got a case."

"Want to tell me about it?"

After rinsing, I headed back that way, still looking over the file. "That's a negatory. But I'd like to keep that option open. You know, if I get in trouble."

"So, you'll be telling me all about it by tomorrow afternoon. Have you talked to your dad?"

"Negatory times two. This guy seems to be very precise in what he's burning down. I'm assuming there's no insurance angle?"

"Not a single one. Different owners. Different insurance companies. We can't find a single thread connecting them."

"Hey," I said, thinking about the news show I'd seen. "Do you guys have any idea who those Gentlemen Thieves are? Those bank robbers?"

He perked up, clearly interested. "No, do you?"

"Darn. Not really. They just look familiar." I glanced toward the ceiling in thought. "Like their shape. I could swear I've seen them somewhere."

The door opened, and Cookie waltzed in with her twelve-year-old daughter, Amber, in tow.

"Well, if you figure it out, give me a call, okay?"

"Will do."

Cookie offered an absent wave to Ubie, barely taking note of him. But he noticed her. Both his pulse and his interest rose. So either he was still pining over Cookie or he was having a heart attack. I voted for pining.

"Hey, Robert," she said, dumping an armful of groceries on my counter. "I'm going to try out some of these appliances before we send them back. Who knows, I may wonder where they've been all my life."

"What is all this anyway?" he asked, indicating the boxes with a nod of his head.

Amber spoke up then. "Hey, Uncle Bob." She gave him a quick hug. "This is Charley's attempt to cope with her feelings of insecurity and helplessness. In a sad effort to gain control over her life again, she has turned to hoarding."

"For heaven's sake," I said, offering Cookie my best glower, "I'm not a hoarder."

"Don't look at me." She pointed to the fruitcake of her loins.

"We watched a documentary at school," Amber said. "I learned a lot."

"Obviously, but for your information, I am not attempting to hoard control over my sad . . . helplessness."

"Oh, yeah?" Her eyes narrowed into a challenge if I'd ever seen one.

"Yeah," I said, following suit, trying not to grin.

"Then why do you wear that gun everywhere you go?"

"Why does everyone have to give Margaret a hard time?"

She raised one brow. "You've never carried one before."

"I've never been tortured within an inch of my life before, either."

"My point exactly," she said, but her face softened, and I realized I shouldn't have brought that up. Apparently my being tortured not fifty feet from her had caused her no small amount of distress. Or nightmares. "And I'm sorry for making it so rudely," she continued.

Cookie put a hand on her shoulder.

"No," I said, stepping forward and taking her lovely chin into my hand. "I'm sorry that happened, Amber. And I'm very sorry you were so close when it did."

I'd never told her that the man who attacked me had been in the room with her for God only knew how long before I showed up. I'd never even told Cookie, and I never kept secrets from her. But I had no idea how she would take it, knowing that the wreckage from my life had spilled over into hers. Had almost gotten her daughter—and herself, for that matter— killed. I just didn't know how to tell her.

"Well, I wish I'd been closer," she said, a vehemence thickening her voice. "I would've killed him for you, Charley."

I pulled her into a hug, her graceful body more bone than flesh. "I know you would've. Of that, I have no doubt."

"Am I interrupting?"

I looked past Amber as my sister, Gemma, walked in. She had long blond hair and big blue eyes, which was a bitch growing up with, getting asked questions like, "Why aren't you pretty like your sister?" Not that I was bitter.

Gemma and I weren't super-close growing up. Her insistence that our stepmother was not an alien monster sent from a tiny settlement some- where on the seventh ring of Saturn had tainted any rapport we might have had, sibling or otherwise. But now that she was a psychiatrist, we could talk about the fact that our stepmother was an alien monster sent from a tiny settlement somewhere on the seventh ring of Saturn like two grown adults. Though she still didn't believe me.

Amber turned. "Hi, Gemma," she said before heading to my computer. Or trying to head to my computer. "Can I update my status before I do my homework, Charley?" She craned her neck so she could see over the wall of boxes. Hopefully she'd find the computer. I hadn't seen it in weeks, but surely it was still where I'd left it.

"Sure. What are you going to say?"

"I'm going to tell everyone Mom had *the talk* with me." She air-quoted the pertinent information.

I snorted and regarded Cookie with a questioning brow. "The one about the birds and the bees?"

"Oh, no, not that one," Amber said. "We had that one ages ago." As tall as she was, I still lost her when she entered the forest of square trees. But her voice was coming through the boxes loud and clear. "The one about how guys are really aliens sent to Earth to harvest the intelligence from young, pliant brains like mine. Apparently, I won't be completely safe from their techniques until I'm thirty-seven and a half."

Cookie shrugged a brow.

"She's right," Uncle Bob said, pouring himself a cup of coffee. "I'm actually from Pluto."

Gemma put her bag down and came over for a hug, a tradition we'd only recently started partaking in. I hadn't seen her in a couple of weeks. After the torture thing, she was coming over every day. But between work and her pretending she had a social life, her visits had dwindled to a slow trickle.

"I see you took our last talk to heart." She offered me her stern face, the one that used to make me giggle. Now it just made me appreciate her lopsided sense of reality. Like I took anything she said to heart. We'd been related way too long for that. "Do you think you have enough small kitchen appliances?"

"We're working on that," Cookie said as Uncle Bob gave Gemma one of his big bear hugs.

"Yes, we are," he concurred.

"Well, good," Gemma said, stepping into the kitchen to see what Cookie was up to. "I just came to check on things, see how you were doing."

"Okay, well, thanks."

"How are you sleeping?"

"Alone, sadly."

"No, I meant *are* you sleeping?"

I figured I could tell her about how I roam my apartment all night like a paranoid drug addict, checking and rechecking the locks, making sure the windows were shut and the door was soundly bolted. I could explain how I would then go to bed only to lie there conjuring images of burglars and serial killers with every creak and groan the old building had to offer. But then she'd only insist on medicating me. A prospect I refused to consider.

"Of course I'm sleeping. What else would I be doing at night?"

"*Not* sleeping." She appraised me with a knowing gaze, probing, measuring my reaction. Freaking psychiatrists.

I let a carefree smile part my lips and said, "I'm sleeping just fine."

"Good. Because you look a little sleep deprived."

"Is that your years of training talking?"

"No, that's the dark circles under your eyes talking."

"I'm not sleep deprived."

"Wonderful. I'm glad."

She wasn't glad. I could feel suspicion on her every suspicious breath.

So, Cookie was here to check out my new appliances that I would never use. Amber was here to use my computer, of which they had two in their apartment across the hall. Uncle Bob came all this way just to give me a file. And Gemma came over to check on me. I hadn't had this much company since I had my apartment-warming party and invited the UNM Lobo football team. Only about twelve of those guys would actually fit inside, so the party spilled out into the hall. Mrs. Allen, the elderly woman in apartment 2C, has never stopped thanking me. And every time she did, her voice got this husky tone to it and she would wriggle her brows. I always wondered just what happened that night to make her so appreciative. Maybe she got a little on the side. Or copped a few feels. Good for her either way.

But with this many people in my apartment, and with all of us surrounded by a jungle of boxes, I was beginning to feel claustrophobic. And wary. Especially when Cookie kept throwing secretive glances at Ubie. I should have known she was too dismissive of him when she came in. She usually grinned like a schoolgirl at a boy band concert. They were totally up to something.

I faced my well-meaning but garishly obnoxious group of friends and/or family members, trying to decide, if this were a video game and they'd all been turned into zombies, which one I'd take out first. "Okay, what's going on?"

"What?" Gemma asked, her expression the picture of innocence.

Her.

Uncle Bob rubbed his five o'clock shadow. Amber peeked over a stack of boxes, her huge blue eyes watching warily from afar. Or, well, a few feet away. Cookie was looking at me from behind a set of instructions for the electric pressure cooker, fooling absolutely no one. Unless she could read instructions in French. And upside down. And Gemma propped onto a barstool to examine her nails.

"We've been worried about you," Uncle Bob said, shrugging one shoulder.

Gemma nodded. "Right, so we thought we'd come over and make sure everything was okay."

"All of you?" I asked.

She nodded again, a little too enthusiastically.

My brows slid together, and I regarded Uncle Bob, my expression a mask of bitter disappointment, knowing he'd cave before anyone else, the old softy.

He held up a hand. "Now, Charley, you have to admit, your behavior has been a little erratic lately."

I crossed my arms. "When is my behavior *not* erratic?"

"She has a point," he said to Gemma.

"No," she replied, mimicking me by crossing her arms as well, "she doesn't."

I sighed in utter annoyance and strode around the breakfast bar to get to Mr. Coffee.

"Did the stain come out?"

"What stain?" I asked, pouring a cup of Heaven on Earth.

She pointed to a section of my living room I referred to as Area 51, where a huge pile of boxes cleverly disguised as a mountain sat. It served a purpose: to conceal that area of the room. That particular section. That black hole of turmoil and disorder. I'd shoved box after box over it as they came in so I didn't have to look at it, so I didn't accidently get sucked in by the gravitational force of millions of solar masses. I knew how crazy it sounded, but burying the place where I was once cut to pieces, shoving it under a mountain of shiny new products, seemed like a good idea at the time.

I figured I could call it a monument. No one ever questioned art.

Gemma's expression grew sympathetic. "The stain. Did it ever come out?"

Boy, she wasn't pulling any punches this trip. All the times she'd come over, she never talked about that spot. That stain. The one where my blood and urine had spilled over the sides of the chair as Earl Walker sliced into me with the confidence and precision of a surgeon.

"Intervention time, huh?" I asked, chafing under her scrutiny.

"No," she said, rushing to placate me. "No, Charley. I'm not trying to control you or take away even an ounce of your autonomy. I just want to try to get you to see what you are doing and why."

"I know why," I said, my tone even, my voice dry. "I was there."

"Okay. But do you understand *what* you are doing?" She looked around, indicating the stacks and stacks of boxes.

I drew in a deep ration of air, letting my irritation slide through unheeded, then took my cup and headed for my bedroom, the only safe haven I had left at this point. "You could take every single thing out of this room right now, and I would be fine with it." I waved my hand in the air. "Do you understand that? Peachy as a Georgia plantation."

"Do you mind if I test that theory?" she asked.

"Knock yourself out."

As I continued to my room, she walked toward Area 51. I paused and watched as she took a box down and handed it to Uncle Bob. He stacked it on top of the wall Cookie had been working on earlier. And the protective coating around my shell cracked. Just barely. Just enough to cause a quake at the very base of my being.

I knew exactly what was underneath those boxes. If she took away many more of them, the chair I'd been bound to would show through. The bloodstain in the carpet would reappear. The truth would scream in my face. I felt the sting of metal sliding through layers of skin and flesh. Nicking tendons. Severing nerves. Welding my teeth together to keep from crying out.

"Charley?"

Uncle Bob said my name, and I realized I'd been standing there, staring at the mountain of boxes for some time. I looked back embarrassed as everyone waited to see what I would do. The pity in their eyes was almost too much.

"You know," Cookie said, coming around the breakfast bar, "you are so strong and so powerful, sometimes we forget—" She looked back at Amber, not wanting to give too much away, then she continued, her voice softer. "—sometimes we forget that you're only human."

"I won't ask you to take a box away until you're ready, Charley," Gemma said, stepping closer. "But we'll take one box away from that spot every day until that time comes."

It was so odd. I'd never been afraid of a chair before—or a stain in the carpet, for that matter—but inanimate objects seemed to take on a life of their own lately. They were beasts, their breaths echoing around me, their eyes watching my every move, waiting for the opportune moment to strike. To cut into me again.

When Gemma spoke this time, her tone was so gentle, so unassuming, I had a hard time holding up my wall. "But only if this is okay with you. Only if you're comfortable."

"And if I'm not?"

I wondered if it was wrong of me not to want to deal with anything beyond lethargy at that moment in time. I'd just been robbed blind by a parking attendant, accosted by a demon, manhandled by the son of Satan, and withheld vital information by a group of nuns. I didn't know how much more of this I could take.

She put a hand on my arm. "Then we'll be here until you are."

After offering her an appreciative smile, a horrific thought hit me. "But not, like, literally."

An idea sparked in Gemma's eyes. "Yes," she said, her lips inching into a sly smile. "Literally. We're going to move in."

"Oh, can we have a slumber party?" Amber asked.

Gemma beamed at her. "We most definitely can."

Shit. This was going to suck. Until I let Gemma fondle my boxes, I'd never get any peace.

"Fine, play with my boxes if it makes you feel better."

"Oh, man," Amber said. "We never get to have slumber parties."

I cracked open another smile until Gemma, on a roll, said, "And I'd like you to do one more thing."

"Soak your contacts in lighter fluid?"

"Now you're just being hostile. I'd like you to write a letter every day. One a day to whoever comes to mind. It can be a different person every day, or the same person throughout. But I want you to tell that person in the letter how you feel about him or her and something general, like how you're doing or what you did that day. Okay?"

I took another sip, then asked, "Are you going to read them?"

"Nope." She crossed her arms in satisfaction. "They are for you and for you alone."

"Can I write one to Uncle Bob telling him what a geek he is?"

"Hey," he said, straightening when the attention landed on him. "What'd I do?"

I fought back a giggle. I guess if nobody read them, it'd be okay. I'd had enough psychology to understand what she was doing, but if no one was going to see them, then she'd never know if I wrote them or not. This was clearly a win–win.

"And I'll know if you've written them or not, so don't make a promise you don't intend to keep."

Crap. "How will you know? I'm a really good liar."

She laughed out loud at that. I bit back a retort. Mostly because Uncle Bob, Cookie, and Amber laughed, too. W T F?

After announcing my chagrin with an expertly placed death stare, I asked, "You'll leave me alone if I do all this?"

"Are you asking if I'll stop coming over and diving into your mountain of boxes?" When I shrugged an acknowledgment, she said, "No. We will get through that mountain." She put an arm over my shoulders. "Together. All of us." Everyone nodded in agreement. "Every day, at least one of us will take a box down until you can watch us do it without wincing."

I frowned. "I didn't wince."

"You winced," Uncle Bob said.

"I didn't . . . Whatever."

I was in a nightmare that consisted of well-meaning friends and family members who deserved to be in a locked cell with an anaconda. Not for very long. Just long enough to give them a few nightmares every night for the next month or so.

The thought made me happy.

Another knock sounded at the door, this one harder, more demanding.

"Really, guys?" I said, pounding over. Who else could they get to tag-team me?

Without putting a lot of thought into it, I swung open the door with the dramatic flair of a silent screen actress.

What I saw on the other side—who I saw—stole my breath. Surprise rocketed through my nervous system as I watched Reyes standing there in a fresh T-shirt and jeans, casual as lemon pie, like he hadn't just killed a man. Like he hadn't just dragged me across a warehouse and thrown me onto a cement floor. Like he hadn't just disappeared when I was trying to have a civilized conversation with him. Served me right.

He folded his arms over his chest and leaned against the doorjamb, his eyes sparkling in appreciation. "I wanted to make sure you were okay."

"Why wouldn't I be?" I asked.

His gaze wandered over me, his interest not subtle in the least. "How's the kid?"

He had just fought a demon for me. He had just saved my life, yet he stood there like he hadn't a care in the world. I shook my head and said, "He's okay. A little traumatized, but he's in good hands. He's Deaf."

"I know."

"How?" I asked, surprised.

"I watched you talk to him for a while."

I pressed my lips together, then said, "Stalker."

"Nut."

I gasped. "Neanderthal."

"Fruitcake."

"Ape."

"Psychopath."

Why did his entire repertoire of insults question my mental stability? I scowled up at him and leaned in. "Demon."

He wrapped a finger in the bottom of my shirt and pulled me closer. "Then that would make you a slayer, wouldn't it?" he asked, his voice like deep, rich velvet.

I breathed in the heat that spiraled around him. He gave me every ounce of attention he had to offer, focused like a leopard focusing on his prey, just long enough to cause a warmth to crack open and spill into my chest. Over my stomach. Between my legs. Until, that is, he spotted Uncle Bob. His gaze glided past me to where Uncle Bob sat.

In a rush of panic, I realized I still had a house full of unwanted guests. And one of those unwanted guests was Uncle Bob, the man who put Reyes away for ten years for a murder he didn't commit. But it wasn't Ubie's fault. All evidence pointed to Reyes. Earl Walker had made sure of it.

Maybe Reyes wouldn't remember him.

I whirled around and gaped unappealingly. "Hey, guys. I want you to meet Reyes."

Cookie dropped something, but I didn't dare take my eyes off Uncle Bob, hoping he wouldn't give himself away. Not that I had a snowball's chance that Reyes had actually forgotten the man responsible for his conviction, but even snowballs could dream.

Uncle Bob, clearly surprised to see him, fought his emotions a minute, trying to figure out what to do before he made a decision. With a nod of acknowledgment toward Reyes, he leaned over and shut Cookie's jaw for her. She caught herself and smiled sheepishly. However, he wasn't close enough to Gemma to close hers without great discomfort. Amber seemed a tad thunderstruck as well. She'd strolled around the wall of boxes and stared, her eyes wide with wonder.

I was glad to know it wasn't just me. Reyes seemed to affect every female within a two-mile radius the same way.

But Uncle Bob was a different story. I felt a fire spark and flare inside

Reyes. An emotion I could refer to only as hatred. Unfortunately, he had every right to feel animosity for a man who put him, an innocent man, in prison. And worse, Uncle Bob had recently told me he knew in his heart Reyes was innocent. But there was nothing he could do. Every ounce of evidence had pointed directly at Reyes. Surely Reyes couldn't blame him completely.

Uncle Bob had been sitting on a stool. His expression was one of regret and resignation. He stood and walked forward, resembling John Wayne charging into battle, knowing he wouldn't survive.

"Maybe we should take this outside," he said as he strode forward.

If what Uncle Bob just did, knowing what he now knew about Reyes, was not heroic, I didn't know what was.

Uncle Bob's presence seemed to knock the self-assured wind out of Reyes. A thick cord of tension stretched between them while a battle raged within him. A battle between doing the right thing and doing what his upbringing—the one from the underworld—begged him to do. I felt it twist and claw at his emotions. He was practically drooling to get at Ubie. To rip him to shreds. Something that came as easily to him as breathing did to me. But he held still. Too still. Possibly afraid to move. Afraid of what he'd do.

After an epic battle, he tore his gaze off my uncle and dropped it back to mine. "I just wanted to make sure you were okay," he said, and I felt him withdraw inside himself, as though he could dismiss Uncle Bob and everything that happened just like that.

"You're welcome to stay," Uncle Bob said, and I locked my jaw to keep it from coming unhinged.

"I agree!" Amber shouted. When everyone turned and gawked at her, she ducked back behind the boxes and said, "Sorry. That just kind of slipped out."

I looked back and Reyes was smiling at her. A sweet, understanding gesture that took my breath away. His anger ebbed instantly, the shock of it like a splash of cold water on a hot summer day.

Realizing how rude I'd been, I said, "Reyes, I don't think you've been officially introduced to anyone." I turned to the people who had ambushed me, trying not to hold it against them. "This is my sister, Gemma; my uncle Bob; and Cookie."

"And me," a tiny voice said from beyond.

"And somewhere behind that wall is Cookie's daughter Amber," I said with a chuckle.

He didn't unfold his arms but offered them each a nod in turn.

Uncle Bob elbowed Gemma. She snapped to attention and cleared her throat. "It's nice to meet you," she said.

When Reyes's gaze landed on her again, he frowned in thought. Then recognition flitted across his face.

She read him easily. "Yes," she said, holding out her hand for a shake. "We've met, just not officially." Gemma was with me the very first time I saw Reyes. When we were in high school and Reyes was being abused by Earl Walker, the man he thought was his father.

After a tense moment where I wondered if he was going to reject her offer outright, he took her hand into his. I didn't miss the soft gasp that rushed through her lips when he did so. Not that I could blame her.

Cookie had yet to fully recover. He tilted his head in greeting as though tipping an invisible hat.

The smile that stole across her face was the stuff of legend. Or, well, Rice Krispie treats: soft, sweet, and on the verge of melting into a lump of sticky goo. She offered him a breathy hi, and it took every ounce of willpower I had not to chuckle. Not because I was worried about embarrassing her. Embarrassing her was one of my main goals in life. Right behind designing wedgie-free boxer shorts.

No, I'd been hit with another emotion. As afraid as I was to leave Uncle Bob and Reyes in such close proximity, I stepped over to the wall of boxes and looked behind them at Amber.

"Sweetheart?" I said, wondering what was going on.

The emotion pouring out of her was so strong, so palpable, I was having trouble concentrating on anything beyond it. Reyes had to feel it, too. I looked back. He was eyeing me with concern.

"Amber, are you okay?" I asked.

She was sitting at my desk with her face down, her long dark hair an impenetrable curtain of waves. "I'm okay," she said, keeping her face hidden.

Cookie came over then and tried to peek over my shoulder. "What's going on?" she asked me.

"I'm not sure." Had we hurt Amber's feelings before when we turned to look at her? I wasn't really getting hurt, but whatever she was feeling was overpowering anything else. Twelve-year-old hormones were a tricky thing. She'd seemed fine thirty seconds earlier. Because I didn't know what else to do, I asked, "Would you come meet Reyes?"

She looked up at me then, and I could see tears pooling in her blue eyes. She ducked back down, embarrassed, and let me lead her forward.

"This is the one they call Amber of the Kowalski clan," I said, trying to lighten the mood. "But she's a heartbreaker, so guard yours well." I winked at Reyes.

She strolled forward, her eyes locked on the ground, her shoulders concave, insecure.

He studied her, tilting his head for a better look. She was tall for a girl and really tall for a twelve-year-old girl, but her height gave her a grace that other girls her age lacked. Like a gazelle.

"Amber, can you say hi?" Cookie asked.

With her gaze still averted, she shook her head.

Cookie seemed mortified. She pushed a long lock of hair over Amber's ear. "I'm so sorry," she said to Reyes, shaking her own head in helplessness. "She's usually so vocal."

"You save her?" Amber finally said, talking to her feet. "You watch over her?"

Before any of us could question her, Reyes said, "Only on really special occasions."

What were they talking about? Amber didn't know about Reyes. How could she know he had saved my life? On several occasions, in fact.

She looked up at him then, her lashes holding a shimmering tear at bay. "I know what you do. I know what you are. They think I don't, but I do. And I know you were here that night."

"Amber," Cookie said, a nervous smile twitching the corners of her mouth, "how could you know that?" Cookie suddenly grew afraid, and I knew where her thoughts were headed. What would Reyes do to her if he knew Amber was aware of his existence? "She doesn't know what she's talking about."

"See? They don't know, and they don't trust you like I do." She took a step forward. "You've watched over Charley her whole life. Kept her safe. And that night, if you hadn't come—" Her breath hitched, and before any of us knew what she was doing, she ran forward.

Reyes stepped back as though uncertain as she flung herself at him.

She wrapped her arms around his neck. "Thank you." She turned in to him. "Thank you so much. You saved our lives."

After an awkward moment where Reyes resigned himself to being accosted by a twelve-year-old, he let his arms fall loosely around her. She squeezed tighter.

I stepped forward and rubbed her back, my heart swelling with adoration. I didn't realize she knew Reyes had shown up the night Earl Walker attacked me. I didn't realize she knew anything about what had happened.

She looked over at me, then whispered into his ear. "I know what *she* is, too, but I would never tell anyone."

Reyes offered her the most charming grin I'd ever seen. A soft giggle of delight bubbled out of her before she backed out of his arms. She sidled close to me, her eyes taking on that dreamlike luster I knew so well.

"You coming in?" I asked.

He winked at Amber, then turned to me. "Not tonight. I have business."

"Of course. But I really want to talk to you about—" I thought about how to say *demon possessions* without saying *demon possessions*. "—the occupancy issues we've been having."

One corner of his mouth tilted into an almost grin. "About that, I really need you to stay in your apartment for the next few days."

"Can't, but thanks for asking."

He glanced around, then said with a menacing tone, "Don't make me insist."

"Seriously?" Did he honestly think that would work?

He dragged in a deep gulp of air, then seemed to give up. After a moment of thought, he touched the bottom of my shirt again. "I'm glad you came to see me."

I rubbed my fingertips along the back of his hand. "I'm glad you're free."

A breathy scoff escaped him like I'd said something funny.

"What?" I asked.

He stepped closer, even with Amber there, even with Uncle Bob behind me, rubbed a thumb over my bottom lip, and said, "There is a fine line between freedom and slavery."

9

Two drinks away from girl-on-girl action.
—T-SHIRT

"You okay?" Uncle Bob had asked after I closed my front door. As always, the air crackled with electricity in Reyes's wake. But I thought it was sweet that Ubie would be concerned about me. He was the one quaking in his discount loafers. He was beginning to understand what Reyes was capable of, and quaking in his loafers was a very appropriate response. Especially since he was the one who put him behind bars.

"I'm fine, thanks. How are you?"

"Late," he said. "I have a date."

I tried not to look too surprised. "With a person?"

He frowned. "No, a soda machine. Of course a person."

Amber giggled, recovering from Reyes's presence faster than her mother or Gemma did. I gave them a few minutes to absorb everything while I teased Ubie, who only had to recover from his near near-death experience. I was so glad Reyes hadn't ripped him to shreds. I liked him much better un-shredded. Unlike, say, my preference for lettuce or heavy metal guitar solos.

Getting the feeling I was going to have company for a while, I headed toward my shower. "Well, you better get home," I said to Ubie. "You can only keep a date tied up in the basement for so long before they become resentful."

Just as I entered the bathroom, I heard him say, "Talk to your dad."

Not likely. The shower felt wonderful, even with a furry beast knocking me to and fro. I hadn't seen this much action in one day for over two months. My body didn't know what to do. How to act. It wanted my sofa—which might or might not go by the name of Sharon—and cheese puffs, but I realized I was going to have to wean off both. Slowly at first. Maybe I'd downgrade to a recliner and cheese crackers, ease off gradually, then try something healthy like cleaning house and eating an apple.

I shuddered at the thought. Cheese puffs were so comforting. And they were orange. No, I probably shouldn't rush into anything. I came up with a plan B. Clean house while eating cheese puffs. Comforting and productive.

After Artemis dived into the earth below me, I stepped out of the shower and dressed in a pair of plaid lime green pajama bottoms that had no smart-ass saying whatsoever. But I made up for it with a top proclaiming SARC- was my second favorite -ASM word. Ready to face the masses again, I went back out into the living area.

Cookie and Gemma were in the kitchen, trying out all my cool new gadgets. Hopefully, I'd get a meal out of their efforts. Amber gathered her books when I came out and she stepped over to me. "You're really loud in the shower," she said.

I could only imagine what Artemis knocking me into the wall repeatedly sounded like from out here. "Yeah, I tripped."

"Seven times?"

"Yes."

"Oh, okay. Well, I just wanted to say that I'm sorry, Charley. I didn't mean to do that. With Reyes. I didn't mean to embarrass you."

"Embarrass me?" I gathered her into my arms. "Amber, you could never embarrass me."

"Never?" she asked.

"Never."

"One time, I yelled across the store to Mom and asked her if she wanted the regular or the super-absorbent tampons. I added that, according to the box, the super-absorbent were for those heavy days. Then I asked her to rate her heaviness on a scale of one to ten."

"Okay, you could."

"Then while we were standing in line, I asked her why she was buying three boxes of Summer's Eve in the middle of winter."

I set her at arm's length. "Wow."

"I know, right? I had no idea a person could turn so red."

"So, we've established that, yes, you could indeed embarrass me. But you didn't. I'm sorry that you know so much of things no twelve-year-old girl should know about."

"I won't tell anyone. I promise."

I looked over to see what the chefs were doing. When I saw that they were busy, I leaned in to her. "What exactly do you know?"

She smiled. "I know you're the grim reaper."

That realization knocked the wind out of my sails.

"And I know Reyes is the son of Satan."

"H-how do you know all of this?"

"I have really good hearing. And I can listen to all kinds of conversations even while I'm doing my homework."

"Really?"

She snorted. "I swear, you guys act like I go deaf every time I open a book." With an evil cackle, she headed toward the door. "I can hear other things, too. Before you came around, I had no idea a man could make a girl scream like that. Reyes seems very talented."

Certain my eyes resembled tea saucers, I took a quick peek at Cookie to make sure she wasn't paying attention to us. While I'd never had relations with Reyes other than in my dreams and once while he was incorporeal, those relations were . . . very satisfying. And apparently Amber knew it.

"Don't worry. Mom doesn't know."

"That Reyes is very talented?"

"Oh, no, she's extremely aware of that part. She just doesn't know that I know that Reyes is very talented." She giggled again, a sound that conjured images of a mad scientist in the making, and just before she closed the door behind her, she said, "But don't stop on my account."

Oh. My. God. Cookie was going to kill me.

"So what were you two talking about?" she asked.

I jumped, then smoothed my pajama bottoms. "Nothing. Why? What do you think we were talking about?"

She frowned at me. "Do you think she's okay?"

"Oh, I think she's just fine." The little smarty-pants.

She went back to whisking some kind of batter as Gemma dumped in a powdery substance. I could only hope they were baking brownies. Brownies were like spare batteries. One could never have too many in the house.

"I'm going to sleep with you," Gemma said as she eyed the concoction and rationed in a little more powder.

"You're not really my type, but okay. How kinky are we talking?"

"Do you think it needs more?" she asked Cookie, inspecting the bowl.

"One can never have too much powdered sugar," Cookie said. Then she pointed a whisk at me. "I think you should bottle Reyes and sell him on the black market. We'd be rich."

I stepped closer. "Dude, what are you whisking?"

"Having recently been in the same room with the hottest man on the planet, I'm probably whisking my virtue." She chuckled. "Get it? Whisking my virtue?"

Gemma laughed as she measured in more powdered sugar. I took a gander at Cookie's bowl and scooped out a dollop of white heaven. "So, icing?"

"Yes, we're trying out your new cake pans."

"I bought cake pans?" That was so unlike me.

She wriggled her brows. "And you bought a margarita mixer."

Uh-oh.

I soon found out Gemma had ulterior motives in hanging with me and drinking like a fish on dry land. I could read it in her body language, in the shifting light in her eyes, but mostly when she said, "I have ulterior motives."

She was determined to help me sleep if she had to get me plastered to do it. So she and Cookie were trying out a frozen margarita mixer I'd ordered during a low point in my downfall. For one week, all I could think about was drinking margaritas—well, that and running my tongue along Reyes's teeth—but I didn't have salt—or Reyes's teeth. I'd also lacked the energy to leave my apartment to get some—or the desire to stoop low enough to beg Reyes to let me lick his teeth after what he did—so I could only wish for a margarita. And dream of Reyes's teeth.

I'd secretly hoped a margarita would magically appear in my hand, but that would mean I would have to put down the remote, and God knew that was not going to happen.

It was a vicious circle.

But Gemma rarely drank. Maybe a glass of wine with dinner. And I drank only on special occasions. Like Fridays and Saturdays. Cookie on the other hand . . .

"Wooooooohooooooo!" Cookie raised her arms in triumph. No idea why. "I haven't had thith much fun thince . . . thince . . ." She seemed at a loss for coherent words, but she recovered quickly and pointed toward the door. "Thince Reyeth Farlow walked through that door!" She turned back to me, her expression full of awe. "And, my god, doeth that boy know how to walk."

Cookie stood on the other side of the breakfast bar, trying to bake brownies in my new electric pressure cooker. While the apartment smelled really good, I didn't have high hopes for a chocolate fix anytime soon. The cooker beeped and she turned to check it right before she disappeared. It was weird. She was there one minute and gone the next. And her disappearance was quickly followed by a solid thud, the sound echoing off the kitchen floor. I thought about hurrying to her rescue, but didn't trust my own legs at that point. Gemma was draped over the arm of my sofa—which might or might not go by the name of Melvin—and Aunt Lillian, who swore those were the best margaritas she'd had since that beauty pageant she entered in Juárez, was facedown on my floor. No idea why.

"You're missing out, Mr. Wong. I don't know what Cookie put in these, but they're pretty amazing." I saluted the boxes that surrounded him, downed the last sip of margarita—or Cookie-a-rita, as they'd been recently dubbed—and decided to get a jump on my letter writing Gemma insisted upon as a form of therapy. Usually therapists stuck to journaling, so letter writing was an interesting twist.

I figured I'd write a letter to Santa. Christmas had come and gone, but I'd missed it, as I was not talking to anyone except for the salespeople for the Buy From Home Channel at the time, and they didn't seem to want to spend Christmas with me.

I'd had Christmas dinner with Cookie and Amber, of course, and Gemma and Uncle Bob had both come by bearing gifts and a special, sticky kind of depression, but I really didn't remember much beyond that. Though there was an incredible chocolate cheesecake somewhere in there. The rest was a blur.

I took out pen and paper and jotted down my thoughts.

> *Dear Santa,*
> *What the fuck?*

That was about all I could manage, and it got me nowhere fast. I felt no better for the effort. Gemma's therapy techniques sucked. I still couldn't get Reyes out of my head. The image of him letting Amber hug him was too precious. And not what I wanted. I wanted to be angry with him, to shake my fists and snarl, but he'd been fighting demons for me. To keep me safe. It was so freaking hard to stay angry with a guy who was secretly fighting a war in your honor. Damn it.

I herded Gemma to the bedroom and lay down beside her only to stare at the ceiling for two hours straight. Then the wall. The nightstand. The skull-clad tissue dispenser. After hours of nothing but frustration, I eased Gemma's arm off my face and slipped out of bed. I was really hoping that margarita would help me sleep like it had Gemma and Cookie, but it didn't. When I was trying to stay awake for weeks at a time, all I could do was drink copious amounts of coffee just to fight it off. Now I wanted to sleep and couldn't.

The sandman was an ass.

I realized the one person missing from their little ambush was Garrett Swopes, a skiptracer who often worked with my uncle Bob. I hadn't seen him since I almost got him killed. For the second time. But surely he wasn't holding that against me. He hadn't come by and I hadn't had the desire or the energy to leave my apartment, so I hadn't heard from him in two months. Not a phone call. Not a text. Not an email. Double gunshot wound or not, that just wasn't like him.

I decided to hunt him down. He probably wasn't the same since his near-death experience. He'd seen me. When he died on the operating table, he'd seen what I looked like from the other side, seen what I did on a daily basis. That had to be hard on anyone.

And yet I had no idea if he remembered it. As the escalator to Heaven,

I had certain responsibilities that I'd tried to explain to him once. But seeing was believing. Maybe it pushed him over the edge. Maybe the reality was much more disturbing than the idea.

I pushed my feet into a pair of slippers, threw on a jacket, and headed that way.

Driving at three o'clock in the morning had its perks. Like little to no traffic, so I made it to Garrett's house in record time.

I knocked on his door and waited. That man took forever to answer in the wee hours before dawn. I knocked again. I'd always wondered something: If a skiptracer is arrested and skips, who searches for him?

"Charles!" he growled from behind the door. "I swear to God if that's you . . ."

How did he know? I decided not to say anything. To surprise him with my presence.

The door swung open and he stood there shirtless and disheveled. While I didn't have a particular thing for Garrett, he did make a nice vision. He had mocha-colored skin and smoky gray eyes that alighted on Margaret but dismissed her just as quickly. He was in the biz. Surely he understood my need to pack iron even in my pajamas.

"What's up?" I asked, way more cheerily than I felt.

"Are you kidding me?" He rubbed an eye with one hand.

"Nope." I charged through him and went straight for his sofa. But his house was really dark. Weird. "I haven't seen you in forever. I thought we should talk."

"There is such a thing as being too presumptuous."

"You know, I get that a lot. Got any coffee?"

After exhaling loudly so I wouldn't miss his annoyance, he closed the door with more force than I felt necessary and strode to the kitchen. "What are you doing here?"

"Bugging you."

"Besides that."

"I didn't realize I had to have a reason to visit one of my best friends on planet Earth."

"Are you trying to stay awake for days at a time again?"

"Nope. Not trying. Just doing."

He'd been rummaging around the kitchen, and while I couldn't see what he was doing, the rummaging sounds stopped. I waited. Maybe it was the best-friend statement. Clearly he didn't know he was one of my best friends. He must've felt really honored. Or horrified. It was a win–win.

"Here."

I jumped. He was standing right behind me, handing me a wineglass. "You're serving me coffee in a wineglass?"

"No."

"Is this coffee-flavored wine?"

"No. Drink." He tilted the glass toward my mouth.

I took a sip and . . . "Hey, that's not bad."

"Drink it all and I'll give you a ride home."

"Dude, it takes more than one glass of wine to inebriate me. Remember what I am?"

"Annoying."

"That's so uncalled for."

He sat beside me on the sofa and stretched out his legs. He'd slipped on a pair of jeans, but his feet were bare. They brushed up against a pile of books. I didn't even know Swopes could read.

"You're having problems sleeping?" he asked.

"Kind of." I leaned nonchalantly forward to check out the titles. "Not really. I want to know why you've been avoiding me."

He put his feet on the carpet and sat forward, too, clasping a beer in his hands. He scrutinized the carpet a good minute before he said, "I haven't been avoiding you."

The books he had were all on the spiritual realm, heaven and hell, demons and angels. His near-death experience must have affected him more than I thought. "You haven't been to see me in two months."

"And you haven't been to see me in two months. That's not avoidance on my part, Charles. That's self-preservation."

Crap. "I knew this was because I keep getting you shot."

He sank back into the sofa and sipped his beer. "Is that what you think?"

"It's not like I can blame you. I'd steer clear of me, too, if I kept getting myself shot." I took a sip of wine. "That didn't come out right."

He took a huge gulp, downing the beer in three seconds flat. When he stood to get another, I stayed him with a hand on his arm. But I did not get the reaction I'd expected. The one I'd grown used to. He stepped back emotionally. Almost cringed inwardly at my touch.

The emotion shocked me. I didn't realize I disgusted him now.

That was an eye-opener if I'd ever seen one. "I'm sorry," I said, putting the wineglass on a side table. "I better go. We'll talk later."

"No," he said, but I was already headed for the door.

He rounded the sofa and slammed the door the second I opened it. Standing behind me, he released a slow breath. "I'm sorry, Charles. I didn't mean to hurt you. I forget that you feel things, that you glean emotion off other people."

I turned to him in askance. "So, what? You're going to try to control your emotions around me? Pretend I don't disgust you?" A hitch in my stupid breath gave away the fact that his reaction had hurt. He'd never hurt me before, not like that, and we'd had some doozies. Why now? Why should I even care?

But I knew. He'd always thought I was crazy, but I'd never disgusted him before. The realization brought tears to my eyes.

"Disgust?" he asked, his brows drawn sharp in consternation. "Is that what you think?"

A breathy laugh escaped me. "Please, Swopes. You can't hide your emotions. I felt them like a punch in the gut. It's okay. I just need to go."

"You may feel emotions, but you suck at reading them if you got disgust out of that."

"Garrett, please let me leave. I'm sorry I woke you."

"Hell no. Sit down." He pointed toward the sofa while keeping the other hand planted firmly on the door.

Fine. He didn't need to get all huffy. I sat back down and only then did he take his seat again. I got the feeling he didn't trust me.

"Now, why do you think that you could ever disgust me in any way?" he asked.

"You're avoiding me, for one thing."

"So that means I'm disgusted by you?"

"You don't want to talk about what happened," I tried again. While I didn't want to talk about what happened to me, I was all for talking about what happened to him.

"Okay. What happened?"

"You died."

He stared at me unblinkingly.

"You died and you came to see me. Do you remember?"

"I need another beer."

I let him get up for a beer but followed. He opened the fridge, popped the top, and downed the whole thing without stopping. After tossing the bottle, he took out another and sipped it more slowly. I sat at his pint-sized kitchen table, and he strolled over to join me.

"Can you tell me what you remember?" I asked when he sat down. When he just stared at the bottle in his hands, I said, "Do you remember anything?" I knew he did. He had to have. If not, he would never have reacted in such a way.

"I remember everything."

I blanched at the thought. "Like what?"

He inhaled deeply and said, "I remember being drawn to your light. I remember that little girl crossing through you. I remember Mr. Wong and the dog."

"Is that what bothers you? What you saw me do?"

"No." He looked at me point-blank. "Nothing about you bothers me, besides the fact that you knock on my door at three in the morning. There's other stuff you don't know about."

I frowned at him. "Like what?"

"After I saw you, I went somewhere else. I just figured I was going back into my body since I wasn't dead anymore."

"How did you know you weren't dead in the first place?"

"My father told me. He sent me back. I haven't seen him since I was ten. He was an engineer for a U.S. company in Colombia. He was kidnapped. Normally they just want a ransom, but something must have gone wrong. We never heard from him again. He just disappeared."

"But you got to see him?" I asked in awe. All the crossing-over stuff was still such a mystery, even to me.

"Yes. He sent me back. I was pissed." He turned to look out the window into the black night. "I didn't want to come back. I'd never felt anything like that."

"I've heard that before. It makes me happy to know that death is just a phase, that we go to another world and it's wonderful. But you said you went somewhere else?"

"Yes. After I saw you. And it's not always wonderful."

"I don't understand."

"I went to hell, Charles."

I stilled. "You mean that metaphorically, right?"

"No. I don't."

"You mean literally? Hell? As in fire and brimstone?"

"Yes."

I sat back, stunned.

"And I learned things. I wasn't there by accident. I was sent. To learn. To understand."

"To understand what?"

"What your boyfriend did for a living."

He didn't have to elaborate. I knew he was talking about Reyes. Who else?

"Do you have any idea what he is?"

"The son of Satan."

His expression showed his surprise. "And you're okay with that?"

"Swopes, he escaped from hell, okay? He's not a bad guy. Well, not totally bad."

He scoffed and rose from the table. "Then you need to see what I've seen."

A ripple of fear shimmied through me. "What?"

"He was a general there, you know. The son of evil, yes, but he rose through the ranks of hell all on his own. He was a skilled assassin and he lived for the taste of the blood of his enemies."

"He wasn't exactly raised in a nurturing environment."

"So, you're going to make excuses for him all night? Why did you come here?"

"I wanted to know how you were. Sorry."

I got up to leave again, but he stopped me with one thing he said: "He was sent here. For you."

I turned back to him. "I know he was sent here, but to get a portal. Any portal. Not for me specifically. Then he saw me and fell in love. So he escaped the bonds of his father and waited for me."

"He fell in love?" The astonished expression on his face told me exactly what he thought of me. "He didn't escape anything. He was sent. For you in particular."

"You can't believe that."

"Oh, no. You're right. I mean I was only shown it in hell. Surely my sources are mistaken."

"Swopes, people don't just go to the netherworld, then come out unscathed."

"The fuck they don't. I did. Then I was dragged out by a force of some kind. And I never said I was unscathed."

Well, if anything would affect the psyche, it would be a trip to hell. I didn't know what to say. "What was it like?"

He waved his beer in the air. "You know. Hot. Lots of screaming. Lots of agony. I would not recommend it for a vacation spot."

"How do you know about—? Who told you about Reyes?"

The look he placed on me was filled with a seething kind of hatred. "His father."

I sank back into the chair. "So, you two just struck up a conversation over an open pit, compared notes on death and agony?"

"Something like that. He wanted me to see, Charley."

"See what?"

"What his son was." He lurched forward as though trying to will me to believe him. "What he did."

"We all do things we aren't proud of."

He laughed harshly and scrubbed his face with his fingers. "You live in your own little world, don't you?"

"Yes, and I like it here."

"Well, let me tell you this: I know what he is and I know what you are and I know what will come down if he gets you. I am not about to let that happen."

Oh, wonderful. "Come down? What, like hell on Earth?"

"Like the worst kind of hell on Earth. Charles, he was sent here. For you. To make all of his father's dreams come true."

I stood to get a drink of water. "What you saw, what they told you, isn't real. He wasn't sent here. He escaped. He came here on his own."

"Is that what he told you?"

"Yes," I said, combing his cabinets for a glass.

"I never figured a grim reaper would be so gullible."

Screw it. I could get a drink at home. There were few things I hated more than having my intelligence questioned.

I closed the cabinet door and leaned over him as he sat at the table. "So, you've been to hell, huh?" When he nodded, I offered a candy-coated smile, patted his cheek, and said, "Sweet dreams."

10

Facing your fears builds strength.
But running away from them builds hamstrings.
—BUMPER STICKER

I drove home seeing red. Literally. A cop pulled me over and those lights were freaking bright. I would probably have red blotchy vision for days. After a little flirting which got me nowhere and a mention of who my uncle was which got me everywhere, I drove the rest of the way a little calmer and a lot slower. Despite the hostilities, Swopes's house was a nice reprieve from my cluttered abode. I examined the area when I drove up, paying close attention to the sinister shadows and dark corners. I hadn't been out this much in weeks. And going out at night, at such a deserted hour, felt strange. Unsafe.

I locked my doors and headed inside the building only to be struck with the need to check out every nook and cranny before ascending the stairs to my apartment on the third floor. I stepped with my back to the wall, constantly checking over my shoulder. If ever there was a time to carry a flashlight, it would definitely be at night.

After tiptoeing back into my room, trying not to wake Gemma, I opened my top dresser drawer and took out a picture. *The* picture. The one I'd obtained a few weeks ago and hadn't looked at since.

I heard the toilet flush, and Cookie peeked into my room. The overhead light from the kitchen stove drifted around her, allowing me to make out her silhouette.

"Charley, is that you?" she asked, her voice rough and sleepy.

I wondered if she was still drunk. Angling the picture down so I couldn't actually see it, I said, "No, I'm Apple, Charley's evil twin."

"Can't you sleep?"

I sat on the edge of my bed. "Not really. I keep getting conflicting intel."

She sat beside me. "About what?"

After a soft laugh, I said, "Are you going to be able to get up in the morning?"

She smiled. "I'm good. I get over inebriation pretty fast."

"You were passed out on my kitchen floor."

After an indelicate snort, she said, "Like that was the first time."

She had a point.

"So, what's up?"

"I don't know what to think about Reyes."

"Oh, honey, who does? He's an enigma wrapped up in sensuality padlocked with a dozen chains of desire and topped off with a razor-sharp ribbon of danger. There are more layers to him than a billionaire's wedding cake."

My brows shot up. "Sensuality?"

"I know. It's more than the fact that he is the hottest thing ever to walk the face of the Earth, but that part is just so hard to get past." She noticed the picture in my hands. "What's that?"

I bowed my head. "Do you remember when I went to the building I'd first seen Reyes in? That abandoned apartment building where that crazy woman was squatting?"

"Yes. She'd been the landlady when Reyes lived there. Back when you were in high school."

"Exactly. Well, she gave me this." I passed the picture to her, but held on to one corner and said, "I have to warn you, it's really explicit."

Surprise showed on her face as she took it and held it up to capture every particle of light the room had to offer. Her brows furrowed at first as she tried to make out the image; then they narrowed as dawning emerged. Slowly, the image came into focus. Her lids widened. Her mouth opened in a silent testament to her understanding. Then her eyes watered and she covered the lower half of her face with her free hand.

As though she were witnessing a car accident, she seemed unable to look away. I didn't have to look again to know what horrors the image held. It had been branded into my brain the minute I laid eyes upon it.

The ropes. The blood. The bruises. The shame.

She finally spoke from behind her hand. "Is this—?" Her breath caught in her chest and she swallowed before beginning again. "Is this Reyes?"

"Yes."

Her eyes slammed shut and she slapped the picture against her chest as though trying to cradle him. To protect him. I noticed a shiny trail spill over her lashes.

"My God, Charley. You told me, but—"

"I know." I wrapped an arm in hers.

She hugged it to her and patted my hand.

I let her have a minute to absorb what she'd seen. To get her emotions under control.

The picture was, I believed, a trophy. According to Reyes's sister, Kim, Earl Walker would take explicit photos of Reyes, then hide them in the walls everywhere they lived. And they were on the move constantly, so that could have been dozens of places. She said the pictures were blackmail, meant to keep Reyes in line. That could be, though I tended to think they'd be more like souvenirs. Keepsakes from his exploits. But why he would put them in the walls baffled me. If they really were trophies, wouldn't he take them? Why leave them where they could be found—and had been, in Ms. Faye's case—and used against him?

Then I realized that Earl probably wasn't in any of those photos. They were all of Reyes.

In the picture Ms. Faye had given me, Earl seemed to purposely shame Reyes. That was the worst part of it. He'd tied him up and blindfolded him, though I'd had no trouble recognizing Reyes's perfect form. His mussed dark hair. His full mouth. The smooth, fluidly mechanical tattoos along his shoulders and arms. The rope bit into his flesh. It reopened wounds that appeared to have been healing. He looked about sixteen in the picture, his face turned away, his lips pressed together in humiliation. Huge patches of black bruises marred his neck and ribs. Long garish cuts, some fresh, some half healed, streaked along his arms and torso.

I could never erase the image from my mind, though I'd considered trying electroshock therapy just to give it a try. It would have been worth it. And yet I kept the picture. To this day, I had no idea why I didn't burn it the minute I got it.

"I can't imagine what his life was like," Cookie said, staring off into space.

"Me neither. He saved mine tonight. He fought off a demon that was hell-bent on ripping my throat out."

She tensed in alarm. "Charley, are you serious?"

"Yes. I've been so angry with him, but all he's ever done is save my life. Again and again growing up. I'm not sure I have the right to be angry with him."

"Maybe you're not."

"What do you mean?"

She bit down, hesitated, then said, "I know you, Charley, and I don't think you're really mad at anyone but yourself."

I straightened. "Why would I be mad at myself?"

She offered me a compassionate smile. "Exactly. Why would you be? And yet here you are. As always. Angry with yourself for . . . for what? Because Earl Walker broke into your apartment? Because you were attacked? Because you couldn't fend him off?"

I frowned. "You're wrong. I'm not mad at myself. I'm great. I'm full of awesome sauce. Have you seen my ass?"

She threw an arm over my shoulders and squeezed. "Sorry, kiddo. You're not fooling anyone except maybe yourself. So, what do you think about this guy who goes by the title of son of Satan? Any hope for him?"

She slipped me the picture back, facedown. I kept it that way. "There might just be. The jury's still out."

"Well, tell it to hurry. That guy needs to come around more often. He's like a Brazilian supermodel drenched in sin."

"That's a good description."

"I think so. But I have to ask: Why Apple?"

It was odd. Sleeping with Gemma and having Aunt Lil, even passed out in the belief that she'd gotten stone-faced drunk, in the other room did prove comforting. Not terribly, especially when Gemma started whimpering in her sleep or when she slapped me for being a pirate—that girl had issues—but enough to help me get some rest.

I still woke up pretty early, though. Partly because construction workers started their days earlier than God. But mostly because Gemma was rushing around, trying to find her pants. She was wearing them when I herded her to the bed, so I wasn't even going there. But she kept running into things. Thank goodness I wasn't terribly attached to that macaroni statue of Abraham Lincoln. If I didn't know better, I'd say she was still wasted, and I could hardly wait to see what Cookie looked like.

I hopped in the shower again, more as an icebreaker to the day than anything. Disturbing images kept dancing around my head: Garrett in hell. Reyes fighting the demon from yesterday. Cookie trying her hand at pole dancing. It might have worked had there been an actual pole, but I gave her extra points for her ability to mime it.

After dressing in jeans, a chocolate brown cowl-neck sweater, and old, faded boots that gathered at the ankles, I stepped out of my room to face another day outside my humble abode. It was too bad, really. These days, I liked the innards of my humble abode much better that its outtards.

But there were cases to solve and people to bug the ever-lovin' crap out
of. I figured I'd start with Harper's infamous stepbrother, see how bad he
wanted her gone. Or to drive her insane. That possibility had been at the
back of my mind for a while. He would definitely benefit with Harper
out of the way. At the very least, his inheritance would double.

Wondering where Aunt Lil had gotten off to, I grabbed my bag and
sunglasses and headed for the door. Unfortunately, someone beat me to it.
A tap sounded a heartbeat before I reached the knob. I opened the door
and found the last person on the planet I would expect to see gracing my
doorstep.

Undeterred, I slipped my sunglasses on. "I was just leaving," I said to
Denise, the stepmother from hell. Then a thought hit me: Maybe Garrett never went to hell. Maybe he ended up in my parents' house by mistake. That would explain the screams and the moans of agony.

"Can I talk to you?" she asked. "It won't take long."

Denise was one of those women that other people thought was sweet.
She had a nice smile and a great sense of theatrics. But she was about as
sweet as a starving pit viper in a basket of rats. At least to me, the step-
fruit of her loins.

We'd never really gotten along. She'd started openly disliking me
when I kept bugging her to tell me stories about her childhood, what it
was like to run with the dinosaurs. After that, she'd give me these glares
made of liquid nitrogen that could instantly freeze the best of intentions.
I'd learned my most effective glares from that woman. That was something to be thankful for, I supposed.

With a long, taxed exhalation, I stepped to the side and invited her in
with a gesture. She stopped short when she saw the condition of my apartment, and I secretly begged her to say something. Anything. Any excuse
to kick her ass out of my apartment. I had to put up with her at family
functions, and I did so willingly around Dad and Gemma, but not here.
Not in my sacred space. She could bite me if she thought I was going to
grin and bear her condescending glances under my own rented roof.

She seemed to recognize this fact. Her survival instincts kicked in. She recovered with a blink and eased farther inside, sidestepping a box and a pair of khakis.

Trying not to wonder how Gemma was faring without her pants, I led Denise to my living area—about five steps from the door—sat down, and offered her my best scowl. "What can I do for you, Denise?"

She sat cattycorner to me and squared her shoulders. "I just wanted to ask you a couple of questions."

"And your phone isn't working?"

She bristled under my sharp tone. It wasn't like her to endure my attitude without a fight. Demureness was not in her blood. She must really be desperate. "You aren't accepting my calls," she reminded me.

"Oh, right. I forgot. So, what can I do for you?"

She took a tissue from her bag, took off her sunglasses, and made a show of cleaning them.

Finally, and with great care, I opened. I let myself feel the emotions coursing through her. Most of the time, I kept myself closed off. There was simply too much out there. I'd learned to control what and how much I absorbed when I was in high school. Before that, life had been . . . challenging. Especially around the step-beast.

Emotion rushed through her in spades, the worst of it like a lightning strike, knocking the breath from my lungs. Fear. Doubt. Grief.

Someone had died. Or someone was going to die. Those feelings were way too strong to be associated with anything other than death.

"First, I want you to know that I believe in you. In what you can do."

So the woman who made my childhood—my abilities—a living hell now believed in them. Oh, yeah. Someone was going to die. Maybe it would be her, but I didn't want to get my hopes up.

"Awesome!" I said, faking enthusiasm. "Now we can be besties."

She ignored me. "I've known for a long time, Charlotte."

She'd always refused to use my nickname. The gesture would make us seem close, and we couldn't let that happen. Her friends might look down their noses at her.

"You have to understand that it was hard raising you."

I couldn't help it. I snorted. Loud. Then laughed. "Raising me? Is that what you call it? What you did to me?"

She ignored me my entire childhood. Unless I'd embarrassed her in front of her friends or was bleeding profusely, I was of no consequence to her whatsoever. I was nobody. Invisible. I was dust beneath her feet.

Not that I was bitter or anything.

"You don't have children, so I don't expect you to understand."

I decided to share an anecdote with her to help her better grasp the situation. "Anyone with children should know, sometimes when you ask little Charley who broke the lamp and she says she doesn't know, what she's actually saying is, 'It was a guy with pale, see-through skin and bad hair who may have died from the blunt force trauma to the head but more likely bit the dirt from the multiple gunshot wounds to his chest.' But that could just be me projecting."

"Your circumstances were unusual," she acquiesced, examining her sunglasses.

"Ya think?"

She bit back a retort and I almost smiled. I wasn't sure when I'd become so cruel. She was clearly in pain. But payback was a cold, hard bitch. I'd have to be one more often.

Ever the stalwart soldier, she marched onward and asked, "Will you give me the message? The one my father left for me?"

I couldn't help it. My mouth fell open and I almost scoffed aloud. Now? After all these years she decides she wants to join the club and I'm supposed to remember a message given to me by a departed when I was in the low single digits? What the bloody hell?

"Okay, well, I was like—" I lifted my eyes to the big calculator in the sky. "—I don't know, four or five, so that was how many years ago? Math isn't really my thing."

"Twenty-three," she offered.

"So, I was four."

"I know," she said. Her fingers tightened around her bag. "But I also know how amazing that mind of yours is." She looked at me pointedly. "Clearly you never forget anything."

"You do have a point. I still remember quite profoundly the slap you gave me in front of the crowd at the park. And the time you dragged me off that bike at the beach. By my hair. And the time I tried to tell you what your father said and how you went ballistic on my ass, screaming at me as we drove to Dad's bar." I leaned in. "You spit in my face."

Her lips thinned in regret. Damn, she was good. If I didn't know her better, I'd say she was actually sorry for what she did.

"I was in shock at the park. What you did was—" She inhaled, then let that accusation drop and moved on to the next. "And your hair caught in my ring. I told you not to get on that bike and you disobeyed me."

If the heat of anger could manifest outside my body, she'd have been nuked right then and there. A charcoal briquette in the shape of Hitler, because she really did resemble him in an odd, disturbing kind of way. What I did? How dare she.

"And if you will remember, I wasn't even aware that my father had died when you told me you had a message from him from the grave. How was I supposed to respond to that, Charlotte?"

"By spitting in my face, apparently."

She lowered her head. "If I apologize, will it help?"

"Not especially."

"Will you tell me anyway?"

The sadness in her eyes, the remorse, ate at my resolve. Not much. Kind of like a mouse nibbling a tiny speck off a hunk of cheese the size of Mount Rushmore. But enough to have me saying, "I honestly don't remember the exact message, since you're asking. It was something about blue towels. Or maybe towels that weren't really blue. Fuck, I don't know."

Okay, I only used the F-word because I knew how much she hated it, but it did little good. She was lost in thought, trying to remember what I could possibly be talking about. Then something sparked in her memory. Recognition flitted across her face. "Wait," she said.

"How long, because I really do have things to do."

She stood and turned her back to me. "What did he say about the towels?"

After taking a deep breath, I said, "I told you, something about the fact that they weren't really blue. I think he said it wasn't your fault."

The sadness hit me like a blast of acid. It caused my eyes to sting. My chest to contract. I closed against it, shut down my ability to absorb emotion, and forced nonacidic air into my lungs.

Then she turned and kneeled in front of me. Kneeled. On her knees. Awkward. I tried to scoot away from her, but I was already at the end of my sofa—which might or might not go by the name of Consuela. My expression had to show the distaste I was feeling.

"It wasn't even about me," she said, her face glowing with awe. "It was about you. He was trying to tell me about you."

"You're in my bubble."

"He was trying to tell me how special you are."

"And you didn't listen." I tsked. "How surprising. But, no, really, you're in my bubble."

"Oh," she said, glancing around in surprise. "I'm sorry. I'm—" She sat back on her chair and smoothed her slacks. "I'm sorry, Charlotte."

I had no idea how her father had sent her a message about me from the grave, or how she made such a connection when it was apparently about blue towels. And, sadly, I didn't much care.

"Is that all you needed?"

"No."

"Well, that's the only message I have for you today. Unless you want the one about how much work I have to do. That's an important one." I picked my bag up off the floor, replaced my sunglasses, and stood to walk out.

"Can you tell when someone is about to die?" she asked before I got far.

I knew it. With bowed head and gritted teeth, I said, "I'm not sure." Sadly, I had the uncomfortable feeling that I could. That I always could. But it was one of those nagging little notions in the back of my mind that I ignored. Like when Cookie wore purple, red, and pink together. I just pushed it to the back of my consciousness. I didn't know how to explain that to someone like her, so I didn't try. "It's possible." I tilted my head to the side and looked her up and down. "Yep. I'd start looking at burial plots if I were you."

She didn't take me seriously in the least, which was probably a good thing, since I was pulling her spindly leg.

Standing as well, she stuffed her tissue in her bag and said, "If you notice anything of that nature, will you please give me a call?"

"Absolutely. I'll put you on speed dial."

She walked to the door, then turned back. "And just for the record, I wasn't asking for me."

I let her leave, waited a good five minutes, then headed out the door myself, dismissing her from my mind completely. Or doing my darnedest to.

According to their sign, the Veil Corporation was dedicated to the exploration and development of alternative fuel, and Harper's stepbrother, Art, was apparently a big deal there. Since I didn't have an appointment, I was told to wait in the lobby. Not a place I liked to wait. So I told the receptionist who I was and explained that if Art wouldn't see me, I'd come back with a couple of officers and a warrant. I was shown up to his office in a matter of minutes. I loved it when that crap worked. Honestly, a warrant for what? Art must have something to hide.

He didn't seem especially happy to see me when his assistant showed me in. He stood and offered his hand, but he wasn't happy about it.

Unfortunately, the guy was good-looking. He wore a three-piece suit and had a movie star face with short brown hair and naturally tan skin. But the pièce de résistance was his eyes: silvery gray with a hint of blue, fringed in long, dark lashes. Damn it! I hated it when bad guys were that good-looking. It was so much easier to think the worst of them when they looked the part: scraggly with a greasy smile and rotting teeth.

Though it did help that I could see hints of his mother in him. Oh, yeah, he was scum. And I would prove it the first chance I got.

After offering me a quick shake, he gestured for me to sit, then did the same. "Mind explaining why you felt the need to threaten me, Ms. Davidson?"

"Not at all. I needed to see you and I needed to see you fast. I've been hired by your stepsister—"

"I know, I know." He held up a hand to stop me. "Mother told me all about it."

I was the talk at dinner? Cool. I loved when that happened. But I had a personal bias against grown men who called their mothers Mother, so that was another strike against him. Maybe it would counteract the good-looking-as-heck thing.

"As I'm sure she did you," he added.

"Me?"

"Yes. I'm sure you got an earful about how Harper just wants attention and how it all started right after my parents' marriage."

I assessed his emotions, but he wasn't angry. Or particularly guilty. Until I said, "Harper said you set fire to her dog's house. With him in it."

"She said that?"

Guilt radiated off him, but something else was stronger. Anguish. His feelings were hurt. He stood and faced the window. "It was an accident. She knows that."

"And she told me as much." I could make out the faintest of smiles on his face from the reflection in the tinted glass when I said that, and realization struck. Hard. "Holy crap, you're in love with her."

"What?" He turned to me, his face a mask of indignation.

My mouth thinned. "Really?"

"Shit." He came around his desk and closed the door to his office before continuing. "How did you—? Look—" He raked a hand through his hair as I tried not to grin. "Of course I love her. She's my sister."

"Art, she's your *step*sister, and she's gorgeous. I've seen her, remember?"

He sat back down. "She doesn't know. Not really."

"Why?" I asked, flabbergasted.

"It's complicated. But we've been close for years."

"Wait a minute," I said as realization dawned. "You were her contact. You helped her when she disappeared those three years, didn't you?"

He pursed his lips. "How much of this will get back to my mother?"

"Unless it involved this case directly, none of it. And I can't see how knowing you'd help your stepsister is her business."

"Yes," he said with a reluctant nod. "And it was the hardest three years of my life."

He really did love her. "Well, I have to admit, you've just thrown a wrench into my theory. I really thought it was you."

"Sorry."

He wasn't. I could tell.

"But you believe her, right?" His brows rose, his expression full of hope.

"I do. Can you give me your thoughts? I mean, surely you've formed a few theories over the years."

"Nothing that ever panned out," he said, seeming disappointed in himself. "I've tried for years to figure it out. One time I'd think it was the kid from next door who had a crush on her, then I'd think it was the furniture delivery man. Things would happen at the oddest times. Sometimes Harper would be home, sometimes she wouldn't, so my mother's theory about Harper just wanting attention is bullshit."

I was glad he thought so. "Was there anyone else in the house growing up? Anyone who would have easy access to Harper's room?"

"Sure, all the time. We had relatives, cousins, maids, cooks, gardeners, caterers, event planners, assistants, you name it."

"Did any of those people live in the house?"

"Just the housekeeper and sometimes a cook. We went through a lot of those. My mother is not the easiest person to get along with."

I could imagine. "I need to ask you something difficult, Art, and I need you to keep an open mind."

"Okay," he said, growing suspicious.

"Do you or have you ever suspected your mother?"

His face froze in thought. "No." He set his jaw. "No way."

"But your stepdad's health is failing, right? If anything happens to Harper, you and your stepmother get it all."

He shrugged a shoulder in resignation. "That's true, but we get a small fortune anyway."

"Maybe a small fortune isn't enough. Maybe your mother has been trying to, I don't know, drive Harper insane so she can declare her incompetent or something."

"I understand why you'd think that, but she's not that greedy. I've been thinking about this for a long time. My mother wasn't lying. It all started right after they got married. I'd only met Harper a couple of times before the wedding, but she was just a normal girl."

"And afterwards?"

"Afterwards, she'd changed. And despite what my mother thinks, I don't think it had anything to do with their marriage." He leaned forward and leveled those hawklike eyes on me. "I think something happened to her during my parents' honeymoon. Something that's connected with all of this."

"She didn't mention an incident."

"I've done research on PTSD, Ms. Davidson, and looking back, I think Harper had the symptoms. She was only five, for God's sake. Who knows what she's repressed."

"Well, you're definitely right about that. Bad memories can be repressed. I'm glad she had you, though. Someone in her corner."

"Me, too." He grinned and sat back. "I wonder if she's ever going to let me live that fire down."

"I wouldn't count on it."

11

Since killing people is illegal,
can I have a Taser just for shits and giggles?
—T-SHIRT

Maybe Art was right. Maybe Harper had repressed something. An inciting incident that set this whole thing into motion.

If anyone would know, it should be her first therapist.

I called Cookie and after going through verbal instructions on how to turn the ring volume down on her phone, I got the information for Harper's first therapist, a psychologist named Julia Penn. She was retired, and Cookie couldn't get any contact information other than an address. She lived in Sandia Park just over the mountains. I had a thousand and one things I wanted to do today, including check on Harper and Quentin, and pay a couple of old friends a visit, namely Rocket, a departed savant who lived in an abandoned mental asylum. But I decided to pay her a visit anyway. It shouldn't take too long.

I drove on the historic byway of Turquoise Trail through a rich landscape to the prestigious San Pedro Overlook, an affluent community at the base of Sandia Park.

Struck by its beauty, I called Cookie back.

"Did I not mention the ring thing is bothering me today?"

"Cook, how can you have a hangover? You were fine at four-ish this morning."

"It hadn't hit me yet. It hit me later. Around seven twenty-two. Are those Gemma's pants?"

"Yep."

"How did she—?"

"I have no idea. Look, I just called because screw this apartment building crap. Since we can't have the cool apartment, I say we move out here."

"That's a great idea," she said.

"I know, right?"

"Except, you can't pay your rent."

"All the more reason to move."

"And houses out there are priced higher than you can count."

"It sounds silly when you put it that way."

"You know those women in nursing homes who have to be restrained around the clock because they mix up everyone's medication and steal all the bedpans?"

"Yes," I said, wondering what I was walking into.

"That's going to be you."

She was probably right. If I lived that long.

I drove up to a stunning adobe casita with a three-car garage and a manicured lawn, wondering if I could afford something like that if I sent all my purchases back and sold Misery. Behind it were the Sandia Mountains and in front, gorgeous red-rock canyons. Julia met me out front and led me around the house to the back.

"I got a call from Mrs. Lowell," Dr. Penn said as she showed me to an outside patio behind the house. She had a fire burning in a kiva fireplace. "I've been expecting to hear from you. But I didn't expect you to show up on my doorstep."

Wonderful. Had Mrs. Lowell called the PTA as well? Maybe Harper's childhood friends? Or her second-grade teacher and high school volley-ball coach. She must have been on the phone for hours.

Dr. Penn, an averaged-sized woman with long gray hair pulled back into a hair clip, motioned for me to sit, her outdoor furniture elegant to the extreme. "I can't talk about the case. I'm sure you know that."

"I'm aware that you can't talk specifics, so I was going to ask some more general questions. You know, things that could apply to anyone."

She offered me an impatient smile.

"Do you know what the symptoms of PTSD are?"

"Are you going to attack me, Ms. Davidson?"

"Not at all. I just want to make sure you know the symptoms."

"Of course I know the symptoms."

"Did you not recognize them in Harper? It sounds to me like they were genuine."

"Do I come into your office and tell you how to run your investiga-tions?"

I thought a minute. "Not that I'm aware of, but I haven't been in my office for a while now."

"Then please, Ms. Davidson, don't tell me how to diagnose a patient. I think I've had a few more years of experience than you."

Snobbish much? "So, what you're trying to tell me is that you screwed up but you can't take it back because it would look bad."

"You can see yourself out, yes?" She rose and started for her back door.

I stood as well. "Or did Mrs. Lowell pay you to misdiagnose Harper? To keep her drugged and compliant?"

If my stepmother'd had money, I had no doubt in my mind that she would have done that very thing. To shut me up. To keep me from caus-ing trouble or embarrassment.

She turned on me. "I am a psychologist. I rarely recommend drugs and am not licensed to prescribe them." She turned to her fireplace. "Every psyche is different. Some are more fragile than others. Harper missed her father, what she once had with him. She saw Mrs. Lowell as a threat. It's all in the timing."

"Ah, the marriage. But what if something else happened? Looking back, knowing what you know now, could she have had a form of PTSD?"

With a sigh of resignation, she said, "It's possible. But I even tried regression therapy."

"You mean hypnosis."

"Yes. I shouldn't be telling you this, and I only am because Harper hired you and her stepmother said to cooperate, but she lost a chunk of time. A week, to be exact. She couldn't remember anything about the week she spent with her grandparents. Nothing at all."

"And she'd stayed with them during the Lowells' honeymoon, right?"

"Yes, but they doted on her hand and foot. Now, that is all I can tell you. The Lowells are very good friends of mine. I've already overstepped the bounds of confidentiality."

"I just have one more question."

With a beleaguered sigh, she said, "Fine. What is it?"

"Are you renting or did you buy this outright?"

When I'd asked Dr. Penn about her house, she became slightly volatile, accusing me of accusing her of taking payoff money to be able to afford her luxurious lifestyle. I really just wanted to know if she was buying or renting. Clearly we'd gotten off on the wrong foot.

On the way back to the big city, I called Gemma for more intel. "So, how's the head?" I asked.

"What the hell did Cookie put in those margaritas?" She sounded like she had a cold. It was funny.

"Your guess is as good as mine, which is why I only had one."

"Oh, my God, I had like twelve."

Being the loving, nurturing sister that I was, I laughed. "Let that be a lesson."

"Never drink twelve margaritas in a row?"

"No," I said with a pfft. "That's totally acceptable. Never trust Cookie."

"Got it. Have you seen my pants?"

"Speaking of which, how did you get home without them?"

"I borrowed a pair of your sweats. I ran into a convenience store with them on. I talked to neighbors out in their yard when I pulled up. And only after I got inside did I realize they had 'Exit Only' written across the back."

"You stole my favorite sweats?"

"I wanted to die."

"It's weird that sweats would make you suicidal. I'd analyze the crap out of that if I were you."

"Do you actually wear those in public?"

"Only when I go out in them. Hey, how hard is it to diagnose PTSD?"

After a long pause, she said, "Charley, I know why you're calling, and yes, hon, it's painfully obvious you're suffering from posttraumatic stress disorder."

"What? No. I'm talking about a client."

"Mmm-hmm. And does this client have brown hair and gold eyes and talk to dead people?"

"Subtle. Don't make me yell into this phone," I said with an evil smirk. Twelve margaritas would make that thought very unappealing.

"Oh, for the love of God, please don't."

"Okay, then focus. It's not for me. Really. How easy is it to diagnose in a child?"

"Well, unless the patient doesn't remember anything that happened to him or her, then it's pretty easy. I mean the symptoms are fairly universal, although each case is a little different. No matter what happened, it should be fairly straightforward. Anything from a car accident to a natural disaster to soldiers exchanging fire on the battlefield can cause it."

I decided to take a stab in the dark. "What if something happened to a young child, but she didn't remember what it was? Or maybe she saw something? Or heard something? Can that cause PTSD?"

"Absolutely. But that happens even to adults. I once had a case where a woman was in a car accident and couldn't get to her crying son. She couldn't see him, but she could hear him. And before help could arrive on scene, he passed away. She heard his last cries."

"Okay," I said, interrupting her. "I don't like this case."

"I didn't either, but I have a point."

"Fine, then, but make it quick."

"Afterwards, she had what is referred to as hysterical deafness, or psychosomatic hearing loss."

"Like the guys who go off to war and go blind for no apparent reason."

"Exactly. Their minds can't absorb the horrors they've seen, so the brain refuses to process visual information. The visual cortex shuts down. It's completely psychological. But those are pretty extreme cases. PTSD is usually much less blatant, so oftentimes people don't even realize they have it. Like, say, a PI who was held captive and suffered great physical and emotional trauma."

"Are we back to this again?"

"Charley, let me hook you up with a friend of mine."

I straightened. Now she was talking my language. "Is he cute?"

"*She* is a very good psychotherapist. One of the best in the city."

"Wait," I said as another thought occurred to me.

"No more waiting."

"What if this happened decades ago? Would it have been harder to diagnose PTSD back then?"

"Possibly. PTSD has been around since the dawn of man, but it only gained notoriety as a diagnosis around the eighties. Then it took a while to catch on."

"Thanks." That might explain how Dr. Penn had missed it. Why she looked so hard at other causes of Harper's illness. I had to find more about what happened to Harper during her parents' honeymoon.

I decided to do a quick drive-by at Pari's place to check on Harper. The shop wasn't open yet, it was still early for a tattoo parlor, but Tre was there looking at Internet porn. He had good taste.

"Where's Pari?" I asked him.

He shrugged and I sensed a jolt of hostility. "She's out."

Uh-oh, trouble in paradise. He seemed really bummed. Not enough to hold my attention, though. I looked past him at the pictures of clients Pari had on her wall and pointed. "Hey, those are the Bandits."

I stepped closer to the pic of the ragtag team of bikers. They owned my favorite mental asylum, for some bizarre reason, and the picture was of my favorite three bikers ever: Donovan, Eric, and Michael. They were showing off their tats, each of them posing like bodybuilders, but something about them clicked in the back of my mind. I'd seen them out of context recently, in another situation, another environment. It was odd. Something about their shape. Tall, medium-tall, and just plain medium.

"Okay, well, I'll just be back here."

Tre shrugged, his acknowledgment barely noticeable.

I wondered about the Bandits as long as my ADD would allow me to, then moved on to my childhood dream of being an astronaut and how I would've tried to save the world if a comet were headed toward Earth. I concluded that the human race was doomed.

"Hey, Harper," I said, ducking into her closetlike room.

She'd been looking out a window the size of a business card and turned to me. "Hi."

"Do you have a minute?"

"Really?" she asked, indicating her surroundings with her upturned palms.

"Right," I said. "I hope Pari is treating you well."

"She's kind of different."

"That she is."

"Did you talk to Art?"

"Yes, and he's definitely not our guy."

"Oh, I know that. I was just hoping he might have figured something out."

"Well, he did have some pretty interesting comments," I said, my clever meaning disguised in a subtly subversive way. "He seems to think something happened to you while you were staying with your grandparents."

She stood again, her jaw set in frustration. "It always comes back to that, but I just don't remember. For some reason, by the time my family got me into therapy and I'd started to analyze what could have happened, I'd completely forgotten that week. It's not all that unusual. I mean, how much about your childhood do you really remember?"

She had a point. Even my childhood was pretty spotty, and I could recollect anything if I wanted to. I couldn't imagine how much a normal kid would forget.

"But he said you'd changed after you came back."

She looked at me, confused. "He hardly knew me. My parents dated and got married before we knew what happened. Let's just say we were not brought into the loop on that decision."

"That's weird. I wasn't brought into the loop with my parents' marriage either."

"Really? How old were you?"

"Twelve months."

She giggled. "I can't imagine why they didn't ask your opinion."

"I know, right? Well, if you don't have anything, I guess I might have to actually do some investigative work."

She grinned. "Isn't that what you do?"

"Oh, yeah, sure. Right." I nudged her with my elbow. "I am a PI, after all." Telling her I could talk to the dead and often used them to help me solve crimes might be awkward at this juncture. It would be best if she thought I had my crap together instead of scattered from here to Timbuktu, like, say, the crap on a cattle ranch. "Have you checked out Tre? He's well worth the effort."

Her shoulders raised in modesty. "Not yet."

"Well, see that you do, missy. Hard manly flesh like that shouldn't go to waste."

"Okay. I promise."

I stepped out of Pari's shop just as my phone rang.

Speaking of whom, "Hey, Par."

"Where the heck are you?"

I stopped and looked around. "Right here. Where are you?"

"You're here?"

"Here where?"

"Charley."

"Pari."

"You're supposed to meet my dates."

"Oh, right. That's where I am. I'm almost there."

"Are you sure? Because we're on a pretty tight schedule."

"Positive." Knowing it'd take me forever to get a parking space, I took off in a full-out sprint. I may not look good when I got there, but I'd be damned if I was late. Or, well, later.

Fortunately, the Frontier was a mere two blocks away. I thought about ordering a *carne adovada* burrito and a sweet roll before sitting with Pari and—did she say dates? As in more than one? But she might hurt me. Still, their sweet rolls were a thing of beauty.

The Frontier was an odd sort of place just across from the University of New Mexico. It ran the length of several partially divided rooms. I finally found Pari and her dates in the very last one. There weren't many people in that part. Several students were having a Bible study group in one corner, and a homeless man named Iggy sat at a booth off by himself. Pari and her dates—literally, as there were three men sitting with her—were stashed in the farthest corner.

This wouldn't be awkward at all.

She brightened when she saw me and motioned me over, looking only mildly ridiculous in her sunglasses, knowing I would be there.

"Hey, you!" She stood for a hug. "I haven't seen you in forever. How weird that we'd run into each other here."

Oh, okay, we were playing that game. I wished she would've filled me in. I thought we were playing the I-have-trust-issues game. Why else would she want me to sit there and measure their honesty while she grilled them?

"This is Mark, Fabian, and Theo. Guys, this is Charley. She sees dead people."

I rolled my eyes. I closed them first so no one would see, but the minute my lids locked down, my eyes did somersaults.

She laughed and patted my back hard enough to dislodge my esophagus. Maybe she was perturbed that I was late. "Just kidding." She waved a dismissive hand at them. "Nobody can see dead people. You should join us."

Before I could answer, she shoved me into the nearest chair. This was going to be the worst dates I'd ever been on. Though she had good taste, I'd give her that. They all had varying degrees of dark hair and tan skin. Mark and Fabian were Hispanic, and Theo was Caucasian with something else thrown in for good measure. Possibly Asian.

"So, Mark," she said, sitting beside me, "have you ever been arrested for kiddie porn?"

Oddly enough, my forehead dropped into the palm of my hand.

But Mark was good-natured enough to laugh it off. "Well, so far nobody's found my stash."

After an appreciative laugh, she turned to Theo. "How about you?"

Theo was a little less accepting. "Am I being interrogated?"

Pari snorted. "What? Absolutely not. But have you?"

After an hour of the guys pretending they weren't on an interview and me pretending I was just there to eat despite the fact that I never got any food, I came to one, noticeable conclusion: Pari was a big fat liar.

"So?" she asked after they'd left. I was exhausted. Trying to read every emotion while wading through hers was like trying to sprint in five feet of water.

"So?" I asked in return.

"Sooooo?" she asked again, believing that drawing out the O would make me spill quicker. She raised her brows and waited for my answer.

"Pari, the only one who lied throughout this entire conversation was you."

She balked. "You were reading my emotions?"

"Par, I can't weed through them like you obviously think I can. I can't pick and choose. It's an all-or-nothing kind of gig."

"Oh. So?" She raised her brows expectantly.

"Well, I did manage to figure out three things."

"Wonderful." She shimmied in her chair and settled in for the telling of my great and mighty insights.

"You're afraid of squirrels. You've never been to Australia. And you're a convicted felon."

Her face fell. "I could've told you that."

"Yes, but you didn't. Now, why is that?"

With a defensive shrug, she said, "It was a long time ago. I was really young."

"How young?"

"Twenty. Okay? Now, what did you think about—?"

"What were you convicted of?"

"Chuck, we aren't here about me. So, which one did you like?"

"They were all three pretty great, though I'm having a hard time seeing you with an investment broker. But you have good taste, I'll give you that. So, what were you convicted of?"

"Fine," she said, grinding her teeth. "In a word, hacking."

I could not have hidden my surprise if someone had paid me to.

"What? I was young."

"You're a computer whiz?"

"*Was. Was* a computer whiz. Now I'm not allowed near a computer. It's the terms of my probation."

"So, that means you've been on probation for almost nine years."

"Yeah. I got ten years' probation for hacking into a federal vault and funneling money to my mom's bank account. I thought it would be funny. And it was until I got caught."

"You funneled money?"

"Eighteen dollars."

"Wow." Apparently everyone knew how to funnel money but me. I was so behind the times. "I just never knew. But really? Only eighteen dollars?"

"That's why I only got probation. Like I said, I just thought it would be funny." Her shoulder lifted into an innocent shrug. "And I'd get bragging rights. You have no idea how addictive bragging rights are in the hacking world."

"Obviously. But you have a computer in your office."

"I can have one for business purposes." She raised a finger to make sure I knew she was serious. "No Internet of any kind."

"But you do have Internet. I saw Tre looking at porn on your computer."

"What?" She seemed appalled.

"Like you don't do the same thing."

"Yeah, but I don't work for me. He does."

"That's why you were trying to rewire everything," I said, the truth hitting me like a brick.

"He was looking at porn?"

"You were trying to hide the fact that you have Internet."

"Yes, yes," she said, growing annoyed. "It's so frustrating. I can't even have a computer with a modem. So I have to work around that."

"I am so in awe of you right now. I always wanted to be a computer whiz, and I would've been if not for Paul Sanchez."

Her brows rose in question.

"He told me computers were alien technology and they used them to track us."

"Weren't you abducted by aliens once?"

I nodded. "Exactly why I stopped going around them. By the time I figured out Paul was wrong, I'd sailed past my prime. Now, thanks to him, I can hardly program a universal remote."

She blinked. "So, about my dates?"

"You can do better."

I looked up into the eyes of the bartender Dad had hired, only she was looking at Pari, and the invitation dripping off her in spades was like looking at a waterfall of sin and sensual degradation. A fact that was not lost on Pari if the dreamy expression on her face was any indication.

"I'm Sienna—" She slid a card across the table toward Pari. "—if you want to interview me."

One corner of her mouth lifted into a wickedly dimpled grin before she turned and started out the back door.

"So," Pari said, gathering herself in a rush of emotion, "you're just going to walk away?"

Sienna flashed a gorgeous smile and walked back to us. And I was so not doing the interview thing again.

"I have to get something to eat before I die. And I need a mocha latte. Do they have those here?"

Pari shrugged, suddenly very disinterested in anything I had to say.

"Thanks for caring, Par."

"What do you do, Sienna?"

The woman sat in my seat when I stood, making it clear I was not welcome. I felt so appreciated. I strolled to the front and ordered a *carne adovada* burrito, a sweet roll, and a café mocha. Then I had to figure out how I was going to pay for it. I pulled out my cards. Three of them. Everything I had left.

"Okay," I said, trying to cipher in my head, "put three twenty-seven on this one." I handed it to her. "And two fifty on the flowery one." I handed her the flowery one, too.

The girl took the cards from me and rolled her eyes. I could've knocked the shit out of her. She'd have good reason to roll her eyes then. But knocking the shit out of rude people wasn't my style. Heckling them every chance I got was. Hopefully she'd screw up soon. I didn't have all day.

"And four whatever is left on the blue one that looks like a camel died on it." She went to take it from me, and after snatching it back, I leaned in and said, "If it's not too much trouble."

She gritted her teeth and said, "Not at all," before jerking it out of my hand. Then she mouthed the word *loser* as she swiped it and punched in numbers. Oh, yeah, this girl was going down. She had no idea who she was messing with. And, sadly, she didn't seem to care.

I hoped her drawer came up short at the end of her shift. Karma's a bitch.

She pushed the sales key on the register, and an alarm went off. Damn it. Did my card not go through? Maybe I mixed them up. But why would an alarm go off? Didn't the little machine just decline the card and go on its merry way?

The manager, a twenty-something guy who would forever look like he'd just gotten his braces off and was late for a chemistry exam, ran over with a humongous smile on his face.

"You won!" he said, his enthusiasm more than I could bear at the mo-men—

Wait. I'd won?

"It's our anniversary, and your order has been randomly chosen as today's lucky winner," he said, squealing like a kid on a roller coaster. He clapped his hands together, his excitement suddenly infectious.

The surly girl's mouth dropped open, and I couldn't help the smug expression I offered her. Oh, the agony of it all. The anguish. The torture! In your face, girlfriend.

No. No, I had to be the bigger person. It wasn't her fault she was born a *loser.* I mouthed the word. It was infantile, but I did it anyway. She rolled her eyes again.

I turned to the manager with an expectant smile. Maybe I'd won a cruise. Or a yacht. Or a small island. "I won?"

"You won," he said. Everyone around me started clapping. Except for Iggy, the homeless guy in the corner. He didn't seem to care. But everyone else was super-excited for me. "You won a year's supply of our famous sweet rolls."

I stilled. This . . . this couldn't be real. A year's supply? "No way!" I shouted. This was so much better than a yacht. Especially since I lived in a desert.

"Yes, ma'am," he said. He hurried to the back, then reappeared with a booklet of some kind and a camera. After the surly girl took pictures in which I was fairly certain she cut off my head, I walked to the back room again to wait for my burrito and was congratulated by a few customers as they passed by my table. I felt like a celebrity. Like I'd won the lottery. Or an Academy Award.

Since Pari was busy being seduced by an Egyptian goddess, I decided to give them some alone time. And to let my nerves calm down a bit. That little adrenaline rush was more taxing than I thought it would be. I strolled back one room and sat in a center booth.

As I sat waiting for my number to pop up on the marquee, my mouth watering as I imagined the red *chili* in the burrito and the butter dripping off the sweet roll, I decided I had to get out more. Two months without the sugary goodness of a sweet roll was entirely too long to wait. What the hell had I been thinking?

I hadn't been thinking. I'd gone crazy. Gemma was right. I had a disorder. I'd have to see if there was an OTC I could use. Like a salve. Or a medicated powder.

I was so into my musings that it took me a while to sense the darkness sitting nearby. So close, I could taste it on my tongue. The raw acidity of rotten eggs filled my mouth and nostrils until my stomach heaved in reflex. I fought the feeling and looked to the side toward a man staring at me in a tweed suit and tan fedora. He had his legs and hands crossed and looked like he could have been a professor at the university.

"This is quite an honor," he said, nodding an acknowledgment.

He had a smooth English accent, the tenor to his voice pleasant but not very deep. His smile was kind and affectionate, but I didn't miss the darkness lurking just behind his eyes. Still, if this was a demon, why wasn't he scrambling toward me with drool dripping off his chin? Wasn't that what they did?

"To be close enough to you to taste the sweetness of fear wafting off your flesh." He tilted his face up and drew a deep ration of air in through his nostrils. Then he closed his eyes as though savoring what he found there.

And he was right. I was afraid. I couldn't move, I was so afraid. What if he came after me? What if he pounced? I'd be dead before I could say, *Um, Reyes?*

He refocused on me with a sheepish expression. "Forgive me. I've heard stories of the girl with no fear, so please excuse my surprise."

"Surprise of what?"

"You're afraid of me."

"I'm not afraid of you," I said, lying through my chattering teeth.

"Of course you are."

"Those stories were exaggerated anyway."

The next expression he offered held more wolf than sheep. "I doubt it. Something happened. Your aura has been damaged. So it would be horridly unfair of me, but I'm finding it difficult to hold back. I seem to want nothing more than to rip out your jugular with my teeth and smell the copper in your blood."

"I have a guardian."

"But I'm here on a mission," he said, ignoring me. "I have a message."

"Have you tried texting?"

"If the boy will stop hunting us, we will leave you alone to live your life and die naturally, though I have to warn you, traditionally reapers don't live long in corporeal form. Still, you shan't die by our hands. We will not interfere in your life in any way. We'll only—" He turned up a careless palm. "—watch from afar."

That was disturbing.

"But when your body dies," he continued, lowering his head in warning, "you're fair game."

"The boy?" I asked.

He smiled. "Rey'aziel."

"Reyes is hunting you?"

"You didn't know?"

I shook my head. It seemed the only movement I could manage. "No."

"Did you think he just happened upon my soldiers at that ridiculous contest?"

"You mean the fights?" I asked, frowning. "I hadn't given it that much thought."

"He has been hunting us down like dogs."

"Not like dogs." I shook my head once more. "You don't deserve the high praise of such a comparison."

A lecherous grin stole across his face. "There she is. The girl with no fear. It is no wonder he is obsessed. He always was such a clever boy."

Surely he was talking about someone else. Reyes was no more obsessed with me than he was with dryer lint. He just needed me alive for this war that supposedly hovered on the horizon. He'd told me so on several occasions. "So let me get this straight," I said, trying to wrap my head around the goings-on of the underworld. "He stops hunting you, and you stop attacking him."

"We have never attacked him, dear girl. We have no need of him just yet."

"I would beg to differ. I saw what your demons did to him in that basement."

"Touché, but that was only to get to you. We can get to him anytime. Those tattoos are there for a reason, love. You, on the other hand, are protected. A treasure not so easily gained. But you do have part of it correct. If he stops hunting us, he'll live much longer in his physical form, fragile as it is. No more stab wounds. No more gashes of which to tend."

I jerked to attention. "Gashes?" The bandages he had at the fights.

"You have no idea what the boy has been up to, do you? He's grown up. Become quite the warrior, if his ability to down my soldiers while hardly breaking a sweat is any indication. But you care for him." He turned a curious gaze on me. "Perhaps I could make a deal with you instead."

"What?" I asked, realizing I was actually negotiating with the devil. Or, at the very least, one of his minions.

He unfolded a hand and held it out to me, palm up. "Come with me now. Your death will be quick, and you will rule by my master's side."

"Your master? Meaning Satan."

"That is one colloquialism, yes."

"Why on all that is holy would I do something like that?"

"Because you have no idea what you're capable of. What you can do defies everything you have ever known. But right now, you are just a silly girl running about in an ape suit. You'll be so much more powerful when you shed it. You will shine like the brightest star and you will have just as much power as one."

Okay, so this guy seemed to know what he was talking about. "Tell me what I'm capable of."

He leaned in, his eyes black caverns behind the light brown of the human's he inhabited. "Anything you can imagine."

Again? Really? "Why do you want me so bad? There have been other reapers."

"But none like you, my dear. We want you, but we need both of you to gain the advantage. You are so close to doing our jobs for us anyway, we'd just like to be around when the gate is actually opened." When I questioned him with my eyes, he asked, "What do you think happens when the key of darkness is inserted into the locket of light?"

He raked a salacious gaze from the top of my head to the tips of my booted toes. I felt violated. And repulsed.

"It's like opening a door directly from hell and straight into the heart of heaven. How many soldiers do you think can slip through before that door is closed? We just have to be at the ready when it happens."

He couldn't possibly be saying what I thought. "So, you mean if Reyes and I get together?"

"Yes, well, there's a bit more to it than that, but that's the basic idea. Why do you think the master made the son? It wasn't because he longed for a family, if that's what you're thinking."

I was starting to feel sick. The acrid smell of him made me dizzy. That combined with the constant surge of fear had me almost doubled over with nausea. But I didn't dare take my eyes off him.

"I'm going to have to turn down your kind offer," I said, praying he'd leave so I could run to the bathroom.

"Pity. But I do understand. The human mind is so limited, it's hard to see past the rotting flesh of humanity to bigger and better things." He seemed so civilized, so educated.

"Is the accent yours?" I asked.

"No, it belongs to the ape I'm wearing. But I like it. I think it suits me." He rose and adjusted his tie almost joyously. Then he walked around, bent over, and whispered in my ear, the acrid smell of him over-powering. "Tell Rey'aziel hello from Hedeshi." He straightened and pointed to the coupon book on my table. The one I'd just won. "That was my gift to you, by the way. A token of my admiration."

When he turned to walk away, a handful of college kids a couple tables away started clapping, their faces alight with appreciation. He stopped and offered them a regal grin. They were applauding as though we'd just given them a theatrical production. But that's exactly how it would look from their end. Anyone watching would think we were ac-tors, probably rehearsing for a performance at the university. How could the conversation we'd just had been real?

Hedeshi held up a hand in true thespian style and took a bow as I sat dumbfounded. He bowed again as he left; then all eyes turned toward me. Waiting to see what my exit would entail. They were about to be very disappointed.

I looked down at the coupon book for a year's worth of sweet rolls. With shaking legs, I stood and smiled to our audience, then walked over to Iggy and handed him the book. Knowing I would never make it to the bathroom, I ran out the back door and almost emptied the coffee I'd had on the way over onto the pavement as a cat watched me, her ears twitching in curiosity. Then I took a deep breath, straightened my jacket, and summoned Angel.

12

When I want your opinion,
I'll remove the duct tape.

—T-SHIRT

After dry-heaving in front of God and beast alike, I started toward my apartment building on the next block, then remembered I'd left Misery at Pari's. I had to stop and lean against something every so often. My hands and knees shook. Even my elbows shook. And quite possibly my hair follicles. Bile slipped up my throat, and I swallowed it down in several quick gulps. Trying to calm myself. Trying to collect my wits and focus.

The moment his name came to mind, Angel appeared. He glanced around and then glared at me from underneath his bandanna. "How are you doing that? And why are you blue?"

I sipped on the cool air before asking, "Where is he?"

I didn't have to clarify. Angel knew exactly whom I was talking about, and if anyone would know where Reyes was, it was him. He'd been keeping tabs on him ever since the son of public enemy number one got out of prison. I knew it and I knew why. Angel was hoping Reyes would keep his distance, would stay away from me. Not that he told me that outright, but I knew enough about Angel's feelings toward Reyes to know exactly why he would keep tabs on someone he was so afraid of.

He kicked the rocks at his feet. "Why?" he asked, his disappointment evident.

"Because if you don't tell me, your mother will never see another penny."

His expression held a hint of resentment, but I couldn't help that now. "He's at the Paladin Lodge down the street."

I straightened in surprise. "A hotel? I thought he was living with Elaine Oake."

"Look, you asked. I told. I have no idea where he's living. But right now, he's at that hotel."

Fair enough. "Room?"

"One thirty-one."

"Thank you."

I dismissed him and started for Misery.

I parked several spaces down from number 131 and hoofed it to Reyes's room. The hotel wasn't horrible. Especially for one that rented by the hour. I'd been to worse. On a scale of one to five, I'd give it a two-ish, but at least there were no blatant drug deals going down in the parking lot. Always a good sign.

When I got to the room, the door stood ajar just enough for a stream of evening light to slash across worn, dark carpet. I drew Margaret and held her with both hands, barrel pointed to the ground. Like in the movies. If I could actually hit something when I shot, I'd have felt safer, but at least I looked cool.

"Reyes?" I asked, peeking inside.

When I didn't get an answer, I nudged the door open with Margaret's barrel, an act that only sounded naughty. A ray of light revealed a boot propped on a small table by a kitchenette. I recognized Reyes's signature style instantly. His boots were a combination of ropers and street cycle, and I coveted them horridly.

After glancing around for any other occupants, I stepped cautiously inside. He sat ensconced in shadows, so I couldn't see his facial expression to gauge his mood. The only sentiment wafting off him was pain. Beside his boot on the table sat a bottle of whiskey and a roll of duct tape. That meant only one thing: He was hurt and probably hurt bad. Duct tape was Reyes's answer to stitches. And surgery. He healed so fast—we both did—that we rarely needed to go to extreme lengths to recover. The exception for me was when Earl Walker had taken a knife to me. The exception for Reyes was when a group of demons had gotten ahold of his physical body while his incorporeal one had been away. And it was a big group. Over two hundred, if I had to guess.

He didn't move when I repositioned the door where he had it. His heat drifted around me, warming me, calming me. I was still shaking when I'd parked, but his heat was like a salve for my nerves.

"Nice room," I said, glancing around.

The whiskey bottle was half empty, and I wondered if he'd drunk it or used it as an antiseptic on his wounds. Probably a little of both.

"I thought you were staying with Elaine."

He spoke at last. "I thought we agreed you'd stay in your apartment."

"You agreed," I said, lifting a notepad to inspect it. I couldn't read the writing. "With yourself apparently, because I remember refusing to."

A black jacket lay tossed over a chair, and take-out containers filled the trash cans. At least he'd been eating.

"Did she kick you out?" I asked.

"She served her purpose."

Surprised, I asked, "And what purpose would that be?"

"She had connections. I needed those connections to get a trainer for the fights. I couldn't get in otherwise."

The fact that he was just using her should have horrified me, but elation swept through me with the knowledge. "So you just tossed her aside and moved into a seedy hotel?"

"Something like that."

I picked at receipts and other notes scattered on the dresser. "I've seen her house. I'm not sure you made a wise decision."

"Why are you here, Dutch?"

His brusqueness pricked. He was really having issues with me lately. One minute he wanted to pull me into his arms, and the next he wanted me out of his sight. Fine, I'd give him the message and leave him to it. I holstered Margaret and said, "Hedeshi says hello."

Every emotion in him fled instantly, like he was a roiling ocean growing completely calm in a matter of seconds.

After a long, drawn-out silence, he asked, "Did he hurt you?"

"No. We had a very nice conversation, in fact. And he helped me win a year's supply of sweet rolls, but I gave it to Iggy."

"What did he say?"

"Oh, you know, he talked about the boys back home, the fact that he wanted to rip out my jugular and drink my blood, your father's plan to take over the world."

He looked to the side in thought. "I knew there had to be someone behind this. It's too organized. Too well thought out."

"Well, he wants you to know if you'll stop hunting them, they'll leave me alone, allow me to die of natural causes." I scoffed. "Like that's going to happen."

I saw him clench and unclench his fists. "They're liars, Dutch. Each and every one. They would lie when the truth would sound better. They have no intention of leaving you alone, no matter what I do." He took the bottle, and just before downing a swig, he said, "They want you more than they want their next breath."

"I figured as much, but why didn't he just kill me then? Why go through all the theatrics?"

"Hedeshi isn't stupid," he said after putting the bottle back. "He knows he can't fight your guardian. He has no defense against her. The moment he attacked, she would have been on him, and he knew it. They will have to attack in a group to get past Artemis." His lips softened as he examined me. "He upset you." It wouldn't have been hard for him to pick up on that. Probably the minute I drove into the parking lot.

"Only a little." When he didn't say anything, I asked, "You've been hunting them? Is that who hurt you?"

He examined his bandages. "They're very strong."

"I could tell. You broke that man's neck, and he still came after me." I ran my fingers along the chipped edge of the dresser I was leaning against. "How is that possible?"

"As long as they're inside, they make the human body almost indestructible. Once they vacate that body, it will die if it has been mortally wounded."

The last time demons had escaped onto this plane, there were hundreds of them. There was no way Reyes could fight them all, even with Artemis's help. "Do you know how many are here?"

"Not many," he said with a shrug. "And there aren't that many people who are genuinely clairvoyant."

"So, you know who they're targeting?"

"Yes."

"And, what? You're going to kill them all?"

He raked his fingers through his hair, exasperated. "To stop a war between heaven and hell from spilling out into this world? Yes."

He had a point, but still. "Reyes, you can't kill these people."

"I just need to kill the demons inside, but sometimes the human has to be sacrificed to obtain that goal."

"Well, then stop." I pulled a chair out across from him and sat down. My eyes were adjusting and I could just make out the sensual line of his lips, the fringe of his thick lashes, the frame of mussed hair. His wide shoulders were bare, and duct tape shimmered over one of them and across his abdomen. No bandages. No gauze. Just duct tape. How sanitary could that be? "You can't kill innocent people."

"That man last night wasn't innocent, if it makes you feel better."

"Sadly," I said, curious about what the man had done, "it does, but only a little." I rubbed my arms, still fighting off the effects of my encounter with the Englishman. "What happened?" I asked, nodding toward the tape.

He took the bottle of whiskey again and downed about a third of what was left before replacing the cap. "I was mugged," he said after wiping his mouth on the back of a hand.

As he'd said before, it was doubtful a human could do that to him, but I dropped it. He was never one to share with the class anyway.

He lifted a gray T-shirt off the back of another chair and pulled it on with great care. When he settled back, it took a lot for me not to sigh aloud. He looked really good in gray.

"I thought it was almost impossible for demons to get onto this plane."

"It is. These are left over from our last encounter."

A jolt of surprise shot through me. "You mean from when they had you in that basement?" I had destroyed them then. The light inside me proved a powerful weapon. "There were more?"

"They're like cockroaches. Once they escape onto this plane, they can hide for centuries as long as they stay out of the light."

He'd told me before, they'd been banished from the sun when his father was cast from the heavens. It was now lethal to them.

"They weren't all in that basement, but most of them were. Still, this is organized. Way more organized than anything the lesser brethren would be capable of. I'm not surprised Hedeshi is behind it. He was always such a suck-up."

I was hoping to get more answers before he went gallivanting onto the battlefield, hunting down the suck-up. This was a rare opportunity. Having Reyes Farrow all to myself without someone trying to kill us, or without women standing around gawking. Well, *other* women standing around gawking. I didn't count.

"What am I capable of?" I asked, changing the subject again.

He filled his lungs to capacity and accepted my query with grace. "Only you can know that."

The room grew darker by the minute with the setting sun. I stood and leaned toward him until I could smell the earthy essence he'd been born with. Like a lightning storm in a dessert desperate for rain. "I want to know, Reyes. You keep telling me I'm capable of so much more. I want to know what."

His eyes shimmered with interest. "I'm not lying. I don't know."

I took the bottle and shoved away from the table so I could rinse the taste of bile out of the back of my mouth. After taking a swig of a liquid acidic enough to melt the paint off a Chevy, I swished it around, then swallowed. My eyes watered as it seared my already raw throat; then I handed the bottle back and strode to look out the window. I had to ease the thick curtains aside to see onto Central as rush hour traffic came to a head in the evening gloom.

"Every reaper is different in physical form," Reyes said. "And most never fully come into their powers."

I turned back to him, so thirsty for information, I was not above begging. "What do you mean? How many of us are there?"

"Not as many as you might think."

The room had grown even darker, so I reached over and turned on a lamp. It helped, but Reyes still sat in shadows.

I eased back into the chair and waited as he took another drink from the bottle and I realized then that he was still bleeding. Dark spots were seeping through the T-shirt. I tried to tamp down my alarm.

"You're not really called reapers on the other planes," he said, placing the bottle carefully back on the table. "That's a human reference."

"Wait, other planes? How many planes are there?" I asked, surprised by his word choice.

"How many galaxies are there in the universe? How many stars? It's hard to know exactly. Suffice it to say, many."

"I—I had no idea."

"Not many do. And in answer to your question, there is a new reaper born on this plane every few hundred years. There's no set time, really."

I stilled. "But you told me before, you'd been waiting for me. That every time a new reaper was sent, you were disappointed because it wasn't me. How long have you been here?"

He frowned in thought. "I'm not sure exactly. Maybe fifteen centuries."

Stunned, I asked, "What the heck were you doing all that time?"

He studied me. "Waiting."

For me. That Englishman said he'd been sent for me. Was he telling me the truth? Did Reyes's father send him for me specifically?

"So a new reaper is born every few hundred years. Are they immortal or something?"

"No. Not their physical bodies. Most don't live more than a few years, in fact."

"Why?"

He considered me a minute, then said, "Think about your childhood, Dutch. What it was like growing up with your abilities."

Memories flooded my cerebral cortex instantly. My stepmother's horror. The loss of good friends once I tried to tell them who I was. What I was. The distractions in class when departed showed up, which often ended with me going to the principal's office.

"Now think about having those abilities in a world teeming with superstition and fear. Many were killed as children. Of those who weren't, most became hermits. They were shunned by their own people, never fully accepted. You are truly the first of your kind who has thrived among them."

I didn't know what to say. "What happens when we die?"

"You have to understand, your body is the anchor for the portal. It's the part that got you onto this plane."

"But if my body is gone, what happens? Will I still be the portal?"

"Yes." He nodded. "You were a portal long before you ever took human form."

"So, if—when I die, I'll still be the grim reaper?"

"Once your body ceases to exist, you become powerful a hundred times over, but you'll also change. You won't have that human connection, and every reaper changes over time. They lose their sense of humanity, though some didn't have that much to lose in the first place. Humans were not kind to them."

"If that's the case, why did you try to let your body die?"

He leaned his head to the side. "Back to that?" When I shrugged, he said, "Because it was the draw, Dutch. The bait they could have hooked you with. And they succeeded, in case you've forgotten."

"But they could've taken you. Once your corporeal body passed, they could've taken you, right?"

His mouth curved knowingly. "They would've had to catch me first."

"The Englishman made it sound like it would be easy to track you down, because of your tattoos, the key."

"The Englishman?"

"Hedeshi. He's in the body of an Englishman."

"Ah. Well, there are ways around that as well."

Certain he wouldn't tell me what those ways were, I kept on track. I was actually getting somewhere for the first time in forever.

I shifted in my chair, leaned forward in enthusiasm. "Okay, so, if I'll become that much more powerful, what am I capable of while still alive?"

"I wish I knew. It's hard to know for certain. Like I said, most of your kind don't live long."

"But you've told me repeatedly I'm capable of more."

"And you are. That doesn't mean I know exactly what."

I decided to reword my question. "I've been told twice now that I am capable of anything I can imagine."

"That's true."

Well, this wasn't frustrating at all. "I can imagine a lot," I said, challenging him. "So, can I shoot fireballs from my hands, because I can totally see myself doing that."

The look he offered me was full of both humor and affection. "No."

"Then I've been lied to." I copied him and tossed a foot onto the table. Denise would be horrified.

"Who told you this?" he asked.

"The Englishman, for one, and Sister Mary Elizabeth, for another."

"And she lies to you often?"

"No," I said, frowning defensively.

"She did not say you could do anything you can imagine. She said you are capable of anything you can imagine. Not the act, Dutch, but the consequence."

"I don't understand the difference," I said, feeling thick.

"Think about it. If you could shoot balls of fire from your hands," he said, pausing to laugh, "what would happen?"

I looked away from him in disgust. "I don't know. I could make a car explode, maybe."

"Then *that* is what you are capable of. The consequence, Dutch. The result."

His meaning started to take root in my mind, muddled as it was. "So, if I wanted to blow up a car, I could do it, I just couldn't do it throwing fireballs from my hands." I squinted, tried to get a firm grip on his meaning, lost it, clawed to get it back, let it slip, gave up with a heave of resignation. "Nope, I don't get it. But the bottom line is, if I can imagine it, I can do it, right? So, I can kill people with my mind?"

"If you believe you could live with yourself afterwards, sure."

"That's a good point. Can you kill people with your mind?"

A soft grin spread across his face. "Only if my mind tells my hands to carry out its orders."

The smile that I felt widen had to look as diabolical as I felt. "So, I can do more than you can?"

"You always could."

I hadn't gotten this many answers from Reyes in, well, never. I decided to tease him a bit. "You still owe me a million dollars."

"Take off your clothes."

"No."

"I'll give you a million dollars to take off your clothes."

"Okay." I lifted my sweater, then paused. Pulling it back down, I said, "I thought you didn't have any money."

"I don't. But you can still take that off."

"I have more questions," I said, ignoring him.

"I'd have more answers if you'd take that off."

I got the feeling the only reason he wasn't closer to me, running his fingers up this sweater himself, was because of his injuries. They must be really bad. "I have to tell you about Garrett."

"I'm breathless with anticipation."

"He went to hell." When Reyes didn't comment, I said, "He met your dad."

He turned the bottle on the table until he could read the label. "Dad doesn't usually entertain visitors."

"He made an exception. He showed Garrett what you were like growing up. Serving in his army. Rising through the ranks. He said your father showed him what you did."

"My father showed him all this? The greatest liar the universe has ever known?"

"Are you saying what he saw wasn't true? It didn't really happen?"

After a thoughtful pause, he said, "I was a general in hell, Dutch. What do you suppose that entailed?"

I dropped my gaze to the matted carpet. "Why don't you tell me?"

"So you can hate me even more?"

I looked up in surprise. "I don't hate you."

His jaw flexed in reaction. "There is a fine line between love and hate, or haven't you heard? Sometimes it's hard to decipher exactly which emotion is strongest."

I raised my chin. "I don't love you either."

He lowered his head and watched me from underneath his dark

lashes. "Are you certain? Because the emotion pouring out of you every time I'm near you is certainly not disinterest."

"That doesn't mean it's love."

"It could be, I promise you. Take off that sweater and give me ten minutes, and you'll believe beyond a shadow of a doubt you're in love."

13

Drink coffee!
Do stupid things faster and with more energy.
—T-SHIRT

After several rounds of why I should and should not take off my sweater, I decided to give it a rest. Literally. I lay down on the bed only to discover it was straight out of an episode of *The Flintstones*. Rock-hard mattress. Rough, scratchy bedspread. Lumps where dinosaurs apparently slept. But I was tired and Reyes didn't seem to be in a hurry to get anywhere for once in his life.

I watched as he walked around the table to join me, his movements forced, painstakingly cautious as he tried to walk with as little agony as possible. I had never seen him in so much pain. His T-shirt had several large circles of blood and several smaller blotches. I didn't bother offering to take him to urgent care. He wouldn't have gone if I'd put Margaret to his head and insisted.

"Don't even think this means I'm taking off my sweater," I said.

He chuckled and lay next to me. The bed dipped minutely under his weight, and he exhaled loudly when he finally managed to settle in. I turned toward him. He lay on his back with an arm thrown over his forehead, the position both charming and sexy at the same time. His profile was that of a Greek god. Perfect dimensions. Exquisite lines.

"This bed is really hard," I said, boxing my pillow and wiggling for a more comfortable position, which was not easy with Margaret hogging the bed.

"You should straddle me. I'm harder."

My eyes flew open and I almost looked before I caught myself. I would not be baited. And he was injured, for heaven's sake. "So, next question. Why do you call me Dutch?"

He grinned from under his arm. "I don't."

I frowned at him, not that it did any good. "You call me Dutch all the time. You've always called me Dutch."

"You know, for someone who knows every language ever spoken on the planet, you're not very good at siphoning meaning when you need to."

"What do you mean?"

"Think about it."

"Fine." I thought about it. I rolled the word over in my mind and on my tongue until his meaning became clear. I gazed at him in astonishment. "Seeker. You're saying 'seeker' in ancient Aramaic." The word only sounded like *Dutch* because I'd always associated it as so. It actually had more of a *ts* sound than a *ch,* and the *u* was smoother, more drawn out.

"Bravo."

"You've been calling me 'seeker' all this time?"

"It is what you are. The seeker of souls."

"Wow." For some reason, that knowledge made me happy inside. Like a mocha latte would have if I could've afforded one. I was learning so much, I didn't want it to end. And him being too injured to storm off in his manly way and go on a quest to slay the Englishman was awesome. More time with *moi.*

"I like that," I said.

"Your elders chose well from within your race."

I smiled. Then blinked. Then frowned. "My race? I have a race?"

"Of course."

"So, wait. For real? Do I have a family like you? One from another plane?"

"Yes."

My head snapped up. I hardly expected a straight answer, much less an affirmation. "Really? I have another family?"

"Yes."

This was boggling. I didn't know what to think.

"I don't know that much about them, so don't strain too much."

"Are they . . . are they grim reapers?"

"Only the one who is chosen to cross onto this plane is a seeker. You come from a race of very powerful light bearers. They would never have sent you normally. A seeker of your . . . standing isn't sent to do such menial tasks. But you were the youngest and the most powerful among them, and they knew I was here."

It was one thing to go my entire life not knowing anything about why I had the gifts I had. It was another altogether to get so many answers— answers I'd been begging for my whole life—all in one huge gulp. And for Reyes to talk about it so casually, so nonchalantly, like it didn't mean the world to me to know about my heritage. I tried to remain calm. I could handle this with grace and dignity. Not as I wanted to, like those women on *The Price Is Right*.

Then his meaning sank in. "Wait, are you saying I was chosen because of you?"

His lids were closed behind his arm. "If I had to guess, I'd say they felt I was here to start the war. My father created me to help him bring about the end of humanity. So they sent you." He turned to me, the green and gold flecks in his eyes sparkling brightly against their rich brown background. "We are enemies, Dutch. A princess and a pawn, each from opposing sides." One corner of his sensual mouth lifted. "They would be quite disappointed knowing how we've gotten along."

I leaned up and looked down at him. "So, what? I'm supposed to kill you or something?"

He ran a fingertip over my mouth. "Yes. It is why you were sent."

"Well, that sucks." So, there's a guy hotter than a Rolex from Sal's Pawnshop living on Earth, and they send *me* to kill him? *Me?* Clearly I came from a race of crazy people.

"You could do it," he said, his mouth thinning in regret. "You could kill me. Destroy the opposing portal and cut off my father's doorway to this plane. The last reaper tried." He averted his gaze. "He failed, so they sent you."

"Reyes, that's ridiculous. I couldn't just kill you. You're way stronger than I am, and . . . and you know how to fight and crap."

Offering me an unconvinced grin, he said, "When the time comes, and it will come, do it quick. Don't hesitate, Dutch. Not even for a split second."

I had no idea how much of his story to believe. He was from a race of liars. How reliable could his intel be?

I frowned in suspicion. "Don't think that you can win me over by being all noble and charming and insisting I'm powerful enough to kill you. You pushed me," I said, reminding him of the fight the other night. "And you dragged me and shoved me, so don't think that just because you're all sweet now and self-sacrificing, I'll forget that shit." I plopped back onto my pillow and crossed my arms. "That's just not shit you forget."

His eyes shimmered with mischief in the low light. "I never claimed to be a Boy Scout."

I could feel the heat of his gaze, and all I could think was, *My god, he's beautiful.* I took the chance to assess just how badly he was injured. Raising my hands to his waist, I felt the ridges of duct tape along his rib cage and pressed gently. He sucked air in through his teeth and grabbed hold of my wrist. But blood gushed from under the tape and soaked the tips of my fingers through his shirt.

"Reyes, what the hell? What happened?"

He captured my gaze with a determined expression. "If anything happens to me, you need to know they hunt in twos. If you see one, if one comes after you, Dutch, I promise you, there is another one nearby. If you see three, there will be one more waiting in the wings. Never, ever trust them."

"Can't I just do what I did last time when I flashed my nuclear light on them?"

"No." He pulled me toward him until my forehead was on his. "While they're inside a human, they're protected from light. Even from yours."

I hated feeling so vulnerable, so paper thin. "I can't fight them, Reyes. They're too strong."

"You could if you knew how, but you aren't there yet, so don't even try. Just call your guardian and run."

I lay beside him and kept my hand on his ribs. "I'm pretty good at running. I mean, I'm not fast or anything, and I wind easily . . . never mind."

He could've been the poster boy for seriousness when he said, "There's something really motivating about having a bunch of demons on your ass."

"I'm sure there is."

"Just run and don't stop. Promise me."

"I promise I'll try to run without stopping, but I really do wind easily."

I'd managed to wrench a soft laugh out of him. He leaned in to nibble on my ear. Sharp ripples of desire shot through me at lightning-quick speed and pooled low in my abdomen. I couldn't believe it. I finally had Reyes Farrow in the flesh, alone in a hotel room, and he was bleeding profusely. I was the one who would've taken advantage of him given the chance, but now was hardly the time. And it killed me to admit that.

As his mouth moved down my neck, I wrapped my arm around his head and whispered, "Tell me a story about my ancestors. About another grim reaper."

He was quiet for so long, I thought he wouldn't oblige. Then he lay back in thought. "There was a boy named Cynric whose father took him to his village elders. The man claimed the boy was possessed. That he saw spirits and knew things no one could know. After an inquisition that lasted for days, the boy still wouldn't talk. He was stoned to death."

I cringed. "So this isn't a happy story?"

"Not many of them are. Afterwards, the village suffered a rash of sicknesses and deaths. They thought the boy had cursed them before he died."

"Did he?"

"No, another did. He'd only been repeating what his little sister had told him. She was the reaper, not the boy. But she had suffered an illness as a baby and couldn't talk. Only he could understand her." He pointed to his head. "They spoke with their minds and their hearts. In her grief, she became crazed and unleashed her powers without realizing what she was doing. A reaper does not always know what he or she is capable of until great emotional trauma."

"Did the girl live very long?"

He nodded. "Compared to most reapers, yes. Into her seventies, if I remember right. But she had to live with what she'd done. She became a recluse, and eventually insanity took hold."

"That's awful. If she was a celestial being, how could she kill so many? How could she get away with that?"

"Reapers are given agency at birth. They are the seekers of souls, but they may—" He thought a moment. "—they may, on occasion, hunt them down, for lack of a better phrase. It is their right."

"Well, that's a right I'm certainly never taking advantage of."

To lead us no longer into temptation, I tossed my pillow at his ankles, plopped my head at his booted feet, and lay perpendicular to him across the bed. He had given me so much information, I wanted some time to absorb it all, but I didn't want to leave him. Not like this. Not ever, as long as I lived. Or until I had to get back on the case. Whichever came first.

I had another family. An otherworldly family. How cool was that? And I could kill people with my mind. Okay, that part I wasn't actually buying, but I had an otherworldly family. I wondered what their names were. Maybe I had an aunt Myrtle. Or an uncle named Boaz. I'd tried to convince Uncle Bob to change his name to Boaz once, but he refused. Not sure why.

As I lay there, contemplating all the advantages of having an other-worldly family, I felt my lids grow heavy. Reyes's heat was making me sleepy. Having him close by was comforting, and I'd almost fallen asleep when he said, "You could move farther up. You'd be more comfortable if you were farther up."

I chuckled. "No, *you'd* be more comfortable if I were farther up. Perv."

And before I knew it, I was dreaming of Reyes and beaches and Cookie-a-ritas with little umbrellas brushing across my palm. That's when I felt Reyes's fingers brush across my palm. I wondered if he'd done it on purpose. When he rolled on top of me with a growl, pinning me down with his immense weight, I was pretty sure he had. But before I could protest, his mouth was at my ear.

"Shhh," he said, his breath warm. At first I thought he was just frisky, but he seemed rigid, tense, ready to strike. Or beat the crap out of me. What the hell?

I started to struggle, but then felt his fingers at my palm again. Only this time the heat of his touch was instantly replaced by the cool metal of a gun. I stiffened as he unholstered Margaret and tucked her into my hand.

"What—?"

I didn't get far before his mouth was on mine. But while his mouth performed a magic spell, his tongue pushing past my lips, rendering me useless, his hands were doing something else. Then I felt the long cool metal of a knife as he pulled it out of the back of his waistband. He returned his mouth to my ear and whispered, "Call the dog."

My pulse skyrocketed. "Why?" I asked, my voice nothing but a breathless whisper.

He lifted just enough to look into my eyes, his own full of an unspoken apology. "Because this isn't my room."

He kissed me again, his mouth hot on mine, and yet every muscle in his body was stretched taut with eagerness. His heart raced on top of mine, his pulse roaring in my ears. I put my hand over the side of the bed and snapped my fingers.

Artemis lifted into my palm, materializing out of the ground, and nuzzled my hand for a split second before pricking her ears. A low growl rumbled from her chest as the door eased open. She lowered onto her haunches and waited.

The door pivoted slowly, then stopped at a forty-five-degree angle. Not enough for me to make out the intruders. All I could see past Reyes's shoulder was a hand on the doorknob. The intruder started forward a heartbeat before Artemis attacked. With a bark that vibrated against the walls, she bound forward through the half-open door and onto a possessed woman, if the feminine scream was any indication.

Reyes's weight vanished, and in the next heartbeat, another assailant crashed into the room after having been thrown there. The door banged against the wall, and I could see the woman struggling with Artemis on the sidewalk, fighting something she clearly couldn't see in its entirety. Even I had a problem staying focused on Artemis's huge body as she ripped the offending soul out of her.

But before I could see exactly what happened to the demon, the one Reyes was fighting spotted me. He let out a shriek of rage and fought Reyes's hold to get to me. It was the strangest sensation, to be wanted so desperately by a man who took no heed of the fact that his spine was bent so far out of position, it started to crack under the pressure. I could hear the sharp snaps of bones breaking, of tendons ripping and vertebrae dislodging, yet the man couldn't take his eyes off me. He wanted me so passionately, his free arm stretched out, his eyes begging me to come closer.

And they were blue. The man's eyes. I could just make out the demon behind them, the smoky black essence wafting off him, but the host the creature had possessed had blue eyes. So clear, they looked like a swimming pool sparkling on a hot summer day. And they watered as the pressure Reyes was placing on his throat cut off his air supply. But still he didn't care. He clawed his way toward me with one arm, the other having been broken. It lay limp on the ground beside him, useless.

As he lunged for me in one last valiant effort, his reach appeared to lengthen. Black, razor-sharp claws appeared out of the man's hand. The darkness of night did nothing to deter the demon from unmasking himself, from reaching out. I could see only his hand, but I knew at least that part of him was unprotected.

I leaned over the side of the bed, ignoring Reyes as he yelled at me to get back, the claw so close, centimeters away. One more ounce of effort, and he'd shred my face. I held out my hand, palm up, leaned in, and blew. As though blowing magic fairy dust, particles of light from inside me floated toward the demon, landed on his claw, and in one great burst of energy, he screamed and stumbled out of his human host.

Writhing in agony, the demon thrashed along the ground, his high-pitched cries like a thousand jet engines taking off.

Artemis pounced in the next instant, sank her teeth, locked her jaw, and ripped the life out of the beast. Killing it was almost an act of compassion at that point, it was in so much pain. I watched as its thick gaseous blood spilled onto the floor, then evaporated.

Before I realized he was angry, Reyes jerked me to my feet and looked me over from head to toe. Then he focused on my face, his own picture of astonishment. "What the fuck was that?" he asked, anger sharpening his voice.

But adrenaline rushed down my spine and through my body. I looked past him toward Artemis. She was busy sniffing the room with the enthusiasm of a hunting dog on the trail of a fox, certain she'd found the scent of another demon. She jumped through the wall into the next room before I could call her back.

Afraid I was going to be sick again, as that seemed to be my MO lately, I stumbled past him toward the miniscule bathroom near the door. He picked me up when I tripped, but I fought his hold and hurtled myself toward the toilet. The fact that I was spelunking in a porcelain bowl used for years by men with bad aim didn't deter me from my mission. I gulped stale air and swallowed back bile as my stomach heaved unsteadily.

Reyes knelt beside me, and I felt a cool cloth at the back of my neck.

"That's what's driving them crazy." He leaned forward and buried his face against my neck. "The scent of fear—your fear—is like the scent of heroin to a bona fide addict."

"Well, I can't help it," I said.

"I know. It's my fault, and I'm sorry."

I looked up and realized for the first time that the demon had struck him. He had three bloody gashes across his face, the uppermost a mere centimeter from his lower lashes. I took the washcloth from him and dabbed at the cuts.

"Did you kill him?" I asked.

"No. He won't be running marathons anytime soon, but we need to get out of here."

Reyes accompanied me home in silence, probably unsure what to think of me. I wasn't sure what to think of me either, so we didn't really have a lot to think about. He saw me up the stairs and to my door, but I didn't let him help me in. I was tired of suddenly being an invalid, unable to walk and chew gum at the same time.

I opened my door and stepped inside. "Can I put something on that?" I asked, indicating the cuts on his left cheek. He dabbed them with the hem of his T-shirt, sopping up the small rivulets of blood that had escaped. They were already healing, but antibiotic ointment wouldn't hurt.

He ignored me and looked around my apartment. "Call your boy," he said, his tone coarse.

"What boy?" I asked, suddenly very tired. "I don't have a boy." At least I didn't think I had a boy. I couldn't remember ever being in labor, and I was fairly certain that wasn't something a girl could easily forget.

"That kid that always hangs around. Call him."

"Angel?" I asked, and as soon as I thought it, in he popped.

He looked around in surprise, spotted me, then glared from underneath his bandanna. "Are you for real going to keep doing that?"

"Hey, it wasn't even me this time." I pointed to Reyes, and Angel's bravado dwindled.

He took a step back as Reyes took a step forward.

"Stay here," Reyes said to him in a tone that brooked no argument.

But he was talking to Angel Garza. The kid had never met an argument he didn't like. He bit down and squared his shoulders. "You stay here, *pendejo.*"

Reyes was on him before I saw him move. He had Angel by the collar of his dirty T-shirt, his face inches from his own. "Do you have any idea what I can do to you?"

Angel's eyes widened before he caught himself. "I know you can go back to hell."

I struggled to get in between them, pushing at Reyes's hold.

After a moment, Reyes released him and offered him an apologetic gaze. "Stay here for her," he said, softening his tone.

With a shrug, Angel straightened his shirt and said, "For her."

That seemed to satisfy him. He snapped his fingers like calling a dog, and Artemis appeared. She jumped on him, her huge paws leveraging her weight against his chest as her stubby tail wagged in delight. He rubbed behind her ears and nuzzled her neck.

"You stay here," he said into her ear, "and don't let her get into any trouble. Got it?"

When he raised his brows in question, she barked in affirmation, and I suddenly felt very outnumbered.

I frowned at her. "Traitor."

She barked again, completely unmoved by my accusation, and jumped to play with Angel, easily tackling him to the ground. Angel laughed and tried to get her in a chokehold. It was odd how her jaw could open to accommodate the girth of his throat. His gurgling screams of agony seemed to make her happy, and that was good enough for me.

"I just need to make sure they didn't follow us here," he said.

"You should really let me take a look at your wounds."

"The last time you looked at my wounds, you almost passed out."

"That was a long time ago."

"Two months. Give or take."

"Fine," I said, sending him off with a wave. "Go do your cool manly things while I stay home under the ever-watchful eye of a gurgling thirteen-year-old gangbanger."

There was something so wrong with that picture.

I awoke to the cool sensation of a hundred-pound departed Rottweiler sprawled over me as though I were a human mattress. I wasn't really alarmed by the fact that her right paw covered my face almost completely, cutting off my flow of oxygen, or the fact that my legs had gone numb as her shoulder was wedged into my hip bone, but more by the fact that as her head hung over my ribs, she was snoring. Really? Even in death? Snoring just seemed superfluous for some reason.

I had so much to think about—demons, my heritage, my apparent long-term commitment as the grim reaper, a contract I did not remember signing—but nothing beyond the thought of coffee penetrated my cranium. And oxygen. And the fact that I had to pee like a champion racehorse. There was an odd pressure on my bladder that went by the name of Artemis.

I moved a gigantic paw off my face and wiggled out from under the Rottweiler with herculean effort. When I landed on the floor, her head hung off the side of the bed, but she had yet to wake up. I couldn't help it. I leaned in to nuzzle her whiskers. Her lip twitched and formed a snarl every time I kissed her nose. She would have made a great Elvis impersonator.

I managed to get to my feet and make it to the bathroom. After a quick pit stop and a rendezvous with Mr. Coffee, I sneaked to the living room window, careful not to disturb Angel or Aunt Lil as they lay crashed on varying articles of furniture. It still amazed me that the departed slept. Especially with all the hammering going on next door.

Even through the noise of construction, I'd heard a truck pull up. It was too early for a delivery truck to be at Dad's bar, so my curiosity got the better of me. Maybe it was my new neighbors, though that would be silly, as their apartment was still being renovated. My digs could use some renovating. I'd have to talk to Mr. Z later. Convince him new countertops would add to the value of the whole building.

Surprisingly, there was a moving van outside, but it was pulled up to the back of the bar. With curiosity piqued, I hurried to my bedroom window for a better view. Yep, someone was moving in. I looked at the second-floor windows and gasped. Aloud. A man was opening the blinds and dusting off the sills as though readying the place for a new tenant.

In *my* offices.

My father was renting out my offices right out from under me. I was appalled. Offended. And more than a little ticked. After a quick wardrobe check—surely plaid boxers, a T-shirt that proclaimed that I was cooler than refrigerated air, and pink bunny slippers would do for a quick trip across the alley—I put my coffee cup down and headed to my dad's bar. The more I thought about it, the faster I walked. And the faster I walked, the angrier I became.

A crisp wind whipped around me when I exited my building, but I ignored it. My father was renting out my offices. Of all the gall.

I strode past two men struggling to offload a desk and ducked into the bar through the back door.

"Dad!" I yelled, stalking past my startled stepmother, who'd just come in from the front. She'd apparently brought the traitor breakfast. I could only hope he'd choke on it. And past Sienna, the gorgeous new bartender who'd hit on Pari. She wore an appreciative grin when she noticed my boxers.

Gemma stepped out of Dad's office just as I got there, her face a picture of surprise. "Charley, you're not dressed."

"Where is he?" I asked, stepping past her.

"Dad? He's upstairs, I think."

If I'd been in my right mind, I might have paid heed when the tiniest hint of a smirk flitted across her face, I might have caught on to the fact that all was not as it seemed, but I was on a mission. I turned and took the stairs two at a time. Not the easiest thing to do in bunny slippers. And the long leaps caused my boxers to wedge into unmentionable places, but a quick readjustment once I reached the landing set things right.

I stormed into the first office, the one that had been mine for over two years, and found Dad looking out the window with the raised blinds. His tall lean form had been draped in a plaid button-down and wrinkled khakis that looked two sizes too big, and his normally tan, healthy skin had the pale matte texture of blanched flour that just matched his dark blond hair.

No one else was inside. Everything I'd left was exactly where I'd left it. Not a file cabinet or bookshelf out of place.

I stopped behind him and jammed my hands on my hips. "Really?" I asked.

He bowed his head, and I blocked his emotions the minute the sorrow that had consumed him hit me. I breathed deep and shook it off. He'd had me arrested as I lay in a hospital bed. He didn't deserve my sympathy. But he did deserve the brunt of my anger.

"You're renting out my offices? Just like that?" I snapped my fingers to emphasize the hastiness of his actions. I'd been out of them two months, but for some reason, that didn't seem to be the point.

He turned to me at last, looking more haggard than usual. His Popsicle-stick frame seemed bent with fatigue. His clothes sat askew.

I didn't care. I did. Not. Care.

"No, sweetheart, I'm not."

I pointed a finger toward the window. "Then what is that?"

"A ploy," he said, his voice so matter-of-fact, it took a moment for his words to sink in. "A ruse," he continued.

I looked out the window and realized the moving van was completely empty except for the desk. The men below gave my dad an official salute before reloading the desk and sliding the door closed.

Turning back to him, I asked, "What are you talking about? A ploy for what?"

"For you," he said, stepping closer.

I stepped back, suddenly wary.

He took another step but stopped when I offered him my infamous death stare. "You won't take my calls," he said, raising his palms in surrender. "You won't answer your door when I go over."

"Gosh, I wonder why." I turned to leave, but his next statement stopped me dead in my tracks.

"I didn't know how much time I had."

"What?" I asked, suspicion evident in the sharp tone of my voice.

"When I had you arrested, I didn't know how much time I had. I just wanted you out, and I had to do it quick."

With annoyance and zero patience guiding me, I opened my arms in helplessness then dropped them again. "I have no idea what you're talking about."

"I just wanted to do right by you. I just wanted to make up for what I'd done. I got you into this life. I wanted to get you out of it before it was too late."

"So you had me arrested? That was your solution?"

"You can't be a private investigator with a record. Your license would have been revoked." He shrugged. "Mission accomplished."

The smile that slid across my face held anything but humor. "Thanks for having my back, Dad. Appreciate it."

"You left me no choice."

"What?" My voice rose to just below screaming level. "I left you no choice? Are you psychotic?"

"I tried to get you to open up to me, but you don't trust me. You never have. And I didn't know what else to do. I was trying to right a wrong. It's my fault you do what you do. I got you into this, and I just wanted you out of it. Out of danger. When bad guys come after you because of me . . . I'd been pretending up to that point. But I couldn't pretend any longer."

"Well, you picked a fine time to grow a conscience, Dad. As I lay in a hospital bed after being tortured almost to death, you have me arrested." I gave him two thumbs up. "Good call."

He dropped his gaze. "I had no other choice."

"You know what?" I said, stepping toward him. I poked a finger into his chest. "I've thought a lot about how I've always seen you. You were my rock. The only one who believed in me, in my abilities. I always thought you were on my side. But then it hit me. All those years you put up with Denise, with the way she treated me, and instead of defending me, you looked the other way. You never stood up for me. You just reaped the benefits of my ability, but you stood by and let that witch run me into the ground every chance she got."

He looked past me, and I turned to see said witch standing in the doorway, her mouth open in surprise.

I pointed to her and nodded at him. "Yes, that one." When he refrained from comment, I asked, "Did you ever really care about me?"

He snapped to attention in surprise. "Of course, I did. I always have. I just thought—" His voice broke, and he covered his mouth with a fist.

"Make it good," I said, my tone more warning than suggestion.

"You girls needed a mother."

"And you gave us that?" I stepped closer—so close, my image shimmered in the tears pooling between his lashes. "You didn't have my back. You had yours. Go ahead. Rent out my office. I don't care."

Since Denise stood blocking my escape route, I decided to go through the next office and out the front door.

But just as I turned the knob, he said, "I need to know you'll be okay when I'm gone."

In one last valiant effort, I turned back to him, a very clever and timely comeback sitting on the tip of my razor-sharp tongue, but it stayed there, because in the next instant, Dad raised a gun and shot me.

14

Or, well, shot *at* me.

I ducked. Not sure why. But ducking when being shot at seemed like the right thing to do. Used to be, I could slow time, I could literally see the bullet hanging in midair, but since being tortured, I seemed to have lost that ability, because Dad fired and I ducked without even trying.

I fell to my knees and covered my head, then turned to look at Dad from underneath my arms.

He was still holding the gun, a stunned expression on his face.

"Leland!" Denise shouted seconds before plastering her hands over her mouth in shock. Had to give her kudos for the effort.

After taking inventory of my vital parts and feeling no pain, I jumped to my feet. Gemma ran up then and squeezed behind Denise to get into the room. She was quickly followed by Sienna, who was holding a pot of coffee in her hands.

I realized the world was spinning. The sound had sent adrenaline rocketing through my system.

After patting myself down for injuries with shaking hands, I screamed at my dad. "What the hell was that?" But he was still holding the gun on me. He seemed to have slipped into a mild state of shock. "Dad!" I said, trying to get his attention. "It is so official. You are a bad father. Good fathers do *not* shoot their daughters!" I crossed my arms and brought out the big guns. "I am so telling Mom when I die."

"What happened?" Gemma asked, looking from me to Dad.

I pointed to him. "He tried to kill me. That's what happened."

"Dad!" she said, scolding him like one would a child who'd just eaten a bug.

"No, you don't understand." He focused on her just as Uncle Bob rushed in, shoving past Denise. Great. The whole gang was here to witness my murder.

Dad looked back at me, his jaw open. "Watch this."

He fired again.

I ducked again. And fought the dizzying effects of an adrenaline rush that sent me to the brink of unconsciousness. According to evolution, that was not what adrenaline was supposed to do. It was supposed to make me wet my pants, then run really fast as though a bear were attacking. Passing out was so un-Darwinian.

Uncle Bob had his pistol out and pointed at Dad's head before I could say, "What the fuck?"

I'd fallen onto my knees again. The crack of thunder from the gun jolted through me so hard and fast, I felt like the breath had been knocked out of my lungs. I stumbled to my feet as the spin of the world blurred my vision and turned my stomach. I was going to be sick. My body quaked from the inside out. I swallowed hard, trying to keep down the small amount of coffee I'd had earlier.

I felt a heat rush across my skin and looked to my left. Reyes materialized beside me, his massive black robe undulating and making the world sway even more. I felt like a boat on high seas.

He looked from beneath his hood toward Dad, then back at me. "Why is your father trying to kill you?"

I swallowed again and braced myself against the wall at my back. "I have no idea." When he started toward him, I hurried forward to cut him off, stepping in between them. "Oh, no, you don't. He is off-limits, do you understand?"

He took my arm and pulled me into his robes. The scalding heat soothed despite my anger. "Get a handle on this, or I'll kill him where he stands."

I pushed away from him and pointed toward the window. "Out. Now."

With a low growl, he dematerialized, but I could feel him close. He hadn't gone far, and he could materialize and sever Dad's spine before I could cry foul. I had to defuse this situation and do it fast, or my dad would never be able to walk again. Or quite possibly breathe.

After gathering myself, I realized everyone was looking at me. Most likely because I was talking to air. They could just deal with it. We had bigger fish to fry. But the look on their faces stopped me in my tracks. They'd seen me talk to air before. Well, everyone but Sienna. I couldn't imagine that causing the level of shock they were displaying.

Sienna dropped the carafe. It landed with a thud on the floor, and coffee slushed over the sides, but not a single gaze wavered away from me.

"What?" I asked, suddenly self-conscious. I looked down to make sure my boxers were in place. They seemed fine to me. I scanned the faces again. Even though Uncle Bob was holding a gun to my father's head, he was looking at me. Just like everyone else.

Dad lowered the gun. The movement caught Ubie's attention. He turned back to him. "Drop it, Leland."

He did. The gun fell to the floor, but nobody seemed to care. All eyes stayed locked on me. Slowly, and with deliberate care, Uncle Bob kneeled down and picked up the gun, but he looked away for only the split second it took him to grab it.

This was getting weird.

"How did you do that?" Gemma asked.

"What?" I asked, completely confused. "Almost get shot by my own father?" When everyone continued to gape, I decided now was a good time for a rant. "It really wasn't that hard. I just kind of stood here while a crazy man pointed a gun at me—"

"They were blanks."

I refocused on him. "You tried to kill me with blanks?"

"Yes." He nodded, then caught himself and shook his head. "No, I mean—"

"Isn't that counterproductive?"

"The way you moved," he continued, his voice thick with disbelief. "It wasn't real. Nobody can move like that."

"What do you mean?" I asked, growing angry. Did nobody care that my own father just tried to kill me?

He walked up to me and tried to touch my face, but I blocked his hand and stepped out of his reach. He didn't pursue it. Instead he asked, "What are you?"

"Besides pissed?"

"Charley," Gemma said, her voice taking on that gentle therapist tone she was so fond of, "look where you are."

I glanced around and realized she was right. I had been at the door, and now I was at the windows facing the alley. I shrugged. "So I lunged out of the way. So what? I was being shot at."

"But you didn't," Gemma said. "You were here, then you were there. You—" She paused as though unable to come up with the right words. "You moved so fast. It's like you disappeared, then reappeared. I've never seen anything like it."

"I had to know," Dad said. "I had to know you'd be okay. I knew you were different, but I had no idea just how different. Then when Caruso tied me up and went after you with that knife . . . the way you moved. It was like nothing I'd ever seen." Caruso had been one of Dad's collars. He'd sent the man to prison for a very long time. The minute he was paroled, he came after Dad, and in periphery, me. "That's when I realized how special you really are."

I was still fighting the effects of adrenaline rushing through my nervous system, and trying not to seize. "I cannot imagine how you thought that shooting me would be a good idea." I turned to leave, but Uncle Bob stopped me.

"Charley, hon, I need to know if you want to press charges."

A malicious smile spread over my face before I said, "No. Not today. I don't want to have anything else to do with him."

I shoved my way past Denise and plowed down the stairs.

"Charley, wait," Gemma said behind me.

I kept walking. "I am writing a letter to Mom about this."

"Good," she said, trying to catch up. "That's perfect, but there's something you need to know before you get too carried away."

I'd made it all the way to the front door of my building before she caught up with me. "I know," I said, my throat closing in on itself. "I felt it the minute I walked up there."

She took deep, even breaths and said, "He doesn't know how much longer he has."

I turned away from her, refusing to acknowledge the sting in my eyes. "How long have you known?"

"Couple of months. He wouldn't let anyone tell you. He wanted to do it himself, but you wouldn't take his calls."

I crossed my arms, still unable to face her. "I'm still telling Mom."

She stepped behind me and wrapped her arms around my neck. "Tell her hi for me, too."

After leaning my head on her bony elbow, I said, "Okay, but I don't think she likes you as much as she likes me."

Gemma laughed and squeezed me tighter.

Up at the penthouse, Cookie came barreling in as I stood pouring myself a cup of coffee, her eyes wide with worry. When she spotted me, relief washed over her. She walked up, panting with one hand on her chest. "I couldn't find you," she said between pants. "And all your stuff was here. I thought you got killed. Or abducted again."

"Sorry. Here I am."

She held up a finger, swallowed hard, then said, "Charley, I swear you're going to be the death of me."

"Don't be ridiculous. Why would I kill you? You work for next to nothing."

She nodded. "That's a good point."

"I was just over at the office. Dad tried to shoot me. Twice. So Uncle Bob pulled a gun. That man is way faster than he looks."

Her eyes widened again. Then they narrowed in disbelief. Then widened yet again. Then narrowed. Then they did this little mushy thing as she tried to wrap her head around what I'd said. Then they widened some more. Then narrowed. And as entertaining as her eye movements were, I was in my boxers.

"Okay, so I'm going to take a shower. You let that sink in."

"How did the offices look?" she finally asked, and I knew she missed them.

"They are really nice since Bobby Joe refinished them. I like the soft taupe he chose."

"It's so weird that he thought his girlfriend was trying to kill him with peanuts."

"I know, right?" I took my coffee cup and headed that way. "It would have made more sense if he'd had a peanut allergy."

After I got rid of Angel, telling him his shift was up, I took a quick shower and went over my agenda for the day. We weren't any closer to finding out who Harper's stalker was, and that saddened me, but I still had several leads to check out. Cook had already obtained the list of nonresident visitors at the Tanoan Estates, and none of them coincided with anyone from Harper's past that we could deduce.

She also hit me with an address on the Lowells' long-term housekeeper who'd recently retired. I figured I'd start there, then go to the abandoned mental asylum and check on my friend Rocket. I hadn't seen him in a while.

"I also have a list of everyone who worked for the Lowells when they were married," Cookie said as I munched on the breakfast of champions, leftover brownies, "but not many of them worked there for more than a couple of years. Their driver still works for them, and their live-in housekeeper worked for them up until a couple of weeks ago."

"Right, their new housekeeper told me that much."

"Took me a while to track her down. She worked for the Lowells for almost thirty years. You'd think they would know where she lived. I had to ask Donald."

"Donald?" I asked, injecting a purr of interest into my voice. "You're on a first-name basis with Donald?"

"Pffft. He's the Lowells' driver, he's the only one who would give me a microsecond of his time, and he sounds ninety if he's a day."

"Maybe he's a smoker. If he's still their driver—"

"Sorry. *Former* driver. Now he just takes care of their cars or something. He said they just keep him around because they feel sorry for him."

"Interesting. Did you find out anything else?"

She batted her lashes. "Well, he's a Gemini, likes long walks on the beach, and is very attracted to men in kilts."

I swallowed the last bite of brownie and chased it with a shot of luke-warm java juice. "That's so weird. I'm attracted to men in kilts, too." I elbowed her. "Can I get Donald's number in case I have any questions?"

"You wouldn't move in on my territory, would you?"

I gasped and put an innocent hand on my even innocenter chest. "I would never."

She ignored me. "So, after you interview the housekeeper, you're going to check on Rocket?" she asked, a knowing grin lighting her face.

Rocket was an invaluable resource when it came to finding out who had passed and who was still kicking. A departed savant who knew the names of every person who ever lived on Earth, Rocket could give me their status updates in seconds flat. And he was big and adorable and loved to hug. Hard.

But Cook wasn't talking about Rocket, if that mischievous twinkle in her eye was any indication.

"Yes," I said, memorizing the address of the housekeeper she gave me.

"And what about Rocket's neighbors? Going to check on them, too?"

I crooked a brow. "I do have a weakness for guys on Harleys."

She wagged an index finger at me, teasing. "Just say no."

"You don't understand," I said before heading that way. "It's a really strong weakness."

I drove to the housekeeper's residence on the south side, trying not to obsess about the fact that my father had tried to shoot me. Twice. The housekeeper lived in an older part of town. Many of the houses were considered almost historical and they were well kept, as was Mrs. Beecher's.

After I knocked on the door, I took a moment to appreciate the beautiful flowers on her front porch. They were purple. That was about as categorical as I got. A squat elderly woman with light gray hair and soft gray eyes opened the wooden door but stayed put behind the screen of the storm door. The top of her head barely reached my chin, and she had to look up at me.

"Hi, Mrs. Beecher?"

"Yes?" she said, wiping her hands on a dish towel. She wore a floral dress that looked like it'd had more than its fair share of washings.

"I'm so sorry to bother you. My name is Charley Davidson." I held up my ID. "I'm a private investigator, and I was hired to look into a case involving your former employer, the Lowells?"

Her heartbeat skyrocketed and her mouth did this little twitch thing where it thinned for just a microsecond before she caught herself. Then she plastered on her best poker face.

"Look, I understand it's frowned upon to be talking about the Lowells. You were in their employ for many years. But I have their express permission to question their staff," I said, lying through my whitening-stripped teeth. The Lowells had a strong hold on their staff. Mrs. Lowell was a tyrant if I ever saw one.

"Oh, all right, then," she said, seeming to calm. "What can help you with?"

She continued to talk to me through the screen, clearly not wanting me to enter. Poor thing.

"I understand you worked for the Lowells for almost thirty years. Can you tell me anything about their daughter, Harper?"

Her heartbeat skyrocketed again, and she glanced around as though wondering if she were being watched. Just as her replacement had when I tried to question her at the Lowells' mansion.

"I really can't say much. She was very disturbed and they had a lot of problems with her, but that's all I can tell you."

"Yes, I've heard. Do you remember when it all started?"

She glanced at the dish towel in her hands. Fear radiated off her in waves. "It seemed to start right after Mr. and Mrs. Lowell got married."

I nodded. "Did you notice anything suspicious at that time?" I couldn't help but wonder if Harper's stalker wasn't an employee, maybe even a disgruntled one. "Did the Lowells hire anyone new around that time? Or maybe someone quit?"

A thought dawned. I could see it in her expression. But she dismissed it with a frown.

"Mrs. Beecher, anything you can tell me will help, no matter how small you think it is."

She drew in a long draft of air. "It's nothing. I just remembered that Felix started right before the wedding."

"Felix?" I asked, taking out my memo pad and pen.

"Felix Navarro. He kept their lawns for years and—" She paused in thought.

"And?" I asked.

When she refocused on me, her expression was full of regret, like she hated to vocalize her suspicions. "And, well, he liked Ms. Harper. Very much."

"How much?"

"H-he carried pictures of her in his wallet. Several pictures."

Okay, that was creepy. I couldn't help the accusation that crept into my voice. "You don't think he was doing anything—"

"Oh, goodness no," she said, cutting me off with a wave of the dish towel. "Not at all. He was just . . . well, he was very fond of her."

I'll bet. "Thank you," I said, offering her a reassuring smile. "You've been very helpful."

She bowed her head as though ashamed she'd said anything and closed the wooden door.

After making a phone call to have Cook check out the gardener who was fond of little girls and carried pictures of them around in his wallet, I pulled around the side of a mental asylum that had been abandoned in the fifties. I'd found Rocket there when I discovered a love for exploring such mental asylums in college. Partly because of my fondness for old buildings but mostly because of my fondness for departed mental patients. They knew the secrets of the universe, each and every one, and I could talk to them for hours on end. It beat the heck out of homework.

Surprised to discover an abandoned asylum smack-dab in the middle of Albuquerque, I cased the joint for a couple of days, then went in one night when the moon was full of glow-in-the-dark chalk and my belly was full of a cheap, nondescript wine. As I stumbled around the place, oohing and aahing at the forgotten equipment, wondering exactly what one would do with an instrument that looked like garden sheers, there stood Rocket.

I wasn't sure which of us was more surprised by the presence of the other, but once I assured him I was not there to steal his checkers, we became fast friends. However, because of Rocket's minimalist approach to the whole attention-span thing, it took me several visits to discover anything definitive about him. I did find out that he'd died in the fifties. He also had a sister who'd died during the Dust Bowl. She kept him company at the asylum, but I had yet to meet her.

Oddly enough, a local biker gang, the Bandits, owned the asylum in which Rocket lived, and they lived next door. I'd sneaked past them for years despite their tendency to have a slew of Rottweilers on duty at any given time, but the leader, a rough-and-tough type who went by the name of Donovan, had recently given me a key to the place. I had yet to use it, but today seemed like the perfect day to try it out.

And yet I seemed unable to just pull up to the front door. I'd always pulled around the side and hidden Misery behind a Dumpster so I could sneak in without announcing my presence. Apparently that habit was hard to break. After locking her up tight, I patted Misery's fender and went in search of the mighty Rocket. Or I would have had my interest not been piqued by the goings-on behind the Bandits' headquarters.

I looked through the ivy covering a chain-link fence and could just see the back area of the Bandits' yard, where they had an old attached garage. They'd always had a plethora of bikes and parts scattered around the cinder-blocked area, but there was a van parked out back and several guys dressed all in black loading nylon duffel bags into it. Among the guys in black were Donovan and his two sidekicks: Michael, a Brando-esque kind of guy who could look cool in a tutu; and Eric, a tall kid who looked more like a Greek prince than like a biker. But what struck me as most odd was the fact that they were all dressed exactly alike. Eric and Donovan wore black bandannas around their necks, but other than that, there were four men total and one woman with black long-sleeve shirts and black military-style pants. They all wore leather gloves as well and were either wearing sunglasses or had them propped on top of their heads. That was taking the biker club colors to a whole new level, in my opinion. But to each his own.

Still, there was something about their shape. I looked at the three main guys: Donovan, the leader, and his seconds, Michael and Eric. Tall, medium-tall, and just plain medium.

Surely not.

I'd almost left my hiding place and started for the asylum when something fell out of one of the duffel bags. I studied it as Eric picked it up and stuffed it back into the bag, and my heart sank. A white rubber mask. Just like the guys who had been on the news all over the county. Robbing banks. I knew those guys on the video surveillance footage had looked familiar. Of all the asinine hobbies.

How could I have been so wrong about them? They were good guys. I felt it the moment I met them. True, I'd been on the ground and Donovan had propped a boot on my stomach to keep me there, but deep down inside, they had hearts of gold.

I eased back behind Misery and thought about what I should do. I could try to talk them out of it, but I didn't really want to die anytime soon. And they'd clearly been doing this for a while. I could turn them in, but what if I were wrong? Maybe they had a perfectly good explanation for why they were dressed exactly like the infamous bank robbers the Gentlemen Thieves. Maybe they were going to a theme party where the attendees dressed like their favorite villains. Bikers did tend to have some off-the-wall parties. But at ten o'clock in the morning?

Ten o'clock in the morning was prime bank-robbing time.

Damn it.

The van roared to life, and I stepped back to the fence. Donovan tossed something to Eric just before the kid slid the side door closed; then the scruffy leader looked around to make sure no one was watching before jumping in the passenger's side.

That's when a plan formed. I would follow them. If they really were just going to a theme party, I'd go in and tell them what I'd thought and we'd all have a good laugh. But if they robbed a bank, I'd have to come up with another plan. There was no getting around it.

I hopped in Misery and did my best to keep up with them without looking like I was doing my best to keep up with them. For the first time since I got her, I cursed Misery's cherry red exterior. Black would have been better. Or better yet, pavement gray. Then I'd really blend. I'd never longed for an invisibility cloak as much as I did at that moment.

When they pulled up to the Bernalillo Community Bank, I was still hopeful they were just withdrawing extra cash for the party. Someone had to pay for the chips and beer. I parked across the street and waited. They sat idling for a few seconds before bursting out of the van in full bank-robber attire, complete with white masks and semiautomatic weapons.

I let my head drop onto the steering wheel and sat in misery, literally, wondering what to do. Today was just not my day. Between my dad trying to kill me, Reyes trying to kill my dad, and the hottest biker dudes I'd ever met turning out to be notorious bank robbers, I wondered why I'd ever left my apartment. I was just fine there. I liked it there. It was warm and cozy in the same way a prison cell was cozy, but at least no one was shooting at me and no one was robbing it. Not that I knew of.

Wait. Maybe I could still talk them out of it. Maybe if Donovan knew that I knew, he'd be embarrassed and put a stop to the whole thing.

And maybe Charles Manson really was just a misunderstood poet.

But it was worth a shot. I mean, we were friends. Friends didn't shoot friends. Apparently fathers did, but friends were a different story altogether.

I left Margaret in Misery and hurried across the street, past the idling van, and into the bank as stealthily as I could. Which wasn't very. The place was being robbed, so it wasn't difficult to spot a new patron stepping inside. I zeroed in on Donovan instantly. The cool thing was, not one of them had his gun drawn. Fortunately, that didn't seem necessary. Donovan was busy keeping his eyes on the security guard and the patrons who were facedown on the floor. They were so going to be traumatized and I felt bad for them in that regard, but I was still thrilled Donovan wasn't pointing a gun at them, threatening to blow their heads off. That was much more traumatizing in the long run.

The others were seeing to the cash drawers and the vault, and one of them was standing on the tellers' counter, keeping watch. It was Eric. He spotted me and stilled. I thought about smiling and waving but didn't want to look like a *complete* idiot.

When I looked back at Donovan, he was watching me, his arms crossed at his chest, his head tilted to the side as though asking me, *What the fuck?*

I wondered that, too, as I stepped over patrons to get to him.

"Sorry," I said when I stepped on a woman's skirt. Then I tripped on a man's arm. "Sorry," I repeated. When I finally got to Donovan, I did that fake smile thing so I could talk without moving my lips. No idea why. "You're a bank robber?" I asked through clenched teeth, looking around nonchalantly.

Eric, the youngest and tallest of the crew, jumped from the counter and landed solidly next to us. He eased around me, crowded into me, dipped his head until his mouth was at my ear. "Don't we need a hostage?" he asked, his words breathy with adrenaline. I could hear the smile in his voice.

Donovan kept tabs on the room with quick, sharp glances that landed on me at regular intervals. He looked at his watch. "Fifteen seconds!" he yelled before refocusing on me. At least I think he did. It was hard to see past the rubber mask. "I think you're right."

Before I could protest, he turned me around and put one arm around my throat and one around my waist.

I rolled my eyes. "You have got to be kidding me," I said, my teeth still clenched.

"This is going to be fun," Eric said.

"Could you do your job?" Donovan asked him.

"Oh, right." He jumped back and started grabbing the nylon duffel bags that one of the others had brought out of the vault. I couldn't believe that a bank that size carried that much cash. Sirens blared in the distance, and I wondered if I should be relieved or worried. It was a strange feeling. I was on the side of the law. I worked as a consultant for the Albuquerque Police Department. Surely my participation in a bank robbery would look bad. But adrenaline was coursing through my veins, and I couldn't help but wish they'd hurry the heck up.

As the guys started filing out, Michael swaggered up to us. I could tell it was him because no one did swagger like Michael. "A hostage," he said, offering me a nod in greeting. "Cool." Then he walked out to the van like he hadn't a care in the world.

Oh, yeah. These guys were crazy with a side of fries.

Donovan dragged me along behind him, following the others out the door, his hold tight enough to pull my entire length against him. He was such a perv.

"Sorry," I said as I tripped on the guy's arm again. He glared up at me, but really, he saw us coming. He should have moved his freaking arm. It was hard being half-dragged backwards across a floor of bank patrons. And I'd never been accused of being sure-footed. He had to know that after our first encounter.

I clutched at Donovan's arm and said, "This is not winning you any brownie points, mister."

When we got to the door, Donovan whispered into my ear, "Nice to see you, too, beautiful."

I started to respond, but he jerked me out the door and shoved me into the van. I landed in a heap among boots and bags of money. And I was broke. I blinked and looked at them longingly for exactly two-point-seven seconds before reality struck. I couldn't take stolen money. Not even if I lived to see another sunrise, which wasn't super-likely if all the white faces staring down at me were any indication.

The van peeled out and took a sharp curve, sending me crashing between a pair of legs. I fought for balance and pretended the moment
wasn't awkward in the least as I turned back to Donovan. He was on his
knees, keeping perfect equilibrium as he ripped off the mask and stuffed
it into a bag. The others did the same. Eric's demasking revealed an evil
smirk, as it was his legs I'd crashed into, his charming grin accompanied
by dark, sparkling eyes.

When Michael took off his mask, his grin was filled with both humor
and curiosity. But I was more concerned with the fact that everyone had
started disrobing. They peeled off the black shirts to reveal a varying array of T-shirts. Then off came the pants. Donovan wore jeans underneath, but Eric and Michael both wore leather.

The driver also peeled off his mask—or, well, her mask—and tossed
it back, and I recognized her from when I was at the house a couple
months ago. Curvaceous with long hair the color of midnight and strik-
ing hazel green eyes, she seemed to be the only woman within the inner
circle of higher-ups of Donovan's gang. And she could drive like nobody's business. I saw why Donovan chose her, as she took just enough
risky chances to make lights and hurry through turns without drawing
too much unwanted attention.

She looked at me in the rearview mirror and winked humorously. At
least they enjoyed what they did for a living. Something to be said about
that.

"Strip," Donovan ordered, and I realized he was talking to the last
guy. He sat by the back door and had yet to take off his mask.

"Are you for real?" he asked. "She knows who we are."

"She knew who we were before she ever stepped into the bank," Eric
said, becoming defensive instantly. "Get your shit together."

"Fuck you," the guy said. "I ain't going to prison for that skank."
Skank?

"Get your mask off," Donovan said, his tone sharper than I'd ever
heard it. "We're almost at the drop point."

Did he call me a skank?

"And fuck you, too," he said to Donovan. "She sees my face, she can testify in court."

Before anyone could respond, Michael was on the guy. He charged forward, took him by the collar, and jerked his mask off. "She can testify anyway, dipshit." He threw the mask to Eric, who stuffed it into the same bag with the others.

The guy nodded in astonishment. He had blond hair cut so short, he looked almost bald. His skin was leathery from too much New Mexico sun, but his cheeks had a ruddy complexion. I didn't remember seeing him, but I'd been to their house only once, and it had been a very tense situation. "Great," he said, his anger hitting me like a wall of heat. "Now we're all going to prison."

"We're going anyway if this doesn't work," Donovan said. "Quit your whining or get out at the next stop."

The guy worked his jaw as he peeled off his outer shirt as well, but he kept the black military pants on.

"How we doing, darlin'?"

"Ten seconds," the driver said.

Eric zipped the bag just as she took another sharp turn, this time down an alley and into a parking garage. She skidded to a stop, sending me flying forward. And yet I was the only one. I had serious gravitational issues.

The driver grinned down at me.

"Hi, I'm Charley," I said as Eric opened the door and jumped out the second the van stopped.

"I know," she said with a soft laugh. "I'm Sabrina, but I'd appreciate it if you didn't repeat that in court."

"You got it."

I watched as they transferred the money to the trunk of a yellow Hyundai and the bag with the clothes to the back of a green Dodge Ram truck. But the part that fascinated me the most was the fact that Michael and Sabrina peeled a plastic wrap off the sides of the van. I couldn't see what the van now looked like from my vantage, but surely they had just changed its entire appearance.

They wadded the wrap and stuffed it into a storm drain; then Michael tossed Eric a set of keys. He jumped in the truck and started it up as Sabrina headed for the Hyundai while Michael took her place behind the wheel of the van.

"I'm going with the money," the blond said, but Donovan pulled him back in and closed the door.

"We stick to the plan. Unless you want to give up your share and leave now."

The guy sat back, his expression full of anger, and most of it was directed at me.

"Hold on to your panties," Michael said as he charged forward. The Hyundai and the Dodge followed until they were out of the garage; then everyone went their separate ways.

"You just signed our arrest warrant," the blond said to Donovan.

He unsheathed a wicked-looking knife, and my gaze locked on like a laser-guided missile. My chest weakened, the walls caving in as I withered inside myself like paper. I'd felt a knife once as it slipped past layers of flesh and tendon until it hit bone. It was not something I wanted to repeat.

He pointed it toward me. "Either she goes in the dirt," he said, shifting the pointy end toward Donovan, "or you do."

Adrenaline pumped hard through Donovan's body, so if this chain of events surprised him, I couldn't feel it. Without a hint of hesitation, he pulled his Glock and fired. For the third time that day, a gun went off way to close for comfort.

I should've known the day was going to turn out bad when it started with my father trying to kill me. They always went downhill from there.

"Fuck!" the guy yelled, ducking long after the bullet flew past him and broke through the glass of one door.

He'd ducked, too. For some reason, that made me feel better about my earlier reaction. But not about the sound. Nausea punched into my stomach and pushed hard, but I was getting used to the massive adrenaline dumps. I tensed and fought the surge of bile, forcing it down and holding it there.

"Drop the knife, and the next round will never leave the chamber."

The guy tossed the knife right at me, but more as a warning than an attack. It hit my shoulder and landed harmlessly on the metal floor with a clang. I grabbed it before the guy could change his mind. The blade was as long as my forearm, and holding it did little to alleviate the fear coursing through me. I couldn't help but wonder if Reyes had been right. I was afraid of a guy with a knife. Two months ago, that would only have registered about a 4 on my Richter scale, but now the slightest offense seemed to rocket my fear response off the charts.

We hit a rough spot as Michael barreled forward, and then the world went dark. Everyone exited out different doors: Michael out the driver's door, the blond out the back, and Donovan out the sliding side door. He grabbed the last bag and nodded for me to follow him. We were in his detached garage.

Michael was busy taking off yet another wrap; this one had yellow letters that read D & D PLUMBING. Now the van that had been black when I first saw it was white. Clever.

"You kidnapped me," I said to Donovan.

"We didn't kidnap you. We borrowed you."

"You took me hostage."

"Which is like borrowing."

I marched behind him and he busied himself with this task or that one. "Why banks? Why do this?"

He dropped his gaze and fiddled with his gloves, unsnapping and resnapping the strap. "Sadly, we won't see a penny of that money we took today."

"What? I don't understand."

"That was the goal." He lifted his brows into a shrug. "It was always the goal. We had to make it look like we were just robbing banks randomly. Like we just stumbled upon a fresh shipment of cash by accident. Like we didn't know it would be there. Waiting."

I'd wondered how they happened upon so much cash.

He took out a saddlebag and stuffed it with some personal effects. "The deal was we get to keep everything we've taken so far. That's our payoff. But the money from the heist today all goes to one guy."

"And who would that be?"

"The guy who's blackmailing us."

The air siphoned out of my lungs as I laughed; then I realized he was being serious. "You're being blackmailed to rob banks?"

"Stranger things have happened," he said, lifting one shoulder.

"Not to me." When he offered me a skeptical stare, I said, "Well, okay, but this is still a bit out there, even for me. Donovan, what happened?"

"I happened." Eric walked up then. He'd apparently ditched the truck and strolled up to us with hardly a care in the world. "I was jumped one night outside a club by a group of guys, and I killed one of them. This guy filmed the whole thing."

"He has evidence that would put all of us away for a long time. We were there. I watched it happen. Eric was holding his own, so I didn't step in. But we just left the guy there."

"We didn't think he'd die," Eric said. "Those guys fucking started it."

"But if it was self-defense?"

"Not when you're a Golden Gloves champion boxer," Donovan explained.

Michael shoved Eric to the side. "And these dipshits fled the scene."

Donovan gave him a stern look. "He would have gone up for a good stretch either way."

"And when this guy came to us," Eric continued, "he knew everything about banks."

Michael nodded in agreement. "Said he could get us in and out, told us what to take and what to leave, how to avoid the cops, everything."

"Then he set up every job to make it look completely random," Donovan said.

"So, who is this guy?" I asked, hoping they'd tell me.

A slow grin spread across Donovan's face. "I'm going to a lot of trouble to keep your ass alive and unharmed. The last thing I'm going to do is feed you to the wolf."

"But he works at the bank you robbed today, right? That's how he knew about the shipment."

"Yeah," Michael said with a wink, but he was lying. I could feel it as easily as I could feel cool breeze on a hot summer day.

"Thing is, I don't think it was going to stop here. I think he was going to force us to hit one more bank. He's been talking about it for a while. When we told him it couldn't be done, he said he had a guy on the inside. The fact that you made us basically saved our asses."

"We're out," Michael said, a smile playing on his mouth. The same mouth that smirked more often than not, so the smile was nice. Genuine.

Eric was at my back then, too close as usual as he bent over me. "You saved us from ever having to do this again. There's no way he can force us to continue now."

"We're off to Mexico anyway," Donovan said. "This just seals the deal."

"Not for me, it doesn't." We turned as the blond strode in, his movements sharp with anger. "This guy had no idea who I was. That I was even involved." There was something odd about his anger. He wasn't being completely honest, I just couldn't quite figure out which part he was lying about.

"He still doesn't," Eric said.

"But she's seen my face. You insisted on it, remember?"

Donovan grabbed him by the collar, clearly as sick of his whining as I was. "You were the one who wanted in on this. We stick to the plan."

"Since when did the plan involve taking a hostage?"

"I improvised," Donovan said, pushing him away. Then he turned to me with another grin. "How much time do we have until you turn us in?"

Oh, they really were leaving. And they knew I would have to turn them in. I was a little stunned no one was trying to kill me. "As long as it takes me to get free."

He frowned in confusion, so I showed my wrists. The next grin that crept across his face could only be described as wolfish. "I can't make any promises once you're tied up."

I smiled. If Donovan was anything, it was a gentleman. A scruffy, vagabond gentleman, but a gentleman nonetheless. "I think I'll take my chances."

15

Your existence gives me a headache.
Go stand over there.

—T-SHIRT

Twenty minutes later, I found myself hog-tied in a basement-level room in the asylum. Donovan didn't want to take the chance that one of his club members would come to the house and find me all tied up and help-less, so the three of them led me over to the asylum and down a dilapi-dated staircase. Eric found a chair, and the tying commenced. Or, well, the taping. They had no rope, so they brought out the duct tape. Men had such a thing for duct tape.

Eric bent over the back of the chair and kissed my neck. "See you on the flip side, gorgeous. Don't go breaking into anything I wouldn't."

I smiled and nuzzled him between my head and shoulder. He was a good kid. And sexy as all get out. This was such a bad position for some-one like me to be in. Tied up and helpless with three hot guys vying for my attention. I totally needed to get out more.

He nibbled my earlobe a bit, then left before I could even say good-bye.

Michael offered me that cool smirk he carried with such style and bent to kiss my cheek. "I have a feeling we'll meet again," he said before saluting and heading away.

And that left me alone with Donovan.

He kneeled in front of me, his face quite handsome in the low light that streamed in from a single high window. He wrapped both arms around my waist and wedged in between my legs. "You're a brave woman," he said, his smile genuine.

I wanted to tell him about Artemis, because before she died, she had been his dog. I wanted him to know that she was with me and doing well, that she'd saved my life at least twice already, but I had no idea how he'd take that. He probably thought I was enough of a freak without bringing his departed dog into the picture, so I decided to keep that bit of info to myself for the time being.

"You're really going to Mexico?" I asked.

"To start with. Who knows where we'll end up, but things are getting too dicey around here." He rubbed my leg with one hand, his fingers getting dangerously close to the crest between my legs, otherwise known as Virginia. "You could go with us," he said without looking up at me.

He was dead serious, and I knew he'd let me come in a heartbeat if I wanted to. But how could I possibly leave? Some women were the drop-everything-and-run-off-to-Mexico kind of girls, but I was not. I had responsibilities. And a case to solve. And demons after my ass. Come to think of it, running didn't sound like such a bad idea.

Nah, I couldn't leave Cookie. Or Gemma. Or Mr. Wong. Or . . . Reyes popped into my head no matter how hard I tried to keep him out. His shimmering dark eyes and long thick lashes. Who was I kidding? I couldn't leave him either.

Yet kneeling in front of me was one of the sweetest men I'd ever met. Biker or not, he knew how to treat a girl.

True, he duct-taped me to a chair, but that had been my idea.

"I'll let you know where we are when we get there," he said, not waiting for an answer from me. "You'll always be welcome."

"Right," I scoffed, not believing him for a minute. "You'll find some Mexican beauty who makes you want to get married and have *pequeños banditos* for the first time in your life, and you'll forget all about me."

The sadness that washed over him spilled out into me. "Not likely, love." He ran his thumb over my bottom lip, then covered it with his own, taking it between his teeth and suckling before pressing his mouth to mine.

It was a nice kiss, soft and unhurried, and as welcome as a delicate rain on the high plains. It was what I needed. A healing kind of karma swam around me as he pulled my hips to his. I spread my knees and reveled in the feel of his erection against my most sensitive girl part. And I swore if I hadn't been taped down, I would have jumped him right then and there. I was such a hussy.

"I'm not sure you should be doing that, Miss Charlotte."

I broke off the kiss with a breathless gasp. Rocket was standing right behind Donovan, hands on his hips in disapproval.

"Rocket," I said, straightening in the chair. "Donovan was just helping me with . . . my contacts."

Donovan raised his brows humorously.

Rocket furrowed his. "Did you swallow them?"

Rocket was like a giant Pillsbury Doughboy with a kind face and a mushy body, which made him the best hugger around.

"No, I didn't swallow them. He was just—" Before I could come up with another plausible lie, I looked over and saw Strawberry Shortcake, a departed nine-year-old who could make me cringe at forty paces. I hadn't seen her in a while, so it was actually nice to know she was still here and okay. But she wasn't what gave me pause. While she also stood with her hands on her hips, disapproval lining her pretty face, right beside her stood a tiny girl with a short dark bob and overalls.

As Donovan looked over his shoulder, wanting to see what I was seeing, I let a soft smile spread over my face. I turned my palm up, twisting my arm in my shirtsleeve as the tape held it in place, inviting her closer, and said, "You must be Blue."

Her oval face, tiny and so pale, it was hard to make out her features other than her huge dark eyes, was a picture of shock and awe. She'd obviously never seen anyone kiss before. If I'd known that would lure her to me, I would have dragged Donovan in here and made out with him ages ago.

Rocket turned back to her, and he seemed just as surprised as I was to see her standing there.

Strawberry walked up then, her mouth a thin line of disappointment. "Who is he?" she asked, pointing at the scruffy guy who still had his hands wrapped around my ass.

With a grin, I said, "This is Donovan. He just happens to own this building you're standing in."

"I thought you said you were going to go on a date with my brother."

For her sake, I tamped down the horror I felt at the prospect of dating Taft, her cop brother. He was okay as far as guys went, but I'd never felt the slightest inclination to bang him, and that was my criteria for dating. If that primal attraction wasn't there from the get-go, it would likely never show up. Not in my world, anyway.

"No, *you* said I was going to go on a date with your brother." I leaned over and kissed her nose, an act she didn't appreciate but one I enjoyed immensely. "As it turns out, he's all booked up."

"Yes, with gross girls who wear too much makeup. You may not be very pretty, but at least you don't wear too much makeup."

I coughed back a retort. "Thank you, I think. But Donovan's a pretty good guy despite his tendency to rob banks."

"Really?" Her eyes came to life as she looked at him with a whole new perspective. "He's a bank robber like Jesse James? I just thought he was a scruffy biker guy."

I laughed. Who knew the kid would be attracted to bank robbers? "He is a scruffy biker guy."

"Hey," he said, nudging me with his knee.

"But there's more to him than meets the eye."

His mouth curved into something resembling doubt. "Are you really having a conversation with someone else or are you just avoiding the issue at hand?"

"And what issue would that be?"

"That I may never see you again." His expression remained impassive, but his emotions grew somber.

"D," Eric yelled from the stairs, "we have to hit it!"

He took in a deep draft of air and ran his fingers down my jaw and under my chin. "If I don't hear from you in two hours, I'm going to assume you're still down here and send help."

My brows shot up. "I've seen the kind of help you have," I said, referring to his merry band of criminal associates. "I think I'll take my chances."

"I'll call the police," he corrected. "So let me know when you get out of here."

"Okay, promise."

"D! If you aren't coming, can I take Odin? That's a sweet ride."

"No!" he shouted.

"Fine. Shit. Don't blow a gasket."

I sat ogling Donovan, a new appreciation blossoming in my chest.

"What?" he asked, suddenly wary.

"Odin? You named your bike?"

He offered me a wink as he picked up the roll of duct tape. "I was inspired by a crazy girl in a Jeep named Misery."

"You named your car Misery?" Strawberry asked, her face twisted in distaste.

"Look," Donovan said, his expression suddenly severe. "Edwards is not all there, if you know what I mean."

"Edwards?"

"The guy who wanted to take you out."

"Really?" I asked, interested. "Is he cute?"

"The blond in the van who wanted to slice you into itty-bitty pieces."

"Oh, that Edwards."

He laughed. "He got kicked out of sniper training school in the Marines, and he hasn't been the same since."

"The Marines may have been on to something."

"Just watch your back, okay?"

"Consider it watched."

He grinned and tore a strip of tape away from the roll, readying it for more duty. I laughed. "I think I'm secure."

"Nope, but you will be." He ran the tape in circles around the back of the chair and over my rib cage just under Danger and Will Robinson.

The act emphasized their fullness, a fact I was fairly certain he didn't miss.

"That's better," he said, his gaze fixed on the girls.

I rolled my eyes. "Really? This is how you're going to leave me?"

Before I could say anything else, he lunged forward and planted his mouth on mine again. This kiss was anything but gentle. Need and longing radiated out of him as his tongue slipped past my lips and between my teeth. Just like last time we'd kissed, he tasted faintly of beer and cinnamon. I heard a soft moan, and I realized it was coming from me.

His hands rose to my face, his fingers diving into my hair, pulling parts of it loose from the hair tie. He cupped my chin with one hand and angled my head to give him better access. Slanting against me, he deepened the kiss even more. I wanted to mold myself to him again, to feel the hardness of his body against mine, but he'd taped me to the back of the chair. Of course, that didn't stop one hand from meandering back to my ass. He pulled me closer—chair and all—then let his hand slide up to Will, to measure her weight in his palm, to test her peak with his thumb.

"D, what the fuck?"

With great reluctance, he pulled away from me. His lids were still closed when he yelled, "I'm coming, damn it!" Then he focused on me once again. "Not literally, unfortunately." He brushed a thumb over my mouth again. "You are so very special, Charley. I *will* be back."

Without another word, he rose and walked out of the room, his big boots echoing against the walls until I heard a door close above me. I sat stewing in a fog of desire and warmth until I realized I still had an audience. And I couldn't help but notice that Blue's jaw had fallen open. Poor kid.

After a long draw of air to get control of my hormones, I asked Rocket, "Are you going to introduce us?"

"Miss Charlotte, I don't think you should be kissing boys on the mouth like that. Especially in front of my sister."

"You're right." I hung my head in shame. "She's very pretty, though."

"I'll fix your hair," Strawberry said. She stood behind me and ripped the hair tie out, then proceeded to rake her fingers over my scalp. For the love of sunshine, I'd be lucky to leave this place with any hair left at all.

Blue was still as far away from me as she could get without being in the next room, but I could hardly believe I was finally getting to see her. I'd been coming here for years and had never even been offered so much as a glimpse. And she was absolutely adorable. Her short hair curled under at her ears. Her bangs cut to meticulous precision.

After a moment, she took note of the fact that I was looking at her. She closed her mouth and stepped back, her head down and her shoulders concave.

"It was so nice to meet you," I said a split second before she melted into the far wall.

Then I was lifted, chair and all, off the ground and into the most awkward hug I'd ever encountered. Rocket was a hugger. It didn't matter that my face was being ground into his cool shoulder with the unnatural position.

"Where have you been?" he asked, and I couldn't help but notice how air became precious fast when your supply ran out. "You haven't been here in forever."

"Rocket," Strawberry said, her voice nasally with a whine, "I can't reach her hair, and have you seen it? Maybe we should just shave her head and start over."

My eyes flew open. She was probably one of those girls who shaved her dolls' heads. Those girls were creepy.

"No shaving heads," I said into Rocket's shoulder.

"I have no idea what you're saying," she replied. "I'll go find some scissors."

Panic seized me but only for a moment. The departed were limited in what they could do with objects on this plane. Surely she couldn't really get a hold of a pair of scissors.

"Or maybe I can find a knife." She disappeared down the hall.

"Rocket," I said, my voice muffled. "I can't breathe."

And just like every other time he'd picked me up for one of his bear hugs, he let go. I crashed to the ground, the chair cracking and tipping awkwardly back, hovering on the brink of oblivion, until the weight of my head won and I fell to the floor. For the second time in as many days, my big head bounced off the cement when it hit, and pain shot down my spine.

I squeezed my eyes shut to block out the sudden burst of discomfort. And there I sat, molded to the chair with duct tape, my feet in the air and my head lying in some kind of grayish remains.

This wasn't uncomfortable at all.

The sound of motorcycles roaring to life flooded the room. After a few minutes, the rumbling faded as the Bandits—literally—drove off into the sunset. So to speak. At first I wondered how much time I should give them before I managed to escape and call the police; then I wondered if I could escape. What if I couldn't? Would he really call them after a couple of hours? Would I die down here of hypothermia and dehydration?

I looked so unhealthy when dehydrated.

That was not the way to go in my book. Better to die with plenty of fluids in my body. Like at a waterpark. Or during a wet T-shirt contest.

"You look funny," Rocket said, and I figured we could catch up while I lay there stewing in worry.

"Oh, yeah?" I volleyed. "Well, you look fantastic. Have you been working out?"

A huge boyish smile broke across his face. "You always say that. I have new names for you."

"Okay." I looked around to admire his artwork and frowned. As far as I knew, every room in this asylum had been covered over and over again with the names of the departed Rocket scratched into its plaster walls, but the walls in this room, in this huge, cavernous vastness, were completely untouched. I craned my neck to see what I could, taking in the blank canvases around me.

Rocket started for the next room before he realized I wasn't following him. "Miss Charlotte, come on."

"I can't right now, hon." My absent response didn't deter him.

"But I have to show you. Something's going on." He took my arm and pulled me toward the door, grinding my hair in the oily contents even more. The chair scraped along the cement, but the closer we got to the door, the more worried I became. There was no way I was fitting through that door at this angle. Unless I lost my head altogether, which judging by Rocket's strength, was a strong possibility.

"Rocket, wait," I said, but he kept pulling and I kept sliding.

I struggled in the chair, fought against the restraints as the doorframe drew closer and closer.

"Rocket, I'm not kidding."

He stopped suddenly and looked back at me. "Do you think rain is scary?"

"Um—"

But he was gone. He'd already snapped back to attention and refocused on the task at hand. Damn my hesitation.

"Rocket!" I yelled, trying to break his concentration. "I have a question for you." He paused, so I hurried and asked, "Why are there no names in this room? These walls are completely empty."

He cast me a withering look. "I can't touch these. I'm saving them."

"Really?" I asked, fighting duct tape tooth and nail. "For what? The apocalypse?"

"No, silly. For the end of the world."

I stopped. "Wait, what? Rocket, what are you talking about?" Everyone had been hinting at some kind of supernatural war, but nobody had mentioned the end of the world. I was only teasing when I'd said that to Reyes.

"You know, when lots and lots of people die because of the decision of a few men. Or even just one."

"One. You mean a dictator like Hitler? There'll be another Holocaust?"

"Not Hitler. A man pretending to be human."

Hadn't the sisters said something along those lines? A man pretending to be a human. Okay, well that left out half the population, since it was not a woman. "But who? When?" I'd always dreamed of going back in time and killing Hitler pre-crazy time. Any one of a million people would have done the same if only we had a crystal ball. I may not have had a crystal ball, but I had Rocket. And his head was ball-like. And shiny. And I could see through it. He'd work. "Rocket, what man? What will he do?"

"I don't know yet. He may or may not do it. It's all still floating."

I shifted for a better position, grunting a little in the process. "Floating?"

"Yes, like when people make decisions and maybe the person who was not going to die yet does, or the person who was supposed to die doesn't. They are floating."

"So, these decisions aren't carved in stone?"

"No, they're carved in my walls."

"But who, Rocket? Who's supposed to do all of this?" I swore, if he said Reyes, I was going to scream.

He wagged a finger at me. "Uh-uh-uh. No peeking, Miss Charlotte."

This was more information from Rocket than I'd had in a while. He knew things that were going to happen. That was clairvoyance if I'd ever heard it.

I thought of my dad. Wondered how much time he had. "Can I give you a name?"

"But I have something to show you."

"I'm kind of tied up right now. Leland Gene Davidson."

His lashes did that fluttering thing they did when he was shuffling through millions of names. "Three are dead. Two are still alive."

"Okay, but the ones who are still alive, do you know when they're going to die? Is it soon?"

"Not when. Only if."

"But, is he floating?"

"No. Not floating."

Well, this was like driving a supercharged Challenger on the highway to nowhere. I gave up and decided to choose another route. "Rocket, can I tell when someone is going to die?"

He stopped and regarded me with a look of utter puzzlement. "Of course you can tell when someone is going to die. It's your job."

I thought as much. I wondered when I was going to die. "Am I floating?"

"Miss Charlotte, you're the grim reaper," he said with a snort. "You're always floating."

"So, I could die for real? At any second?"

"Yep."

"Oh." That was disappointing. "Well, thanks for giving it to me straight." I blew dust out of my bangs.

"You could be killed by a bicycle. Or crushed by a big rock. Or stabbed with a knitting needle."

"Okay."

"Or even pushed down some stairs."

"Right, I got it. Thanks."

"Or you might be shot in the head with a gun."

"Rocket! I'm good. Seriously, no more elaboration needed." But he grabbed my arm, and all the innocence drained from his face. He wasn't a little boy anymore. He knew too much. Had seen too much. "Or," he said, his voice taking on an eerie depth, "you could be killed by the one you love most. Along with everyone else."

Well, that sucked more ass than liposuction.

He let go of my arm and stood to inspect the area. I knew what he was feeling. I felt the same thing even before Reyes materialized, and I wondered how long he'd been there. Never having been a fan of Reyes's, Rocket disappeared the moment a sea of black robes burst into the room, undulating around me until they settled at Reyes's feet. He spoke from the shadow of his hood, refusing to show his face. "You agreed to be tied up when there is a legion of demons after you?"

"Yes. I didn't really think of it in those terms."

He released an exasperated sigh and started forward. "Someday, I will understand how that mind of yours works."

I snorted. "Good luck. It seemed like a good alternative to dying out-right at the time."

"When exactly was your life in danger?"

"Are you going to help me out of this or not?"

He kneeled beside me and pushed back the hood of his robe to reveal his exotically handsome face. A face that had fresh lacerations over its brow and cheekbone.

Startled, I asked, "You're still fighting them? Hunting them?"

His head cocked to one side. "Did you actually expect me to stop?"

"How long can this go on? How many are there?"

He was inspecting the duct tape. "Only a handful now. There are very few humans on Earth who can see what these can see. My brethren are running out of options."

"You're not killing them, are you? They're innocent. They're just people who happen to be able to see the departed."

"I kill them only if I have to. Are you going to question my every move while you are duct-taped to a chair?"

"Sorry. I was just hoping you'd stop hunting them."

"They won't stop trying to get to you, Dutch. Hedeshi lied."

"I know. I just meant . . . You're getting pretty beat up in the process."

His sensual mouth tilted up at one corner. "Worried about me?"

"No." I added a *pfft* just to emphasize how much I was not worried.

"You didn't look worried with that guy's tongue down your throat."

Great. He did see that. "Jealous?"

"No."

"'Cause you seem jealous."

His lashes lowered as he narrowed his eyes at me, but the high-pitched voice of a departed nine-year-old with masochistic tendencies drifted down from the stairwell before he could reply.

"I found a knife!" Strawberry said.

Holy shit. "Get me out of this," I said to Reyes, wiggling my fingers. "Hurry before she comes back."

16

Don't judge me because I'm quiet.
No one plans a murder out loud.
—T-SHIRT

After Reyes got me out of the restraints then did his usual disappearing act, citing an extreme need to be elsewhere, I exited the asylum and walked past a couple of bikers hanging out at Donovan's. I wondered if they knew about the robberies. Or that he wouldn't be back for a while. Mustering as much nonchalance as possible—and hoping that whatever was in my hair wasn't too noticeable—I started down the street toward a convenience store nearby. This wasn't the safest neighborhood to be walking through, even in the early afternoon.

I scraped my hair back into the hair tie, then dug my phone out of my pocket and texted Donovan, letting him know that I'd barely escaped with my life and my virtue intact. Then I called Garrett.

"Swopes," he said, all business. He had caller ID, for heaven's sake.

"I need a ride."

"You need a therapist."

"True, but I need a ride first."

"Why? Where's your Jeep?" He sounded winded, like he was running. Or having sex. Surely my timing didn't suck that bad.

"Misery's at the scene of a bank robbery."

"I'm not even going to ask." He was learning.

"I'll be at the Jug-N-Chug off Broadway."

"That strip club?"

"No, and ew. The convenience store."

"Oh. I was hoping you'd changed professions."

"Dude, you do not want to see what I look like dancing with a pole. I did it once at a bridal shower, and let's just say it did not end well."

"You pole-danced at a bridal shower?"

"It's a long story. Are you going to come get me or not?"

"I guess. It'll take me a few to get there."

"Well, hurry. I have shit to do. And I could be arrested as an accessory, so I need to get on this." I still had to check on Harper and do some more investigating on her behalf. My imminent arrest as an accessory to bank robbery would cut into my crime-solving time.

"Are you using that handbag that has the word *fuck* written all over it again? I warned you about taking that out in public."

"Not *for* an accessory. *As* an accessory. Just come get me."

"Okay."

I hung up and called my friendish-type contact at the local FBI office. We'd met on a case a couple of months ago, and I liked her. She made me smile, and she hardly ever threatened to arrest me. We got along great. And I knew she'd be a good ally if I happened to show up in the aftermath of a bank robbery as a suspect.

Since I didn't have a candy wrapper to help me with the bad connection I was about to have, I resorted to using vocal sound effects. When Agent Carson picked up, I started my performance. "Agent . . . Agent Carson," I said, panting into the phone.

"Yes, Charley." She seemed unimpressed, but I wasn't about to stop now.

"I—I know who the kshshshshshsh are."

"I'm a little busy right now, Davidson. What is a Ksh, and why do I care?"

"I'm sorry. My kshshsh . . . is kshshsh . . . ing."

"I repeat. What is a Ksh? And why do I care if it is ksh-ing?"

She was a tough one. I knew I should have waited and bought a Butterfinger at the Jug-N-Chug. Those wrappers crackled like Rice Krispies on a Saturday morning. "You aren't listeni—kshshsh."

"You're really bad at this."

"Bank ro-ksh-ers. I know who they kshshsh."

"Charley, if you don't cut this crap out."

I hung up and turned off my phone before she could figure out what I was trying not to tell her and call back. The whole thing would have been more convincing if she'd found me tied up on the floor of an asylum. Luckily, that rarely happened.

I made it to the store in record time, but all I could afford was a banana. They were on sale, and the mocha lattes were ungodly. I totally forgot to ask Reyes for my million dollars. This being too poor to buy coffee was for the birds.

Cookie called just as Garrett pulled up. I'd turned my phone back on as a precaution when a man in an old Cadillac kept asking me if I wanted to sample his antifreeze.

Still trying to blend with the locals, I answered the phone saying, " 'Sup, girlfriend?"

"Are you in a bad part of town again?"

"You know it." I climbed into Garrett's truck and completely ignored him. It was fun. "But I did learn something today."

"Yeah?"

"If you must eat a banana in public, never make eye contact."

"Good to know. So, I looked into the activity around the time all this started, when Harper's parents were married. It's mostly small stuff, except for a murder in the Monzano Mountains, but that was solved. There was also a missing persons case that was never solved, a little boy, but that was in Peralta. As far as I can tell, neither had anything to do with the Lowells."

"Well, okay. Thanks for looking."

"Oh, and that shrink will see you, but only if you skedaddle over there. He's has a couple more appointments today, then he's headed out of town."

"Oh, perfect timing. If you come across anything else."

"I know where to find you."

I hung up and offered Garrett my full-ish attention. Actually, a guy arguing with a newspaper dispenser captured most of it, but what was left, I handed over to Swopes freely.

"*Hola.*"

"So, where are we going, or are we just going to sit here until I run out of gas?"

I was just about to answer when Agent Carson called back. Darn it. I should have turned off my phone again.

I pointed east, ordering Swopes that way, then answered the phone. When I started to do the *ksh* thing, she said, "Don't even think about it. Why is your Jeep at the scene of a bank robbery?"

"Oh," I said, panting again, "thank God you got ahold of me." I swallowed hard. Garrett shook his head and focused on his driving. I was totally behind him on that decision. "That's what I was trying to tell you. I was taken hostage."

"Yes, I've seen the surveillance footage."

"Right, so you know—"

"Do you realize how many years you'll get for this?"

Well, crap. "I really was taken hostage. Kind of. And I can tell you who the bank robbers are."

After a long pause in which I was certain she was recovering from the shock of her good fortune, she said, "I'm listening."

"But you have to let Uncle Bob in on it."

"Okay."

"Are you there now? At the bank? I can be there in a few."

"Davidson, who robbed this bank?"

I let out a long stream of air, stalling as long as I could, letting Donovan get a few feet closer to Mexico, then said, "A handful of men from a local biker club called the Bandits, but I need to talk to you about them before you go off half-cocked."

"I never do anything half-cocked."

I didn't doubt that for a New York minute. "The guys were being blackmailed and whoever set up that gig knew that money would be there, but he doesn't work at the bank. So, who else would know about it? Like maybe an armored car driver? Or the spouse of someone who works there?"

I could hear shoes clapping on the sidewalk as she searched for someplace more private. She whispered into the phone. "Are you saying this was an inside job?"

"That's exactly what I'm saying. These guys did it, absolutely, but they had no choice."

"Well, you're always entertaining, that's for sure."

"Oh, thank you." She was so nice. "I'll meet you at my Jeep."

"I'll be here."

I hung up, then asked Garrett, "Can I hire you for the rest of the day?"

"Sure," he said with a shrug. "I just got off a big case. I can take an afternoon away from the office."

He didn't actually have an office so much as a truck. I took in the vast array of papers and file folders and take-out containers that lined his backseat. "I thought this was your office."

"It is, more or less. I meant that metaphorically."

"While I'm impressed you know what that word means, I have to be honest. I don't have any money to pay you."

"Figures. So where's your Jeep?"

I was a little surprised he didn't know. He must not have been listening to the radio. Surely, the robbery was all over the news. "Well, my Jeep is at the Bernalillo Community Bank, but I need to run a couple of errands first, and I don't have much gas."

"Didn't you just tell that agent you'd be right there?"

"I said I'd be there. I didn't say when. And you're the one who keeps telling me I need therapy." I beamed at him. "Let's go see a psychotherapist."

He shrugged and followed my directions to Harper's current psychotherapist's place of business. It was a small building right out of the seventies, complete with a lava rock exterior and metal beams protruding over the walkway.

I went in as Garrett sat outside in the getaway truck, wondering if he could get arrested for his part in my evading a federal officer. I assured him that was not the case. And he believed me. I'd hate to be in his shoes if I were wrong, and if push came to shove, I was so throwing that man under the bus. I could claim he forced me into his vehicle at a convenience store and held me captive for two hours.

He made a great scapegoat.

I took off my shades and announced myself to a very stoic receptionist before sitting in the waiting area. After a solid twenty minutes, I was finally shown in to the doctor's office. Harper's psychotherapist was a dwarfish man with gray hair and tan, prunelike skin. He sat with his hands folded in his lap and his face set to *no comment*.

"Thank you for seeing me, Dr. Roland." I sat across from him at a ginormous mahogany desk, trying not to read anything into it. "I just have a few questions about Harper Lowell."

"Ms. Davidson, as my receptionist has already told you, there is absolutely nothing about Harper or her treatment that I can share with you. As a private investigator, you should already know that."

I did know that, but he didn't have to actually say anything. He could just sit there while I asked the questions. His own emotions would help me more than he could possibly imagine. "I understand, but Harper hired me, Dr. Roland, and asked me to look into her case."

"Have you seen her?" he asked. "She missed her last appointment."

"She came to see me a couple of days ago when she hired me. When was the last time you saw her?"

"She left in the middle of our last appointment. Very abruptly and very apprehensively. I haven't seen or heard from her since."

I nodded in an open and nonjudgmental way. "Do you know what sparked her sudden departure?"

"Yes."

"Can you tell me?"

"You know I can't."

"But she got a phone call or a text, right?" What else would it be?

He smiled. "Perhaps."

He was lying, so now I had to actually figure out what else it would be. Was it something he said to her? Or maybe something came out during their session. Could something he said have triggered a memory?

Knowing he wouldn't tell me straight out, I asked, "And when did this happen?"

"She missed her last appointment, so a week ago Tuesday."

"Did you call her?"

He seemed to be growing agitated. "I called and left a message, but she didn't return my call."

"What happened to her when she was five?"

With a sigh of annoyance, he uncrossed his legs, adjusted his position, then recrossed them yet still managed to look about as comfortable as a mouse in a boa tank. "Ms. Davidson, I have a client coming in—"

"I believe her," I said, leaning forward and waiting for his reaction to hit me. "I think she has been terrorized methodically and systematically for a very long time. And I truly believe her life is in danger." Judging by the emotion pouring off him, he did, too.

He averted his attention by picking lint off his jacket and said, "I cannot disagree."

"Thank you," I said, glad for an ally. "Without breaking your code of conduct or giving anything away, do you have any idea, based upon what you've learned so far, who is behind these attacks?"

Regret washed over him. "No, Ms. Davidson, I'm painfully sorry to say that I don't."

Crap. Another dead end.

"But I can say that—" He cleared his throat and examined a fruit tree outside his window. "—sometimes our pasts come back to haunt us."

I knew it. Whatever happened when she was five started it all, and Dr. Roland knew it. With a smile of gratitude, I said, "It most certainly does. Thank you so much for seeing me."

He stood to shake my hand. "Can you please have her call me?"

"I'll do my best."

When I left the doctor's office, I had a text from Cookie ordering me to call her.

"I think I got something," she said.

"It better not be the flu, because we have a case to solve, and you're not nearly as good at your job on flu medicine."

"Well, I'm not sure if this will matter, but the Lowells had Harper institutionalized when she was twelve."

A cold bitterness washed over me at the thought of Harper being institutionalized. Then again, I could use that information against Mrs. Lowell. "And I'll bet that's not something they want printed in the society pages. If Albuquerque has society pages. Rich people are weird that way."

"I've heard that. Not that I'd know from personal experience."

"Hey, I'm trying to get us a million dollars. Just hang in there a little while longer."

"You asked Reyes for a million dollars?"

"Yes."

"Okay, well, tell him to hurry. I need a pedicure."

"Cook, how can you think of your toes at a time like this?"

"Do you remember the time we were running for our lives from that guy with that weird eye thing and you were upset because you'd left your mocha latte at his house?"

"I'm not sure I understand your point."

I talked Garrett into taking me all the way across town back to Harper's parents' house in the hopes of catching Mr. Lowell out gardening. Since he was supposedly on his deathbed, the odds were not in my favor, but I could grill his testy wife again for good measure. Mrs. Lowell knew something, and she was damned well going to tell me. And now, thanks to Cookie's prowess with search engines, I knew something, too.

I couldn't have had much more time before everything came out in the open. I had to take advantage of the ace up my sleeve while I could.

Oddly enough, Garrett got through the gate easier than I had the first time I came through. It probably helped that he didn't try to order a taco. We were shown into the drawing room again. I loved being able to say that.

I nudged Garrett with my elbow. "This is the drawing room." An inane giggle bubbled out of my chest.

"You scare me sometimes."

"That happens to me, too. It's weird." I looked at the signature on one of the paintings on the wall. It read *Norman Rockwell*. "Holy cow," I said, impressed.

"Ms. Davidson, really," Mrs. Lowell said, shushing me with a hiss and a glare, and she hurried inside the room and shut the door.

"Sorry. I don't think I've ever seen a Norman Rockwell in real life."

Her chest swelled with pride. "Jason acquired that at an auction in the early aughts."

Did she just say *aughts*?

After Garrett introduced himself, we sat down and I decided to get right to the point. "Can you tell me about the period in which Harper was institutionalized?"

Her face stretched into a mask of humiliation. No idea why.

"As you know, nothing we did was helping, so yes, we had to have her institutionalized when she was twelve."

Twelve? My heart broke for her.

"We tried several forms of therapy there until we found one that worked."

She meant until they found one that shut Harper up.

"Unfortunately, Harper's short-term memory was affected by some of the treatments, but her behavior improved immensely."

Without any further explanation, I knew exactly what kind of treatments she was talking about. Electroshock therapy. She was talking about ECT. My disdain of Mrs. Lowell sank to an all-time low.

"We were able to bring her home, and everything went back to normal for a couple of years. Years, mind you. But slowly her erratic behaviors resurfaced until we had no choice but to ask her to leave." When my brows shot up, she qualified her actions with, "She was eighteen at the time, and we bought her a house. It's not as though we threw her out on the street. Then she married that hooligan just to spite us. That lasted all of five minutes."

"Mrs. Lowell, can you remember anything out of the ordinary happening to Harper around the time you and Mr. Lowell married? Was she threatened or bullied?"

"I've been over this a thousand times with her therapists and the police. The only thing that changed, that would have brought on such extreme behavioral changes, was our marriage. Nothing else happened."

"You're certain?"

When she hedged, glanced at her nails, then began perusing the carpet, I felt it. That quake of doubt. That grain of skepticism rippling through her.

"Mrs. Lowell, anything you can remember would help. Did Harper have any cuts? Did she come home one day especially dirty or frightened? Anything that would have had you believing she had been abused in any way?"

"No." Then she bowed her head. "Not anything that I noticed, but I didn't really know her before Jason and I married. She seemed like a sweet girl. She was cordial and had decent enough manners. But after we came home, she was a very different child."

So one person before their marriage and another after. "And she stayed with her biological grandparents during that time?"

"Yes. They've since died, sadly, but even they were at a complete loss as to why Harper would change so drastically."

"Okay, well, maybe something happened on the trip home. I mean, was there any kind of an accident?"

"None was ever mentioned. Really, Ms. Davidson, this could go on all day."

Crap. I was simply getting nowhere with this case. Not a single clue to go on.

We stood and her young housekeeper showed us to the door again, but this time Mrs. Lowell followed. The housekeeper seemed quite smitten with Garrett.

"I tried to call her," Mrs. Lowell said. "She won't accept my calls. Would you please have her call her father?"

"I'll do my best."

I called Cookie the minute we got in Garrett's truck.

"Are all stepmothers bitches?" I asked her, knowing how awful that sounded. I cringed at the words myself. One of my good friends was a stepmother, and she was the best thing that ever happened to those kids.

"I was raised by my stepmother," Cookie said. And I knew that. That's why I'd called her.

"I'm sorry. I didn't mean it."

"Sure you did, and you have every right to wonder such a thing, hon, after what you've been through with yours. But mine was amazing. If not for her, my childhood would have been drastically different, and not in a good way."

"Then I'm grateful for her, too."

"Thank you. I'll let her know. Did you need something?"

"Affirmation."

She chuckled. "What kind?"

"The kind you just gave me."

I told Garrett to head to the bank. I couldn't imagine Agent Carson would wait for me much longer. My phone rang as we were headed over to the scene. Of course, everything would be back to normal now, but Agent Carson might be a bit miffed at me for not showing immediately.

"Where the hell are you?" she said in answer to my "Charley's House of Edible Thongs."

"Sorry," I said, cringing at her tone, "I was making a delivery. Edible thongs are very popular right now."

"So are prison uniforms."

"Are they edible? That seems to be my best selling point."

"If you are not here in two minutes—"

"Here!" I shouted into the phone as we pulled into the parking lot across from the bank in question. "I'm here." I put one hand over the phone and whispered to Garrett, "She's so sensitive."

"Where here?"

"Turn around."

Her short, dark bob swiveled to her left.

"Other way."

She did a 180 and spotted us parking.

"Here I am." I waved through the windshield. "And just in the nick of time. Whew."

Before I got out, I turned to Garrett. He kept his gaze front and center, waiting for me to vacate the premises. He'd been quieter than usual. Well, okay, he was always quiet, but not deathly quiet. Not I've-been-to-hell-and-I'll-never-be-the-same quiet.

I crinkled my chin and said, "Do you want to talk about it? What it was like to be in hell?"

He turned on me so fast, his movements reminded me of Reyes's. His silvery eyes locked on to mine, his gaze hard, his jaw locked. When he spoke, he did so with eerie purpose, each syllable precise. "Do you want to talk about what it was like to have razor-sharp metal slice through your flesh until it scored across bone?"

Goodness. He was in a mood all of a sudden. "So, that's a no?"

He quirked one corner of his mouth, but the gesture held no humor whatsoever.

"Okay, well, good talk," I said, feeling blindly for the door handle.

He went back to staring out his windshield.

When I got out, Agent Carson stood tapping her toes on the pavement. I had no idea people really did that.

"So, what makes you think this was an inside job?" she asked. No hello. No how's the wife and kids. Just business as usual. I liked her.

"I was told so by the robbers."

"And their names are?"

"I told you, the Bandits."

"The Bandits are a motorcycle club two-hundred strong. I need the names of the men who entered the premises at gunpoint, held a group of patrons hostage, and took currency that did not belong to them out of that bank." She pointed across the street for reference.

"They didn't actually pull their guns," I said, correcting her. "They don't unless they have to. I've seen the stories on the news."

"Charley," she said, a sharp edge of warning in her voice.

"Okay." I filled my lungs and released the air slowly, sorry for what I was about to do. "I don't know all of their names," I said, lying. For some reason, I couldn't bring myself to tell her about Sabrina. She was a girl. No one would suspect her. Who's to say if I saw the driver's face or not? She was in it to help my biker guys, and for some reason, I felt I owed her for that. "The three I do know, the three who are being blackmailed, are Michael, Eric, and Donovan. There are two more, but I don't know their names. Oh, wait," I said, rethinking that. Donovan had mentioned blondie's name. "There was a blond guy named Edwards. He wants to take me out."

She wrote down everything I told her. Without looking up, she asked, "Really? Is he cute?"

"No, I mean, like to keep me from testifying, he wants my head on a platter."

"You just make friends wherever you go, don't you?"

"It's weird, right?" Then I leaned into her. "They're not bad guys, Agent Carson. They were being blackmailed, for real."

"You've said that, but no one held a gun to their heads in there."

I knew she'd see it that way. She had to, and I couldn't blame her, but I had to at least try to get the other guy convicted as well. He had just as much to do with this as my biker guys, if not more. No one except me blackmailed my friends and got away with it.

17

I meant to behave.
There were just too many other options.

—T-SHIRT

After giving my statement of events to Agent Carson, I fired Garrett, claiming irreconcilable differences, but told him to keep his schedule open just in case; then I headed home, craving sweet potato pie for some reason. That banana didn't last long. And I felt dirty after eating it.

I started up the staircase to my apartment, then noticed I grew warmer with each step that led to the third floor. And there were a lot of steps. When I reached the landing, the heat emanating off Reyes was scorching, and I couldn't tell if he was hot and bothered or just angry. Possibly a little of both.

The hallway sat in total darkness, and either the wiring had gone wonky again or Reyes had unscrewed the lightbulbs. I fished the keys out of my bag and walked to my door in the void of illumination. It's not as though it was a long or particularly hazardous journey, although with Reyes Farrow waiting at the end of it, it could turn that way quickly. I felt for the lock and inserted the key.

"Do you have my money?" I asked, feeling like a mob boss. Or a pimp.

"I need you to stay in tonight," he said, completely ignoring me.

My door gave, and I asked, "You coming in?"

"No. I just came to tell you to stay in tonight."

"Is that an order?"

"Yes."

I looked over my shoulder. I could just make out his shadow. "You should tread softly. The caffeine is wearing off."

He walked up behind me. I felt him raise an arm over my shoulder and brace it against the doorjamb. God, he was good at that.

"Why?" I asked, dropping my keys back into my bag. "Why stay in tonight?"

"You know why."

"Are they coming after me?" I asked, only partially kidding.

He leaned in until his mouth was at my ear. "Yes."

I couldn't decide if the shiver that ran along my spine was conjured because of the image his words had provoked or the heat of his breath rushing over my skin. He smelled like smoke and ash, thunder and lightning.

"Are you in love with him?" he asked, his deep voice soft with uncertainty.

I turned to face him in surprise. "Who?"

He lowered his head and looked at me from underneath his lashes. As dark as his eyes were, they still shimmered in the low light, the gold and green flecks like reflectors in the pale glow of a full moon. "You know who. The guy you were kissing today."

"Which one?" I asked, teasing him.

But he didn't bite. A sharp ache wafted off him, but I couldn't tell if it was physical or emotional. Surely my macking on some guy in an insane asylum wouldn't hurt him. He'd been living with his stalker, for heaven's sake.

He curled one arm around my waist and pulled me softly against him. "I just came to tell you to stay in," he said before leaning in to kiss my neck. He stayed there a moment, breathing me in, then dropped his arms and walked away. The air cooled instantly in his wake.

"Wait, Reyes." I hurried after him, took the stairs two at a time to keep up with his urgent need to be away from me.

"I just came to tell you to stay in."

"Reyes, for the love of Pete. And his dragon." I grabbed his arm and turned him toward me. We were on the second-floor landing then. It still had lights, and I could see him more clearly, including the fact that he was carrying a duffel bag over his shoulder. Blood had soaked through the front of his shirt in streaks, and I was certain he was covered in duct tape again. "I thought that would heal faster."

He examined his shirt and cursed. "It did. These are new. It won't take long, though."

I tamped down my alarm. It would do me no good. But my fear was uncontrollable. "Are they here?"

His head tilted in thought, measuring the energy around us. "I don't feel them now, but I did before you got here. I think they've figured out where you live."

"Wonderful. And as gallant as the intention is, you are in no condition to be hunting them down and going all ninja on their ass."

He looked himself over again, one corner of his mouth lifting into that charming half grin of his, the one that sent butterflies somersaulting through my stomach.

"I could've been a ninja," he said.

"Yes, you could have, and the Japanese nation would have been proud to have you. Now, come on." I tugged at his arm and he followed me back to my apartment. "You can go around covered in blood for only so long before someone calls the police and has you committed."

When I dropped my hand, he took it into his own, laced his fingers with mine, and followed me back up the stairs hand in hand. The contact was sweet and sexy and gave jolts of delight with every step I took. Damn him.

But it wasn't until we got into my apartment that I saw the extent of his injuries. He was literally covered in blood.

I closed the door behind him in horror. "Is all that yours?"

He took inventory of my apartment, then turned back to me with a shrug. "I don't think so."

"And you're burned." I rushed forward to inspect the back of his shirt.

"One of them tried to light me on fire."

"A demon?" I asked, cringing when my voice came out as more of a squeak that only dogs could pick up.

He nodded. "They're crazy. What's with the boxes?" He nodded toward the mountain of boxes, the only ones left in the whole apartment. Cookie had cleaned me out except for those in Area 51. I could now see Mr. Wong, thank goodness, his gray presence oddly comforting.

I tossed my bag onto the breakfast bar. "That is a black hole. Don't go near it. It's Gemma's idea of therapy. She thinks I have a mild form of PTSD."

He'd turned and was checking out my fake dying plants. "You do."

"Yeah, well you have issues, too, mister." I could just see the side of his face.

He flashed a nuclear grin. "I never said I didn't. Can I use your shower?"

While I wanted to say, *Only if I'm in it,* what I said was, "Sure, but I have to warn you, you might have company in the form of a huge, thirsty Rottweiler." Then I cleared my throat to cover the surge of pleasure that rushed through me at the thought of Reyes Farrow naked in my bathroom. Or naked in any room, for that matter. "Oh, and I'm all out of duct tape, if you're looking to patch yourself up afterwards. I might have some Scotch tape, though, if you're desperate."

He raised his duffel bag. "I'll manage."

When he closed himself in my bathroom, I let out a long breath and headed for Mr. Coffee. Either Albuquerque had a population explosion chock-full of exquisitely hot men, or I was just really hormonal.

———

Thirty minutes later, Reyes opened the door to the bathroom in a pair of jeans with a towel draped over his shoulders. And damn, what beautiful shoulders they were. He had replaced the old duct tape with a fresh application around his abdomen, but he was covered in old wounds, wounds that were healing quickly but still left dark purple streaks across his torso, shoulders, and the side of his neck. He took the ends of the towel and scrubbed at his head, then leaned against the doorjamb. "How is that therapy?"

I had yet to tear my eyes off him. When I did, I realized he was examining the boxes again. "Oh," I said, stirring a second cup of coffee and walking over to him. "Gemma wants someone to take one box off every day until I can do it myself. It's ridiculous. She says it will help me heal."

He stole my coffee, took a sip, then handed it back. "She's right."

As I gaped at him, appalled that he would side with my sister over me, he tossed the towel onto the sink and pulled on a plain dark gray T-shirt. I headed for my sofa, which might or might not go by the name of Malibu Barbie, but turned back to him before I reached it.

"Where did you get that?" I asked him, indicating the shirt with a nod. I wanted to know where he got everything. Where did he get his jeans and his shoes and the duct tape that he used to hold himself together? Where did he get food and water, and what had happened when they released him from prison? Was his BFF Amador there to pick him up? Amador was Reyes's only friend. I knew they were very close. Closer than Reyes and I would ever be, most likely. Surely Amador wouldn't have left him hanging. Or maybe that had been Reyes's wish, to be left alone, to fend for himself as he'd done his whole life. I sure hadn't been there for him. I'd been licking my wounds in my girl cave.

He tugged the shirt down, then headed my way—only he didn't stop when he reached me. I held the coffee cup out to the side as he walked into me and kept walking, guiding me back, his lean body comfortable against mine.

"It's a loaner," he said.

"From Amador?" My voice was nothing more than a husky whisper.

He wrapped an arm around me and continued back. His inky lashes, spiked with water, made his eyes glisten even more. My apartment was hardly roomy, so we couldn't possibly go much farther. But we kept walking until I bumped into something. I froze when I realized what. Area 51. We were standing in the midst of Area 51.

I pushed against him, but he didn't budge a centimeter.

His playful expression turned serious. "Sit down."

I reached to put the coffee cup on a box, but missed, my shaking hand fumbling until the cup dropped faster than I could manage to catch it. Just as it was about to hit the carpet, Reyes scooped it up. Hot coffee splashed out and over his hand, but he didn't seem to notice.

He rose to his full height again and said, "Sit."

On the boxes? No way. With jaw set, I shook my head.

He placed the cup on an end table, took me by the shoulders, and turned me to face the black hole.

"This is just a space," he said, easing closer behind me. He wrapped his arms around my stomach. "It means nothing." He bent and kissed my collarbone. My neck. My ear. "It's your space. Not his."

Earl Walker. He was talking about Earl Walker.

He pushed a box aside, sending it crashing to the ground. My stomach flexed in response, so he tightened his arms and held me until my nerves calmed. Until the crack in my shell began to mend.

"Point taken," I said, making the time-out signal with my hands. "Play time is over."

Ignoring me, he reached out and pushed another.

I bucked against him, but his hold was unbreakable. He kept me pinned to the spot and pushed another box off the mountaintop. It tumbled to the ground. Then another. And another. All the while keeping me locked against him.

The heat emanating off him soaked into my clothes and hair, the scent earthy and rich. His corded arms and strong hands held me so tight, fear didn't really have a chance to take over. When he pushed another box and three plummeted to the ground, not a single drop of adrenaline escaped into my nervous system.

He reached a bare foot around me, kicked one out of his way; then we stepped closer and he kept pushing and shifting boxes with one hand while holding me to him with the other until only one object remained in Area 51. The chair.

This time, adrenaline did flood my nervous system, and I couldn't take my eyes off it even though it was like any other chair. It belonged to the small table I'd tucked into a corner in my kitchen. Cheaply made with rickety legs and a rounded back.

Reyes wrapped me tighter with both arms and took another step closer. I put my foot on the seat and pushed to keep my distance.

"It's just a chair," he said, his voice careful, soothing. "It's your chair. Not his."

"And I'm just a girl," I said, trying to explain to him that while I might have some supernatural standing out in the universe, here on Earth, I was just as human as anyone else.

He wrapped a hand around my throat and whispered in my ear. "Yeah, but you're mine. Not his."

He bent over my shoulder and slanted his mouth across my lips.

When I reached between us to caress the bulging outline in his jeans, his breath caught in his chest. He tensed to a marblelike hardness, then broke off the kiss and stared down into my eyes. His glittered with an emotion unsettlingly close to anger. "Are you in love with him?"

"Who?" I asked, basking in the sting of ecstasy pooling between my legs.

"The one from the asylum."

"Donovan?" I asked, breathless.

"If you are, you have to send me away." He buried his fingers in my hair and held my head back against his shoulder, his determination impenetrable. "You'll have to do it. I'm strong enough to leave now." He groaned when I brushed my hand over the outline of his erection again. Grabbing hold of my wrist, he stared down at me, a warning in his eyes. "I'll not lie with you if you love another."

His dialect took on that old-world quality it sometimes did despite his years on Earth, reminding me he was from another place, another time.

I reached up and pulled him down until his mouth was on mine again. If I loved anyone in the universe, it was this man, this god who'd risked his life for me countless times. Who'd asked for nothing in return. Ever.

He gripped my hair and tilted his head to the side to deepen the kiss, his tongue teasing and exploring as he sent a hand up my shirt. In one lightning-quick move, my bra hung unfastened and he cupped Danger in his palm. A shiver of pleasure raced over my skin with his touch. With his other hand, he unbuttoned my pants and pushed them over my hips. My abdomen tingled with excitement as he broke off the kiss again to peel my clothes off completely with an impatient fervor. Cool air washed over my skin, but he stepped close again, enveloping me within his warmth. Then he edged me closer to the chair.

With one knee, he nudged my legs apart and sat me down facing the back. I gripped the wooden slats, no longer worried about what the chair represented but electrified by the prospect of what could happen in it now.

He leaned over my shoulder and questioned me with his expressive eyes.

We'd never been here, in this place. Not flesh to flesh, physical form to physical form.

"It's been a very, very long time," he said, his deep voice less certain than usual.

I reached up and traced my fingertips along the outline of his mouth, full and sensual. He kissed my fingers then parted his lips and grazed his teeth along the sensitive tips. The heat of his tongue scorched my skin as his own fingers slid up my thigh, causing my nerve endings to quake with the rush of elation his touch evoked until he reached the apex between my legs and pushed inside me.

I gasped. Liquid heat flooded my abdomen. He slid his other hand down my back and gently pushed me forward, coaxing his fingers farther inside me. I tensed as a ravenous desire rippled through me. Gripping the chair harder, I spread my legs even more.

With a growl, he covered my mouth with his own. The rhythmic rocking of his fingers that matched the thrusts of his tongue was almost my undoing. A biting arousal stirred and churned, pulsating like a cauldron of lava in my abdomen. Sweet tendrils of ecstasy spread throughout my body, stinging with a hungry need.

When he kneeled beside me and took Will's peak into his blistering mouth, I almost cried out at the instantaneous jolt of pleasure. The tendrils turned to claws. I wrapped my arms around his head, buried my fingers in his hair as he suckled Will and coaxed me closer and closer to orgasm.

Before I could come, he took hold of my hips and lifted me out of the chair to stand before him. His sudden absence was like being doused in ice water. I blinked to attention as he sat back on his heels and stared. I should have been self-conscious. He was still fully clothed while I stood completely naked, but the stark admiration glistening in his eyes, the raw desire, eased every insecurity I'd ever had.

"My God," he said, rising onto his knees.

He took hold of my wrists, locked them behind my back, and trailed tiny kisses over my stomach. Waves of delight shot to my core when he dipped inside my belly button. Then he parted my legs and lifted one over his shoulder, giving his mouth access to that most sensitive area. I clutched the back of the chair for balance as his scalding tongue coaxed me back to the edge of sanity. To the fringe of madness. I welded my teeth together and grabbed his hair, a pulsing need rocketing through me.

My legs shook, so weak with longing I could hardly stand.

The closer I got to orgasm, the more I wanted him in me. I pulled at his hair. Ripped at his shirt. He paused and jerked it over his head. Then I tugged him to his feet. My hands shook as I worked to unfasten his pants. With rushed movements, he pushed his jeans over his hips and exquisite buttocks. His erection stood firm, pulsing with anticipation. And it was my turn to stare in admiration. A fine sheen of sweat covered his powerful body, making him even more alluring, even more exotic.

The hills and valleys that made up his sensuous form were like a work of art and the evidence of his arousal was no exception. I raked my fingernails over the length of him and watched in fascination as his muscles contracted in response. Before he could stop me, I dropped to my knees and took him into my mouth. He hissed in a sharp breath.

"Dutch," he said, locking a fist in my hair and fighting for control.

I looked up and his eyes blazed with unspent desire. I knew the feeling, wanted him to experience more of it. Drawing him in deeper, I grazed my teeth along the smoothness of his erection, reveled in the feel of blood rushing through it.

He tightened his hold on my hair as though trying to stop me. "Wait."

But my arms locked around him to keep him close. His breathing grew labored. Tormented. On the inside, he trembled with the force of it, with the passion he held in check. He tensed each time I drew him inside, groaning until I'd milked him to the brink of orgasm.

Left with no other choice, he jerked me off him and pinned me to the floor, his body rock hard against mine. Without waiting a moment longer—unable to wait a moment longer—he spread my legs and pushed inside me. A shock of pleasure ripped through me so hard and fast it stole my breath. I clutched at his back, bit down on his shoulder, kicked at his hips, but he just wrapped me tighter in his arms and drove, faster and faster, harder and harder, the pressure bubbling and building until I came with a violent burst of white hot sparks. They cascaded over my skin and rushed through every molecule in my body like a shower of light, spilling through my entire being, crashing against my bones like the sea. I had imploded, and all that was left were shimmering flakes of gold.

In exquisite agony, Reyes buried his face against my neck, clawing at me, growling as his own orgasm shuddered through him, his body vibrating with pleasure. He quaked in the wake of it, panting on top of me, letting the orgasm run its course.

"Fuck," he said at last. He relaxed and lay beside me.

I opened my eyes to look at him. "What?" I asked, worried.

He grinned. "Just fuck."

"Oh."

His dark lashes fanned across his cheeks as he lay in stunned satisfaction. I ran my finger along their fringe, and he frowned with a chuckle.

"Now I know the true meaning of perfection," I said.

His eyes blinked open, and he stared at me with a deep appreciation. "You need to get out more."

"So everyone tells me."

But I hadn't been kidding. It would never be better than this. Better than him. Reyes was the apex. It was all downhill from here. He was heaven and hell at once, angel and demon. I wondered how long I could keep him. How long I could call him mine.

He turned onto his side, rested his head on an arm, and put a large hand across my belly. With a mischievous grin that transformed his handsome face into that of an angel's, he asked, "Do you know where the gods keep their nectar?"

I narrowed my eyes in suspicion, and said, "No idea."

His hand slid down my stomach and between my legs. I sucked in a sharp breath as he leaned in and whispered in my ear, "Let me show you."

After two more explorations of our stamina, a shared roast beef sandwich, a shower, and another exploration of our stamina, we lay on my bed, entangled in sheets and towels. Reyes wrapped me in his arms and was almost asleep when I said, "Who knew that all this time the nectar of the gods was in my va-jay-jay?" He laughed softly and let sleep overtake him, but I could not stop looking at his handsome face. At his sensual mouth and strong jaw. His straight nose and thick lashes. He was a miracle. A godsend. And a pain in the ass, but so was I, so I couldn't fault him that.

I heard my front door open, so I disentangled our limbs, threw on a pair of pajamas, and headed out to the living room. Cookie was putting something in one of my kitchen drawers.

"Do you know what time it is?" I asked her.

She turned to me and raised a sucky thing. "This is a turkey baster. I'm not sure why you ordered seven, but I'm only letting you keep one."

I had no idea either. "It's after midnight. What are you doing?"

"I watched a scary movie and couldn't sleep."

"How many times do I have to tell you? If you're going to watch scary movies, do it when I'm around so I can giggle when you jump." There was nothing more fun than watching Cookie's eyes glaze over in fear. Besides what I just did with Reyes.

"I know. So, how was your day?"

"Well, I was in a bank robbery, taken hostage by the Gentlemen Thieves, almost arrested as an accessory, and had one of the most interesting evenings of my life. Speaking of which, did you know the nectar of the gods is in my va-jay-jay?"

She shot me a mortified look of horror. "What the hell is a va-jay-jay?"

But I could tell she knew. Deep down inside. Otherwise, why the horror?

"Wait, what happened over there?" she asked, nodding toward Area 51.

"Reyes has been giving me therapy, though I don't think he's licensed."

She gasped and dived toward me. "Oh, Charley, I need details. And an oil-on-canvas if you can get one done."

18

That which doesn't kill me
had better run pretty darned fast.

—T-SHIRT

"Where are you going?" I asked Reyes as he climbed out of bed.

"To your sad excuse for a kitchen."

I gasped. No one insulted my sad excuse for a kitchen and got away with it. But then he flashed his nuclear grin and I forgot what the problem was instantly.

"Got anything to eat?" he asked.

"Does green, fuzzy stuff count?"

"I'm not really into health food," he said with an even more dazzling grin.

When he walked by the dresser, the fact that I had taken out his picture that morning, the one of him bound and blindfolded, hit me with a jolt of panic. He didn't even look at my dresser. He would never have seen it, but the panic that rushed through me stopped him in his tracks. I had to remember he was like me. He could feel emotion as easily as I could. Could sense it and taste it in the air. And my panic hit him hard enough to stop his forward momentum. I'd given myself away.

He turned to me, curiosity cinching his brows together. "What?" he asked, a half grin still lighting his face.

"Nothing. I just thought, I thought you were leaving."

A deep suspicion stilled him. "Why are you lying to me?"

"I'm not. I mean, I am but only because there's something I don't want you to see."

Without thought, he looked around. He didn't spot it. It lay facedown, half covered by file folders and a brush and quite possibly a box of feminine products I had yet to transfer to my bathroom.

He turned back to me and crossed his arms. "Now I'm curious."

I pulled my lower lip between my teeth. "What if I asked you not to be?"

"You don't trust me?"

"It's not about trust. Not really. Not on your end."

He shifted his weight in thought. "So, it's about trust on your end? As in, should I trust you?"

"Kind of, yeah. Or you'd see it that way."

"What way, exactly?" He looked over his shoulder in confusion. If the picture had been a snake, it would've bit him, then he would've killed it in his manly warrior way. But, yes, he was that close.

"How about we go out and grab a bite?"

"Is it this?" he asked. Without looking behind him, he reached back and slid the picture off the desk.

"How'd you—?"

I stopped before digging my hole any deeper. He still had his beautiful gaze locked on mine when he brought the picture forward, but the minute it dropped, the minute his eyes landed on the image, a cold shiver of astonishment hit me. He blinked in shock.

I rose to my knees and crawled across the bed toward him. "Reyes—"

"Where did you get this?"

The next emotion to hit me was not anger or pain, but betrayal. Distrust.

"I just . . . A woman gave it to me. She found it in the apartment you were living in when I first met you. She'd saved it."

"But why would you keep it?"

The storm of torment that swept through him made me light-headed. It made my chest contract and my heart ache. "I don't know. I haven't looked at it once since the first time."

He rushed forward, and a blast of anger hit me. Finally, something I could deal with. "Then why keep it, Dutch?"

I raised my chin. "I don't know." How could I tell him I never wanted to forget what he went through? What either of us went through at the hands of that monster?

He strode out of the bedroom, picture in hand. I hurried after him as he headed for the stove. He was going to burn it. That was probably best, but for some reason—for some bizarre, inexplicable reason—I lunged for it and grabbed it away from him.

An astounded glare stole over his features. "Give it to me."

"Can you tell me what happened?" I asked him, knowing full well he'd never open up to me that much. Not enough to tell me about his past with Earl Walker. I could hardly blame him, but it was worth a try.

"How about I burn that and we forget all about it."

"I can't," I said, trying to curb the pain in my chest, but he felt it anyway.

With a growl that sent my heart racing into overtime, he wrapped one hand around my throat and the other around my waist. From there, he led me back against the wall.

"Don't you ever feel sorry for me, Dutch. The last thing I need is your pity."

"It's evidence, Reyes. If what you went through is ever questioned again, we'll have proof. And I don't feel sorry for you. I empathize with you."

The grin that spread across his face no longer sat at a playful angle. It held more animosity than warmth. More intimidation than affection. And my heart broke. I thought we were beyond this. Apparently not.

He leaned in, the heat of his anger like molten lava on my skin. The visceral reaction from my body anytime he was near seemed to multiply triplefold. I inhaled through my teeth and he paused. After a moment, he placed his forehead on mine and leaned in to me, seeming just as unable to fight the attraction as I. But in his eyes, I had betrayed him. He didn't want me looking into his past, and that is exactly what this picture represented.

When he spoke, his voice was even, his tone distant. "The minute you can tell me the difference between sympathy and empathy where that picture is concerned, you give me a call." He pushed me back in warning before grabbing his duffel bag, heading out the door, and slamming it shut behind him. I slumped back against the wall and fought to fill my lungs.

Cookie came over the next morning with new intel on the case, and I fought to keep the telltale signs of sadness at bay.

"Okay," she said, reading from her notes as she made herself a cup of coffee, "it seems that the gardener Mrs. Beecher told you about, Felix Navarro, died a few months ago."

"Well, that would explain why he's no longer their gardener. Anything suspicious about his death?"

"No. His daughter told me he died of natural causes, nothing to investigate."

"Well, then, he's definitely not our guy. If he did have all those pictures of Harper in his wallet, maybe he was just really fond of her." I took a sip of coffee and sat at my breakfast bar. The boxes in the apartment had dwindled down to almost nothing. Cookie had made tons of headway in the last two days. The only boxes that remained were the ones from Area 51.

"He was," she said. "His daughter told me he carried pictures of all his kids, and he considered both Harper and her stepbrother, Art, part of his family."

"Oh, well, that's sweet."

"It is. Very. Though I can see why Mrs. Beecher would see it as suspicious, considering everything that happened."

"True."

She flipped to the next page. "Oh, and your uncle Bob called. That guy torched another building early this morning."

"Same guy?"

"It would seem so. I wrote the address on the file." She pointed to a file folder lying on my kitchen table. "Apparently the arsonist pulled someone out of the building kicking and screaming before he set fire to it."

I sat my coffee cup down. "Well, at least he's civic minded."

She nodded and continued to stir her coffee as I went to grab my bag. "Okay," I said, "call me if you get anything else."

"Will do."

Just as I headed for the door, I glanced at the file folder. The recognition didn't hit me until I'd shouldered my bag and reached for the doorknob. I stopped, remembered the address, and whirled around so fast, the world tilted off center. Hurrying back, I tore the Post-it Note with the address of the latest fire off the folder. Then the world tilted for another reason entirely.

When I pulled up to the scene of the fire, the smell of smoke billowed in through Misery's vents, acrid and irritating. Firefighters were still working on it, shooting water in the air from huge red trucks. The whole area was taped off, and bystanders stood off to one side, watching the firefighters do their job, filming the massive wall of smoke on their phones.

I stepped out and looked up. No way was this an accident. No way was this a coincidence. This was it—the very building I'd been talking to Reyes about not three hours earlier. The one where I'd first seen him. The one where the picture was found.

I called Cookie. "Hey, hon. I need you to check something out for me."

"You got it."

"I want you to get that list of all the addresses the arsonist has hit. It's in the folder. Then crosscheck those with the known addresses Uncle Bob had on Reyes Farrow when he was first arrested for Earl Walker's murder. I have his file in the cabinet."

"Right, I remember it." Her words were drawn out and wary. "Do you think there's a connection?"

"That's what I intend to find out. Or, you know, for you to find out." I hung up and strolled to an officer on duty. "Where's the woman?" I asked him.

"Excuse me?" He started toward me with his palms up in warning. "You need to stay one hundred feet back."

"The woman the arsonist dragged out before he torched the place. Where is she?"

The guy glanced around. "How did you know that?"

"I'm working with APD on this case under the supervision of Detective Robert Davidson." When he didn't budge, I showed him my PI license and my APD ID that identified me as a consultant. "Would you like Detective Davidson's number?"

Before he could answer, I heard Uncle Bob's voice. "Charley," he said, lumbering up to me. His knee must've been bothering him again. "I didn't expect you to come over. As far as we can tell, the building was empty except for that one woman. She is not happy to be out."

I nodded. It had to be Ms. Faye—and, no, she would not be happy, but worry of a different nature knotted my gut. It must've shown.

"What is it, pumpkin?" Uncle Bob asked.

I offered him a weak smile. "Maybe nothing. I just . . . I hope it's nothing."

"Hon, if you know something about this case—"

"I'm not sure I do. Cookie's looking into it now. If I get anything, I'll call."

He nodded.

"So, could Ms. Faye identify the arsonist?"

"Nope. Said it was too dark, but he was tall and thin."

I wouldn't exactly call Reyes thin, but I could see where Ms. Faye might. She had an odd way of seeing the world.

"Your Agent Carson has some pretty good leads on those bank robbers."

"Yeah, sadly," I said.

"Friends of yours?" he asked, his brows raised.

"Very good friends of mine. Well, except for one. He wants to take me out. And, no, not on a date," I said, before he could ask.

"Oh, you mean like *take you out* take you out."

"Exactly."

"Well, glad we got that clear. How's your other case coming along?"

I gave him my defeated expression. The one where my lips looked very much like they belonged in the duck family. "It's not."

"I'm sorry, kid. Let me know if I can help."

"Thanks, Uncle Bob. And be careful with Ms. Faye. She has an arm on her—"

"Oh, no, already learned that." He rubbed his shoulder. That woman was a menace.

I climbed back into Misery, going over what I knew to be fact in my head. Reyes had smelled like smoke. His shirt had been singed and he had scratches on his face, something Ms. Faye was very capable of, even with him.

For once in my life, I prayed I was wrong.

Since I was close, I decided to check in on Harper before heading to my next stop. I walked in the back to the sound of an ink gun buzzing away. One of them must've been working on a friend, because they didn't open for hours.

I found Pari at her desk. "Hey, you, how's Harper?"

"What did you do?" she asked, fumbling to find her sunglasses.

"Nothing." I felt it was better to play innocent now while I could still lay claim to it. "Why? What'd I do?"

She slipped them on, then strode toward me. "Sienna is gone. She went back to New Orleans."

I backed out, holding up my hands. "We didn't do anything. She was into you, not me."

"She came over yesterday, shaking and freaking out, saying something about you not being what you say you are." She leveled a furious glare on me. "How did she find out?"

I couldn't help but notice a smile on Tre's face as he inked an octopus on a college kid's back. The work was incredible. Behind the octopus was a labyrinth of steam-powered mechanisms. Wheels and cogs working together to push the hands of a huge clock that covered his left shoulder blade. But Tre was smiling for a different reason altogether. I was so thick sometimes. The guy was totally into Pari. He was thrilled that Sienna was gone.

I led Pari to a more private area. "My dad tried to shoot me. I ducked. That was it."

"Your dad tried to shoot you?"

"Only twice."

She lowered her head in defeat. "Sienna and I really connected. I thought she could be the one."

"You've been seeing her for a day."

"And it was a great day," she said, her defensive hackles rising.

"Have you ever thought about looking closer to home?" I asked, hedging.

"What do you mean? Like, in my family? Because that's normally frowned upon."

"No, like in your house." I nodded toward Tre as he added shadow to a tentacle.

At first her face contorted with a jolt of revulsion; then she rethought her expression. I could hear the cogs clicking as she peeked around the wall to take another look. "He is hot."

"Duh."

"But he's just so . . . I don't know, slutty."

"You're one to talk. Wait a minute." I cast her a knowing smile. "You're worried about the competition."

"Am not."

"Are too."

"Am not."

"Are—"

"Boss!" Tre called out, his voice full of mirth. "If you're finished talking about my awesomeness, your client has decided on a color."

She straightened. "Oh, that's me. Tell Harper hey for me."

"You got it."

I wound toward the back room, but Harper wasn't there. I checked the whole area, including the front of Pari's parlor. No Harper. Darn. I was running out of time.

Since Mrs. Beecher had been so helpful the first time I spoke with her, I decided to question her again, only this time I'd focus on what Harper was like when she'd come back from her grandparents' after the Lowells got married. I parked in front of her house again, admired her purple flowers again, and knocked on her door, wondering where Harper could have gotten off to.

Mrs. Beecher pulled open the solid wood door, but stayed behind the screen like last time. However, unlike last time, she seemed annoyed at my being there. Couldn't blame her. I annoyed the best of them.

"Hi again," I said, waving inanely. "It's just me. I was wondering if I could ask you a couple more questions."

She glanced over her shoulder, then said, "I have dinner on."

"Oh, it'll just take a minute."

After pressing her mouth together, she nodded. She wore a gray dress this time that matched her hair and eyes, and a pale yellow apron.

"Awesome, thank you. I understand Harper stayed with her grandparents while the Lowells went on their honeymoon. Do you remember anything odd about that trip? Did Harper seem like she'd been abused in any way? Or bullied? Anything out of the ordinary?" I took out my memo pad again, just in case she gave me some juicy tidbits, because the best tidbits were juicy.

"Not especially." She shrugged and thought back. "She'd come in every evening after playing out in the sun with the neighbor kids all day. Got a horrible sunburn. Other than that, she had the time of her life. She loved it out there on her grandparents' estate."

I paused, then ran my tongue over my bottom lip. "She'd come in?" I asked in surprise. "You mean, you were there? You were at her grandparents' house with her?"

Her smile stretched as false as a bad face-lift. Suddenly every movement she made was calculated, every expression rehearsed. "I was, yes. I just assumed you knew that."

"No. No one mentioned it." Was it really so easy to dismiss the help like they didn't exist?

A ripple of unease radiated off the woman, and I realized I might have assigned the wrong source to the fear I'd felt the first time I met her. I'd assumed she was afraid of speaking to me because of Mrs. Lowell and what she might do. I'd never imagined . . .

No, I couldn't jump to conclusions. Besides the fact that I wasn't that strong a jumper, this was a sweet old lady. Sweet old ladies didn't stalk children. They didn't terrorize them or bully them without a reason, and what reason would anyone have to oppress a five-year-old child?

I decided to play my ace, see if she'd show her hand. I waited a heartbeat, then said, "Well, when I talked to Harper a couple of days ago, she didn't mention you'd been with her. But you didn't notice anything out of the ordinary?"

The moment the words of left my mouth, Mrs. Beecher's emotions went wild like I'd hit the jackpot on a slot machine. But she was a pro. Her poker face was a thing of beauty. The emotion roiling underneath her calm exterior was like a summer hurricane as seen from the calm of space.

I stood there stunned. The housekeeper? Seriously? She was four feet tall and as round as a muffin.

"I'm sorry I keep asking the same question," I said after a quick shake to recover. "We're just really worried about Harper. Any information you have will help."

She suddenly seemed more fragile than fine china as she craned open the screen door and hobbled to the side. "Certainly, certainly. I'm sorry for being so rude. You come on in." Even her voice quivered more than it had when she first answered.

Oh, yeah. This was going to end badly.

I wondered who else she had inside. A burly beefcake who did all her dirty work for her? A crazy daughter who followed her every order? She didn't look like the type who would kill a rabbit and put it on a little girl's bed, but stranger things had happened.

Forcing my feet forward, I stepped inside the spider's web.

"Can I get you some tea, dear?" she asked.

So you can lace it with arsenic? I think not. "Um, no, thank you, I'm good."

We stood in the foyer, and I couldn't help but notice the seventeen million photographs she had of one man. They spanned his entire life from the time he was an infant until he was probably in his early forties. Her son, perhaps? Grandson?

"Now, what else would you like to know?"

Well, what I wanted to know was how on Earth I was going to prove that this sweet old lady had been threatening Harper practically her whole life. But I didn't think I should ask her that. I totally needed evidence. Or a full confession in high def.

She looked past the foyer, but I couldn't tell at what. Sadly, I couldn't turn and look, too, without seeming suspicious, and I wanted this woman to trust in the fact that she had me completely and utterly fooled.

"I know this is silly," I said, rolling my eyes with a helpless smirk, "but Ms. Lowell insists someone is trying to hurt her. Can you tell me what you remember from that time at her grandparents? Do you remember when the *supposed*—" I added air quotes. "—threats started?"

Her smile softened with relief. As far as she was concerned, I was just as gullible as her employers had been all those years. But I had to admit to more than my fair share of bafflement. Why would this woman terrorize a five-year-old girl? Then continue to do so her entire life? So much so that Harper had to be institutionalized? The mere thought was horrific.

I looked at the pictures that surrounded us. Maybe she had some help. It didn't take a genius to realize there was something a tad left of kilter about the guy in the pictures. His blue eyes seemed a little too bright. His brown hair a little too unkempt. His expressions a little too feral. He reminded me of Gerald Roma from grade school, who used to burn ants with a magnifying glass. He was never quite right. It was weird that he spontaneously combusted during finals week our freshman year in college. Payback was a bitch.

Mrs. Beecher chuckled and led me farther inside. "That girl and her imagination, I tell ya. She started telling stories when she was around five and never let up." She strolled all the way into her kitchen. I peeked into every nook and cranny I could along the way, trying to assess exactly what I was dealing with.

As luck would have it, Cookie called, her timing impeccable. "I'm sorry," I said, pushing the icon to accept the call, "will you give me a minute? I have to take this."

"You go right ahead, dear."

I turned and walked a few feet away toward an open door just off the kitchen, and I found it interesting that the closer I got to that door, the more apprehensive Mrs. Beecher became.

"Hey, Cook," I said, all cheer and goodwill. But before she could respond in kind, I said, "Yeah, I'm here talking to Mrs. Beecher now. This case is a dead end. I can't find any evidence whatsoever of what Harper Lowell was talking about." My words calmed the woman a bit, so I took another few steps that way.

"Okay," Cookie said, catching on, "are you in immediate danger?"

"I don't think so, but one never knows with cases like this."

"What can I do?"

"Sure, I can meet Uncle Bob for coffee. Can you call him and have him meet me at that address you gave me?"

"I can definitely do that. Do I need to get emergency over there?"

"Oh, no. That's okay. Just tell him to take his time. I'm almost finished here."

"Okay, calling Ubie now. Be careful."

"What? You like to look at naked men on the Internet?"

"I mean it."

Darn. Didn't even get a rise out of her. What good was harassment if she didn't rise to the occasion? I hung up and took one more step closer to that door. I couldn't see past the thick blackness, but it was cooler than the rest of the house, possibly a basement of some kind. Nothing good ever seemed to come of basements, so I started to turn back, when I heard a loud thud. A sharp pain exploded in my head; then the world tumbled around me in a series of somersaults and painful bounces.

I landed in a heap of hair and body parts at the bottom of a very solid set of stairs. One would think pine gave more than that. But crap on a cracker, that hurt.

I curled into a fetal position, cradling my head and gritting my teeth against the pain shooting through every molecule in my body. Above me, I heard a door close and then Mrs. Beecher's feeble steps descending the stairs. She moved at a pace that would have given a baby turtle a run for his money. A cast-iron skillet hung from her hands, and I was fairly certain that was what started my tumultuous journey into the unknown. Who knew cast iron was so hard?

I still needed evidence of her involvement in Harper's case. Right now, all I had was an assault with a skillet by an elderly woman who could claim dementia and most definitely get away with it in court. With every ounce of strength I had, I forced my muscles to relax, my body to go limp like wet noodles. Uncle Bob was on his way. Maybe I could wrap this case up before he got here.

My eyes had watered and the air felt cool against the wetness on my cheeks, but that was the only positive I could wring out of the situation. Well, that and the fact that I could probably outrun Mrs. Beecher if push came to shove. She was about halfway down the steps at that point, so I decided to save my mental strength and ponder what it would be like to live in a world where butterflies ruled and humans were their slaves.

It didn't help. All I could think about was the pain shooting through Barbara, my brain. Normally, I didn't pay a whole lot of attention to Barbara—she didn't get out much—but today was her day to shine. I was certain parts of her were oozing out of Fred, my skull.

As I lay there channeling spaghetti, Mrs. Beecher headed toward a stack of shelves and started rummaging through old boxes, probably looking for a rusty old hacksaw to dismember me before she buried my parts in this very basement. I couldn't help but notice it had a dirt floor. Convenient.

Then I heard something else. I looked up as Harper tiptoed down the stairs. I glared at her, but she rushed down the minute she saw me.

"Charley," she whispered, glancing around in horror, "what happened?"

"What are you doing here?" I asked through gritted teeth, trying not to move my lips. Not sure why. I wanted nothing more than to hold my head and writhe in agony.

Harper spotted Mrs. Beecher. She put a hand on my shoulder as recognition dawned on her face. "I remembered something, so I came over here."

"You really need to leave. She may not look like much, but that woman has a wicked left hook." I glared at her over my shoulder. "Freaking cheater. How the fuck did she wield a cast-iron skillet? She's the size of a tennis ball." But I'd lost Harper. She was staring at Mrs. Beecher's back, a combination of astonishment and anguish in her eyes. I had anguish in my eyes, too, but for a completely different reason.

"Harper," I whispered, trying to coax her back to me. Thankfully, Mrs. Beecher seemed to be unable to hear anything under a dull roar. "Sweetheart, what do you remember?"

Harper's huge brown eyes glanced down at me but didn't quite focus. "Her grandson," she said, her voice barely a whisper. "Dewey was a little older than me. He lived with us. With Mrs. Beecher in her apartment."

The pain ebbed slightly, the throbbing becoming almost tolerable. "What happened, hon? She stayed with you at your grandparents' house while your parents went on their honeymoon. Did her grandson hurt you?"

Her expression was so distant, I was afraid she wouldn't answer. But after a minute, she said, "No. Not me." She put her hands over her mouth. "A little boy. I think he killed a little boy."

My eyes slammed shut in a feeble attempt to block the mental image her words had conjured.

"Mrs. Beecher found Dewey. He was trying to wake the little boy up, but he couldn't. That's when she saw me."

I looked back at her. "Mrs. Beecher? She saw you nearby?"

"Yes. We were playing hide-and-seek in the barn, but Dewey got mad when the little boy found him. I'm not really sure what happened, but they started wrestling. Dewey got him down and sat on him until he stopped struggling. Stopped breathing." Harper shut her own eyes, and tears spilled out from them. Then she jumped, remembering more. "I came here. I came to ask Mrs. Beecher why she did it. Why she covered it up."

Mrs. Beecher had apparently found what she'd been looking for. She was headed back our way. I had to hurry. "Harper, what did she do? What did Mrs. Beecher do that day when you were in that barn?"

"She grabbed me." Harper refocused on her arms. "She had sharp nails and she shook me. Said that Dewey had accidently killed a rabbit. A white rabbit. And that if I ever told anyone, he would do the same to me. Then she put the rabbit in a suitcase and brought him back to the city with us."

My shock must have shown.

Harper nodded as sadness welled in her eyes. "But it wasn't a rabbit. I remember now. That little boy is buried somewhere on our property. In a red suitcase."

My lungs seized. Cookie told me there'd been a missing child from Peralta around that time, and Peralta and Bosque Farms sat back to back. It was hard to tell where one stopped and the other began. The case had never been solved.

Well, it was certainly about to be.

Still pretending to be unconscious, I lowered my lashes to slits as Mrs. Beecher ambled near. I could see just enough to make out her image as she shuffled into view. Carrying an ice pick. *An ice pick.* What the hell? This woman was cold. Harper gasped and huddled over me protectively. It was one of the sweetest things anyone had ever done for me.

The door above us opened, and heavy footsteps sounded on the stairs. Sadly, it couldn't have been Uncle Bob. Not enough time. And Uncle Bob almost always yelled things like, *APD! Get your hands up!* This guy didn't yell anything.

I cringed as the guy from the pictures stepped beside me. Partly because he was ginormous, almost twice the height of Mrs. Beecher, but mostly because shit just got real. Now I'd have to outrun both of them with Barbara oozing out of Fred.

"Who are you?" he asked me. He apparently talked to spaghetti, as I was doing my best impression of a wet noodle.

"This woman wants to take you away from me. We're going to have to plant her in the ground so she can grow."

He lowered his head. "I don't think I want to do that anymore."

"I don't want to either, but I need you here with me, honeybun. Who else is going to do the yard work?"

The yard work?

"I know, Grandma, but—"

The fucking yard work?

"No buts. Now, you take care of her like you did Miss Harper."

He looked over into a dark corner of the basement. Toward a fresh mound of dirt. "Harper was nice to me."

I'd mow her lawn, for fuck's sake. This was honestly about yard work?

She reached up and patted his big shoulder. "I know. I know. But she was going to turn you in to the police. They would have taken you to jail, sugar britches. What would I do without you?"

He shrugged and she cackled in delight, pinching his cheek as if he were four. I was in so much trouble.

Gripping the ice pick like her life depended on it, she looked down at me. "Hold on, though. I have to make sure she's dead first."

She bent to one knee beside me, a laborious act that took her enough time for me to ponder what would happen if the polar ice caps melted. After that played out, I wondered if I should make a run for it or try to reason with Dewey. He seemed to be slightly saner than his counterpart.

"Now, where do you suppose her heart is?" said counterpart asked.

Betty White? She was going for Betty?

Instinctively, my hands shot up to cover her. She was so fragile. So vulnerable. And Mrs. Beecher wanted to jab her with an ice pick? Not on my watch.

The woman jumped back in surprise, and I started to scramble toward the stairs when a weight comparable to a cement mixer landed on my back.

"Oh, that's good, sugar pie. You hold her there. Now, where'd that ice pick go?"

Harper lunged forward, intending to knock Dewey off me, and was surprised when she flew right through him.

Damn. I should have told her. It was hard when people didn't know they were dead. The realization sent them into a state of shock, and sometimes I wouldn't see them again for years. But I really should have told her, because the stunned expression on her face as she turned back and reached through Dewey's head broke my heart.

She locked gazes with me. "I'm dead?" she asked, her voice hoarse with emotion. She sank to the ground, her expression a thousand miles away.

I strained against the weight of Dewey, wondering what the heck his grandmother fed him but thrilled she'd lost the ice pick. "I'm sorry, Harper." I could barely get out the words. "I wanted to tell you."

"What?" Mrs. Beecher asked.

"I called the police," I said, craning my neck. "They're on the way."

She scoffed and turned her back to me. "I need more light. Where could that thing have got off to?"

"They killed me?" Harper asked, still in a daze.

I reached out to her and put my hand on her knee. "Yes. I'm not sure who exactly. Do you remember what happened?"

"She's talking, Grandma."

"Well, sit harder."

He took her advice and bounced, and all I could think was, *Oh. My. God.* Where was Uncle Bob when I needed him?

Feeling like I was in a horror movie, waiting for evil clowns to appear from under the stairs, I tried to focus on surviving this freak show.

"What are you doing?"

I turned to my other side to see Angel. He wore a scowl of disapproval.

"I'm trying to breathe," I said, trying to breathe. But darkness crept into my periphery.

"Why is that guy sitting on you?" Then he saw Harper. "Oh, hey."

He nodded an acknowledgment, but she was still in shock. She raised her hands and looked at them, turning them over and over.

"I don't suppose you could push this guy off me?" I asked him.

"I guess I could try."

"So, like, soon?"

Angel frowned, then focused on Dewey and concentrated. After a few seconds, he pushed. And Dewey went head over heels.

Sweet potato pie.

I scrambled for the stairs again while fighting the tilt of the Earth. It kept throwing me against the wall, and I realized I probably had a concussion. Unfortunately, Dewey recovered and reached over the stairs, grabbing my leg and pulling it out from under me.

This was going to hurt.

Yep. My chin hit a step, clashing my teeth together. This was so much like a thousand horror movies I'd seen.

Dizziness played a huge part when I tumbled right back down the stairs.

I held up my hands and said, "You need to calm down."

That was when Dewey wrapped his large hands around my throat. Someday I'd realize telling people to calm down had exactly the opposite effect.

"Hold her still, sugar. I can't find that danged ice pick. I'll have to use the skillet."

"You need to stop thinking like a human," Angel said.

"You are not helping. Go get Reyes."

"I'm here," Reyes said from a corner. "Watching you get your ass kicked. Again."

His thick black robe undulated around me, not helping at all with the sudden onset of motion sickness. This was definitely the incorporeal Reyes. The Beechers couldn't see him.

When Dewey's grip slipped for a split second, I said to Reyes, "Do something."

"Can I break her neck?"

"No."

"Can I break his neck?"

I had to think about that one.

Mrs. Beecher was headed my way, skillet at the ready.

"You have to . . . save . . . Fred and Barbara," I said. With Dewey's hands around my throat, I sounded like a cartoon character. A fact that could not possibly be appealing. Really, how long was he going to let this go on?

"I'm trying to let you come into your powers."

"Fuck my powers. Do something."

Reyes dematerialized and rematerialized beside me. I heard the sing of his blade; then Dewey's grip relaxed, his expression morphed into surprise, and he fell to the floor. Reyes had severed his spine, though it would take the doctors a little while to realize it. There would be no outside trauma. Reyes cut from the inside out.

Mrs. Beecher stopped, her face just as shocked.

"Mrs. Beecher," I said, coughing and sputtering like a Yugo, "put that frying pan down this instant."

19

When life hands you lemons say,
"Lemons? What else have you got?"
—BUMPER STICKER

Uncle Bob showed up in his own sweet time and ordered a team of investigators as soon as he got to the Beechers' house and saw me wrestling with Mrs. Beecher. That woman was so much stronger than she looked. Reyes kept wanting to sever her spine, and Angel kept telling me to stop thinking like a human, whatever the hell that meant.

After watching Uncle Bob tackle her to the ground—an image I would cherish forever—I gave my statement to him; then he drove me to the Lowells' mansion. Harper was in the backseat, still stewing in her own astonishment. Two patrol cars followed behind us, and another detective from Ubie's precinct was en route to the scene. The Lowells were about to be scandalized.

I still wasn't exactly sure who had done the terrorizing—Mrs. Beecher or Dewey on Mrs. Beecher's orders—but it didn't really matter in the grand scheme of things. Neither would be able to do it again.

Uncle Bob put a hand on mine. "Now, just tell them that Dewey told you where the boy's body was, okay?"

"You say that like I haven't done this a thousand times," I said, cringing at the sound of my own voice. It was odd what a crushed larynx did to the midtones.

"I know. Sorry, pumpkin."

"It's okay. Harper says she remembers where the suitcase is. The only place it could be. Dewey had started a new garden when they got back. It has to be there."

He turned a worried expression on me. "This is not going to be pretty, hon. If you need to leave—"

"Oh, hell yeah, I'm leaving. The minute Harper shows us the grave, I'm out of there."

"So this is it," Harper said, coming to terms with her demise.

I turned around to face her. "I'm so sorry you've passed, hon."

"Have you known this whole time? That I was dead?"

"Yes. It's what I do."

"So, no one else can see me? I'm—I'm a ghost?"

"I'm afraid so. But you can cross through me whenever you're ready. Your family is waiting for you on the other side. Your mother. Your grandparents. They'll be so happy to see you."

She nodded. "I know. I think I've known they were waiting for me this whole time." Her voice cracked. "I wonder how long I've been dead."

"Well, you came to see me two days ago, but Mrs. Beecher knew you'd been gone longer than that. That's how I knew she did it. But your psychotherapist said the last time he saw you in his office was almost two weeks ago. So it had to be—"

"That's it." She stared in thought. "I was in a session with Dr. Roland and I was telling him about a trip I was going on. He asked me what color my suitcase was, and everything came rushing back. Dewey killing that boy. Mrs. Beecher putting him in that red suitcase." She covered her mouth. "What kind of people do that? She lived with us for over two decades. How could we not know?"

"I was a little floored myself when I figured out she was involved. I think she is very good at fooling people."

We pulled up to the speaker box. "Whatever you do," I told Uncle Bob, "do not order a taco. They're very sensitive about that."

He nodded, flashed his badge, and said, "Open that gate. I have a warrant."

And the gate opened. Just like that. No haggling or bartering. I totally needed to become a real cop. It probably paid better.

Mrs. Lowell met us on the steps to her house, as did her son, Art. He was dressed in a nice suit and tie, and Mrs. Lowell had been spit-shined herself. She wore a long evening gown and pearls. Clearly we'd interrupted their evening plans.

"Now what?" she asked as I got out of Ubie's SUV.

He hurried around to intercept.

Despite their duds, they seemed upset. I got the feeling they'd been arguing when we arrived.

"Mrs. Lowell, we have information about a missing child. He's been gone for over two decades, and we believe he is buried on your property."

She huffed, indignant. "Oh, for the love of—"

"Your former housekeeper," I said, interrupting her tirade before she became too invested in it, "buried him here, knowing no one would look on your property. Why would they? The boy was from Peralta."

She paused and ogled me like I'd lost my mind. I looked from her to Art, knowing he would take Harper's death hard.

"Can we go inside?" I asked him.

"I can't get ahold of Harper," he said as he waved Uncle Bob and me inside. "She hasn't returned my calls for over a week. Have you talked to her?"

I swallowed the lump in my throat. "That's the other reason we're here."

Two hours later, I found myself hiding in the Lowells' bathroom as the digging crew lifted a red suitcase out of the turned earth. It was exactly where Harper had said it would be, under a patch of garden that Dewey had tended for over twenty years. Unlike Mrs. Beecher, Dewey's actions would speak of remorse and regret.

An entire team had been dispatched to the scene, and along with it came camera crews and reporters galore. I almost felt bad for Mrs. Lowell. This definitely would taint her image, no matter how innocent of wrongdoing she was. But when Uncle Bob told her Harper's body had been found, the hard shell she'd encased herself in shattered. Her shock was so complete, so devastating, the pain of it almost doubled me over. She really did care for Harper. There was no denying it.

And I also knew she had nothing to do with that little boy's death or the subsequent cover-up. Her surprise was utterly genuine.

Art took Harper's death hard. He ensconced himself in a room upstairs, but even the thick walls of the Lowell mansion could not block the waves of agony that poured out of him.

And I stood hiding in a bathroom, fighting for air among the fragments of a broken family. Their suffering was only beginning, and even though I was still not allowed to see Mr. Lowell, I felt his pain spill down the stairs like a heavy fog.

"I can't be here anymore."

I turned to Harper. She stood looking out the bathroom window, watching the workers excavate the grounds, a dozen officers surrounding the taped-off area.

"I need to go before I can't go at all," she said.

I couldn't feel emotions off the departed as I could the living, not until they crossed, but the anguish on her face spoke volumes. She looked up toward the second floor, and I realized she was worried about Art.

"He's in love with you," I said.

She looked at me in surprise before a sad smile thinned her lips. She really was beautiful.

"He told me he was your contact."

She nodded. "Yes. We'd kept in contact the whole time. He even flew to the island to visit me a few times."

"Why didn't you guys ever hook up for real?" I asked her.

"We did. Kind of. When I came back, Art insisted that we get married, but I couldn't get past the fact that according to society, we were brother and sister. I hurt him so bad when I said that I wanted to wait."

"I'm sorry." Family was so important. If I'd learned nothing more these last three days, it was that.

Harper walked toward me, purpose in her eyes, and with one last glance toward Art, she crossed. I didn't see the pain and fear she'd suffered through all those years. I didn't see her being terrorized or the nightmare she suffered through from her time in the mental asylum. What I did see was her father picking her up and carrying her on his shoulders as she pointed out his route through the trees behind the house. I saw her dog, a golden retriever named Sport, who would lick her toes until she couldn't stand the tickling any longer. And I saw the first time Art kissed her. She was in high school, watching him at a basketball game. He'd been hurt and was in the locker room. She hurried to check on him. Gasped when she saw him being strapped onto a stretcher. Almost fainted when she saw the odd bump of the arm secured at his side, the bone straining to break through the flesh.

He'd covered his eyes with his other arm, hiding his anguish. She rushed forward, and before she knew what was happening, he wrapped his hand around her head and pulled her down until her lips were on his.

And then she was through.

Ever the romantic, the agony of lost love was my undoing. I let a series of sobs quake through me, and when I felt I could face the world despite the obvious swollen eyes to match my swollen jaw, I stepped out of the bathroom and asked an officer to drive me home. The Lowells would have a lot to deal with in the coming weeks, and I could only hope Art would be okay. According to Harper's memories, he hated chocolate, but I chose not to hold that against him. No one was perfect.

But really? Chocolate?

As I was getting into the officer's car, I heard a familiar female voice. "Charley Davidson."

I straightened and turned to Agent Carson as she walked across the driveway toward me. It figured the FBI would be here. It was a missing persons case, after all. "Hey, Agent Carson."

Before she could respond, Uncle Bob walked over to us. "Are you leaving?"

"Yeah, Uncle Bob, you remember Special Agent Carson."

She took his hand. "Detective. Your niece has a knack for solving cold cases."

He smiled proudly. "Yes, she does."

"I'm impressed, as usual. Someday you'll have to share your secrets," she said to me.

"I could tell you, but then I'd have to kill you."

"Fair enough. I was wondering if you'd look over a couple of cases for me. One is very old and is as yet unsolved and one is my own personal one-that-got-away."

I shrugged. "Sure, as long as you don't get your hopes up."

"My hopes never get out of hand, if that's what you mean."

"Then you can bring them by—" I was about to say *my office,* but realized I no longer had one. "You can bring them by my apartment."

"Or her office."

I turned to see Dad walking over to us. He stopped to stand beside Uncle Bob, his expression sheepish but hopeful. Ubie must've called him when he realized I'd been injured, but I wasn't sure I could handle Dad's presence at that moment. My heart hurt bad enough. And my head hurt. And my eyes were icky and swollen.

He put his hands in his pockets. "Are you okay?" he asked, and I wondered what Ubie had told him.

"Good as gold."

"I'm glad. And I'm moving you back into your offices. Pretending I can keep an eye on you, no matter how ridiculous the notion, will give me peace of mind. And you can glare at me and make faces behind my back and hate me forever, but when you're ready to talk, I'll be there. Without judgment and without a hidden agenda."

I looked out over the Lowells' vast estate. "If I make faces at you, Dad, it won't be behind your back."

He nodded. "I'll come for your stuff this weekend."

Agent Carson's brows rose in interest. "Perfect. I'll drop the files by next week, if that's okay?"

"Sounds like a plan," I said, ducking into the patrol car. Dad wanted to give me a ride home. I could feel his intentions thick in the air, his eagerness to be with me, but that was a cake I'd have to take in small bites. Still, I thought of Harper. The memories of her dad despite her stepmother's seeming indifference. I had a feeling Dad and I would be best friends again someday.

I looked back at Carson. "How goes the bank job?"

Uncle Bob grinned at her. "You're pulling bank jobs? Isn't that a little against the FBI code of conduct?"

She grinned. "What? There's a code of conduct? Nobody told me." She handed me her card. "And this case is turning out stickier than I'd hoped, but you were definitely right about the inside guy. Now to prove it." She nodded toward the card. "Use that if you hear anything else."

I winked at her, then closed the door before anyone else could walk up unexpectedly and wrench my heart into pieces.

Cookie called on the way home. I picked up and said, "No cast iron in the house. Ever."

"Got it. Making a note now. How was it?"

"Exhausting. And Mrs. Lowell isn't quite the monster I imagined her to be."

"Maybe Denise isn't either."

"Seriously?"

"Okay, I'm putting these feet to bed. Let me know if you need anything. Like an ice pack."

I jumped in alarm. "Did you say ice pick?"

"No."

"Because no ice picks in the house either. Ever."

"Got it. Making a note now."

The officer, who remained silent all the way home, thank the gods, dropped me at my front door. I offered the most grateful smile I could manage, then set out in search of a long, hot shower and a strong cup of java. But, naturally, the minute I stepped out of the patrol car, I was hit with all kinds of dark emotions that I'd learned to associate with dark people. Feral people. Possessed people.

I'd started to get right back in the car, when I heard an English accent from the shadows very near me. "I wouldn't, if I were you."

Wonderful. It was my new friend from the old country. I knew this day had gone too smoothly. My life had been in danger only a couple of times. These things usually happened in threes.

The officer looked back at me. "Is everything okay, Ms. Davidson?"

I so very much wanted to tell him the truth, but there was nothing he could do, and his life would be in just as much danger as mine if I brought him into it, so I said, "Yes, thank you," instead.

I closed the door and watched as he drove off. A hatred so pure it pulsated swirled around me. I could feel at least four of the beasts near, possibly five, lurking in shadows, afraid of the light even though they were protected by human flesh.

The Englishman stepped out of the dark to stand beside me. "Good girl," he said, and I wondered what the unpossessed Englishman was like in real life. He certainly dressed nice. But this wasn't him. This was a fraud, a minion from hell. A demon. I flexed my fingers at my hip, but Hedeshi stopped me again. "And don't call your dog, either. It will end badly for both of you."

Was he right? Could he kill Artemis?

"I take it Reyes didn't stop hunting your pets."

"You knew he wouldn't."

He was right. I did know. "Reyes doesn't really listen to me."

The man leaned over to smell my hair. He took a deep whiff, practically nuzzling my neck, reveling in the scent, while he smelled like rotten eggs. I tried not to flinch when his scent burned my nostrils.

When he spoke, the smell grew stronger. Suffocating. "If I could," he said, his voice soft, sincere, "if I had the time, I would lick the fear off every inch of your body before I bit into your flesh, but no doubt the boy will come soon."

The moon glinted off a silvery blade in my periphery. A blade very similar to the one Earl Walker had used on me. The fear that flooded my system hit so hard and so fast, the edges of my vision grew fuzzy. I wanted to run, but Hedeshi seemed to sense every thought I had.

He put a hand on my shoulder to stay me. "I'll make it quick, Dutch. You'll hardly feel a thing."

"Yeah," I said, my voice quivering, "I've been on the wrong end of a blade before, and I would have to argue with you on that point."

He stepped around until I could see his face. He wasn't tall, but I knew the demon inside gave him immeasurable strength. A humorous smile slipped soundlessly across his face. "You're probably right." His hand shook with excitement as he drew back the blade, and I hoped Dad would be okay with this. With my death. He'd probably take it hard.

Odd that I would think of him now.

Setting my jaw, I figured I should probably give this my all. If I was going to go out tonight, I was going to go out fighting. Or screaming in agony. Either way.

The blade rushed forward, certain to sink into my stomach, which instantly pissed me off. I'd heard death from a stomach wound was a really painful way to go. Reyes was right. These guys were liars. Before I could think about it, I blocked his attack by thrusting his hand to the side with one of mine, diverting the forward momentum. I twisted around, doing everything in my power to avoid the sharp end of the knife.

I still managed to get cut. The blade sliced across my forearm, through my jacket and into my flesh. The sting of the blade rocketed through me, but Hedeshi brought it back around for another try. He lost control for just an instant, and the demon inside the man slipped to the side. I saw him, and the sight stunned me for a moment. Long enough for him to sink the blade into my side. I rocketed to attention and pushed at him as hard as I could. Then I ran because it seemed like the right thing to do.

This was no ordinary demon, as ridiculous as that sounded. His shell didn't swallow light like the void of a starless night. Instead, his sleek black exterior gleamed with a red translucent coating, an iridescent shine. He was something else. Something higher. Stronger.

"Older, actually."

"Reyes," I whispered.

I tumbled out of Hedeshi's reach to the ground and swiveled around to see Reyes standing between us. No wonder I wasn't bleeding from a dozen different stab wounds. Reyes held the man's arm, the sheer strength each of them possessed causing the earth to quake beneath us. I scrambled back only to be brought up short by a hot breath fanning across my neck.

Slamming my eyes shut, I summoned Artemis, my voice nothing more than a breath on the night air. She rose from the earth beside me and lunged toward the demon at my back. Loud, guttural growls mixed with a series of inhuman screams as the demon was ripped from a woman's body.

Hedeshi and Reyes seemed oblivious. They stood there, arms clasped, eyeing each other. The energy radiating off them caused the fabric of time to ripple around me. Their images distorted, warped, then snapped back into place. I blinked to clear my vision. To focus.

The woman lay unconscious, but I felt more demons nearby. None dared come any closer, no matter how bad they wanted to. I could feel their desire, their singular drive, pulsate around me. They craved my blood like a desert craves water, my fear driving them into a mental frenzy. But they refrained from acting on it. Artemis was too powerful. She'd disposed of one demon and now stood hunched over me.

Waiting.

Hoping.

"You can't win," Hedeshi said.

Reyes lowered his head. "You forget who I am."

"Not at all." The man smiled, his teeth gritted with effort as he struggled against Reyes's hold. Shook with it. "You're the boy from the village who got lost on his way to the market. Do you remember why you're here? Why your father created you?"

Another wave rippled through the air with the heat of Reyes's anger. "He created me so he could get out of hell."

"That was only half of it. The other half was for you to find the portal." He nodded toward me. "That particular portal. Why do you think he sent you here?" He leaned in until their noses almost touched. "*You?*"

Reyes eased back. "He sent me after a portal, any portal. Not her." He didn't seem quite as confident as he had before. His brows slid together in thought.

The Englishman laughed. "You really don't remember, do you?"

"I remember everything, like the fact that all you know how to do is lie."

"She's royalty, boy. She's the most valuable pawn we could ever hope to possess. And you think you can keep her to yourself?"

A knowing grin slid across Reyes's face. "She's also the most powerful."

"Exactly," Hedeshi said, his eyes suddenly bright with hope. "Think of what we can do with her. With the two of you together. That's what this is all about. What it's always been about." He dropped the knife and wrapped his hand around the back of Reyes's head, pulling him forward into a brotherly embrace, their foreheads touching in affection. "We will be unstoppable, my lord. The world will fall beneath our feet, and your father will rule at last."

Was he telling the truth? Was Reyes sent for me specifically? He must've sensed my doubt. He turned slightly, watching me from his periphery. "Remember what they are, Dutch. What they do."

"I remember," I said, trying to scoot out from under Artemis, but she plopped a huge paw on my chest, pinning me to the ground.

"Really?" I asked her, and she leaned over with a whine to lick my face. I pulled her head down into a hug, partly to assure her I wasn't mad at her and partly to get a better look at the two men standing before me. That's when I saw where the knife had dropped. Not to the ground as Hedeshi had expected, but into Reyes's hand.

He took hold of the man's head, seeming to embrace him back, and plunged the knife into his gut in one lightning-quick strike. Hedeshi gaped at him, his shock genuine as he stumbled back. "You would deny your father his throne?"

"It was never his," Reyes said, plunging the knife again. Forcing it up his torso. An instant later, the knife reemerged from just underneath the Englishman's chin.

Hedeshi looked at me, his eyes watering in pain. "Just remember what I've told you about him."

I tried to tamp down the horror I felt at watching a man being cut open. "I'll tie a string around my finger."

Another stab wound wrenched a ragged groan from his throat. "He is not what you think he is."

I thought of my father. Of Harper and Art and Pari. Of pretty much anyone I'd ever known in my entire life, and answered him as truthfully as I could. "No one ever is."

Reyes embraced him again and plunged the knife into his side. "Your first mistake was coming for her," he said into the man's ear.

Hedeshi coughed, knowing full well he was taking his last breaths. "And my second?" he asked as blood gushed out of his mouth.

"Believing that you could get past me."

The man smiled and said in the gentlest of voices, "Attack."

And that was pretty much when all hell broke loose.

20

It puts the lotion in the basket.

—T-SHIRT

Five more demon-possessed people lunged out of the shadows like crazed mental patients as Reyes separated into two distinct beings. His incorporeal body dematerialized, reached into the Englishman, and ripped the demon Hedeshi out with a ferocious twist. His corporeal body dived into the darkness, taking on the biggest of the demons approaching, a male who looked like a sumo wrestler. They landed hard and quickly blurred into a tangle of arms and fists.

Unfortunately, Artemis used my body as a launching pad, ridding me of a kidney named Percival and quite possibly Harold, my spleen. I cradled my stomach, then scrambled to my feet and reached for the closest thing at hand—a leaf rake leaning against the building.

That's when I realized Mrs. Allen had come outside to let PP the miniature poodle go potty. PP went berserk at all the action. Mrs. Allen yelled at him to get back inside, but PP was beyond listening to anything she had to say. I scooted back in surprise as he attacked a burly man headed toward me. The guy had enough weight on him to be taken seriously.

Not as much as the sumo wrestler, but I wouldn't have challenged him to a thumb war if my life depended on it.

He crept forward, literally crawling on hands and knees, stalking me in a slow methodical march, victory so close, so sweet, he must've wanted to savor the moment. PP barked and leapt off the ground, sinking his toothless gums into the man's ear.

He cursed and shook off the dog, but Artemis took over from there. She'd already disposed of another demon, leaving a guy around my age lying unconscious in the small square of grass that lined the apartment building. Now she pounced on the heftier man, her snarls of rage enough to cause goose bumps to jut out all over my skin.

I glanced at Reyes and the demon. One incorporeal being against another, his enveloping black robe making much of the fight impossible to see. But what I did see was surreal, otherworldly, and my mind had difficulty processing it. Their movements were so fast, so fluid, it was like watching two oceans collide. Then I looked at his physical form. He had the sumo wrestler in a headlock, one knee jabbed into the man's back. In the next instant, the man's head snapped to the side with a sharp crack. He slumped to the ground instantly. But I knew from experience that wouldn't last long. He'd be back up in a matter of moments.

I tore my gaze away. The Englishman's body lay limp on the paved lot. I gripped the leaf rake and started toward him as PP went after another possessed woman. Hunched a few feet from me, she seemed confused. She wanted me but didn't seem to know why. And when PP nipped at her fingers, she appraised him with a vacant stare as though trying to figure out exactly what he was.

I took the break to check on the Englishman, but the instant I started toward him, I could tell he was already dead. That's when I realized another of the possessed had picked up the knife, his eyes glistening with hunger as he came for me. I met him halfway, pitching forward and lashing out with the rake. Just to stop it. To slow it down.

The bristles of the rake scraped harmlessly across its face, doing little damage, but I did manage to knock the knife out of his hand. He looked to the side, and the distraction granted me enough time to crash into him, another male in his early forties. He seemed unable to believe his luck as we tumbled to the pavement and skidded across the lot. Dirt and gravel ground into my shoulder. He straddled me, took my head into his hands, and started to twist.

He was going to break my neck, and I hated having my neck broken, so I lifted my legs, leveraged my feet up and around his head, then jerked back, knocking him off balance long enough for me to almost make it out from under him. But he threw his weight on top of me.

I fought his hold, elbowed him across the face, and crawled forward, fighting for every inch I gained. Before I knew it, his hands were gripping my head again. He really wanted the kill. When he twisted, I rolled with it, forcing him to go for a better hold. But Artemis finally ripped into him, hurtling herself right through the human's body and dragging the demon out with her as she landed. The man went limp on top of me, and I lay pinned to the ground.

I looked over and realized Artemis had already taken care of the demon inside the man Reyes had been fighting, the sumo wrestler. Only one demon remained. The woman. She came into view as I lay right in front of her, easing over me, drool dripping from her mouth and into my hair.

A mountain lay atop me, and a possessed woman sat studying my every feature as though I were a specimen in a petri dish. I looked to the side just as Reyes sliced through Hedeshi's demon self, cutting him in half at the hips. He'd screamed and started back for more, when Reyes swung again. He severed its head, and with its death, it evaporated like smoke on dry ice.

When another drop of drool landed on my temple, I shivered in revulsion. But at least she wasn't trying to break my neck.

I looked to my other side. PP and Mrs. Allen were gone. She'd probably call the police.

Artemis came into view then, her stubby tail wagging in excitement, ready for more. She hunched down by my side with a begging whine. Reyes stepped beside me, and his incorporeal body reentered his physical one. The robes settled around his shoulders, then disappeared as he dragged the man off. Grateful, I stood, wiped my face and hair, then stepped to the woman, who sat on her knees, now staring at the grass where I'd been.

I knelt down and talked to the demon inside. "This is not going to end well for you."

She looked up at me, her lids fluttering, and said, "Let me go now and I'll spare the woman." Then her brows crinkled and she stared into space again. She was fighting it. The woman. She was fighting the hold the demon had on her.

Sensing the new danger, Artemis crept forward until her jaws were at the woman's neck, her teeth bared and glistening, saliva dripping off her jowls. The demon flinched, and its head turned toward her. Artemis struck in the next instant with a ferocious bark that shook the windows. The demon didn't stand a chance. She yanked it out and tore it to pieces until it was nothing more than a heavy vapor. From there, it evaporated, its immeasurable darkness dispersing in the air.

The woman collapsed into the cold grass, and I turned her head to make sure she could breathe. Reyes bent to help, and only then did I realize that he had fought a demon while his incorporeal self was out of his body. He'd never been able to do that. Normally when his incorporeal self left, he entered a seizurelike state.

I leaned back, regarded him warily. "You—You're—You told me you couldn't do that," I finally said accusingly. "You fought a demon without—" I fought for the right words "—without your soul."

Reyes was checking the woman's pulse. "Couldn't," he said absently before turning back to me. "Can now." He stood and offered me his hand. He seemed distant, hurt.

"That's it?" I asked. "You just can now?" When he only shrugged,

I asked, "Is that all of them?" I hoped that with the absence of Hedeshi, their leader, there would be no more demons to contend with.

"For now." He frowned and looked past the building down the alley. "Until they figure out a better way to get at you."

We were still at an impasse with the picture. And I still had to wonder if he had been cleared of murder charges only to become an arsonist. Why would he burn down that building? Any of them? He'd lived there, but why burn them down?

I had to remember what he came from. I'd been tortured by Earl Walker once and only once, and I had been changed mentally, physically, and emotionally. I became a different animal. What would years of that do to a person? Decades of living and breathing fear, day in and day out? Of being used and abused, beaten and starved, with no haven, no safe place to hide? The thought cinched my ribs around my lungs.

He watched me from underneath his lashes, his expression knowing. "You aren't feeling sorry for me, are you? I would hate to have to remedy that."

Yep, he was still mad. "And just how would you accomplish such a thing?"

The resignation on his face stole my breath. "Believe me when I say you don't want to know."

Before I could manage a reply, a thunderous crack exploded in the air behind him. He turned toward the sound and I looked past him, sensing danger instantly. The world thickened and slowed, but not fast enough. Reyes stepped in front of me as a bullet that had been rocketing toward my head tore through his chest instead. It exited out his back and continued its journey, the metal fragmented, but whole enough to finish what it had started.

Then, in a feat that stunned me to my core, Reyes turned, too fast for me to see, and caught it in midair.

I stumbled back and looked on as Reyes opened his palm to examine the bullet. But he was corporeal. When the bullet hit, he hadn't had time to separate. To try to stop it with his incorporeal self. Blood spread across his T-shirt so fast, I grew light-headed at the sight of it. He coughed, and blood bubbled out of his mouth.

His gaze met mine as he fell to his knees and whispered, "Run."

I rushed forward to catch him and caught a glimpse of the culprit cowering on top of a building down the street. I expected another demon. Perhaps one who'd wised up and decided to bring weapons of mass destruction to the party. But it was the blond biker from the bank robbery. The one who had been kicked out of the military, who hadn't finished his sniper training. I stood there, beyond flabbergasted. Apparently, he *really* didn't want any witnesses.

Anger surged inside me faster than the splitting of an atom. Like a volcano bursting through the top of a mountain, fury erupted out of me in one blinding flash. Windows shattered and shards of glass hung like a menagerie of shimmering color as I walked toward Blondie, determination locking my teeth together. He was reloading the rifle, his movements slow in the adjustment of time, sluggish. He brought the butt to his shoulder, leaned his head over until the image from the scope came into view. Just as his finger started to squeeze the trigger, I reached into his chest and crushed his heart. It beat once, twice more, then stopped altogether. And satisfaction coursed through me like cool water dousing a wildfire.

Blondie grabbed his chest, his mouth dropping open, fighting for air seconds before he fell face-first to the ground.

Reyes appeared beside me. He examined me, the blond, then turned back to where we had been. Where we still were. When I looked back, I saw myself kneeling on the ground, looking back at me, into my own eyes. Reyes's body lay next to me. Before I could make sense of any of it, I awakened to my previous surroundings with a startled gasp, like I had never been outside my own body, like I had not just seen it from a great distance. I looked down at Reyes.

He curled into himself, his breaths hard and shallow.

"Reyes!" I shouted, scrambling toward him and trying to find the wound to put pressure on it. A bullet had ripped through his chest. Even the son of Satan wouldn't walk away after an injury like that.

We heard sirens in the distance, and he struggled to his knees.

"Get me . . . into the shadows." He nodded toward a trash bin. "Behind that Dumpster."

"You need an ambulance."

"No." Anger hit me like a wall of fire. He grabbed my shirt with a bloodied hand and jerked me forward. "I'm not going back, and you're not sending me there." He pushed and fell onto his hands, trying to catch his breath. It reminded me so much of the very first time I saw him, when I was in high school and he was fighting for air beside a Dumpster after being beaten. I'd let him down then. I did nothing to save him, and his life took a definite turn for the worse. I would not let that happen again.

I touched his shoulder, forgetting that he was more wolf than canine, more panther than cat. There was nothing domestic about Reyes Farrow. He could turn in a heartbeat, had proved it a dozen times. But when he did turn on me, when he rocketed from prey to predator, my shock was complete.

He struck so fast, his movements were nothing more than a dark blur. I was vertical one moment and horizontal the next. And he was on top of me, his body rock hard, unbending, unyielding. He leaned into me until his mouth—his sensual mouth that had only recently sent shivers of passion thundering through me—hovered at my ear. The warmth of his blood spread over my chest and shoulders and pooled in the divot at the base of my throat, and I wondered how much longer he'd live. Surely no one could survive that much blood loss. Not even a supernatural being. He sent a thigh between my legs, parting them for a better fit.

"I told you," he said, his voice like a low growl, rippling through me in white-hot waves. "Don't—" One hand wrapped around my neck as his mouth nuzzled my ear. "—ever—" The other slid up my shirt, the pleasure of his touch leaving heat trails in its wake. "—pity—" His hips pushed my legs farther apart; my hands cupped them in reflex. "—me."

His mouth crushed mine, the kiss raw and needy. I wrapped my arms around his waist, then sent one over his steel buttocks, pulling him into me, wanting him inside. Despite our situation. Despite our circumstances.

Only Reyes Farrow could do this to me. Could make me beg for him, no matter the setting. No matter how dire the predicament. And he knew it. He knew exactly what he did to me.

I felt a smile behind his kiss a microsecond before he lifted off me and vanished into the dark. A rush of cold took the place of the heat that had blanketed me. I dropped my arms to the ground. Closed my eyes. Breathed. A whimper sounded beside me. Artemis lay in the distance, watching. Every few seconds, she'd inch closer, crawling on her stomach. Then she'd stop and focus on something in the distance, pretending not to notice me.

One of the men woke up then, his movements slow and lethargic as he rubbed his head, the back of his neck. He tried to make sense of his surroundings, but couldn't seem to manage it. No telling where he was from. Two lay dead, and three others lay unconscious still as the first patrol car skidded to a halt in the parking lot. Right in front of the Englishman's body. And on a building top down the street, they'd find another body, that of a blond biker who was almost a sniper in the Marines, who'd wanted to serve his country but now robbed banks and tried to snipe people.

I covered my eyes with my arms. I didn't care what kind of connections I had, no way was I getting out of this unscathed. This could even put Uncle Bob in the spotlight if he tried to cover any of it up. It could jeopardize his career. His retirement.

A patrolman rushed over to me. He said something I couldn't quite make out, because another realization had washed over me, and I suddenly couldn't think. Couldn't breathe.

I'd killed a man. I'd reached inside his chest and stopped his heart. Like I had the authority. Like I had the right.

My world tumbled back into a familiar place. One of darkness and desperation and denial. Then I was being lifted. Bright lights flickered past. Blue scrubs. Silver instruments. Somewhere in the fog of reality, Uncle Bob appeared. Then Cookie. I felt cool sheets beneath my body and warm hands cupped in mine, and I realized I was in the hospital for the second time in as many months. I heard familiar words: *concussion, stab wounds, fractured ankle.* The last one surprised me. I didn't remember that part. But that's what adrenaline did. It pushed pain aside and thrust you forward.

I forced my lids apart.

Dad was there, too. Close by. As was Uncle Bob, and I knew I could tell them. They would know what to do.

I pressed my mouth together, closed my eyes, and said, "I killed a man."

When I looked again, they glanced at each other, worry in their expressions. "One of the men outside your apartment building? Because it looked like they fought each—"

"No, a man on a roof. A bank robber who wanted to kill me."

Uncle Bob's brows furrowed. "When, pumpkin? We don't—"

"Tonight. Right after I was attacked. He was on a rooftop and I killed him. After he shot Reyes with a fifty-caliber rifle, I reached inside his chest and stopped his heart." Soft sobs drifted out of me as Dad took my hand.

"Sweetheart, that's impossible. If Reyes was shot with a fifty-caliber rifle from a sniper on a rooftop, he would not be alive."

"He wouldn't even be in one piece," Uncle Bob agreed.

"You don't understand," I said, sorrow drowning my words, "I killed a man. I lost control. I killed him."

"Shhhh," Dad said, cradling my head against his shoulder. "You're not like us, hon. I know that. And I don't care who or what you are, I know one thing for certain: Your actions are above the laws of man. I'm sorry for saying that, but it's the truth. You are here for a reason."

"Robert. Leland."

I looked up to see the police captain from Uncle Bob's precinct walk in. Uncle Bob nodded to him, then leaned in and whispered in my ear. "You don't remember anything."

Ever the champion, he was still fighting to keep me out of jail. Or prison. Or the nuthouse. But this was bigger than any of us. There was simply no explanation for what had happened. Then again, what was I supposed to tell them? The truth?

Special Agent Carson walked in right behind the captain.

"You're quite an asset," he said, eyeing me suspiciously. He glanced at Uncle Bob, then back. "You managed to solve four cases in one day. I think this is a new world record."

"Four?"

He counted on his fingers. "The disappearance and death of Harper Lowell. A missing persons case from over two decades ago. The disappearance of several people who seemed to have been drugged and dropped on your doorstep. We've had a rash of those lately. And the apprehension of an escaped serial killer. But come to think of it," he said, looking at his hands, "that might technically be five. Or maybe even six."

"A serial killer?"

He nodded. "You're about to make us one of the most respected departments in the country. One of our consultants single-handedly took down the Englishman, a convicted serial killer who escaped from Sing Sing three months ago."

It figured Hedeshi would have chosen a serial killer as his host. I wondered how on Earth he got him out of Sing Sing.

"And he's not even from England."

I blinked in surprise. "He wasn't English?"

"No, he was originally from Jersey. He just spoke with an English accent. No one knew why. But I have to admit, I think it's odd that all this would happen to you in one day, especially considering the other guy," the captain said.

"The other guy?"

"Yes," Agent Carson said, "it would seem one of the Gentlemen Thieves died of a heart attack on the rooftop of a building on Central. He had a fifty-caliber rifle in his hands, and it looked like he was getting ready to do some damage. It's odd that he would just drop dead like that."

Uncle Bob shifted in his chair.

"That is weird," I said, biting my bottom lip. "I mean, wasn't he pretty young?"

"Thirty-two," she said. "And he just happened to have an uncle whose wife works at the branch that was robbed yesterday. Seems those three were in it together. Something about it being Edwards's idea to blackmail his friends, certain members of the Bandits motorcycle club, in the first place. I don't have all the details yet, but we have the uncle in custody. He's filling in the blanks now."

If my shock didn't show that time, I was going to Hollywood. What a scumbag. Dad and Uncle Bob were busy looking elsewhere—too elsewhere—but no way could this work out so easily. Life wasn't a stack of cards that just magically fell into place when dropped. Unless life was named David Copperfield.

That was it. I would name my life. The minute I came up with a name for my sofa, which might or might not go by the name of Sigourney Weaver, I would name my life. Now I had something to live for. And I had a decision to make, a big decision. What name would incorporate all that life entailed, every aspect of uncertainty, of beauty and surrealism and encounters with crazy people? It would have to speak of the ups and downs life had to offer, like being too broke for daily mocha lattes. If I lived through that, I could live through anything.

After another few minutes of conversation that had my head throbbing, the captain and Special Agent Carson left, but not before one last look back. Agent Carson smiled. The captain eyed me like he really, really, really wanted to get to the bottom of my involvement. That couldn't be good.

I turned to Uncle Bob as we waited for the discharge papers. "This is all way too neat. Way too tidy. They're going to figure out this couldn't possibly have happened the way it looks, and I don't want you in trouble."

"Neat?" Dad asked. "Tidy? That is exactly the way they like it, pumpkin. All wrapped up in a bow. Trust me, it means less paperwork, and that's always a good thing." Dad helped me to my feet. "I got the phones at the office turned back on. And I had Sammy's wife clean the place up." He was bound and determined I'd move back into the offices above his bar.

"So, how are you?" I asked, pretending not to care.

A smile lit his eyes anyway. "I'm okay. It seems I don't have cancer after all." He looked around, then whispered, awe evident in his voice, "Did you have anything to do with that?"

I tried to smile. "No, Dad. I don't have that kind of power."

"It's just—" He bowed his head. "It's just, I had pancreatic cancer."

His words sent a piercing pain through my heart.

"They did every test known to man, and I had it. Then after you found out, after you touched me in the office . . . well, it seems to have vanished."

"When did I touch you?"

"You poked my chest with your index finger when you were chastising me for trying to shoot you."

Oh, right. I only wished I could do cool stuff like that. "It wasn't me, Dad. But I'm glad."

"I'm glad, too," he said, placating me. He didn't believe me for a minute.

Gemma rushed in like a whirlwind on meth. "Well?" she asked, looking from Uncle Bob to Dad to Cookie, then finally at me. "What happened this time?"

After a long moment of contemplation, I said, "Fine, I'll accept counseling, but only from you."

"Charley, while I'm thrilled, completely and totally thrilled, I can't treat you. That would be in violation of my code of conduct."

"Screw the code. Get a new code. I can't see anyone else without them trying to lock me away." I clenched my teeth and said, "Grim reaper, Gem."

She almost giggled in delight. "No, I know someone. I promise, it'll be okay."

"I swear, the minute they bring out a straitjacket, I'm crossing your name off my Christmas list."

"Deal," she said, a satisfied smirk on her face. "But if they do put you in a straitjacket, can I take your picture? You know, for research purposes?"

"Not if you value your cuticles."

She jerked back her hands. "That's just mean."

I shrugged my brows. "You mess with the reaper, you get the scythe."

"You don't really carry a scythe."

"So not the point."

Before we went home, I had Cookie drive me to the convent. Dawn had just barely peeked on the horizon, but this was important. Quentin had to know he would be okay. That it was safe to go out. He needed that weight off his shoulders.

We were met by a very austere-looking mother superior, and I couldn't help but wonder what qualifications it took to become the supreme mommy figure. Clearly a mean death stare was a prerequisite, but what else? Surliness? Advanced algebra?

She showed us into the kitchen again as Sister Mary Elizabeth brought Quentin down. He looked half asleep in his pajamas, and his hair had been trimmed, but it still brushed his shoulders. He rushed into my arms, then realized I was hurt.

"I'm sorry," he said, his signs and expression sincere. He put on his sunglasses and pointed to a bandage on my arm. Thankfully, the knife had barely grazed both it and my side. "What happened?"

"The same thing that happened to you, only from the opposite end. Other people who were possessed attacked me, but I wanted you to know, it's safe now. It's okay. They won't come after you again. The being that instigated it all has been killed."

Relief washed through him, and I led him to a table to sit down.

"Are you okay here? Have they been slapping your hands with rulers or anything? I've heard nuns do that."

The mother superior cleared her throat. Apparently, she knew sign, too.

"We enrolled him in school," Sister Mary Elizabeth said, hardly able to contain her excitement. "At the School for the Deaf in Santa Fe. He'll live there during the week, then come home on the weekends."

Quentin didn't seem quite so thrilled. He pressed his mouth together.

I leaned into him. "Are you okay with that?" When he shrugged, I asked the sister, "He'll come home on the weekends?"

She smiled. "Here." She put a hand on his arm. "He'll come here until we can find a more permanent home. Oh!" She looked at me. "And he can stay with you every so often, too, if you'd like."

"I'd love," I said. I glanced over my shoulder at Cookie. "I have a feeling Amber will be wanting to learn ASL."

Cookie nodded and offered me a dreamy expression. "He is darling."

When I signed what she said to Quentin, he blushed and offered a soft thank-you, only he spoke it, his vowels clipped and his voice deep and soft.

"Okay," Cookie continued, "I'm in love."

Quentin tapped my hand. "I have a name sign for you."

I straightened in surprise. "Really? Wow."

He took his right hand, splayed his fingers, and formed a modified eight where his middle finger was bent forward slightly more than the rest. Then he touched the tip of it to his right shoulder and twisted it up and out away from him, shaking it ever so slightly.

I put my hands over my heart. It was the sign for *sparkle,* only from the shoulder. He was telling me that I sparkled. I felt a sting in the backs of my eyes, and he dipped his head sheepishly. I couldn't help it. I threw my arms around his neck. He let me hug him a solid minute before asking, "Can I stay with you sometimes?"

"I would love for you to stay with me sometimes."

I leaned in and kissed his cheek to the abrasive sound of the mother superior clearing her throat again.

"Well, that boy is a living doll," Cookie said as we made our way to the third floor of our apartment building.

"Isn't he?"

There were still cops outside, still investigators combing the area inside and out of yellow caution tape. They had taken my clothes as evidence, but the only blood on them, besides mine, was Reyes's. Would they know that? Was he in a DNA database somewhere?

"How's your head?" she asked. "Are you okay?" She was such a dear friend. She put up with so much from me. And it was a wonder she was still alive, all things considered.

"Yeah, I'm okay."

"Good." As I turned to unlock my door, she slapped me upside the head. Fred thrust forward and knocked against the doorjamb.

I turned back to her, aghast. "That head is concussed, I'll have you know."

"I know. And I'm glad, for your information."

"That's not a very neighborly attitude."

"You almost die right outside the apartment building, and you didn't think to, perhaps, yell my name? Call out for help?"

"And what would you have done, Cook, besides get attacked coming to my rescue?"

"You know, that excuse is going to get old one of these days." Her eyes watered, and she looked down. "Do you know how I felt when I found out Earl Walker had tortured you not fifty feet from me?"

The chambers in my heart squeezed shut.

Against my better judgment, Cookie needed to know the truth about what it really meant to be in my life.

I leaned back against my door and folded my arms. "Amber was there," I said, my voice a mere whisper.

Alarm rushed through her. "What? Amber was there last night?"

"No. *That* night. When Earl came."

Her alarm ebbed, and she took a step back. "I don't understand."

"When I walked into the apartment," I said, unable to stop a floodgate of tears as they pushed past my lashes, "Earl was there. And so was Amber."

Cookie's hand flew to cover her mouth. She'd had no idea, and I'd been too much of a coward to tell her.

I wiped at my cheeks, angry that all I seemed to be able to do lately was cry. Because crying helped so much. "She was asleep on my sofa." I saw the image in my mind so clearly, and my stomach lurched with the thought as bad as it had that night. "He had a gun to her head."

She covered her whole face and shook as a sob wrenched through my chest. I tightened my arms and curled into myself. I was about to lose one of the best things that had ever happened to me, but she had to know the truth.

"As long as I was quiet and cooperated, he said she'd live. You'd both live. He let me lead her to your apartment. She was so sleepy, she never saw him. But he was there because of me, Cookie. Amber almost died because of me."

After a long moment of contemplation, she took a deep breath and tilted her face toward the heavens. "No," she said, steeling herself. "No. Earl Walker used Amber to get you to do what he wanted. And it worked, Charley. He knew it would. This is not your fault."

I gaped at her. "It's entirely my fault. All of it."

"Charley," she said, putting a hand on my shoulder, "I told you this before. You do incredible things, and I get to be a part of it. That incident was one in a million. And it's over. We have to move past it. The odds of anything like that happening again are astronomical."

"Do you even pay attention?"

"That captain said it himself. You solved four cases in one day. Four, Charley. That's—that's unheard of. And you captured an escaped serial killer. You saved who knows how many lives. And I got to help. We'll just have to be more careful in the future. We need better locks, right? We've already talked about that. And a security system."

It would hit her later. Anger. Regret. Despair. And she might even hate me a little. Better to hate me for almost getting her daughter killed than for actually accomplishing the feat.

In the meantime, I'd just turned Cookie into a slightly older version of myself. She'd probably be up nights, checking and rechecking the doors and windows, turning the tiniest of sounds into a full-blown home invasion. I could totally see why she liked being my friend. Working for me.

"Is everything okay, pumpkin toes?"

I turned toward Aunt Lillian as she melted through the door. I was just about to answer her when the landlord walked by. "Ladies," he said, a lecherous grin on his face.

"Traitor."

He chuckled and knocked on the door to the end apartment.

Cook and I perked up, our interest aroused. I wiped my cheeks, and we leaned together, hoping to get a look at the new tenants.

"I got that other key for you," he said. Then he ogled us from over his shoulder, wiggled his brows.

I rolled my eyes until they were staring into the face of Barbara.

The door opened, slowly at first, and I fought back a bizarre kind of excitement. It was like opening a present, trying to discern the contents inside, guarding your expression not to show disappointment if it came to that. And perhaps it was the concussed state of Fred and Barbara, or the delicate state of Betty White, her fragile chambers beating between pangs of pain and desperation, but when I saw Reyes Farrow open that door, I was pretty sure I seized.

Cookie inhaled so sharply, Reyes looked past the landlord and directly at us. His eyes glistened in the low light as he looked me over. I did the same to him. He had a bullet wound in his chest from a fifty-caliber that would have ripped another man apart, and yet I felt no evidence of pain or signs of physical weakness from the blood loss. No doubt he was covered in duct tape underneath his dark red T-shirt. The one where the sleeve openings weren't quite large enough to hang loosely over his arms, so they formed to his biceps instead, caressing them, embracing them.

After he finished examining me, he spoke, his voice like warm brandy on a cold night. "You can just give it to her," he told Mr. Zamora.

"Oh." Mr. Z stammered a bit in surprise, then handed me the extra key to Reyes Farrow's apartment with a delighted leer on his face.

Reyes nodded toward Cookie congenially. "Cookie," he said, addressing her with reverence. He moved to Aunt Lil. "Lillian," he said, and if Aunt Lil had died with her dentures in, I was pretty certain they'd have fallen out at that point. Then he leveled his smoldering gaze on me, tilted his head in interest. "Dutch." He offered me one last look—a look full of promise and desire—before stepping back and closing his door.

We stood there, the three of us, our jaws firmly planted on the floor. Aunt Lil recovered first. She nudged me with her elbow and said with a cackle of delight, "I think you guys should make some more of those brownies, 'cause that boy looks hungry."